DEATH WHERE THE BAD ROCKS LIVE

"An exciting and quirky mystery that seamlessly shifts between past and present, offering a number of finely delineated characters and a strong sense of life on the reservations and the beauties of a hostile land."   —*Kirkus Reviews*

"Manny Tanno is not your typical hero. He's a horrible driver, doesn't like to rush into a gunfight, suffers from diabetes, isn't the stud in the barn he used to be, and doesn't have all the answers. I can't tell you how refreshing this is. He's an imperfectly perfect hero . . . *Death Where the Bad Rocks Live* isn't simply about murder but about reconnecting with the past, with ourselves, and protecting what is ours. Perfectly paced, intricately woven, and fascinating are just three phrases that come to mind for the second book in the Spirit Road Mystery series. Truly worth reading."   —*Fresh Fiction*

"The investigation is engaging and the locale symbolically fascinating."   —*Genre Go Round Reviews*

DEATH ALONG THE SPIRIT ROAD

"A mystery novel that grabs you by the lapels and refuses to let go . . . This is storytelling at its best and C. M. Wendelboe is a new author to watch."

—Margaret Coel, *New York Times* bestselling author of *The Perfect Suspect*

"The pacing of the novel . . . is distinctly native, something I haven't read since the departure of the old master, Tony Hillerman."

—Craig Johnson, *New York Times* bestselling author of

Hell Jun 2013

Berkley Prime Crime titles by C. M. Wendelboe

DEATH ALONG THE SPIRIT ROAD
DEATH WHERE THE BAD ROCKS LIVE
DEATH ON THE GREASY GRASS

DEATH ON THE GREASY GRASS

C. M. WENDELBOE

BERKLEY PRIME CRIME, NEW YORK

THE BERKLEY PUBLISHING GROUP
Published by the Penguin Group
Penguin Group (USA) Inc.
375 Hudson Street, New York, New York 10014, USA

USA | Canada | UK | Ireland | Australia | New Zealand | India | South Africa | China

Penguin Books Ltd., Registered Offices: 80 Strand, London WC2R 0RL, England
For more information about the Penguin Group, visit penguin.com.

This book is an original publication of The Berkley Publishing Group.

Berkley Prime Crime Books are published by The Berkley Publishing Group.
BERKLEY® PRIME CRIME and the PRIME CRIME logo are
a registered trademark of Penguin Group (USA) Inc.

Library of Congress Cataloging-in-Publication Data

Wendelboe, C. M.
Death on the greasy grass / C.M. Wendelboe.—Berkley prime crime trade paperback ed.
pages cm.
ISBN 978-0-425-26325-9
1. United States. Federal Bureau of Investigation—Officials and employees—Fiction.
2. Indian reservations—South Dakota—Fiction. 3. Dakota Indians—Fiction. I. Title.
PS3623.E53D43 2013
813'.6—dc23
2013007213

PUBLISHING HISTORY
Berkley Prime Crime trade paperback edition / June 2013

PRINTED IN THE UNITED STATES OF AMERICA

10 9 8 7 6 5 4 3 2 1

Cover illustration by Richard Tuschman.
Cover design by Rita Frangie.
Interior design by Laura K. Corless.

ALWAYS LEARNING   PEARSON

ACKNOWLEDGMENTS

I would like to thank my editor, Tom Colgan, and agent, Bill Contardi, for their continued patience; Craig and Judy Johnson for always being there with answers to my oddball questions; the staff at Little Big Horn College at Crow Agency for their generosity in allowing me research time and materials; Crow Agency police officer Neil White Hip and Oglala Sioux Tribal police officer Derek Puckett for their local insights; Montana State DCI Agent Klostermeier, Kevin Klostermeier, who likes his lattes stirred, not shaken; Campbell County (Wyoming) coroner Ton Eekhoff for happily confirming my worst fears; Steve Hamilton for his killer logo; Doris Rogers for her constant encouragement; my wife, Heather, whose proverbial red pen and tech support made it possible to write another mystery; and all the readers who keep returning for more guidance along the *Wanagi Tacanku*, the Spirit Road.

The Crow country is a good country. The Great Spirit has put it exactly in the right place: while you are in it you fare well; whenever you go out of it, whichever way you travel you fare worse.

Arapooash (Sore Belly),
Apsa'alooke Chief, c.1830

CHAPTER 1

Sun-bleached wood creaked under Willie With Horn's weight as he made his way up past others who were sitting in the stands waiting for the Real Bird Little Big Horn Reenactment to begin. He took the steps two at a time, balancing an iced soda in each hand, careful not to spill any on other spectators. He dropped beside Manny Tanno in the top row and handed him a Pepsi.

Manny pressed the cold cup against his forehead. He was sweating but not nearly as badly as Willie was in the broiling afternoon heat. He took a bandanna out of his back pocket and dried the sweatband of his Stetson before placing it on an empty space beside him.

"You should have listened to me and dressed for the weather." Manny sipped lightly, careful not to drip any on the camera dangling from the strap around his neck. "Don't see me sweating my nuts off, do you?"

Willie laughed.

"What?"

"Don't see me sitting around looking like some damned tourist."

"We can't be tourists: We're Indians."

"No? Just look at you." Willie exaggerated looking Manny up and down.

"What?"

"An FBI agent should have some dignity. Especially one as mature as you."

"What's that supposed to mean?"

"For a man your age, you look silly. Just silly. And half the people here must think so, too, the way they're gawking at you."

A ten-year-old boy in the row below had turned in his seat and stared slack-jawed at Manny. An elderly couple several feet over and a row down gave Manny the once-over, as did another couple huddled together on the other side of Willie. Their heads snapped around when Manny caught them gawking. "I don't see a thing wrong with how I look."

Willie shook his head. "For starters, no one else in Garryowen, Montana, would be wearing a damned Hawaiian shirt. For another thing, your scrawny legs jutting out of those baggy shorts make you look like you're riding a chicken. And it wouldn't hurt to lose that Kodak relic hanging around your neck."

Manny sipped his soda. "I don't care what people think. I'm on vacation."

"Don't get me started on that again." Willie's face turned a darker shade. "I can think of a dozen other places we could have gone on vacation. We could have driven through

Yellowstone. Or hiked up to the Medicine Wheel like I always wanted. Maybe gone rafting Sharpnose or Washakie Falls in the Wind River. But no, you had to drag me up here to Crow Agency."

The boy a row down sat backward staring at Manny. Manny scowled back at him, and he turned back and retreated to the safety of his mother's ample arms. "But this is history."

"I can read about history. What I can't read about is what's it like to have a grizzly nipping at my butt in Yellowstone."

"Just be grateful we can be here," Manny said. "Wasn't too many generations ago we wouldn't be welcome on Crow land, let alone see Lakota involved in the reenactment."

As if to punctuate Manny's speech, men dressed in cavalry uniforms, sitting astride equally uniform brown horses, trotted onto that patch of ground between the bleachers and the river where the action was to play out. A gelding toward the front thrust snapping jaws at a mare beside him, the rider jerking the reins, the horse rearing for a momentary protest before settling down.

The announcer emerged from behind the bleachers, tapping the PA mic as he walked. The boy in front of Manny clapped his hands over his ears against the feedback, then the noise was gone, replaced by the soft voice of the MC. He waved his hat toward the far end of the field. A dapper cavalry officer, sitting tall wearing a gray fringed jacket, rode parallel to the bleachers, leading thirty cavalry officers past the spectators. The MC introduced Steve Alexander in the role of Custer. Manny joined the crowd clapping and Willie elbowed him. "You're supposed to root for the Indians."

"I'm on vacation. I'll root for whoever I want."

Alexander, the announcer continued, had been playing Colonel Custer at the Real Bird reenactment for twelve years, and the crowd clapped again. Alexander took off his hat and bowed for the crowd, his long, blowing blond hair slapping his horse's face. He put his hat back on and led the troopers off the field.

"Where's us Indians?" Willie asked.

Manny jerked his thumb behind them, and turned in his seat. On a field behind the bleachers, Indians in various costumes assembled. Some wore only loincloths barely covering muscular legs, while others wore full leggings adorned with geometric designs and beaded bottoms. Red and yellow and blue face paint contrasted with the dark skin of the Indians.

Where the cavalry horses were uniformly plain, the Indians' horses showed off their own unique prairie palette of colors that matched the style of their riders. Black and yellow lightning bolts were hand painted in descending strikes along the flank of one horse, yellow and red dappled another's neck, black paint circled another's eyes, blue streaks on yet another's rump faded to white all the way to the tail tied tight with red and yellow dyed leather.

"The cavalry used .45-55s back then."

A voice behind the bleachers boomed over the announcer. A cavalry reenactor stood in front of a trooper's half-tent in back of the bleachers, cradling a Springfield rifle in his arms. The gun's muzzle carelessly covered a half dozen people gathered in front of the man. Yellow ribbon sticking out of the rifle's action added color to the man's talk. The soldier, wearing sergeant stripes on his muslin sleeves and leather suspenders tight over a bulging stomach, twirled a long white handlebar mustache. "Yeah, fifty-five grains of black powder in these babies could shoot an Indian from his horse at five hundred yards. In the hands of the right man."

"And if you were that man . . ." A teen in short shorts winked and let her comment dangle.

The sergeant looked around, took a nip from a hip flask,

and quickly hid it. "If it were me, those Indians wouldn't have made it as close as Custer let them." His eyes locked on Manny's and he quickly turned away. Even dressed in his disguise of Hawaiian shirt and khaki shorts, Manny looked Lakota. "That's why I'm supposed to shoot one of the chiefs first."

"Which chief?" a man nibbling on a corn dog asked. He wiped mustard with the back of his hand onto his trousers, to match the dried mustard dotting the front of his BILLINGS OR BUST T-shirt. "Looks to me like there's more chiefs than there are Indians."

The sergeant began laughing, but stopped abruptly as he glanced up at Manny. "Why, the same chief as every year: the one with the yellow face paint, riding a gray pony with blue lightning bolts on its neck. Soon as I shoot, he feigns being hit and slumps in the saddle. That's the cue for the other Indians to come riding down on us, toward the river."

The sergeant leaned his rifle against a tent pole and excused himself. "Got to see a man about a horse," he told his impromptu audience as he began unbuttoning his suspenders while he made his way to a blue Porta-Potty. "Just sit in the bleachers and enjoy the show," he called over his shoulder.

Manny turned back to Willie. "Last call before the show starts. Sure you don't need to go to the crapper?"

"Quite sure."

"Hate to have you miss any of it 'cause you had to run to the big-hole potty."

Willie shook his head. "My bladder's quite healthy. You just want me to fight my way through all these people to get you another soda."

Manny drew back. "I'm ashamed of you, thinking that." He held his cool soda to his forehead. "I'm good here. But if you're going to get yourself another pop, grab me an Indian taco. Light on the hot sauce, please."

Willie sighed and stood, excusing himself as he stepped down each flight of bleachers on his way to the taco stand.

Manny turned in his seat. The fifty or sixty mounted Indians had assembled on the field behind the bleachers, and they trotted toward the field in front, which only a few moments before had been occupied by the soldiers.

More feedback, more squealing that caused the boy in front of Manny to cover his ears again. As he had with the cavalry, the announcer introduced those who would play the Lakota. Manny recognized the names his uncle Marion had held up to a growing boy as true heroes: the Minneconjou warriors, Flying By and White Bull; the Oglala warrior, Low Dog; and the Cheyenne warriors, Wooden Leg and Two Moon. Out of respect for the memory of their greatest warrior, the MC didn't introduce Crazy Horse, for no one in this reenactment could have played him, a warrior like no other, a warrior who had never even sat for a photo.

The rest of the Indians were represented by teens, some younger boys, from Crow Agency, sitting on their horses as if they were born together. The ponies shook and their sleek muscles twitched, not from the heat or from the proximity of other animals, but from a desire for the action to begin. Like their riders. Muscles tensed as reenactors kept their horses in line with just the pressure of their knees, with a loving pat on the neck, with a special word whispered into an ear. Manny marveled at the control the boys exerted over their horses, recalling a time in his life when he'd held such power over a pony. A time when Unc showed him the old ways, which included the time-honored talent for riding bareback.

The announcer's voice abruptly fell silent, and he tapped the microphone. He motioned to a kid who was sitting beside singers with drumsticks who were poised around a drum.

The boy ran out onto the field in front of the bleachers and began chasing speaker wires to find the open line.

Manny set his soda beside him and grabbed the camera from around his neck. He saw the Indians ready to ride after the cavalry, and looked around for the chief with the dubious honor of being the first to get shot to start the reenactment. Manny spotted the chief with half his face painted yellow, sitting on a gray gelding with blue lightning bolts painted on its neck. He was looking toward the bleachers, towering above smaller warriors. He was older by far than the others, and his gray was bigger than the other horses to support the man's bulk. His belly hung over his fringed trousers, and his man-boobs jiggled as he fought to control his horse. He picked at the face paint streaked with sweat.

"See, I told you: you look like a damned tourist, taking pictures like you never saw Indians before." Willie handed Manny the Indian taco. "Satisfied?"

Manny nibbled at it. "Could have used more salsa."

Willie began to argue when the announcer's voice once again boomed loud over the speakers. He started telling the story of Lewis and Clark as two men in buckskins walked onto the field in front of the bleachers. Two Crow Indians in full regalia, feathers flicking the wind, joined the buckskins from the opposite side of the field.

The mock meeting between the Indians and the adventurers over, the MC continued to explain to the crowd the Treaty of Fort Laramie in 1851, and how it contributed to the Great Sioux War and later the destruction of most of Custer's 7th Cavalry.

"When does the action start?"

"Shush!" Manny wiped taco meat from the corner of his mouth.

The announcer finished with treaties made, treaties broken. He stood for a moment in silence, before turning to an American flag waving beside the drummers. "Our National Anthem," he proclaimed, and everyone in the bleachers rose, the sudden shifting weight making the old wood groan. After the National Anthem was finished, the MC spoke into the mike. "Now, the Crow Nation Anthem"—he smiled—"the good guys."

The singers' voices began high at first then dipped low, in tune with the drum, the heartbeat of Indian Nations. The singers seated around the drum struck with precision, eagle feathers tied to drumsticks, bouncing hair falling in eyes. Their beat reminded Manny of polka music and in some deep way, he was certain that was why he liked that music so much. Thum. Thump. Thum. Thump. Manny found himself tapping the bleachers with his shoe, much as he had done that first time he heard the beat, that first time as a boy when he had fallen in love with the music.

The song over, the MC donned his Stetson. "I give you the 7th Cavalry," he said, and stepped off the field.

"Now we'll see something." Manny took the dustcover off the camera lens as he waited for the show to begin. Two abreast, the cavalry soldiers trotted onto the field. The sergeant with the loud mouth and empty whiskey flask rode at the front. They unsheathed rifles as they rode, took Remington and Colt pistols from holsters, waiting for the charge of their sworn enemy.

Loud whooping and hollering accompanied the Indian with the yellow face paint. He kicked his horse and rode full gallop toward the troopers. The sergeant dragged out his role, carefully taking aim at the chief, waiting until he'd ridden close before firing. Even though Manny knew the round was stage ammunition, he jumped just as he got off his own shot with his Kodak.

The chief slumped over his horse as the sergeant predicted, then rolled onto the field. On cue, the rest of the Indians charged the cavalry, smoke filling the field, yelling drowning out gunfire.

"Garryowen," Custer's field song, filled the air as the trumpeter in front of the line of cavalry raised a brass bugle to his lips, signaling troopers to make a charge of their own, with both sides firing en masse. Soon, the reenactors disappeared in the black powder smoke that hung low over the field.

Alexander in the role of Custer rallied his troops as the final charge by the Indians began. Shooting. Yelling. Smoke lingering on the field. Thick enough that Manny could taste the powder, seemingly untouched by the wind, as if staying there to remind spectators of the carnage that day in 1876, as if the smoke were playing a role in obscuring the soldiers' dead bodies from those who would come after to mutilate them.

As suddenly as the firing had started, it stopped, replaced by an eerie silence. Fallen cavalry and Indians lay motionless on the ground, their horses milling about as if waiting for the fight to start again. One bay lit out across the Little Big Horn with a splash, while a riderless paint dropped its head to graze at the edge of the field.

Clapping spectators arose from their seats, high-fiving the reenactors for their performance. When the clapping subsided, people grabbed their padded stadium seats, along with empty bottles and paper plates, and began the treacherous descent from the bleachers. Manny was finishing his Indian taco while he and Willie waited for the crowd to disperse.

"Looks like one wasn't so lucky." Willie chin-pointed to

one of the Crow youngsters, red and yellow war paint smudged with grass stains, sitting on the ground and rocking back and forth, holding his wrist that turned at an odd angle. One of the soldiers squatted beside the boy, talking to him as they waited for the paramedics. "Casualty of war," Willie said, finally starting down the bleachers.

The chief with the yellow face lay where he'd been "shot," while his gray nickered over the top of him, wanting more action. Another Indian walked past him, nudged him with the toe of his moccasin, and said something in passing.

Two women dressed in Lakota patterned deerskin dresses walked toward the boy with the broken wrist. One bent to yellow face as she walked by.

And screamed.

Manny stood on tiptoes to see over the heads of those still making their way down the bleachers. The woman backed away and her hands flew to her face to muffle her screams, blood dripping between fingers and smearing her cheeks.

Paramedics responding to broken wrist diverted to yellow face. They dropped their jump bag beside the body and gingerly rolled him over. One grabbed a stethoscope from around his neck, while the other one cut away the man's shirt. Within moments, they put their gear back into their bag and stood. Paramedics are interested only in the living.

CHAPTER 2

Levi Star Dancer reined his lathered pony beside White Crow. Levi's horse snorted to greet the taller man sitting on his paint gelding as if he'd been born to it. But then, Crow warriors were born with horses' withers beneath them. "Took you long enough to catch up. *Levi.*"

Levi swatted at his friend's head, but White Crow laughed and ducked.

"You know I do not like that. I am Star Dancer of the Whistling Water clan."

"It is what the White man calls you. *Levi.*"

"I do not like it."

"You liked it when they gave you the name and the blankets." White Crow was right. The horse soldiers had given him a name and blankets and food in exchange for his scouting. But Levi would have scouted for nothing had he known they were going after the sworn enemy of the Apsa'alooke, and he need never have been saddled with a White man's name.

White Crow extended his long brass glass and looked out across rolling hills that seemed to move. Buffalo grass and gamma grass, tall this year, undulated with the rising and falling of the wind that blew over from the mountains to the west.

Any other day, it would have been serene. Any other day, Levi would have thanked the Creator for such wonderment. Any other day: except the day that Colonel Custer chose to die. "Any sign of the others?" Colonel Custer had dismissed his Crow scouts before the fighting began, and they had scattered to parts unknown.

White Crow shrugged and handed the glass to Levi. "I saw them ride to where we fought the Lakota at the Rosebud eight days ago."

Levi extended White Crow's looking glass. The Lakota, enemies of the Crow, had fought ferociously under the command of Crazy Horse at the Rosebud. Levi wanted no more run-ins with that warrior.

Levi squinted against the sun as he put the long glass to his eye. Puffs of smoke from a hundred guns showed like puffs from a pipe across the valley. The pop-pop-popping of gunfire reached them, and Levi counted the seconds between the puffs and the sound: a mile. Perhaps more. He and White Crow had ridden out just in time.

"Colonel Custer is a fool. We told him . . ."

"We told him not to attack the camp." Levi adjusted the telescope and tried to spot where Custer and his men were fighting for their lives. Warriors like ants wiggled through wind-moving prairie, while the Greasy Grass, bright light shimmering off its shallow water, meandered below the battle, oblivious to the fighting going on above it. "The river will be stained red this day. Just be grateful the colonel ordered us to leave."

White Crow bent to his paint's neck and grabbed the water bladder tethered to the pony's mane. He took a long pull and handed it to Levi. "Those Lakota and Cheyenne will have Custer's liver for dinner. I wonder what happened to the others."

Levi shrugged and allowed the cool water to snake its way down his parched throat. He handed the deer bladder back to White Crow and glassed the battle. "The last I saw Goes Ahead, he was on the heels of White Man Runs Him and Hairy Moccasin." He closed the glass and handed it back. "And they were as angry as we were."

White Crow brought a white muslin tobacco pouch from his saddlebag. He opened the drawstring and started rolling a smoke. "I could have killed Custer myself. Accusing us of being cowards."

Custer had done them a favor telling them to leave, telling them he would not fight with cowards. But Levi and White Crow, as well as the other Crow scouts, would have stayed. And they all would have been dead, just like Custer's soldiers would be dead before the sun settled over the rolling hills. More popping. More soldiers dying, though at this distance, Levi could only imagine which group of fighting men was the horse troopers and which was the Lakota and Cheyenne.

Levi spat, his throat dry, and he bent to his own water bladder, the sudden familiar groaning like meat boiling inside his bowels. He doubled over as he leaped from his pony, dropping his rifle on the ground. He ran bent over clutching his belly.

He cursed the running sickness, feeling the food sloshing

in his gut, praying he would make it over the hill before he messed his pants. Again. White Crow's laugh followed close behind him, but it did not matter: He had made it to the far side of the hill, away from his friend's prying eyes, and he tested the wind before he squatted. His afternoon meal shot out of him like some of those hot gushers in the mountains to the west, his cramping instantly gone as it always was after an episode. Always he prayed for an *ak'bari'a*. Always he prayed for a healer who could cure him.

Finished, his muscles felt as if he'd just completed a foot-race, and he remained squatting, the tall grass hiding his embarrassment. He grabbed his journal and began tearing off a page before he caught himself. He closed the book, and instead yanked out a handful of buffalo grass. Paper was far too scarce to use to clean himself. He stood on shaky legs as he pulled his pants up and cinched the drawstring. He took deep breaths before he made his way back, knowing White Crow would needle him.

Cries. Loud, angry cries. War cries!

Levi dropped to the ground. He scrambled to the edge of the hill, keeping low, peering between tall prairie grass just as White Crow fired his muzzle-loader. Its sound was so different from the repeater Levi carried, which he had left beside his pony when he had run for the grass moments ago.

White Crow stood, powder horn plug in his teeth, shaking violently. He spilled powder over his arm. He frantically rammed another ball down the barrel, as two Lakota rode hard up the hill. They kicked their horses' flanks, rifles shouldered. Both fired as one. The bullets struck White Crow full in the chest, dust kicking off his breastplate. He dropped the buffalo horn, spilling powder onto the earth. He fell faceup, his lifeless eyes, accusing eyes, finding Levi's stare.

The short, stocky Lakota dropped off his horse, knife in

hand as he ran to White Crow. He dropped and skidded on his knees beside the corpse. Pooling blood from the chest wound was clumping beside the Lakota's knees. He lifted White Crow's hair to make the scalp cut, just when the tall Lakota, still sitting on his pony, shot his shorter friend in the back. The tall one swung his leg over his pony and dropped to the ground. Levi drew in a breath that he feared would be heard, and his hand went naturally to his gut, where this man had shot him two years ago while trapping beaver near the Valley of the Giveaway. This one called Eagle Bull.

The stocky warrior rolled over onto his face, gathering his arms beneath him, looking back, his pleading, disbelieving eyes watching Eagle Bull lever another round and shove his rifle barrel against his head. Blood and gray matter spilled over the stocky man's back and peppered White Crow's bare legs.

Eagle Bull looked around and nudged his dead companion with the toe of his moccasin before turning to White Crow. Eagle Bull slid his knife from the sheath, made the scalp cut in one motion, and lifted White Crow's scalp. He tucked it into his fringed shirt and stood. He walked to the place where Levi had dropped his rifle and picked it up, blowing dust from the action.

Levi unsheathed his own knife and crouched, judging the distance, judging the time it would take to rush Eagle Bull. Eagle Bull stopped, his hand tightening on his rifle, his head turning toward Levi hidden in the grass. Levi realized he would not get two steps before Eagle Bull saw him and shot. A Crow—enemy of the Lakota since oral history told of their conflicts—was understandable. But why had Eagle Bull killed his own friend? Levi held his breath as he wiped sweat from his hand on his trousers. Anyone evil enough to kill a comrade for the honor of a Crow scalp and his pony would gladly kill an enemy.

Eagle Bull, his head swiveling and eyes darting like an owl listening for the mouse, stepped toward Levi. Levi relaxed his muscles, for he knew tight muscles reacted slowly, and prepared to rush Eagle Bull. Another step. Eagle Bull lifted his head up, testing the wind. Levi thanked the Creator his mess was downwind from where the Lakota stood with rifle clenched, looking for someone else to kill.

Levi looked away. *The eyes draw the eyes*, as he had learned from a lifetime of hunting the same type of warrior that now had the upper hand mere feet away.

Eagle Bull shrugged and relaxed his grip on his rifle. He turned to Levi and White Crow's ponies and gathered their reins. He swung his leg over his own pony's back, leading the other horses down the hill. He stopped and looked over his shoulder, as if taunting Levi, before resuming the slow walk toward the huge enemy camp just across the Greasy Grass.

Levi waited until he could no longer hear the snort of Eagle Bull's pony before he stood and walked to his friend. White Crow lay with blood clotting in his open eyes from the insulting, bone-deep cut encircling his head.

Levi shuddered. He jumped at the screech of the owl. He jerked his head around, but he saw no owl plying its grisly trade near his dead friend. Levi shuddered anew. White Crow's *ira'xaxe*, his soul, remained near his body.

But he knew he had heard it. He had heard the owl's lament, the soul grieving for the man, who moments before had breathed the air of a free-ranging warrior. And Levi would forever hear that cry as it wrenched at the fringes of his consciousness.

CHAPTER 3

Willie skidded to a stop, narrowly missing a suicidal doe ante-lope crossing the road. The dust settled just as she reached the ditch on the other side. She stopped and looked back over her shoulder before snacking on gamma grass. Willie breathed deeply and turned to Manny. "Maybe if you'd had your brake shoes replaced this heap would be able to stop safely."

"You're the one that wanted to drive."

"Only because I want to come off this vacation alive."

"What's that supposed to mean?"

"You know just what I mean." Willie looked sideways and continued down the gravel road. He didn't have to explain: Manny's crappy driving continued to scare Willie. Since Manny had returned to Pine Ridge from Virginia, he had seri-ously wrecked four cars, and he'd had a minor accident with Willie's truck. *Okay, so it wasn't minor to Willie. But I fixed it. And if they had mass transit here in the outback, I wouldn't have wrecked those.* Willie wisely insisted on driving to Crow

Agency from Pine Ridge, and he wouldn't let Manny near the wheel. Of his own car.

"At least let me change the music."

Manny reached for the CD, but Willie slapped his hand away. "You said come up with some compromise, and I have. Now sit back." Before leaving on their vacation, Manny told Willie he'd have to shitcan his powwow CD. And Willie countered that he wouldn't ride all the way to Montana listening to Manny's polka.

"Then come up with something else," Manny had told him.

And Willie had. He turned up Three Dog Night, the back woofers thudding the rock song. At least it was easier on Manny's ears than ZZ Top.

Willie turned the music down a notch. "Don't you beat all."

"What?"

"This." Willie motioned to the road. "I'm supposed to be on vacation and I'm stuck here with you."

"We could have been stuck here with the ladies."

Willie rolled his eyes. "Another of your great ideas. 'Get away from the women for a week,' you said. 'If we miss them, that'll tell us if we love them,' you said. Now I'm at Crow Agency with you for God knows how long."

"Is it my fault the SAC called me?"

"You didn't have to answer your cell."

"He knew I went to the reenactment. He knew I was there when the yellow-faced reenactor got killed. What better way to start an investigation than actually witness the death." The Special Agent in Charge of the Rapid City Field Office had agreed to "lend" Manny to the Billings office for the duration of the investigation. The Billings office had no Native American agents. The SAC felt Manny would be an asset, to cut through Indian red tape, and thought, mistakenly, that Manny preferred working reservation cases. "Besides, this looks like nothing more than an accident. Some boob put the wrong ammo in the gun. A day at Crow Agency and we're out of here. Maybe catch Old Faithful before heading back to Pine Ridge."

Willie shook his head. "Must be more to it than that, or the SAC wouldn't have pulled you off vacation."

Manny looked away but Willie caught it. "There is more."

Manny nodded. "BIA here says the victim, Harlan White Bird, owned an auction house in Lodge Grass specializing in Indian artifacts. Had a huge auction at the end of the reenactment every year. They think there might be some connection. They think it was no accident."

>‹›‹›‹

A dispatcher smiled at Willie, then frowned when Manny showed his FBI ID wallet. Dispatch was directly inside the front door of the justice building, and the dispatcher looked the part of the building guard. Beneath her denim shirt she flexed muscles that Manny was sure she could back up, and she held her glare long enough to tell Manny that federal law enforcement wasn't any more popular here than on Pine Ridge. She pointed toward a conference room down a long hallway, her smile lingering on Willie a moment longer.

A black-uniformed Bureau of Indian Affairs officer sat at a long table across from a Crow Agency tribal policeman. The tribal policeman, with thin legs sticking out of jeans frayed where the bottoms met his scuffed boots, sat crooked in a chair, one foot on the table, picking his teeth with a pocketknife.

"Chief Deer Slayer." The BIA chief stood and smoothed his black uniform before offering Manny his hand. He towered over Manny, his grip strong, but not crushing. He held the air of authority Manny had seen in other BIA chiefs. He jerked his thumb toward the tribal policeman. "This is Matthew LaPierre. We call him Stumper."

Stumper looked up from his all-important tooth picking and caught Deer Slayer's scowl. He swung his leg down and stood. He was shorter and thinner than Manny, and the tension in his grip, as tight as the coil of braided hair hanging down his back, belied his small stature. He grinned at Manny's shorts and Hawaiian shirt. He ignored Willie as he dropped back into the chair, picking his teeth as he counted ceiling tiles.

Manny accepted the iced tea Deer Slayer's secretary handed him, and Willie grabbed a chair opposite Deer Slayer. "So what do we got? Word is, you fellas think there's more to White Bird's death than accidental?"

"Stumper." Deer Slayer pointed at his subordinate.

Stumper dropped his boot from the tabletop and slid his chair close. He tossed a manila folder across the table. Inside were preliminary photos taken by the BIA evidence tech, along with Harlan White Bird's information.

"Looks like Harlan was a busy man this year. Spent three months in jail this spring. Thought he owned an auction house?"

"He did," Stumper answered. "Being a drunk was just his hobby."

Deer Slayer glared at Stumper and turned to Manny. "Even though Harlan was an alkie, he was the foremost expert on Plains Indian artifacts from here to the West Coast. He owned the only auction house in the Rocky Mountain region specializing in genuine Plains Indian items."

Manny flipped through Harlan's file. "He have an auction every year at the end of the reenactment?"

"When most tourists are here." Stumper grinned at

Manny's garb. "When most gullible tourists are here for the Real Bird reenactment."

"So Harlan sold to us 'gullible' tourists'?" Manny envisioned Harlan hawking fake Indian artifacts on the sidewalk in front of an auction house. "Did he sell imitations?"

"He sold enough of those." Stumper smiled at Manny and Willie. "To fools that wanted authentic Indian artifacts. But after the repros and the stuff slapped together by workers in Hong Kong were sold, he'd start with the real McCoy. Artifacts that would cost me a year's wages to bid on."

Willie thumbed through the file. "How is it that Harlan could have been shot with a live .45-55 round? Don't they have people checking guns before the show?"

Deer Slayer stood and walked over to a card table. Next to a bronze buffalo skull a coffeepot was steaming. He picked up the pot and held it out to Manny and Willie. They shook their heads, and Deer Slayer replaced it for the next unsuspecting coffee guest. "That's the problem. The folks organizing the show have prop men that check and double-check the guns right before the action starts, making sure there's only blanks in them. They've never had an incident involving live ammo."

"Then what makes you think it was something more than an accident?"

"Him." Deer Slayer nodded to Stumper. "He thinks he had a vision that Harlan was murdered."

"It wasn't a vision." Stumper locked eyes with Deer Slayer. "It was a hunch. Call it police intuition."

"And why didn't any other officers with twice your experience have these intuitions?" Deer Slayer turned to Manny. "Stumper here's been on the force four years, and sometimes he acts like your garden-variety rookie."

Stumper ignored Deer Slayer and turned his chair to face Manny. "Someone replaced blanks with live rounds. I've got two officers asking everyone leaving the grounds if they have any photos or videos of the reenactment."

"You sound sure the ammo was substituted."

"Of course it was switched," Stumper snapped at Willie. "Whether or not it was on purpose—with the intent of killing Harlan—is another matter."

"Then I suggest you three take a look at Harlan's shop."

Stumper scowled at Deer Slayer. "Us three? I thought the FBI did their own investigations. I got my own methods."

"Being Agent Tanno's liaison while he's here at Crow Agency, you'll assist him any way you can."

Manny turned to Stumper. "Then we better take a look at Harlan's shop."

Stumper glared a last time at Deer Slayer. "Sure, Agent Tanno. Just as soon as we talk with the killer."

CHAPTER 4

Stumper stopped in front of a door marked INTERVIEW. "Don't mind if I sit in on this, do you? It might be entertaining."

"Entertaining?"

Stumper smiled. "Wait till you see this guy. He's a candidate for the rubber room."

Stumper held the door for Willie and Manny. The cavalry sergeant Manny saw earlier, whose shot started the reenactment, sat in a captain's chair holding his head as his elbows rested on a long, oval Formica table sporting numerous cigarette burns along the outside edges. The sergeant's own cigarette had burned down, threatening to scorch the side of his head, and it was only a matter of time before the smoldering butt would add another insult to the embattled table.

Manny eyed the cigarette and patted his empty pocket. Even after he'd quit last year, he still craved a smoke. "Put your cigarette out, please."

The sergeant dropped it into an empty Orange Crush can. It hissed and a small tendril of smoke rose from the can.

Manny nodded to the other door opening into the squad room area. "Make sure that's locked," he told Stumper.

The sergeant jumped as if he expected rubber hoses and bright lights to come out. "We just need to make sure no one interrupts us."

The sergeant said nothing and nodded. *Or did he shake?*

Manny introduced himself and Willie, and the sergeant had started to rise when Manny put his hand onto the man's shoulder that shook as much as his nicotine-stained hands. One of the sergeant's suspenders had fallen off his shoulder, and he'd missed two buttons on his fly. Stumper was right: The man was a basket case, and the last thing Manny needed on vacation was to pick a basket case up from the floor. "Just sit back and relax, mister."

The man considered Manny's shirt and shorts. "Don't you FBI agents usually wear a suit and tie?"

"I'm in disguise," Manny answered.

"Ian Tess." He seemed to accept Manny's explanation as he offered his hand, which lacked the firmness of Stumper's and the strength of Deer Slayer's, instead feeling lifeless like the body of the man he'd just killed. Manny wiped his sweaty hand onto his shorts. "This never happens at Gettysburg."

"What's that?"

"Gettysburg," Tess repeated. "I participate in the reenactment there every year, and nothing like this ever happens."

"You mean you never killed anyone at one of these before?"

Tess looked through reddened eyes from Stumper, smiling as he leaned against one wall, to Manny. Manny rolled the only other chair in the room close to the card table and sat, careful not to gouge himself on the broken chair arm. Manny had long ago learned that the best attribute of an investigator was silence, knowing when to wait until the person decided to get their burden off their chest.

"Back there they check our loads before the shooting starts," Tess said at last. "We never have anything on our uniform belts except powder. Never a ball to ram on top of the charge. And they check it many times before the battle begins."

"And this is the first you've killed anyone?"

Tess sat back in the chair and his face flushed. He leaned across the table, and Manny smelled the whiskey on his breath. "Of course I never killed anyone," he said, annoyance entering his voice, and Manny was glad Tess was starting to come around to the land of the living. He reached for his cigarettes, but Manny placed his hand on his arm.

"You didn't know someone had switched a live round with the dummy. Tell me what you did this afternoon leading up to the battle."

Tess slumped back in his chair, his eyes softening, grateful that someone had confirmed he was no murderer. "After I loaded the Springfield, the prop man checked my rifle and stuck the yellow ribbon in the action."

"And the rifle was in your possession the whole time?"

"Whole time?"

"Even when you went to the port-a-potty?"

Tess straightened up and a smile crossed his face. "No, it wasn't. I left it there when I got the two-minute warning and ran to the blue house."

"I saw you run for the port-a-potty," Manny said. "There were people around your tent."

Tess nodded. "People come to these events 'cause they love

history. They love it when I fold a little history into the events. Some background on cavalry equipment. Weaponry. Stuff like that. Anyway, I finished in the crapper just in time for the reenactment to begin. Everyone had cleared out—probably sitting in the bleachers. Even the safety man was gone."

"Safety man?" Willie asked. "As in the man that checked your rifle?"

Tess nodded. "The second safety check of the day."

Manny scooted his chair closer to Tess. "Like Gettysburg, multiple safety checks?"

"Just like Gettysburg." Tess shook his head. "Making sure no accident happens. But it did somehow."

"Tell me about this second safety man." Manny took a notebook from Stumper, not to actually take notes, but to appear to be taking notes. It's what people expected an interviewer to do.

Tess looked at the ceiling before dropping his head and nodding to Willie. "Tall guy, like him. But not nearly as heavy. And sloppy, too."

"How so?"

"Wore an old T-shirt that looked like he served last night's dinner on it."

"Indian?"

Tess nodded. "But don't ask me what kind. They all look alike." Tess looked to all three men in the room and slid his chair back from the table. But there would be no escaping his stupidity. "Sorry, but you guys know what I mean?"

Manny waved it away. "What did the second safety man do?"

"Well he checked my rifle, of course."

"Did you watch him?"

Tess laughed nervously. "What's to check. He opens the

rifle's action and checks that there's a dummy chambered. Then sticks the yellow ribbon back in the gun."

"Did you watch him?" Willie asked. He leaned over the table, and Tess backed up as he craned his neck up.

"I went in my tent for a moment while he did that."

"To take a nip?" Manny asked.

Tess's hand automatically went to his back pocket. "You know they don't allow booze at the reenactment."

Manny shook his head. "I don't care about that. Could you give a description to a police sketch artist?"

Tess rubbed his eyes. "Wouldn't do any good. All I know is he was an Indian."

Manny had stood and started for the door when Tess stopped him. "What happens to me now?"

Manny looked to Stumper and Willie. "Somebody that looks Indian will come get you soon. Just sit tight."

Tess leaned on the table and once again cradled his head in his hands as he rocked back and forth. "Nothing like this ever happens at Gettysburg."

CHAPTER 5

Manny squirmed in the seat as he tried to stretch out his legs. "I offered to sit back there," Willie said. "I don't feel sorry for you."

Manny leaned over and rested his arms on the seat back. "If I can't fit back here, just think what it'd be like for you." He tapped Stumper on the shoulder. "How far is it to Lodge Grass?"

"Twenty minutes," he said as he turned onto I90. Stumper retrieved his can of Copenhagen from his back pocket and stuffed his lip. He had started putting it back when Willie reached over and snatched the can. He started filling his own lower lip, and Manny scowled at him. But just for a moment. Willie was fighting his other addiction, alcohol, and Manny could overlook his tobacco habit for the moment.

They started around a '60s International pickup missing the hood, the seventy-year-old-going-on-ninety driver pedaling as fast as she could. She glared at the tribal Tahoe as it went by and thrust her middle finger high out the door as they passed. Stumper chuckled.

"That funny?" Manny asked.

Stumper shook his head. "Not that, it's us. It's ironic that you and this big ugly Lakota sitting beside me are working a criminal case with me, a Crow. Wasn't but a century ago and we'd be fighting for each other's scalps."

Willie reached over and flipped Stumper's braid. "Who's to say we won't come away with a scalp today?"

Stumper flipped his hair back and slapped Willie's hand away.

Manny was quick to intervene. "Hate to have pulled you away from anything important."

Stumper shook his head. "The only thing you pulled me away from is another methamphetamine case. I get tired of working those."

"Same as us." Willie worked the snuff into his lower lip. "Not a week goes by that we don't have some new meth case dumped in our laps." He rolled his window down to spit. "It's ruining our kids."

"But it comes onto the rez at odd times. Keeps us second-guessing where it's coming from, who's bringing the shit onto Crow Agency." Stumper rolled his window down and spit. Manny scrambled to the other side of the seat just as droplets of tobacco juice splattered where he'd sat. "And if that were my only problem, it would be bad enough. But we got Della Night Tail."

"Meth head?"

"Pain in the ass. She's our chronic bitcher."

Willie laughed. "I'll put our Crazy George He Crow or Henry Lone Wolf against any complainer you got."

Stumper started passing a stock truck hauling yearling heifers, and he quickly rolled up his window against the odor.

"There's no bitcher like Della. She's a professional. She reports her old man, Little Dave Night Tail, missing about once a month. Like she did this morning."

"Little Dave use meth?"

Stumper shook his head. "Little Dave just doesn't come home about every other payday. He lays carpet for an outfit out of Hardin, and claims he needs to tie one on now and again. Claims the carpet kicker trashes his knees, and he drinks to kill the pain."

"But you don't believe him?"

Stumper looked at Manny in the rearview mirror. "If I were married to that witch Della, I'd manage to stay away every chance I could, too. What I think is that Little Dave got himself some stray tail in Hardin, which makes it hard for us. Every time he doesn't come home, Della gripes to the tribal council, and we all know what direction shit rolls."

Willie drew his legs under him and tried to turn in the seat. He just didn't fit. "If he's anything like our drunks, he's on the backside of a twelve-pack of Budweiser, and he'll stagger home when the beer runs out. I know."

Willie caught Manny's eyes in the rearview mirror and he quickly looked away. Willie struggled daily with the booze, and talk of Little Dave Night Tail only reminded him of the comfort a bottle of whiskey or a cold six-pack could bring.

They took the off-ramp to Old Highway 87 onto Main Street. If a town of five hundred souls had a Main Street. "Where'd you get a nickname like Stumper?" Manny asked.

"Yeah." Willie slapped his arm. "Where'd you get that goofy name?"

Stumper leaned his head out the Tahoe and spit. The wind caught it and blew brown tobacco juice back onto his arm. "Some dude from Billings robbed the Little Big Horn Casino my first year on the job. I got there in time to shoot the guy as he ran out the door."

"Doesn't explain your name."

"My aim was a little off." Stumper turned onto Hester Street. "I was shooting a .357 Magnum then, and the ER docs in Billings couldn't save the guy's arm. He's working in a prison laundry folding clothes one-armed." Stumper laughed. "Or should I say one-stumped. So the name stuck."

Stumper drove past a rusting street sign proclaiming they had turned off Hill Street when they reached Taft. They turned down a gravel street and Manny caught sight of yellow crime scene tape encircling a large pole building. Harlan's gray-sided auction barn sat at the end of a dead-end street. In Manny's last home in Arlington, Virginia, such faults of street planning would be referred to as cul-de-sacs. Here at Crow Agency, it was just one more street that ran out of money before it was connected to another.

Stumper pulled up in front of police warning signs that had been posted at Harlan White Bird's auction house. The sign proclaimed the business had been seized as evidence. "Odd for a business to be located on a dead end." Manny unfolded his legs from the backseat and stretched his hamstrings. He needed to get some road miles in his running shoes, even on vacation. "Wouldn't think that'd be good for business."

"Didn't matter." Stumper stuffed his can of Copenhagen in his back pocket before Willie could grab it. "Harlan did enough business that people came from all over the country. He could have held his auction in an outhouse and still drawn a crowd. Besides, Harlan was paranoid as hell. Insisted it was easier to watch anyone coming up if the place set on a dead end."

Willie walked to the corner of the windowless building and back. He tapped the security keypad hanging on one side of the door. "Did Harlan have a reason to be paranoid?"

"The quality of the artifacts he gathered for auction would be reason enough for someone to break in."

Stumper walked to the door and stood on his tiptoes as he felt for the key above the jamb. Willie reached up and grabbed it, smiling as he handed it to Stumper. "Don't say a word, big man."

Willie backed up, feigning hurt feelings, his hands held out in front of him. "All I was going to say is that's a hell of a place to hide a key. For someone so paranoid."

"Who else knew Harlan stashed his key there?" Manny asked.

Stumper paused. "Probably everyone on Crow Agency. Certainly everyone in Lodge Grass."

Stumper had inserted the key when Manny stopped him. "Aren't you going to disable the alarm?"

Stumper turned the lock and opened the door. "Security system's been shot for the better part of a year. Harlan never got around to having it fixed. And yes, most everyone knew about that, too."

They followed Stumper into the building as he felt his way around the wall for the light switch. The fluorescents flickered for a moment before catching, a steady humming filling the huge room.

Stumper caught Manny's slack-jawed stare. "Winter was Harlan's slow season, and he'd clear the tables so the local kids had a place to play ball."

Manny nodded to basketball hoops on portable stands on one end of the building. "It's certainly big enough to play ball in here."

Stumper led them to where Harlan had arranged wall-to-wall display tables clustered together according to the type of relic. They'd been set so close together that there was just enough room for prospective bidders to walk between them as they inspected the artifacts. Manny walked awed among the tables, the largest collection of authentic Indian artifacts outside a museum he'd ever seen.

"Did I lie about Harlan's annual auction being impressive?"

Manny turned away from Stumper and started walking the displays. "You didn't lie."

"Look at this." Willie stood hunched over a table two rows down and Manny joined him. Willie pointed to a cradle-board, Crow by the beaded diamond pattern at the top and bottom of the board, tapering slightly at the bottom. Red and yellow beads set on light blue formed the background. Three deerskin ties to hold a baby at the center of the board lay stiff and twisted from years of hard weather. A yellow plastic tent with the item number on it sat in front of the cradleboard for prospective bidders to match up to bid sheets.

Manny brushed past Willie, stopping at a table displaying metal trade axes, some still secured in ash handles with buf-falo sinew, others pegged in place with square nails, each with its own plastic tent and number assigned. Ornately decorated axes, more ceremonial than practical, were laid out side by side. Their beaded and quilled handles of various colors vied with blades in various stages of brown and black and bluish patinas.

On the opposite end of the table, Harlan had arranged knives of different lengths and different functions. Skinning knives were displayed next to hunting knives, next to knives used in ceremonies.

Manny had started walking past when his eyes clouded, his focus drawn to one knife apart from the others: a warrior's knife. A killing knife. Manny bent over, one hand resting on the table for stability, his other hand reaching out. He touched a dark stain on the blade near the hilt that he knew was ancient blood. He tried pulling his hand away, but it remained on the blade as he fought the physical connection to what he witnessed somewhere deep in his clouded mind.

And then the stench of blood. The stench of pain. The stench of death. He swayed in the heat, the intense heat, of that June day overlooking the Greasy Grass when Colonel Custer fought Lakota and Cheyenne warriors. The heat, always the heat, caused Manny's vision to shimmer. A warrior squatted and peered through thick reeds at his friend in the open field just out of the protection of the tall buffalo grass. Two Lakota rode up a hill, their war cries loud, their horses' flanks whipped with quirts, tongues lapping the air as they bore down on the luckless warrior caught in the open.

Manny felt the need to scream a warning to the warrior caught alone. But this was a Crow, sworn enemy of the Lakota, and Manny hesitated. Shots erupted in Manny's head, the ringing in his ears followed by resounding disbelief. The first Lakota had jumped from his pony, run to the fallen Crow warrior, and dropped to his knees. One hand had grabbed his enemy's hair and the other had held a knife poised to slice. Even before he had been able to make the first scalp cut, he had been shot in the back by his own comrade's rifle. Manny tried shouting.

And his throat closed shut watching the other Lakota coolly murder his friend. He looked down only to make sure before he dropped to his knees and slid the knife around the base of his friend's scalp, lifting the bloody souvenir. The warrior slid the knife into the sheath on his belt, along with the Crow scalp and that of his fellow Lakota. The man mounted and rode slowly away from the killing field. The knife—the scalping knife—fell to the ground unnoticed.

Lights overhead flickered and caught, the humming

bringing Manny back to the present. He shook his head to clear his mind, the strength returning to knees that had nearly buckled. The last thing he felt like putting up with now was some fleeting vision he couldn't possibly need—or want—to interfere with his investigation.

Manny staggered and turned his back on the table with the knife display, concentrating in front of him on the table hosting bow and arrow displays. In the center of the table lay a Crow bow made of mountain sheep horn and covered with rattlesnake skin. It lacked a bowstring, yet Manny knew enough about them from archery in his youth to tell that a very powerful man must have strung the instrument.

Various deer- and elk-skin quivers surrounded the bow, some ornately beaded, others painted on the tanned hides with geometric patterns of forgotten clans. Harlan had arranged single arrows around the quivers, the different fletching with various types of feathers as sure to identify the makers as if they'd left palm prints behind. Manny picked up one arrow and ran the dried, century-old feather fletching carefully over his hand. A warrior was nocking the arrow, a spike buck deer was feeding on an elderberry bush. Once again, Manny shook his head to clear the images flooding his thoughts. "Harlan must have been quite organized," he said, gesturing to the tables categorized by type of artifacts to maximize the bidders' inspection.

Stumper laughed and waved his hand over the room of wall-to-wall tables. "Only in this was Harlan ever organized, and only because he knew the smoother his auctions went, the more money he made. And Harlan was all about money." Stumper turned to a table holding rifles and handguns. Ammunition was still in original boxes, some pristine, others torn and weathered, spilling out graying bullets sticking out of rust-colored casings.

Manny started walking past the knife displays, turning back to the scalping knife. Hairs were standing at attention along his arms and the nape of his neck. He swayed, unsteady, as the face of the warrior emerged slipping the knife from his belt sheath. Ageless stains on the blade exposed the blood of another's tribe. And obscured the blood of his friend's—his own. Manny felt his legs buckle, and Willie caught him.

"You okay?"

Manny nodded.

"You getting visions again?"

"Never."

"You're still in denial."

Manny forced a smile. "What, you're offering me a twelve-step program for vision seekers?"

"Suit yourself," Willie answered. "But I think you need to talk with Reuben. They're becoming more frequent."

Older brother Reuben, the only sacred man Manny knew—or trusted in these matters—had only riddles as to how and why the visions crept up on Manny at odd times. "I'm okay."

Willie shrugged and moved on to another table, while Manny moved in the opposite direction. He bent to a beaded elk-skin dress lying neatly beside an eagle feather fan. A chief's daughter's dress. Imperfect rows of red and black and yellow glass trade beads told the story of a Blackfoot woman making the dress over a warm fire one frigid wintery night.

And the red catlinite pipe next to it, the stem and bowl properly detached. An old man had passed the pipe around to guests in his tipi over a hundred winters ago, saving his pipe adorned with ermine skin and hawk feathers only for ceremonies. Manny was aware that he knew it had belonged to a Cheyenne elder. He knew, yet he drove it from his mind.

Visions just didn't happen without a reason, without the Creator's hand guiding him. At least not to a City Sioux.

"Quality is an understatement." Willie had walked a row over and stood in front of a table displaying pottery. He clasped his hands behind him as he leaned over, examining the relics.

Stumper picked his teeth with his pocketknife as he stopped beside Willie. "Things were simpler back in the day."

"You got that right," Willie agreed. "Men had to hunt and fight and protect the *tiospaye*. The hard stuff. All women had to do was some fleshing and cooking. Take care of kids."

Manny nudged Willie. "Go back home and tell Doreen women had it good back then."

Willie backed away, his eyes widening. "You're not going to tell her what I said, are you?"

Manny smiled. "The mad Lakota woman? Not on your life. She'd be as likely to kill the messenger."

Willie breathed a sigh of relief. Doreen Big Eagle had put her brand on Willie last year and held him by the short hairs. They even talked of setting a wedding date.

Stumper leaned across the table and winked at Willie. "Sounds like your honey's got you where she wants you, big guy." He backed up when Willie leaned across to grab him. "Now us Crow warriors, we wear the breechclouts in our families."

"Bullshit," Willie said. "You're no different than us."

"We are. Back in the day, we did the fighting and hunting. Swapped stories over campfires while the women did the simple things, everyday things, like set aside what to use for TP when you finished your morning constitution."

Willie shrugged. "Guess they used paper, same as the settlers. Same as the soldiers."

Manny shook his head. "We NDNs didn't have a lot of paper to go around. I'm thinking knowledge of the softest prairie grasses was worth their weight in corncobs."

"You're probably right." Willie put his hands on his hips and looked around the tables. "Anything missing?"

"What the hell do I look like?" Stumper asked. "A psychic?"

Willie started around the table, and Manny stepped between them. "Do you have an auction flyer?"

Stumper stood with his neck craned up, glaring at Willie, holding the stare long enough to show Willie he wasn't intimidated by someone so much bigger. Stumper turned and led them through Harlan's office door, a portal to a different world than the neat organized room they'd just left. Gone was any façade of organization and tidiness, buried somewhere in all the clutter and trash littering the office. The large room appeared smaller because of the amount of garbage strewn about. Manny stepped over empty beer bottles, many half-full of stale brew. The decaying yeast-malt odor caught in his throat and he turned away.

A half-smoked Chesterfield sat where it had died on the edge of Harlan's desk, imprinting the wood with another black mark. *Who the hell smoked Chesterfields anymore?* Yet, Manny resisted the urge to snatch the snipe and the matchbook beside an overflowing faux rattlesnake ashtray and light up. *Did Willie struggle like that? Standing among all the beer and booze bottles in Harlan's office, did Willie feel the overwhelming urge to grab a beer?*

Manny picked his way between two file cabinets piled high with cases of Budweiser. A four-pack of Mike's Hard Lemonade sat atop the beer as if Harlan had crowned it king of the office. *Lemonade for hot summer nights, no doubt.*

"Harlan always live like a hog?" Willie moved an empty bottle of Beaver Tail Ale from the desktop. "And always drink the good stuff?"

Stumper laughed and kicked a bottle of Moose Drool from the chair leg before dropping into the railroad chair missing one arm. He propped his feet on the desk and grabbed a paper clip from it. "Harlan was like those competition eaters that stuff as many eggs or hot dogs in their mouths as possible. Except he liked his booze. He took his drinking seriously. I guess I'd call him a professional alkie." Stumper laughed again and started picking his teeth with the paper clip as he nodded toward the cases of Budweiser stacked on the file cabinets. "He kept those for guests. And yeah, he always lived like this. When he had auctions, he shut the blinds so no one could see what a pig he was."

Willie tossed the beer bottle into the round file and it broke. Harlan wouldn't have minded. "It would take me a month in my worst days to drink this much." He motioned to the beer. "He must have had a lot of guests."

Stumper leaned against the chair and the rusty springs squealed in pain. "Harlan hated to drink alone, and the door was open to other competition drinkers like him."

"Anyone in particular came around for free beer?"

Stumper nodded. "Sampson Star Dancer."

Manny brushed an empty Cheetos bag on the floor and sat on the corner of the desk. "You know this Star Dancer?"

"Who doesn't."

"Star Dancer," Willie breathed as if he knew the name. "Star Dancer."

And in Manny's collective memory, he'd heard of the Star Dancers of Crow Agency, too. "Seems like there was a Montana state senator years ago named Star Dancer."

Stumper nodded. "Good memory. Smoke Star Dancer. Held the state office for six terms."

"Any relation to Harlan's drinking buddy?" Willie picked up papers from the desk, and absently put them down. *Keep your mind off the beer*, Manny thought.

"Sampson is Old Smoke's son." Stumper stood and stretched his back. "Or should I say, Smoke's outcast son. Old Smoke never cottoned to Sam's drinking, and neither did the rest of the Star Dancer clan. Sam was a big disappointment for the old man, but at least his daughter amounted to something."

"She around here?"

"She is. Fact is, she's the one that kicked Sam out of the house after Smoke died. As fed up with Sam's boozing as Smoke was, he just couldn't bring himself to kick his only son off the ranch. But Chenoa did. She just couldn't take any more of Sam getting tossed in the pokey and finally gave him the bum's rush." Stumper set cases of beer on the floor to reveal a Montana State Tourism calendar hanging on the wall behind the cabinets. "This is Chenoa."

"Chenoa Star Dancer?" Willie said.

"Chenoa Iron Cloud now," Stumper added. "Face of Montana Tourism."

"Know her?" Manny asked, waving his hand across Willie's eyes. He walked to the wall and grabbed the calendar with the picture of a woman on an Appaloosa stallion. Shiny black hair falling in braids over taut breasts, and a bone choker encircling her muscular neck. She grinned at the camera with perfect teeth, and her gaze seemed to follow Manny as he stepped over trash to stand beside Willie.

"She was my first love," Willie said.

"You've met her?"

"In a way." Willie handed Manny the calendar. "I got her picture hanging up in my locker at the police station back home." Willie's dreamy eyes roamed over the photo. "I've loved her for about twenty years."

"But you're only twenty-three."

Willie shrugged. "I guess it just seems like I've always been in love with her."

Manny turned the calendar to the light and eyed it from different angles. Chenoa's eyes continued to follow him, and Manny suddenly fell under her spell as Willie had.

Stumper grabbed the calendar and hung it back on the wall. "Take a breath you two. She's married. And"—he turned to Willie—"she's older than Manny."

"No way."

"Way." Stumper grinned and leaned against the wall. He'd abandoned the paper clip and stood working the tip of his pocketknife between his teeth. "And there's hardly any makeup on her face."

"If she's older than I am . . ."

Stumper tapped the picture. "Old Smoke was in his eighties when he died, but he looked late fifties, early sixties. Chenoa's got his genes. She never ages. She looks the same as when she was runner-up in the Miss Montana pageant nineteen years ago."

"Who were the idiots," Willie asked, "that awarded her only runner-up?"

Stumper smiled. "There was a bit of a scandal that year. Seems like Chenoa came out for the swimsuit competition wearing a skimpy two-piece. Little more than three Band-Aids. Judges had to ding her on that."

"Oh, I bet they'd have liked to ding her," Willie said, staring dreamy-eyed at the calendar.

Manny turned to Stumper. "Why did Sam hang around with Harlan? Birds of a feather sort of thing?"

Stumper slipped on an empty pizza box as he walked to a door and caught himself on the wall. The latch was broken, probably sometime after the Earth's crust cooled, and Stumper swung the door open. He nodded to a small room. "Harlan let Sam crash here when he needed it. And he needed it often with all the beer he and Harlan put away."

Manny walked past Stumper into a room barely big enough to turn around in. He pulled the string on a bare bulb suspended from the ceiling. Two surplus military cots hugged a wall stained brown with tobacco juice and beer suds. Budweiser cans overflowed a cardboard Miller High Life box doubling as a trash can.

"Not nearly big enough for someone named Sampson," Willie said, ducking to avoid the bulb swinging from a breeze through a broken window.

"Don't let the name fool you," Stumper said, careful not to brush up against anything filthy in the room. "Sam's a runt, and the room fits him just fine. Smoke thought Sam would grow up tough with a name he had to defend."

"Sort of like 'A Boy Named Sue'?"

"Sort of."

"Did it?"

"Did it what?" Stumper asked Manny.

"Make him tough?"

Stumper shrugged. "He was a tough one in 'Nam, from what I hear. But back home, he was just some drunk staggering down the street that people laughed at and veered around so they wouldn't waffle him."

Manny nodded to the other cot in the room, a blue wool military blanket with USN in faded white lettering adorning the front. A piece of wood had been stuck under a broken leg on the cot, yet it still listed to the starboard. "Harlan crash here, too?"

Stumper shook his head. "That one's for Itchy. Harlan just passed out in his chair."

Willie and Manny looked to Stumper for an explanation. "Itchy Iron Cloud. Cubby's—Chenoa's husband Cubby's—kid brother. They kicked Itchy out of the house when he started getting into more trouble than he was worth while still in high school. Harlan lets him crash here with Sam when he needs it."

"Drunk?"

"Some of that. More a drug problem than the booze with Itchy."

Willie brushed past Stumper and stepped into the doorway, eying Chenoa's photo. "So if I get this right, Chenoa's brother, and her husband's brother, both hung with Harlan?"

Stumper smiled. "Just a nice, little dysfunctional family, don't ya think?"

Manny followed Stumper out of the tiny room back into Harlan's office. He slipped on a Twinkie wrapper and caught himself on the edge of a filing cabinet, spilling a stack of flyers onto the floor. Manny bent and grabbed them. "The Beauchamp Collection," Manny read aloud, placing the stack back on top of the cabinet.

"A unique chance to own a piece of history," Willie read over Manny's shoulder. "You heard of this?"

"Who hasn't?" Manny grinned.

"Well, excuse the hell out of me," Willie said, giving Manny a dirty look. "I don't get up here to Crow Agency often."

"It's not like I get up here either."

"Then how you know about this Beauchamp Collection?"

"I just know things." Manny smiled again, waiting for that to sink in. "Look, the sale of this collection's been all over the news. I just didn't realize Harlan was the consignee."

Stumper tapped the flyer with his finger. "This collection has been advertised for months on the Internet, and every western newspaper you'd ever pick up. Every serious relic collector in the country—if not the world—will want to bid on the items."

Manny spread the flyer out on the top of the filing cabinet. It listed items ranging from parfleches used to carry personal items, to quivers stuffed with arrows made of local hickory, some tipped with stone points and others with metal trade points. Buffalo robes traced to pre-reservation days were listed next to Pendleton wool blankets used by fur companies plying the mountain region.

"Commission from this collection alone would have set Harlan up for life."

"If he actually had provenance for all these." Willie ran his finger down the list. "In college, we studied relics being sold from private collections and even museums that assumed authenticity. Common con nowadays is to pass off fakes with contrived documentation."

"Harlan was always careful about verifying authenticity," Stumper said. He grabbed his can of Copenhagen, but put it right back in his pocket when he saw Willie eying it. "That's why Harlan spent time in jail this spring, for beating the starch out of that artifaker that consigned fakes he claimed were genuine." Stumper tapped the flyer with his pocketknife. "Harlan had provenance for everything. At least in the Beauchamp Collection."

"You saying some of these other relics he listed at auction weren't genuine?"

"Most are genuine, but most have been handed down from generations in families. The only provenance is word of mouth, and the only thing going to auction was Harlan's opinion that it was ancient." Stumper stood and closed his pocketknife.

"Now, the Beauchamp Collection—that's different. Harlan had documentation from the great-grandson of the original owner, Blaise Beauchamp. Proof in spades, from what Harlan bragged." He dropped back into Harlan's railroad chair, careful not to let the broken arm gouge his side. "Especially that item in the middle: the journal."

Manny had been reluctant to wear the reading glasses stuffed in his pocket. He had lost his and borrowed Clara's spare pair before he'd left for vacation. But now he needed them, and Willie and Stumper exchanged smirks when Manny donned the paisley-framed glasses with rhinestone-studded bows. Manny kept quiet, content to let them read whatever they wanted into the glasses as he read:

Journal of Levi Star Dancer, Crow scout attached to the 7th Cavalry, Company E. Only journal of any Custer's scout known to exist.

"People from all over the country and some from overseas came just to bid on the journal," Stumper said. "There have been prospective buyers parading through here all week."

"And this Levi Star Dancer is Chenoa's ancestor?" Willie said.

Stumper nodded. "Levi Star Dancer is Chenoa's great-grandfather."

"What's the connection to Beauchamp?"

"Not entirely sure, but I think Levi Star Dancer and this trapper Beauchamp were good friends. At least they lived among the Whistling Water clan at the same time. I asked Harlan about the journal that day I drew security here . . ."

"Did Harlan need security?"

"He thought he did," Stumper answered. "He had advertised the Beauchamp Collection extensively, and he didn't want to take any chances. Especially with the journal." He nodded to a small safe in the corner, the door standing open. "That's the only real security he had here, and I doubt if he ever used it."

Manny bent to the safe, one of those hundred-year-old monsters that stood two feet high, but weighed more than a piano, the actual space used to store things about a foot square. "If he stored anything in there, it's gone now."

Willie whistled and tapped the flyer. "If Harlan's flyer was right—and if he could provide the provenance on the only journal of one of Custer's scouts—he would have earned a bunch of greenbacks in commission alone."

"He wasn't charging a dime commission for the journal, big man. The entire Beauchamp Collection had been donated, and the proceeds were to go to the Little Big Horn College. And Harlan was donating his commission for the rest of the collection as well."

Manny tossed the flyer on the desk. "Benevolent man, your Harlan White Bird."

Stumper laughed. "Just this once. Harlan didn't have a benevolent bone in his old body when it came to business dealings. Harlan figured—rightfully so—that the Beauchamp Collection was sure to draw bidders from all over the country. From around the world. This would have been Harlan's biggest auction ever. Publicly announcing his intent to donate his commission to the college fund made other folks open their pocketbooks to the other items he was to auction off. Or so he thought would happen."

Manny nodded to a safe in the corner. "Surely that's not big enough to hold this collection. Is part of it . . ."

Stumper held up his hand. "Harlan was smarter than the average thief. Besides leaving the alarm pad that didn't work by the front door so everyone could see it, he hid the collection in plain sight. Table D," he nodded. "Items four through thirty-eight."

Manny and Willie followed Stumper to rows of tables on

the far side of the building to one marked D. "These pieces make up the Beauchamp Collection."

Manny stood with his hands on his hips. The artifacts took up the entire table. "This collection's too valuable to leave out in the open."

Stumper laughed. "Harlan looked like your run-of-the-gin-mill rummy, but he was actually shrewd. He said no one would suspect him of leaving the collection out in the open."

"Hidden in plain sight." Willie walked around the table, squatting and looking at the collection from different angles. "This Beauchamp fella must not need the money if he just donated the artifacts."

"I'm with you," Manny said as he ran his finger over the items on the flyer, matching them with those displayed on Table D. "This collection will yield a fortune at auction." He looked over the flyer at the collection. Beauchamp had donated a pair of women's beaded leggings that matched a quilled vest, the light blue background typical of the Crow. An elk-hide possible bag, a single row of beads adorning the closure, sat beside a painted hide shield and bird's head pipe. Gauntlets and beaded saddlebags were displayed next to an ornate red clay pipe. "Where's the journal?" Manny said at last.

"What?"

"The journal," Manny repeated. "Where's Star Dancer's journal? It's not here."

Stumper brushed past Manny and leaned over the table. "It was here yesterday."

"You saw it?"

Stumper's face lost color and he looked over the next tables. "I didn't see it myself. But it was here."

"How do you know if you never saw it?"

"Harlan stopped the bidder's inspection yesterday,"

Stumper said over his shoulder as he walked the rows of tables adjacent to the Beauchamp Collection. "He wanted security while bidders looked at it during the day." Stumper pointed to an empty table beside Harlan's office. "I drew the duty of standing around over there looking ugly all day picking my nose while people filed in and examined the collection."

Manny held up his hand. "I'm not passing judgment. Just trying to find the journal."

Stumper breathed deeply. He rubbed his forehead as he came back to the table displaying the collection. Except the journal. "All I was supposed to do was hang around in case someone decided to make off with something. As soon as the bidders left, Harlan moved the collection to this table while I hung around the office sipping ice tea. He said no one would dream that he left things so valuable out in the open, and he moved the collection."

Manny looked to the tables adjacent to the Beauchamp Collection. "Well, the journal's gone now."

"Maybe this Beauchamp came back and decided he didn't want to donate the journal," Willie said. He grabbed Stumper's can of Copenhagen from his back pocket and began stuffing his lip.

"Don't you ever buy your own?"

Willie ignored him and replaced the lid. "Maybe Beauchamp decided to keep the journal. Maybe he came and got it."

Stumper laughed nervously as he frantically walked the tables looking for the journal. "If he did, he had a hell of a trip. Adrian Beauchamp donated his great-grandfather's personal items, and the man still lives outside Paris. Harlan said he spoke with Beauchamp the morning I was here for the security detail."

Manny rubbed his head, feeling woozy, needing to eat something. He fished in his pocket for a candy bar. "And Harlan never reported the theft?"

"He would have if he would have known about it," Stumper called from five tables over, still walking the display, looking for the journal. "It had to have been stolen after Harlan left for the reenactment."

"If it is stolen," Willie called to Stumper three rows over. "Doesn't make any sense. If someone stole the journal after Harlan left for the reenactment, there wouldn't be any reason to set Harlan up to be killed."

"Unless Harlan knew who had taken the journal." Manny licked chocolate from the Snickers bar from his fingers, his head clearing. "And didn't have time to report it just then."

"Or knew, but figured it was worth more to him putting the bite on the thief."

"Blackmail?" Stumper had reached the last table and worked his way back. "Guess Harlan could put the bite on someone, particularly if they had deep pockets."

"Maybe that's why he didn't need the commission money," Willie said. "Maybe he found new money from whoever stole it."

Manny walked to the end of the display tables and dropped his Snickers wrapper in a trash can. "Then we're back to figuring who hated Harlan badly enough to substitute live rounds for blanks."

Stumper shook his head as he grabbed his can of snuff from the table. He glared at Willie when he opened it and found it empty. "Harlan was like a Komodo dragon—had no natural enemies." He tossed the can in the trash.

"Even when he was a drunk?" Willie reluctantly handed Stumper his can of snuff.

Stumper nodded. "Even drunk. Some people are mean drunks. Harlan was a happy drunk, especially when he had someone to drink with."

Willie turned away. Manny caught Willie's shame of the

bottle, but Stumper didn't. "Half the people on Crow Agency owed Harlan."

"But his business dealings?" Manny asked. "Thought he was ruthless."

"He was. But folks on Crow Agency couldn't afford bidding at Harlan's sales. Even when he had less-than-collectibles up for sale. But apart from business, he was generous, whether it was a meal Harlan bought for someone down on their luck, or a cord of wood delivered to someone in the dead of winter, or letting kids use his shop to play ball, people owed him."

Manny tapped the flyer and turned to Stumper. "Somebody wanted the journal. Who would be at the top of your suspect list?"

"I can't think of anyone."

"Didn't you say Sam Star Dancer crashed here? That'd give him access to it."

"He's a drunk, not a thief. And he certainly couldn't have arranged for Harlan's ammunition to be switched."

"Let's find him and interview him."

"I said he's no—"

"Humor me. Sam may not be a thief, but he may have ideas."

Stumper kicked the floor with his boot. "All right. I'll put out the word we need to talk with Sam. But it won't be easy with a drunk like Sam who crashes wherever he gets the urge."

"Find Itchy, too, if he crashed here with Sam."

"All right." Stumper held up his hands as if surrendering. "As soon as we turn over the right rocks and find them, I'll notify you."

Manny smiled and laid his hand on Stumper's shoulder. "What else you got to do? Work those meth cases?"

CHAPTER 6

"Not the friendliest soul I've ever met." Willie watched Stumper's marked Tahoe disappear around the corner of the parking lot. He unlocked the door of Manny's Oldsmobile and draped his arm over the jamb. "Son of a bitch acts like he doesn't want to work with us to find out who set Harlan up. Acts like his shit don't smell."

Manny paused before sliding into the blistering passenger seat, and he pulled his shorts down as far as they would go. He wished he had bought cloth seat covers for the old car. "You weren't exactly the ideal ambassador for the Lakota Nation yourself."

"What's that supposed to mean?"

"Besides using up all his Copenhagen, you were on the prod to climb Stumper's frame the moment you met him."

"Bullshit."

"Bullshit no shit. It was like you felt obligated to be openly hostile to him 'cause he's Crow. Just like in the old days."

Willie looked away, and Manny knew he mulled that over in his mind. The Crow were historic enemies of the Lakota, even scouting for the government in the old days in their hunt for the Lakota. "Maybe I wasn't Officer Friendly with him." Willie rolled the window down. "I guess I'm just upset for being stuck here, especially since I'm not convinced Harlan's death was anything but an accident."

"I hope you're right." Manny flipped open his cell and punched in the Billings Field Office. "I hope this was an accident and we can wrap this up quick. We got a week left on our vacation, and I feel Old Faithful calling our names."

An operator came on Manny's cell, a soft, bedroom voice, much like Clara's last night urging him to come home soon. Clara had been the one to suggest he and Willie get away together, away from work, away from Pine Ridge, and just relax. "So you can have one guy vacation," she had said, and Manny knew what she meant: after he and Clara were married, there would be little guy time for Manny to get away. And right now, Manny regretted coming to Crow Agency. If he'd have just listened to Willie, bypassed the Little Big Horn reenactment and headed straight for Yellowstone . . . "Can you connect me with Special Agent McGinnis."

After a brief pause, McGinnis came on the line. "Get that accidental death taken care of?"

"I need you to call a guy and get him patched through to me."

"Minute." Papers shuffling on the other end. "All right. Shoot."

"Guy named Adrian Beauchamp." Manny spelled his name phonetically.

"Okay. Where?"

"Outskirts of Paris."

"Georgia?"

"France."

"Do you know what time it is there?" McGinnis said after a long pause.

Manny quickly calculated Paris time. "A little after two in the morning. And your point?"

"My point? You want me to wake up some poor bastard at two in the morning so you can talk to him about an accident?"

"Might not be accidental."

McGinnis sighed loudly into the receiver. "You want me to call this Frenchman now?"

"Bob, if you'd rather work this reservation case yourself, I'll call Beauchamp . . ."

Manny let the threat hang, enjoying the long pause on the other end of the line as Bob McGinnis weighed working a case on Crow Agency. "Damn you, Tanno. Spell this guy's name again."

><><><><

"Do you really think the journal could be that important?" Willie pinched snuff into his lower lip, carefully stuffing less Copenhagen in than when he'd pinched from Stumper's can. "With everything else of value up for auction, someone could have taken many things of great value."

"A journal of one of Custer's scouts? That'd bring megabucks."

"It'll be next to impossible to off the journal in the black market." The strong tobacco odor brought up urges and Manny rolled the window down. "The thief could have taken any number of other items that hadn't the publicity the Star Dancer journal had." Willie stuck the car in gear and started out of the parking lot of the Justice Building.

"Unless theft for sale wasn't the motive. Brings us back to that blackmail theory."

Willie stopped and turned to face Manny. "Stumper never saw the journal. He assumed Harlan had it in that cedar box. There's the possibility that Harlan sold it sometime yesterday before he left for the reenactment."

"So you think Harlan stole the journal, sold it, and was going to claim that someone came in and lifted it during the show?"

Willie raised an eyebrow. "Remember Stumper said Harlan was paranoid, built his auction house on a dead-end street so he could better monitor people coming."

"Go on."

"If he was so paranoid, why didn't he fix his alarm system? Why didn't he repair the broken window in the spare room? I'm thinking he didn't because he wanted to point to those places as a way a thief could gain entry unnoticed."

Manny smiled, proud that Willie was working things out on his own. Just one more step toward his becoming a top investigator.

"Or maybe the journal's a diversion."

Manny fumbled with Willie's iPod, which he'd wired into Manny's car as a condition of going on vacation together. Willie reached over and hit the power and Creedence Clearwater Revival faded away.

"Maybe Harlan was into something else, and the disappearance of the journal is just a diversion."

"Don't get more of a diversion than getting killed."

Willie nodded. "I guess we can assume Harlan wasn't counting on that."

"You're talking us right into an extended stay on Crow Agency."

Willie slipped his Ray-Bans on. "I'm just spouting shit here. I'm sure by tonight we'll close this as a tragic accident, then Stumper and the BIA can worry about what became of the journal."

They took the I-90 Hardin exit and pulled in to the Custer's Revenge Motel. Willie stopped in front of a faux hitching rail replete with rusty horseshoes nailed to the weathered top rail. Manny started to get out, but Willie made no move to shut the car off. "You staying out here?"

"The less time I got to spend in that place the better." He nodded to their motel room. "That's the last time I let you book a room."

"What?"

"What do you mean 'what'? Did you think a motel by the name of Custer's Revenge would be Indian-friendly? The last time I looked, we were still Indians."

"The staff is friendly enough . . ."

"But lazy as hell. The lights don't work half the time, and that bathroom's a nightmare. That crack in the toilet seat pinched my butt last night and I thought it'd never let go."

Manny laughed. "You could have yelled a little softer. You woke me up."

Willie shook his head. "Custer's Revenge. By the looks of the place, we're the only business the place has had all year. Custer's Revenge."

"Could have been called Montezuma's Revenge."

"That's all I need, a case of Montezuma's revenge and trying to fight that toilet seat from grabbing my ass." Willie spit tobacco juice out the window. It slid down the side of Manny's Oldsmobile. "And this?"

"What?"

"This?" Willie wiped his mouth with his bandanna and slapped the green metal dash. "Don't see why you ever got rid of your nice Accord and bought this."

Manny feigned pain as he wiped the dust from the dash of his '55 Olds. "The Accord had a ton of miles on it. It kept nickel-and-diming me to death. Besides, there's more metal here than my Honda had."

Willie nodded. "Guess the more iron you have the less likely you'll be hurt when—not if, but when—you have your next wreck. Next year at this time, this thing will look like every other rez rod prowling Pine Ridge. And"—he shook his head—"you should never buy a car you can't push. And this one's too heavy to push."

"You're the one who insisted on driving my car rather than your truck."

Willie shifted in the seat. "Just because you said this heap had air-conditioning."

"It does," Manny said. "It just doesn't work."

"I can live sweating my butt off without air. But between the lumpy bed and the toilet seat and wrestling this thing around without power steering, I woke up feeling like I'd gone ten rounds with the Turtle Tree boys."

"When was the last time you tangled with those rowdies?"

Willie's hand shot to his cheek, still sporting a faint discoloration. "Two weeks ago when I backed up Hollow Thunder. Point is, that bed about beat me to a draw."

"My bed's just fine."

"And the hot water? Do you like your hot water running out halfway through?"

Manny had done the two-step this morning when the shower turned as cold as a mountain stream partway through. "I notified the manager. Besides, we're not exactly rolling in the dough. It was the most cost-effective room we could get."

"Cost-effective? That's just another way of saying you're cheap."

"Frugal."

"How frugal?"

"They gave me a veteran's discount."

"How frugal?"

Manny looked out the window. "$22.90 a night."

"What! Does that include that rough TP? I got a paper cut with it last night."

"Oh, bull." Manny swore he'd gotten wood chips in his butt last night from the paper. But he wasn't going to admit it to Willie. "So it's not Charmin. When you're trying to be frugal, you have to skimp on some amenities."

"The softest toilet paper a man can use isn't splurging. It's the highest on the priority list." Willie slapped Manny on the arm. "You're just cheap. For the rest of the trip, I'll make the reservations. I'm willing to pay a little bit more for a good night's sleep. And for a butt that isn't healing from a thousand unkind cuts."

Manny opened the door, but Willie made no move to follow. "So you're pissed, and you're going to sleep out here tonight?"

Willie looked away. "I'm going to catch an AA meeting in town."

Manny put his hand on Willie's arm. "Wish I could be of some help."

Willie shook Manny's hand off and turned in the seat. "What could you possibly do? How could you possibly know what real addiction is? It's not like you got much stress to deal with."

Manny wanted to confess he struggled with his smoking habit. And his weight. And his stress level soared with his on-again, off-again relationship with Clara, reaching an all-time high level now that they were engaged. And his guilt over the Red Cloud homicide. And his relationship with his brother Reuben. Manny knew stress.

Willie forced a smile and slapped Manny on the leg. "I know you just want to help. But I'll be all right as soon as I hunt up that meeting."

Manny closed the car door and leaned in the window. "We'll watch some TV tonight when you get back."

"The TV doesn't work."

Manny watched Willie as he drove out of the parking lot. *Damned that Olds has got nice lines.* He turned to their motel room. His key caught and stuck partially into the lock. Manny pushed on the key and the door swung in, unlatched. He tried pulling the key out, but it remained jammed in the lock, and Manny made a mental note to notify the desk clerk in the morning.

Manny clapped, but the light didn't come on. He clapped again. And again, hoping no one saw him clapping like a fool. He had turned to leave for the manager's office when he clapped a last time. A wagon-wheel chandelier missing two bulbs flickered on and washed the room in dirty light. It hung low enough that Manny had to duck around it as he plopped onto a stained blue sofa. A spring jabbed him in the butt, and he moved to the opposite side of the couch. He had started taking his boots off when his cell phone rang.

"I've got your man on the line," Bob McGinnis shouted in the receiver as if he'd been hollering all the way to Paris. "But he's hard to understand. His English isn't very good."

"'Bout like your French?"

"Piss on you, Tanno."

There was a short pause while McGinnis patched Adrian Beauchamp through. Between the language differences and the fact that Beauchamp had been awakened in the middle of the night, Manny strained to understand him.

"The *gendarme* said you need to speak with me right away, Monsieur Tanno."

"*Oui, mon ami.*" Manny didn't trust his French any further and switched to English, speaking slowly. After explaining he had examined the Beauchamp Collection, he asked Beauchamp about the artifacts he had donated for the auction.

"These things belonged to Great-Grandfather Beauchamp . . . Blaise. He spent time trapping Crow country before the Custer Massacre, but he left Crow country some months before the battle."

The line went quiet and Manny wondered if they had been disconnected, when Beauchamp continued. "Blaise moved back east in your country. Started a trading company that dealt with Indians in your west." Beauchamp laughed. "Your Wild West. Anyway, he made his fortune in trade before returning to France. He lived out his days here. The *gendarme* who woke me said the collection has caused much trouble in your country."

"We're not sure the collection has caused any trouble. We are just covering our bases."

Beauchamp chuckled again. "Like your baseball. You wish to swat a home run."

"Hit a home run," Manny corrected. "Tell me about the journal you donated."

"Ah," he said after a long pause. "I sent the journal along with other artifacts *sur un coup de tête*. On a whim."

"How is it that Blaise came to own a journal belonging to Levi Star Dancer?"

"Ah, I regret I cannot say. I have never read the journal. It is in English. I speak your language, but do not read it so well. My son Emile who fell in love with all the things Indian, and especially with Crow culture, has read it so many times he can recite it from memory. As a young boy, he and his friends would play with the collection. Emile always insisted on being the Indian."

That's a first: a White man wanting to be an Indian. "Can I speak with Emile about the journal?"

Beauchamp laughed. "Emile became tired of everything Indian as he grew. No, Emile discovered that women are so much more interesting than a musty hundred-years-old book someone scribbled in. *Volages.* Children are so . . . fickle these days. Emile is away."

Manny felt his headache spreading across his forehead. "When will he return?"

"Whenever the snow melts," Beauchamp laughed. "He and his lady friend found mountain climbing. He may be back tomorrow. He may be back next week. I will have him call you, Agent Tanno."

"*Merci*, Monsieur Beauchamp."

Manny had begun disconnecting when Beauchamp stopped him. "One thing, Agent Tanno. Emile once said that the journal holds the Star Dancer clan in a bad light. And an Indian by the name of Eagle Bull more so."

"In what way?"

"I do not know, my friend. But I will have Emile call you immediately when he returns."

Manny closed his phone and fished into his suitcase for his bottle of aspirin. *Great, the journal might have been a motive for killing Harlan.* "Or it may be nothing more than a musty, hundred-year-old book," he said aloud, hoping he was right.

CHAPTER 7

Levi Star Dancer sat cross-legged on the floor of the tipi, thick buffalo hair tickling his bare legs. But Levi found no humor in the tickling, and he focused on slowing his breathing. He grabbed one shaking hand with the other and hid it under the blanket spread across his lap, for this was a moment most solemn.

His eyes wandered around the tipi, to the smoke from the fire in the center rising and escaping through the smoke hole. His eyes fell on possible pouches hanging inside the lodge containing everyday things: cooking items and hunting and fleshing items. He forced his mind to focus, to concentrate on the light blue pony beads making up the background on the bags with seed beads forming a red diamond hourglass on the supple elk-hide pouches. Eyes roaming anywhere but on Pretty Paw sitting beside her father across from Levi.

He chanced a sideways glance at Broken Rib, sitting with legs drawn under him at the *acoria*, the place of honor at the rear of the lodge. Wolf tails sewn to the heels of his moccasins fluttered as the old man repositioned his legs, working out a cramp, the tails a reminder that Broken Rib struck coup on an enemy. Many times.

Broken Rib packed his pipe and brought a flaming twig from the fire and touched the tobacco. Sweet aroma filled the small space. The old man drew in the smoke, oblivious to Levi and his daughter, watching the smoke rise, a contented purring coming from him like the purring of the *iishb'iia*, the mountain lion.

Levi fought the urge to begin the conversation, unsure if his shaking voice would give Broken Rib the impression that Levi feared him. So he sat looking straight ahead as the old warrior finished his smoke and emptied the ashes in a small bowl to be offered to the four winds later. He carefully and reverently separated the bowl and stem and slid them into a deerskin pipe bag bearing the same geodetic designs as the possible bags. He turned and placed the pipe bag beside him.

Broken Rib turned to Levi and finally broke the silence. "Pretty Paw believes you are here to ask my only daughter in marriage."

Levi nodded and cleared his throat as he remembered what he had rehearsed. "She will be my first," he blurted.

The old man's eyebrows rose. "She may be your first, but she will also be your only wife, the way the world changes. If I allow the marriage."

Levi waited quietly for Broken Rib to continue. "What happened at the Greasy Grass two moons ago was a great victory for the Lakota and Cheyenne." He spit into the fire as if in disgust. "But it will be a victory as hollow as horns of a buffalo on a hungry anthill. The horse soldiers will return. In even greater numbers to avenge the soldier leader with the sun-bleached hair. And they will ask you to scout for them once again."

Levi straightened. "I want to raise a family." Finally, he had gathered courage enough to tell the man seated across from him. "My scouting days are over. I want . . ."

Broken Rib raised his hand. "These things you want—they will have to wait. You will have to scout for the soldiers looking for our enemies when they ask."

Levi felt the rage build, bolstering his courage to confront the old man. "So you are saying you will not allow the marriage until I am done with the soldiers?"

Broken Rib shook his head as he grabbed a lodge pole and stood, arching his back. "I do not think she can wait that long." He turned and faced her. "How long, my daughter?"

Pretty Paw rubbed her belly. "The child grows faster than I wish. Soon, I will not be able to conceal the baby even with skirts big enough for you."

Levi bit his lip, breathing to keep his temper controlled. This was Broken Rib's lodge, and Levi would remain silent until spoken to.

The old man arched his back, popping noises coming from worn joints older than Levi had any hope of attaining, and he looked away. By Crow standards, Broken Rib lacked attractiveness because of his size. Towering over every warrior in the camp, people considered him too tall to be handsome. Yet, his very stature drew people to him, asking his advice, seeking out his wisdom. After a long pause, he looked down at Levi still sitting on the buffalo robe. "How many ponies will you give for my daughter?"

"Father!" Pretty Paw grabbed onto the lodge pole and

struggled to stand. Both men watched her, neither wishing to insult her by helping her. Her belly protruded and she leaned back to ease the pressure. She faced her father, her face flushed, her jaw tightening, reminding Levi why he loved her so. "This is not about ponies."

Her father began speaking, but she interrupted him. "No one else would marry me if they knew." She rubbed her belly. "This baby is not even Levi's. You know that. Yet he would be a father to another man's child."

Broken Rib backed away from his daughter. "This I know is the truth. The trapper—Beauchamp—is without relatives. I should never have let him share my lodge."

Levi nodded; in some small measure it pleased the old man to insult the Frenchman in the worst way a Crow warrior could. *Beauchamp is without relatives, for certain. And without honor for leaving his responsibility of fatherhood behind. If I were close enough to lay my hands at the man's throat . . .*

"But he did share your lodge." Pretty Paw's voice rose, her hands cradling her belly. "But to ask Star Dancer for ponies . . ."

Broken Rib raised his hand and she quieted. "Now it is time I talk over you, my daughter." He took her hand and eased her back down onto the buffalo robes covering the tipi floor. "I may be poor by Crow thinking, but there are those that say I am rich in wisdom. I believe First Maker gave me such wisdom for times such as these." He hunched over and sat cross-legged beside Pretty Paw and stretched his feet to the fire, rubbing his toes.

"Tell me, my daughter, what would people think if they knew Beauchamp was the father of the baby growing inside you?"

"They would shun me. You know that. And they would

shun the baby whenever he or she comes. But this man"—she nodded to Levi—"wishes to be with me."

Broken Rib smiled for the first time. "In the words of the White men, Levi wishes to make an honest woman of you."

Pretty Paw looked down.

"People can be cruel in times like this." Broken Rib's braids danced on his chest. "And the baby would have no one." He nodded to Levi. "He is of the Whistling Water clan, but babies could not—by our custom—ever belong if they are born out of marriage."

Tears formed at the corners of Pretty Paw's brown eyes. Levi started to go to her, to wrap his arms around her and tell her all would be right. But he resisted and sat immobile, listening. "What am I to do Father? You don't want Levi to walk beside me, and I cannot live in peace among our people with a fatherless baby . . ."

Broken Rib touched Pretty Paw's leg and she stopped. "Here is the future: Levi will give me four ponies for your hand, one for each of the four sacred directions that will carry you and my grandbaby through life."

Pretty Paw's face flushed. "Ponies again? Is that all . . ."

"If I allowed Star Dancer to marry you without giving the customary ponies as a gift, people will wonder. They will question. They will ask, 'How is it that Star Dancer receives Pretty Paw's hand and her father demands nothing?' People will add up the days. They will figure out that the baby comes to us when trapper Beauchamp shared my lodge. By Star Dancer giving me ponies, people will believe the child is his." He turned to Levi. "Do you accept my decision?"

Levi dropped his head. "I have but one war pony and one hunting pony. I do not have four others to give."

Broken Rib smiled as he reached around and took the pipe

bag from the tipi wall. "I have four ponies that you can give me."

"Give you horses you already own?"

The old man nodded and slipped the pipe from the bag. He held the stem and carefully inserted the bowl of red stone. "I will hobble four of my finest ponies in the deep earth gash"—he pursed his lips and pointed to the west—"where you led your horse soldiers to the Cheyenne."

"What their maps called Weather Vane Canyon." Levi and White Crow had found a small group of Cheyenne lodges in the canyon, leading the soldiers down a narrow ledge path, single file. They surprised the enemy, who put up a fierce rear guard defense while their woman and children and old men escaped. In the end, only one Cheyenne warrior lay bleeding on the canyon floor. But that had been all right with Levi: He had no wish that the soldiers kill their women and children, even if they had invaded Crow country.

"I will hobble four horses," Broken Rib continued as he opened his tobacco pouch and began tamping the bowl of his pipe. "Tomorrow you go there. Lead the ponies to the village with great fanfare. Everyone will believe they are yours."

"The ponies will be recognized. People will know they belong to you."

The old warrior nodded and reached to the fire for a smoldering twig. "All the better. They will say, 'Star Dancer is a great warrior to steal ponies from such a fierce fighter as Broken Rib.' They will forever respect you, and your courage. As for me, of course I will refuse at first, denying you the privilege of marrying Pretty Paw. But eventually I will accept the ponies, and people will believe I fear Star Dancer."

Levi's mouth drooped.

"What is it?"

"I have no desire that you—a warrior that has been such an influence on our people—be thought afraid of another man."

Broken Rib lit the pipe, the sweet aroma filling the tipi before escaping upward. "To ensure my daughter will have a good future with a good man? It is of little consequence. It is worth what people say."

Levi marveled at the old man's wisdom. *Brilliant.* Four ponies for the hand of a daughter of a respected elder of the tribe was fair. And no one dared challenge Broken Rib's judgment.

>〈〉〈

Pretty Paw walked a step behind Levi as they left the lodge of Broken Rib, careful in the darkness lit only by *Baappaaihk'e.* The Evening Star, bright tonight, giving them just enough light to make their way to the edge of the pond. Levi rubbed moss from the top of a rock glistening from what the White men called fool's gold. He took Pretty Paw's hand and eased her onto the rock. Although she was not far along, pain showed in her face, and Levi knew it was the cloth beneath her dress, pulled tight to conceal her condition to the other lodges, that caused her such discomfort. Levi sat opposite her on a partially submerged log and skipped a rock across the green water. It skipped once and sank. Levi never was good with throwing the rocks.

He took his journal from his shoulder pouch and fished around until he found the stub of pencil and began sharpening it with his knife.

"What do you write about every day in that White man's book?"

Levi licked the tip of the pencil and paused. "Today I write about the happiest day of my life. Today I write how a grizzled old warrior softened and gave his blessing to marry his most beautiful daughter."

Pretty Paw nodded to the journal. "But you always write in it. Surely every day you do not write about such happy things."

Levi frowned. "I write about life. Things that I can look backward on when I am old and forgetful. I write to help me to remember such things."

"And the bad times? Do you wish to remember those as well?"

Levi licked the stub again. "I write about those times, too, so that those coming after us know our troubles. Know what hardships we have seen." *And so someone—anyone—can one day know how Eagle Bull murdered White Crow and the other Lakota.* Levi wanted to talk to Pretty Paw about his obsession with Eagle Bull, but he looked away and closed his eyes. Eagle Bull had shot him in battle, when he was younger, wounding Levi so he would always have the running sickness in his gut. The same wound that would prevent him from ever having a child of his own. Levi had forgiven Eagle Bull, for the two men had faced one another in battle and Levi had lost. But that was before he killed White Crow, killing Levi's friend he had loved since a little boy growing up. That had elevated Eagle Bull into something that warranted Levi's obsession.

Levi dried his eyes and turned back to Pretty Paw. "I could teach you the White man's words." He changed the subject.

She chuckled and held her belly. "Do not make me laugh. It hurts." She leaned back on the rock and dangled her feet in the pond. "I do not have time to sit and learn the soldier words as you did. I have to practice cooking, beading, fleshing out the skin if I am to be a good wife to my future husband."

"You will be a fine wife." He patted her foot. "Besides, what else did I have to do over campfires, when soldiers passed liquor, while others blew that piece of metal in their mouths. Making music. And dancing."

Pretty Paw's eyebrows rose so far they appeared to touch in the middle of her forehead. "Dance? Like us?"

Levi laughed and shook his head. "No. They dance together. They tell me they would prefer dancing with women. But none were in the field. So men danced together."

"And you crept away when the dancing began?"

"I did. Some soldiers were as we Apsa'alooke—nondrinkers. So I joined them away from the others and they showed me the words."

She sat silent.

"But there is another reason you do not wish to learn the words?"

Pretty Paw bent and grabbed a flat stone, skipping it across the pond. Unlike Levi's, it bounced off the surface a half-dozen times before it sank out of sight. "I do not wish to know the words. They look too much like trapper Beauchamp's writing, and his words—like the White man's—are not worthy of learning. Our language is above theirs. Besides"—she smiled—"one Crow in the family writing White man's words is enough. So write if you must, my husband-to-be."

"I will." Levi turned the page and licked the pencil end. "So that people one day will read of us." *And especially read about the murderer Eagle Bull.*

CHAPTER 8

Manny held Clara's paisley-framed, diamond-studded glasses as he scooted his chair closer to the television. BIA officer Matthew Moccasin Top disconnected one of six camcorders and began hooking another to the TV. The four previous camcorders showed Tess shooting Harlan, and Harlan lying in the field after he fell from his horse.

"This recorder is Thelma Deer Slayer's."

"Any relation to the police chief?"

Moccasin Top smiled as he continued working. "We're all related here in some manner." He finished the connection and stepped back with the remote in his hand. "While everyone else was busy recording the buildup to the battle, Thelma went behind the scenes and photographed people just milling about. Including the good Sergeant Tess. I suspect she's got a thing for him."

"Thelma's eighty years old," Stumper said.

Moccasin Top started the tape. "So she's a very old cougar."

The tape began with Thelma panning the area behind the bleachers. Manny recognized the two young Arapaho girls hustling to sell as many reenactment T-shirts as they could as they collected money between two enormous piles of shirts stacked on a makeshift counter.

Manny nudged Willie as he entered the picture. It showed him lumbering toward the taco stand past an old couple. They appeared unsure as to what to order as they stared at the prices scribbled with a grease pen on a whiteboard hanging above the counter. Before Willie left the taco stand and the recording, he slapped salsa on top of Manny's taco.

"Reminds me what a pain in the butt you are."

"Shuh," Manny said as Moccasin Top turned a chair around and sat backward in front of the set. "Here it is."

Thelma recorded Tess standing in front of his tent giving his mini-history lesson to a half-dozen spectators. A girl with jeans ripped on both knees, tight over a ripped seat, listened intently beside a braided Indian boy wearing a sleeveless T-shirt, while Tess held up an 1870s-era mess kit. There was no audio, but Manny could imagine the sergeant's deep voice filtering up to where Manny sat turned in his bleacher seat watching.

"It doesn't show anything we don't already know." Stumper propped his feet on the conference room table and started picking his teeth with his pocketknife. "All this shows is that this Tess character is a blowhard who likes to hear himself talk."

Moccasin Top scowled at Stumper and turned his chair to face Manny. "Thelma had some fascination for Tess. Seems like she spent most of her time filming him." As if to reinforce his theory, the camcorder zoomed in as Tess laid his mess kit down and grabbed his Springfield rifle. Manny recognized the group of people gathered in a semicircle around the sergeant. He took a nip from his hip flask, and a moment later leaned his rifle against the tent pole as he ran out of the picture frame. "This is where he made a beeline for the crapper," Manny said. "And where I stopped watching the people."

"So he got the two-minute warning a minute late." Stumper dropped his boots on the floor and stood. "We all get an attack of groaning gut now and again."

"But this is where it's interesting."

Willie looked at Moccasin Top. "Interesting? Nothing happening." The camcorder stopped moving, permanently zoomed in on Tess's tent.

"Thelma told me she left the recorder sitting on back of the bleachers," Moccasin Top said, "when Tess ran to the big-hole potty. Said she had to go herself." He grinned. "My guess is she just wanted to catch a glimpse of Tess as he was dropping his knickers. She got a little sidetracked on the way back to get her recorder. She found some other old dude to hit on by the T-shirt stand. By the time she came back to the bleachers, Tess had already mounted up and was sitting his horse waiting to fire the opening shot."

"So we got Thelma feeling her oats. This is a waste of time—"

"Here's where we see our man," Moccasin Top interrupted.

Manny leaned forward, squinting. "Shut the lights off."

Stumper hit the switch. "We're not going to see anything."

A man stopped in front of Tess's tent and casually looked around before stepping just inside the tent flap. He grabbed Tess's rifle leaning against the tent pole and reached into his pocket. The tape clearly showed the man opening the trapdoor, prying out the dummy round with his thumb nail, and inserting what appeared to be a live round before closing the chamber. He replaced the yellow ribbon sticking in the action, proof that the prop man had inspected Tess's rifle. His deed finished, he ducked back outside and seemed to smile at Thelma Deer Slayer's camcorder before disappearing off camera.

"The last four minutes just shows Tess returning from the port-a-potty and gathering his rifle and tunic for the show."

"Rewind the tape." Stumper squatted in front of the television. "Let me see the dude's face."

Moccasin Top rewound it and played it back at half speed.

"Shit!" Stumper slapped his thigh. "I know that guy."

"I know him, too," Manny said. The dried mustard on the front of the man's BILLINGS OR BUST T-shirt was as Manny remembered it. "I only saw him for a moment standing around listening to Tess. He's tall. Like Willie. But not so heavy." Manny moved aside to give Stumper a better view. "Where you know him from?"

Stumper leaned back and grabbed his can of Copenhagen from his back pocket. He was slow in putting the can away, and Willie reached over and grabbed it, stuffing the last of the tobacco in his lip. Stumper didn't give his obligatory scowl this time, but ignored Willie as he tapped the screen with his finger. "He was outside Harlan's auction barn two days ago when we responded to that suspicious call."

"False alarm, wasn't it?" Moccasin Top turned to Manny. "Some guy living at the corner where you turn on the street saw a strange car—fancy car from what I remember the call coming in—and some guy walked into the building. The moccasin telegraph got around quick, and the guy knew Harlan was dead. So the neighbor called right away."

Stumper nodded. "This guy was just coming out of Harlan's shop as I pulled up."

"He broke in then?"

Stumper shook his head. "He said Harlan had showed him where the key was. Said he'd forgotten his bid sheet and needed to get it for when Harlan's estate was settled and the artifacts eventually auctioned off."

"When was that?"

"Two days ago," Stumper answered. "Shortly after Sam was there."

"He was there about an hour before," Moccasin Top volunteered. "We had the place on a loose security watch because of the relics Harlan had sitting around waiting for the auction."

"And someone called him in?"

"Naw," Moccasin Top said, rewinding the recording. "Sam has run of the place, and I spotted him when I did my security check. I told him the place was sealed for evidence and he left."

"Harlan ever had a break-in before?"

Moccasin Top shook his head. "Despite what Harlan thought, we're pretty trusting on Crow Agency."

Manny flipped his notebook out, not to take notes, but to prod Moccasin Top to continue with his story. "So you saw Sam coming out . . ."

Moccasin Top nodded. "Carrying a pile of old papers and books. Sam loved to read and Harlan saved him all the mysteries when he finished reading them."

Manny put Clara's glasses back into his pocket, instantly feeling more manly. "Sam always sneak into Harlan's shop?"

Stumper shook his head. "Was no sneaking to it. Like I said before, Sam crashed in Harlan's spare room whenever he felt like it, whether Harlan was there or not."

"Wasn't Harlan afraid Sam would steal some of the relics?"

Moccasin Top laughed. "Sam would be more likely to steal Harlan's beer than any artifacts."

"Tell us you got the dude's name that you caught coming out of the shop." Willie sat on the edge of the chair sipping coffee from a Mighty Mouse mug Moccasin Top had given him.

Stumper spit chew in a round file. "No reason to get his name; his story checked out. The only thing he had in his hands was a bid sheet with items circled."

Willie set Mighty Mouse on the table. "Where I work law enforcement, it's basic police procedure to get names . . ."

"Didn't ask."

Willie shook his head. "Jeza. If that don't beat all."

Stumper turned to Willie, and poked him in the chest. "Look, big 'un. The guy ran in for a second to grab his sheet. End of story. Wasn't like he was running out of the shop carrying stuff from the auction or anything."

Manny slipped between Stumper and Willie. The last thing he needed was to break up a brawl between the two. He motioned to Willie's chair and he sat.

"Tell me what Sam was carrying when you saw him," Manny asked Moccasin Top.

"Just junk." Moccasin Top said. "Like I said, he had old *Billings Gazette* newspapers. Books. It looked like Sam was making a Dumpster run."

"Might he have been carrying a journal?"

Moccasin Top looked down at the floor and kicked a wad of paper. "Hard to say. Could have been."

Manny turned in his chair toward Stumper, who had sat back down and propped his feet on the table. "And the tall man? What did he have?"

"Nothing. He just stood on the sidewalk, smiling friendly like. Said Sam could vouch for him."

"And did he?"

Stumper looked to Moccasin Top. "By the time I heard Moccasin Top had talked with Sam coming out of Harlan's shop, he'd released him."

"And I'll bet you didn't spend a lot of time looking for Sam," Willie said, sitting on the edge of his chair, ready for a rematch with Stumper.

Manny scooted his chair between Stumper and Willie and turned to Moccasin Top. "Can we get a still photo of the tall man coming out of Tess's tent?"

"Sure. Only take a minute." Moccasin Top breathed a sigh, and Manny was certain he was glad to be away from Stumper and Willie. Moccasin Top disconnected Thelma Deer Slayer's camcorder and disappeared around the corner.

Manny dribbled some type of brown liquid from the coffeepot into his cup and sat back down beside Stumper. "Can we hunt up Sampson Star Dancer?"

Chief Deer Slayer poked his head into the doorway and laughed. He spilled coffee on his shirtsleeve and dabbed at it with a bandanna he'd grabbed from his back pocket. "Good luck finding Sam. He crashes wherever he feels like it."

Stumper dropped his feet onto the floor when Deer Slayer came in. "I put out the word to the other officers that we need to talk with him. Itchy, too. No luck yet."

Chief Deer Slayer laughed again and went to the coffeemaker in the corner of the room. "About the only time we see either one is when they get tanked up and tossed in the pokey for public intox. Or shoplifting. Or some other minor offense."

Manny rubbed his forehead, feeling a throbbing pain coming on. He hadn't figured this investigation would drag out this long. He just wanted to sit in the chairs overlooking Old Faithful and watch it erupt on time. "Then let's pay Chenoa Iron Cloud a visit. See if she's heard from her brother."

Stumper shot Chief Deer Slayer a look. "I don't know, Manny. Chenoa's a very busy lady. Besides, she doesn't have anything to do with her brother."

"It wouldn't hurt to at least go talk to her." Willie ran his pocketknife around a fresh can of Copenhagen.

"You two just want to ogle her is all," Stumper said.

Willie smiled. "I can think of worse assignments."

Manny had to agree with him. He recalled the state tourism poster in Harlan's office, how he got lost in that picture. Chenoa's dark piercing eyes had seemed to follow Manny, seemed to beckon him to run his fingers through her shiny black hair. "I think we at least need to talk with her."

Stumper's face flushed, and his jaw tightened. "We don't need to talk with her. We ought to leave her alone."

"That's enough," Deer Slayer told Stumper. He turned to Manny. "What this rude banty rooster here is saying is that Sam is the black sheep of the Star Dancer family. And the only contact Chenoa has with him is when he comes around once a month to pick up his lease check."

"So there's land involved?"

"Considerable," Stumper broke in. "When Old Smoke went to the other side, he left forty sections. Deeded them to Chenoa."

"Didn't Sam get any?"

Chief Deer Slayer grabbed the coffeepot and offered to refill Willie's cup. By the looks of the thickness of yesterday's coffee, Manny was certain it would be an insult to the great Mighty Mouse. "Smoke Star Dancer abhorred Sam's drinking. Said that if Sam didn't straighten up, he'd write him out of the will. And Smoke did. He left a small monthly pittance for Sam. And it's that monthly check that brings Sam and Chenoa together for a few moments every month when he picks it up, or it's dropped off. And when they need Sam to sign ranch papers."

"So Sam is involved in the Star Dancer Ranch?"

Deer Slayer set the carafe back on the coffeemaker, leaving an inch of mud in the bottom. No one likes making coffee. "Smoke Star Dancer set it up that Sam had to approve some things ranch-related: land sales and purchases. Cattle and horse acquisitions and sales. Sam always signs whatever Chenoa wants, 'cause she might just conveniently lose Sam's monthly check."

"Then we do need to talk with Chenoa."

The chief turned to Stumper. "Take Agent Tanno and his dreamy-eyed friend out to the Star Dancer Ranch. But don't upset her. Last thing we need is Chenoa bitching to the tribal council."

Officer Moccasin Top came into the room and passed out copies of the tall man's photo.

"Let's get this over with," Stumper said.

Manny grabbed the photo. "Just as soon as we see if our Sergeant Tess can ID the man."

>◇◇◇◇<

Stumper parked his marked Tahoe beside a Dodge Power Wagon in the Super 8 parking lot. "Can we release Tess when we're done? He's only called me about every two hours since we cut him loose, wondering if he can go home."

Manny nodded. "We know where he lives." And Manny did, too, a mile from what he'd once called home in Arlington, Virginia. But had it really been home, or just somewhere that Manny could hide out from the memories of an orphan growing up on the poorest reservation in the nation? Those memories came sneaking back now and again, the bad times mixed with the good of living with a loving uncle after his parents had died in an auto accident. Thinking back, Manny really wasn't orphaned at all. "We'll let him go as soon as he looks at this photo."

Tess threw open the door on the first knock, looking as if he'd downed a dozen hip flasks. Rings tugged at the spider-webbed skin under his eyes, and his hair stuck upward as if he'd dried it under a rest area hand dryer and used motor oil for fixer. His voice faltered as he teetered on shaky legs, his trembling hand working overtime with his bleary eyes to take the photo of the tall man. "This the guy that switched my ammunition?"

Manny backed away from his buffalo breath. "You tell me."

"Frankie." Tess backed into the room and sat on the edge of the bed. An empty Wild Turkey fifth lay atop a broken Jack Daniel's bottle in the trash can. "He introduced himself as Frankie. Nice guy. Real sociable. Said he was one of the Sioux reenactors. Talked like he did it every year."

"He wasn't dressed like a Sioux reenactor, was he?"

Tess burped, but made no attempt to conceal the odor that reminded Manny of most hog farms. "I wouldn't know a Sioux from a Cheyenne from a Crow. No offense."

Manny waved it away. "None taken."

"Now, put me in the front lines at Gettysburg with a .54-caliber musket and a pocket full of fake minié balls . . ." Tess stopped and looked up at the three lawmen standing over his bed. "But this guy didn't put in fake minié balls. He put in the real thing, and I murdered a man."

Manny sat on the edge of the bed and rested his hand on Tess's shoulder. He slumped, and Manny was quick to keep him talking. "What did you and Frankie visit about?"

Tess sat up and turned to Manny. "That's how he knew."

"Knew what?"

"How to switch my ammo." Tess got up and paced the

room. "He came to my tent. Asked about my cavalry gear. Asked if I had to buy my own rifle, acting like he was interested. Asked if I used period ammunition."

"And you told him you used dummy rounds?"

Tess stopped in front of Manny and looked down at him. "He asked when my ammo was checked and verified to be blanks. He said he was concerned someone might be hurt accidentally. I told him it's double-checked so accidents can't happen. I said it had just been verified an hour ago. He was planning to swap my ammo then, wasn't he?"

"I think he was planning on switching your ammo long before the day of the show."

Tess's legs shook and Manny gently sat him on the bed. "What else do you remember about him?"

Tess rubbed his forehead and looked around. His eyes fell on a fresh bottle of Jim Beam but he made no move for it. "His Cadillac," he said at last. "I thought it odd that an Indian could drive a car like . . ." He stopped, his already red face turning even more crimson as he looked first to Manny, then Willie and Stumper. "I didn't mean . . ."

Manny held up his hand. "Don't worry about it." Manny had heard comments like that all his life: people surprised that an Indian drove a decent car or wore neat clothes or shopped in public with children that were clean and well behaved. "Tell me about Frankie's Caddy."

"Yes, his car." Tess stood and paced the room again, staring at the beige carpet as if the answers were imbedded in the floor. "I was riding my horse out to the staging area, riding past the chief I was supposed to shoot to start things."

"And who you subsequently killed?"

Manny glared at Stumper, smiling at Tess's pain. "You rode past the staging area?"

Tess turned his back on Stumper. "That's when I saw

Frankie leaving. I thought it odd that he didn't even stay for the show, as much interest as he showed. Him being a Sioux reenactor and all."

"The car?" Manny pressed.

"The Caddy. Sure." Tess sat in a chair within reach of the bottle of whiskey. He stared at it as he continued. "It was a new Sedan DeVille. Pearl color, like that iridescent color Pontiac offered before they quit making them."

"Did you get a license plate?" Willie asked.

Tess shook his head.

"Even a partial number?"

Tess stopped in front of Willie, looking up through red eyes. "It never dawned on me to get a plate."

"Anything else?"

Stumper shook his head. "Just tell me the fastest way out of Montana. I'm sticking to being an NCO at Gettysburg. Nothing like this ever happens there."

><><><><

Stumper climbed into his truck but made no move to put his seat belt on. "That was a dead end." He started pulling out of the parking lot. "Waste of time if you ask me."

Willie nudged him. "Would you rather be working chickenshit meth or bogus missing person's cases, pardner?"

Stumper glared at Willie. "Don't see you being much help in there."

Manny leaned over the seat between them. "Tess gave us a good deal of info."

"Right."

"You should clam up," Willie told Stumper. "You might learn something." He turned in the seat. "What do we have to work with?"

"Think what we can do with Tess's seeing Frankie driving

away in a Caddy. We have no plate. Nothing else to distinguish it from any other pearl Cadillac on the road."

"We could put out a BOLO for a pearl-colored Caddy," Stumper blurted out. "That's something we didn't have before. Can't be a lot of those hereabouts."

"The man's not from here," Willie said.

Stumper slowed to allow two kids riding a bike to cross the road, one hanging on to the handlebars for his life as he straightened his legs out to keep them away from the front wheel spokes. "Just 'cause Frankie said he's not from here, doesn't make it so."

"Sure it does."

"How the hell you know that?"

Manny looked at Willie. "What's your thoughts?" Manny always looked for chances to prod Willie, to get him thinking on his own, to steer him in the direction sharp criminal investigators went.

He chin-pointed to Stumper. "Maybe I'll leave him in suspense."

"Come on," Stumper said. "If you know something, let me in on it. I am your liaison, after all."

Willie smiled. "Frankie—if that's his name, which I doubt—wasn't afraid anyone would recognize him. He made no attempt to hide his face. Or his car."

Stumper snapped his fingers. "The car. Folks hereabouts can't afford a hubcap off a Caddy let alone the car. He can't be from here."

"And Tess told us Frankie's an amateur."

Now it was Willie's turn to look at Manny with that thousand-yard stare. "I didn't hear him say that."

Manny sat back in the seat, dragging out his answers, Willie turning in his seat to look at him, Stumper staring at him in the rearview mirror, waiting for an explanation.

"Simple. Would a pro drive something as conspicuous as a pearl Cadillac?"

Willie nodded. "Never."

"Unless," Stumper added, "he's not from here."

"And if it didn't belong to him?"

"It would be a rental." Willie slapped the seat. "What an amateur."

CHAPTER 9

"Stop here," Manny said when his cell phone rang. Willie stopped the Olds at the Lodge Grass off-ramp while Manny scrambled to get his phone from his pocket. Service was little better at Crow Agency than at Pine Ridge, and high spots were at a premium.

"We found someone who recognized the tall man." Manny heard Stumper chewing on something, presumably a toothpick that clinked against the phone as he spoke.

"Someone at the reenactment?"

"Yeah. One of the ladies—Sylvia Cuts The Tree—works the parking area. Tough old bird."

Manny recalled an old woman, walking stick in hand, insulting his Oldsmobile, ordering Willie to "park this piece of shit" away from decent cars.

"She remembered the Caddy. Thought it odd that a skin was driving something that nice." Click. Click. *Damned toothpick.*

Manny covered his phone with his hand and whispered to Willie, "We got a break.

"Sylvia remember anything else about the driver or car?"

Click. Click. "She says the guy was dressed like one of you Lakota. Well, not exactly like you—he didn't wear those silly shorts and loud Hawaiian shirt."

"Just tell me what she said."

Laughter. More clicking. "Sylvia's never seen this dude before, and she's been telling people in cars where to go for eleven years."

"How can she be sure he's Lakota?" Willie asked.

Stumper paused and Manny heard pages flipping on the other end. "She just figured it was one of you guys 'cause he wasn't anyone from Crow Agency she ever met. And she just got the impression he was a bad guy—which rules out any of us Crow."

Manny let that pass. "What else did she say?" Between the heat inside the car, and his soaked bandanna he ran across his forehead, Manny was losing his patience. They needed to get down the road and get some air moving. Willie was right—he should have gotten the air-conditioning fixed.

"Just like Tess, she thought it odd that Frankie left before the show started. When all the Indians were mounting up in the field in back of the bleachers, he took off out of the parking lot."

"Tell me she got a license number."

Clicking against the receiver. "She didn't. But she did notice it had Montana plates. Guess I'll get that description out to car rentals in the area."

"Ask Chief Deer Slayer to put out a TTY on the car and a description of the way Frankie was dressed. He probably changed clothes the first chance he got, but we might catch a break."

"Sure thing."

"And have you located Sam Star Dancer yet?"

Another long pause. "Not yet, but I've still got some follow-up at the reenactment site I need to do. Feel free to hunt him yourself, though."

Manny stared at the dead receiver and pocketed his cell phone. "Guess Stumper's too busy to help."

"Or he just doesn't want to find Sam and have to connect him to Chenoa." Willie started unfolding the impromptu map Chief Deer Slayer had given them to get to Sam's house. "Stumper's starting to get on my nerves." Willie started the Olds down the off-ramp as he drove with his elbows, spreading the map across the steering wheel.

"That's not very safe. Maybe we should pull over . . ."

"Driving with my elbows, I'm still a safer driver than you."

"I still think . . ."

"Look," Willie said, "I'm trying to make up for lost time on this little vacation adventure you've managed to get us into. The sooner we're away from Crow Agency—and that pompous little ass BIA officer—the better I'll feel. That guy's got some leftover animosity for us Lakota."

"And you don't share the same for the Crow?"

Willie ignored him and turned the map that the chief had drawn on the back of a report form. "According to this, it'll be an off-color brown house at the end of the block."

"I think Stumper called it 'shit brown.'"

"Well then, that must be it." Manny pointed.

They drove past Strong Enemy Drive to the end of Red Bird Lane to the only shit brown house on the short block. A once-white picket fence kissed the dirt where it had lain for perhaps decades, rotting wood poking through the weeds, suggesting someone had once cared for the property. Half the shingles had blown off the roof leaving the remaining ones to fend off what little rain Crow Agency got, and the off brown color of the house was as much from mold as from old paint. *Nature's cruel palette.*

They pulled to the curb behind a pink Hummer parked in front of Sam's house. A couple picked their way through weeds and dead bushes and emerged by the front door. The woman drew Manny's attention: tall, lithe, coming toward them like a model on a runway. Her hips swayed seductively inside faded jeans a size too small, and her breasts threatened to burst from a double-breasted Western shirt unbuttoned at the top, revealing cleavage. She met their gaze as she walked toward them, her head slightly high, strong jaw thrust out, ponytail tossed over her back, reeking of aristocracy as she neared.

Willie sucked in a breath when he caught sight of Chenoa Iron Cloud, more stunning, more alluring in person than any tourism poster or calendar. He grabbed Manny's arm. "See who I see?"

Manny nodded. He instantly understood why Montana had chosen her as the face of tourism in the state. Manny imagined her riding across a gentle stream dividing green pastures, snowcapped mountain in the background, looking directly into the camera as she promised anyone who came to Montana the time of their lives.

"And him." Willie chin-pointed toward the man walking just behind Chenoa. He stood a full head taller than her, his broad shoulders sitting atop a narrow waist with the slight Lakota paunch. Gray-tipped braids tied with colored deerskin bounced on his black silk shirt as he walked. "That's Wilson Eagle Bull."

"The rancher west of Oglala running for Senate?"

Willie nodded. "What's he doing here?"

"We're about to find out."

Chenoa and Wilson stopped beside Manny's Oldsmobile. He eyed the crumpled fender of the green machine, while she looked first to Willie before settling on Manny. She grinned as she eyed his legs jutting out of his shorts, while he tried not to focus on the turquoise pendant around her neck, situated between her breasts, rising and falling with her breathing.

"Are you gentlemen looking for my brother?"

"Yes," Manny stuttered. He quickly recovered and grabbed his FBI ID wallet. He flipped it open. Chenoa leaned over and took it. Manny looked away as she read the information.

"Who's this?" Wilson nodded to Willie.

Manny nudged Willie out of dreamland. He grabbed his own ID wallet and showed it to Wilson. "One of my homies," Wilson said, deep voice controlled. Manny could see him speaking at campaign rallies, not even needing a PA system, his mellow voice reaching even those in the back rows. "You're a little out of your jurisdiction, Officer."

Willie nodded and continued staring at Chenoa.

"We're here on vacation," Manny said. "When I got a case dropped in my lap. Willie's helping me. Unofficially."

Chenoa returned Manny's ID wallet. "Doesn't explain why you're looking for Sam." She leaned against the Hummer and crossed her arms. "He must have done something serious this time for the FBI to be hunting him."

"He might have information about Harlan White Bird's murder," Willie blurted out.

Chenoa smiled at him, and the dreamy look in Willie's eyes deepened. "We heard it was an accident."

"Heard the security man screwed up," Wilson added. "Allowed real ammo into the reenactment. How's that murder?"

Manny gave them the headline version that would be buried on page six of the Billings *Gazette* today. When he finished, Chenoa laughed.

"Harlan's death funny?"

She shook her head, Manny's gaze returning to the pendant dangling between her breasts and bouncing with her laughter. "Let's just say Harlan lived longer than he had a right to. The booze should have killed him years ago. Sam, too."

"But Sam is alive. Is he home?"

"He a suspect?"

Manny looked past her but saw no activity around the dilapidated house. "He may have information we need."

Chenoa jerked her thumb toward the house. "He's not here."

"Have any idea where he may be?" Willie finally summoned the courage to speak.

Chenoa shrugged. "We looked at his usual haunts, starting with Harlan's Auction Barn. And Sam crashes in an old school bus parked across from the IGA when he's too drunk to stagger home. Sometimes under a couple nearby bridges. Nada."

"You never said just why you're looking for Sam." Wilson adjusted his buffalo bone bolo tie. "What information could he possibly have?"

"And why are you here?" Manny asked.

Chenoa's smile faded. Her eyes narrowed, fixated on Manny's as she stepped closer. "I didn't know it was a crime to visit one's brother."

"Agent Tanno's not implying anything." Wilson rested his hand on Chenoa's arm a bit longer than Manny thought appropriate. Unless there was something between them. "He's just doing his job."

Chenoa's smile returned. *A practiced smile.* "Of course,"

her voice soft, no traces remaining of anger that had been there a moment ago. "Sam's name is on paperwork for the ranch. In my father's wisdom, he chose to give Sam the power to veto anything I might do concerning the Star Dancer Ranch."

"Has he?"

Chenoa glanced to Manny's car. Stalling. "Has he vetoed anything I've ever done? No, and he'd better not if he expects to get his monthly drinking money."

"Which brings us back to why you're here."

Chenoa's face reddened, but Wilson stepped between her and Manny. "The Star Dancer Ranch is selling my Eagle Bull Ranch forty bred heifers this week. That is, if we can get hold of Sam to sign the papers."

"And if you don't find him?"

Wilson shrugged. "Then I go back to Pine Ridge with no deal."

"Any ideas where we should look?" Willie stuttered.

Chenoa turned to Willie and smiled, a disarming smile that spread across a face framed in just the slightest amount of makeup. Manny glanced at Willie, fearing he'd get a hernia catching the big man when he fell over. "Like I said, we looked in all his usual haunts. But check inside if you want. It's not locked. Sam never had anything worth stealing."

Chenoa turned to her Hummer, and Wilson held the door for her before walking around and squeezing in the passenger side. Like Willie, it looked as if nothing fit Wilson as he ducked his head to clear the doorjamb.

They looked after the Hummer disappearing around the corner, and Willie turned to Manny. "Do you not think it odd that Wilson came here to buy heifers? He's got hired hands that could do that."

Manny elbowed Willie back to the present. "Forty heifers

is a large sale. I'd come myself if my money was on the line. Besides, if you had a chance to take a ride with a lady like that, wouldn't you?"

Willie backed up. "She's married."

"Doesn't mean she's ready for sainthood. Let's check out Sam's crib."

Manny stepped over the broken-down picket fence, between a rusted ringer washer and a dented Dodge fender half-buried in the yard. Or what was once a yard, the sun-flowers growing among thick jagger bushes choking out any semblance of grass. He stepped lightly onto cracked wooden steps that creaked under his weight. He turned back to warn Willie, but it was too late.

Willie yelled as he fell through, rotten boards stubbornly grabbing his legs. His chest stuck out of the porch and he struggled to free himself. "What you laughing about? You could have told me about that step."

Manny held out his hand to help Willie, but he slapped it away as he grabbed onto a porch pole and hoisted himself back onto the porch. Manny waited until he was sure Willie wasn't going to fall through another board, before he turned to the screen door devoid of a screen. One hinge had sprung and rusted and the wounded door sat at a sharp angle against the house missing most of its front siding.

A sparrow flew out of a broken window and Manny jumped. Willie brushed past him and nudged the front door with his foot. It groaned on rusty hinges as it swung inward and banged against a garbage can just inside the room. It top-pled over, spilling beer cans across the dirty and yellow-stained carpet.

Willie bent to pick the cans up when Manny stopped him. "You think anyone coming in here will notice beer cans strewn over *this* floor?"

"Got a point."

Manny led the way across the room, past the kitchen with its two-burner stove caked with last month's government commodities, into what Manny thought must be the living room. A mattress had been tossed beside more empty beer cans, and a greasy pair of jeans occupied an occasional chair missing both arms.

"How the hell can anyone live like this?" Willie stood in the center of the room, careful not to touch anything, shaking his head. "I've seen pigsties neater than this."

"Remind you of any place back home?"

"Too many," Willie answered. "And it doesn't bring us any closer to finding Sam."

Manny looked around the room and smiled. "Sure it does."

CHAPTER 10

Stumper's voice mixed with loud radio chatter in the background.

"What's that about Sam? Tell me you've found him."

Stumper's voice became clearer as he moved away from the dispatch office. "We've turned over every rock where he usually crashes. Nothing. But we found the next best thing—Itchy Iron Cloud. He's climbing the walls in our interview room as we speak."

"Meth?"

Stumper laughed. "He's tweaking big-time. How soon can you get over to the police station?"

"As soon as I get Willie to bring my car around."

><><><><

"We caught him trying to crawl through that broken window in Harlan's spare room." Stumper jerked his thumb at the closed door of the interview room. "The piece of shit's crashing. Big-time. He'll need to score soon or he'll really be climbing walls."

Manny grabbed his briefcase and started to dig out his pocket recorder. "Good thing we got here so quick."

"Too bad you got here so quick. It'd do the little bastard good to suffer a little longer."

Willie smiled. "Stumper's right. The worse off Itchy is, the more he'll want to get back out on the street where he can score. . . ." He turned to Stumper. "What's usual?"

"Itchy will be lucky if he can get enough bucks to buy a quarter gram."

Itchy jumped when they entered room. His head jerked from Stumper to Manny, then widened as he looked up at Willie walking through the door.

Manny drew in a quick breath. Itchy's BO filled the room, a retching odor like a combination of floor cleaner and someone who hasn't bathed in months. Manny walked quickly past Itchy and opened both windows.

Itchy's fingers started tapping the table, sounding more like a dog's nails on a hardwood floor. A cornered dog. "When can I leave, Stumper?" Itchy had stopped tapping the table with his fingers and started tapping the floor with his foot as if he could hear some secret aria no one else could. "I got places I need to be."

Stumper and Willie said nothing as they stood against the far wall, while Manny pulled a chair close to Itchy. He backed away and snatched the faded brown stocking cap off his head. He looked to the door as he began fingering his cap nervously. Manny put his recorder on the table and noted the time and date.

"What's that for?" He dropped his cap but made no attempt to grab it as he clasped his hands together tightly.

"Just to keep us honest," Manny answered, digging out the

small notebook he often used as a prop to distract the interviewee.

"You'll use that against me."

Manny shook his head. "It's harmless. It helps me talk with you."

Itchy wrung his hands that were clamped together as if to stop their tapping. Manny opened the manila folder and studied Itchy's sparse information from previous arrests. "Mr. Iron Cloud—or do you prefer I call you Franklin?"

"Call me Itchy." He forced a smile that showed his choppers had decayed into the typical meth-head grin, teeth rotted by lack of brushing, poor nutrition, and grinding. "Everyone calls me Itchy." He picked at skin underneath his shirt, while he rocked back and forth in his chair, his feet resuming their tapping.

"Okay, Itchy. By your files, it looks as if you spend as much time in jail as out. Problems?"

Itchy twirled his food-matted hair that fell down over his stooped shoulders like dyed mop strings. He had plucked at the hair, frustration caused by being somewhere between tweaking and crashing. "Not me. I got no problems." Foot tapping. Body rocking. "I get a little stinko now and again."

Manny flipped to a summary of Itchy's arrests. Older brother Cubby had raised Itchy when their parents died in a car accident outside Denver. He'd lived with Cubby and Chenoa until Cubby married her, then it was hit-the-bricks time. "Says here your first arrest was at fourteen. Jacked a tourist's car at the Little Big Horn Memorial. Amazingly, they found a Baggie of weed on you when they arrested you."

"Someone planted it."

Manny ignored him and flipped to the next page. "Two months later for shoplifting, and breaking into cars at the casino."

"For which I paid dearly." Itchy picked at his arm, the sleeve wearing thin from the scratching. "Cubby didn't believe it was someone that just looked a lot like me."

Manny handed Willie the folder. "And it's not because of your meth habit?"

"I got no habit." Itchy backed his chair away from the table. His eyes darted to the windows, to four young girls kicking a soccer ball across the grass. "I don't do crank."

Manny stood and walked to the window. The afternoon sun shone on a sky boasting gentle cumulus clouds, and Manny wished he were anywhere on vacation besides in this musty, smelly interview room. He pulled the blinds and turned to Itchy. "You got no habit?"

"I don't."

"Then why are you wearing long sleeves and it's a hundred degrees out?"

"Don't know what you mean . . ."

Manny grabbed Itchy's arm. He tried jerking it free, but his frail attempt was feeble at best. Manny pulled his shirt-sleeve up. The button ripped to reveal tracks on Itchy's arm nestled between open sores that he had been picking.

"Did he have his kit with him when you found him?"

Stumper shook his head. "He had his syringe and rubber tubing last time we nailed him, but this time he dumped it before I could put the habeas grabeas on him. He got away."

Itchy jerked away. "I said I don't do crank. But what's that got to do with me being hauled in here?"

"Ever see this?" Manny ignored him and motioned to Willie. Manny grabbed Itchy's arm and turned it over. A four-inch scar ran the length of the inside of his arm. "He got this when he tried cutting out the bugs crawling under his skin. Isn't that right, Itchy?"

Itchy jerked free and stood pacing the room, his foot

tapping as he walked, picking at one of the many open sores that fought his acne for possession of his face. He turned back to Stumper like he was the only friend Itchy had in the world. "I'm trying to go straight, Stumper."

"Like two weeks ago when we found you shooting between your toes. Something about not being able to find a vein? The only thing you're going straight in is an early grave."

Itchy looked away. Another clump of hair came away from the top of his head. He looked at it for a moment before dropping it to the floor and turning to Manny as his newfound friend. "Can't you just help me? I need to be places . . ."

Manny put his hands on Itchy's thin shoulders and eased him back onto the chair. "We'll talk about help in a moment. But first, we need information about Harlan White Bird."

"What? All I did is help him out around his shop sometimes."

"He pay you? How do you get your crank?"

"I said I don't do . . ."

Manny held up his hand. "Where do you get your money?"

Itchy looked at the ceiling, the floor, and that secret aria started somewhere in his head again and his foot began tapping. "Harlan gave me some lucky bucks for helping him. Or he did." He tilted his head back and turned to one corner of the room as if someone was there sharing his humor. "And Cubby gives me money now and again. What are big brothers for, huh? Anyway, I don't know nothing about Harlan's murder."

Manny scooted his chair back, recognizing Itchy becoming more paranoid. "How do you know it's murder and not an accident?"

A tic started on Itchy's cheek and his hand shot to it as if to calm the muscle. He started picking at a sore instead. "It's all over the rez. Everyone knows Thelma Deer Slayer's camcorder got a guy switching ammo in some cavalry dude's gun. That's why Harlan got killed."

Manny grabbed Frankie's photo from his briefcase and dropped it in front of Itchy. His eyes darted around the room, anywhere but the photo.

"Who is that?"

"I don't know."

"Sure you do." Manny slid closer. "You jumped just now when you saw his photo. Who is it?"

"I don't know. Just some *baashchiili*. Can I go?"

"You're lying, Itchy." Manny moved his chair closer, and Itchy moved his back. "Just like you lied when you claimed someone planted that Baggie of grass on you. And that someone else busted into the cars. I think you know the tall man, and we'll sit here all night until you tell me."

"That's bullshit."

"That's reality." Manny scooted his chair closer. Itchy started moving his back but it butted against the wall. "Who was he?"

Stumper leaned over the table and poked Itchy in the chest. "You said a moment ago he was *baashchiili*. How'd you know he was White when everyone else thinks he's Indian?"

"I don't know," Itchy blurted out. "I just saw him once at Harlan's when I crashed there. Scary dude, but I don't know who he is or why he was there. He might have been there looking at the Beauchamp Collection."

"Why would he want Harlan dead?"

"I can't say. It's not like he fought with Harlan or anything. He was just scary, the way he looked through you when his eyes fell on you." Itchy's foot tapped incessantly, and his eyes darted to the door guarded by Willie and Stumper. "I got to leave."

"Why would he want Harlan dead, Itchy?"

"Let me go."

Manny turned to Stumper. "I think a night in the drunk tank will do Itchy some good." Manny stood and started gathering his recorder and arrest files when Itchy bolted from his chair.

"Don't lock me up tonight. I gotta get out of here."

Manny turned to him, amazed at the man's ability to tremble and shake and still be able to stand. "What did Harlan know that would get him killed?" He put his hand on Itchy's arm and he jumped back, nearly knocking the chair over. "Why would the tall man want him dead?"

"The journal," he said at last, almost a whisper this time.

"What about the journal?"

Itchy slumped in his chair. "Harlan read the journal."

"And you think that's why Harlan was killed?" Stumper asked. "That just your imagination talking again?"

Itchy looked up and stared at Stumper through eyes with pupils as big as liberty dimes. "Me and Sam and Harlan was polishing off a case of Bud last week. Harlan was reading the journal, and Sam was going over the Beauchamp sale flyer."

"What were you doing?" Willie asked. "A gram?"

Itchy's jaw dropped as if Willie had just slapped him. "Just Budweiser that night." His eyes dropped. "Maybe later."

Manny put his finger to his lips and Willie became quiet. Manny turned back to Itchy. "Still doesn't explain why you think that was enough to get Harlan killed."

"Then can I go?"

"Why?" Manny pressed.

Itchy stopped scratching and went back to plucking strands of hair from the top of his head. "Harlan was reading the journal, and all of sudden, he slapped his leg. Said he was in fat city now."

"How so?"

"He said there was shit in the journal that would embarrass people here on the rez. And some family in Pine Ridge. He stuffed notes in the journal and locked it away in his office safe."

"What notes?"

Itchy shrugged and a wisp of hair fell to the floor. "Notes he always writing on. He didn't show me what he was reading and he didn't show me the notes, but I figured they were valuable as he always kept them locked in the safe." Itchy picked at a sore on his temple. A piece of skin came away and he looked at it with fondness before flicking it onto the floor. "Like I was going to steal it. Probably just business notes, anyway."

Stumper leaned close, a stub of toothpick dangling from his mouth. "Did you steal it?"

"Why would I steal a damned old journal?"

"You have a history of theft," Stumper said. "And it was valuable."

"I didn't steal it. I said I didn't even read it." Itchy backed away again. "Can I go now?"

Manny ignored him. "Who stole the journal, 'cause it wasn't in Harlan's safe."

"Ask Sam," Itchy blurted out.

Manny flipped pages of his notebook and held his pen poised above a blank sheet. *Props*. "Why should we ask Sam?"

"He read the journal."

"How you know that?"

"They argued about it. Later that night after I . . . came back, Sam and Harlan argued about it. I crashed, but they woke me up with their fighting and I left."

"Tell us what the argument was about and you're free to go."

"Chenoa," Itchy spit out. "Harlan said he intended

shaking Chenoa and Wilson Eagle Bull down for what was inside the journal. There's no love lost between Sam and his sister, but he would have nothing to do with shaking his own sister down. Sam even offered to buy it."

"With what?" Stumper laughed. "His good looks?"

"Sam had money."

Stumper laughed. "Just about enough to buy a twelve-pack."

Manny glared at Stumper and he leaned back against the door. Manny turned back to Itchy. "Do you think Sam made a deal with the tall man to swap the ammo in the cavalry reenactor's rifle?"

Itchy abruptly stopped picking his arm and the color drained from his face as he leaned closer to Manny in a brief moment of lucidness. "I love Sam like a brother, Agent Tanno, but I'm telling you he was mad enough to take the journal and destroy it. Along with anyone else that might have read it. If he made some deal with the tall man, it wouldn't surprise me."

CHAPTER 11

Stumper filled his coffee cup and held the pot up. "Unlike Chief Deer Slayer, I like mine so it flows."

"In that case, I'll have a cup." Willie held up his Mighty Mouse cup and Stumper filled it. The Mouse's one eye filled up with the liquid, the other clouded with yesterday's coffee stain running down the side.

"Manny?"

"Coffee gives me blood sugar swings. Bad thing with diabetes."

Stumper turned a chair around backward and hung his arms over the side. He nodded to Manny's double-breasted Western shirt and Wranglers bunched up over pointed-toe cowboy boots. "A definite improvement over those funky shorts and Hawaiian shirt." He grinned.

Manny had dropped Willie off at an AA meeting in Hardin yesterday afternoon and gone shopping. "Last Stand

Western Wear. Like you recommended." He frowned as he nodded to his garb. "This isn't me."

"That's what I told him," Willie said. "I can pull that off, but it's just not the grumpy FBI agent getup. But know-everything Manny Tanno didn't pack regular clothes like I suggested."

"It's as close to regular clothes that they had in my size. It's not me."

"And passing yourself off as a Hawaiian tourist is?" Stumper asked.

"Let's say it's my disguise."

Stumper looked Manny up and down. "I second that. No one would believe an FBI agent would wear a sequined Western shirt." He nodded to Manny's boots. "And alligator boots? That part of your new disguise?" Stumper tilted his head back and laughed. "Who wears alligator cowboy boots?"

"It was the only thing in my size that Last Stand had."

"Another reason to pack extra clothes," Willie said. "When you got size twelve double EEs like Manny, you may have to settle for something like those."

Stumper whistled. "Well, if we get any Bigfoot sightings here on the rez, we'll know who to question."

Manny grabbed a Hardin Chamber of Commerce file folder depicting the county museum, complete with all nineteen outbuildings on twenty-two acres. *Maybe Willie will settle for a trip to the museum in lieu of Yellowstone. Wonder if they have discount coupons in their brochure?* "Let's see what you got."

Stumper opened the folder and grabbed a slip of paper. "Avis rental agreement."

"Frankie?"

"Most likely." Stumper set his cup down and started picking his teeth with the edge of the folder. "Billings PD is putting together a photo lineup for the clerk."

Willie scooted his chair closer and looked over Manny's shoulder at the rental agreement. The man renting the pearl Cadillac had scrawled the name Carson Degas on the agreement two days before the Real Bird reenactment. "What's the chance the guy used his real name?" Willie asked.

"Good." Stumper eyed him filling his lip with Copenhagen. He waited until Willie brushed the excess off on his jeans before reaching across the table and snatching it.

"What the hell, I adopt you?"

Stumper ignored him and filled his own lip before replacing the lid and sliding the can back to Willie. "A Carson Degas was arrested in Hardin just before their reenactment was to start on Sunday." Stumper flipped pages in his notebook. "He claimed he was to be in the Hardin reenactment when he got arrested for fighting."

"Hardin's got their own show?" Willie spit into the round file. "Hard to keep up with you Crow."

Stumper nodded. "Hardin's reenactment can be viewed as friendly competition with the Real Bird's. A lot of people go to both. Hardin's starts at one thirty."

Manny nodded, checking his watch for his next blood sugar check. "Twenty miles from here to the Hardin reenactment. That would have given Degas time to leave the Real Bird show and drive to Hardin in time to get arrested. Looks like we lucked out with Degas being in the pokey."

Stumper shook his head as he walked to the coffeepot. "Big Horn County jail says Degas paid his hundred dollars on a guilty plea the next morning and was Gone Johnson."

"Anyone get a chance to show their detention officers Degas's photo?"

"I've been a little busy with a new meth case," Stumper

said. "And dodging Della Night Tail bugging me about Little Dave not coming home."

Manny gathered the folder and turned to Willie. "Then I guess we'll take Thelma's photo and have an all-expenses-paid trip to Hardin."

Willie slammed Mighty Mouse on the table and stood. "Oh that's lovely. Rather than check out Medicine Wheel or Plenty Coup Park, we go to Hardin."

Manny stood and hitched up his jeans that were a size too large. He grabbed the museum brochure. "Hey, they got a museum we can check out. I'll pay the admission."

"It's free," Stumper volunteered.

Manny smiled. "Even better."

><><><><

They parked in front of a Mercedes SUV in back of the Big Horn County Jail. When Sheriff's Captain Miles buzzed them through the security door, Manny mentioned the Mercedes. "Left over from that special police force you guys had here?"

Miles put his finger to his lips. "We don't talk about that."

Manny understood. Black Mercedes SUVs bearing the Big Horn County Department logo had descended on Hardin three years ago. Rumors spread about the level of involvement between the American Police Force and their connection with the Two Rivers Correctional Facility, still empty waiting for phantom inmates to appear. Speculation about town was that Guantánamo was closing and terror prisoners were to be transferred to Two Rivers, bringing hundreds of jobs to the town. It never materialized, and the only one to make out, it appeared to Manny, was the sheriff's office, with a new Mercedes to drive.

Miles led them past two dispatchers, one sitting bored with his head in hands, while the other hunched over a teletype machine, poised to rip off paper when the machine stopped. Miles shut the door and motioned to chairs in front of his desk. "Dispatch said you guys want to know about Carson Degas."

Willie grabbed the picture of the man calling himself Frankie and handed it to Miles. He turned to his computer and began punching keys to access jail records. Degas's booking photo popped up on the screen, and Manny grabbed his reading glasses from his pocket. Miles did a double take of Clara's glasses, and just grinned.

"Getting in touch with my feminine side." Manny tapped the glasses as he leaned over the desk. He studied the picture of the man posing with a jail number in hand in front of his chest, slight smile tugging at the corners of a mouth more a thin slit than lips. Even on the computer screen, Degas's twinkling eyes shone through as if he were happy to be in jail. A brief, evil image fluttered across Manny's thoughts, then was gone as quickly as Degas was from Hardin.

Miles held the picture to the screen. "I'd say this is a match. The deputies have some stories to tell about this guy." He leaned back in his chair and intertwined his fingers across his protruding belly. "They're actually glad not to have to arrest another meth head off the rez." His face got red and he started to apologize, but Manny waved the comment away.

"I'll add Frankie to his alias file," Miles sputtered and turned back to the keyboard.

Manny sat back down. "What can you tell us about Degas?"

Miles tapped the keyboard again. He leaned back and took off his own glasses. He began chewing on the bows frayed from gnawing on them. "Looks like he's from Pine Ridge." Miles chuckled and Manny waited for an explanation. "He'd be easy to find on that reservation—not many White guys living there I'd wager."

"He's White?" Willie stood and looked over Miles's shoulder at the picture.

Miles nodded. "Looks Indian. But he ain't. Man like that could pass himself off as most anything." He turned to Willie. "Know him?"

Willie shook his head and turned to Manny. "Never heard of him back home."

Miles tapped keys. "Deputies arrested him for starting a fight at the Scandinavian Meatball Dinner."

"Local event?"

Miles wiped his mouth with the back of his hand as if he'd just left the dinner. "Very local. Great meatball dinner if you're ever up here for the city reenactment."

"Maybe we'll check that out next year."

Willie kicked him under the desk, but Manny ignored him. "Looks like he pled guilty the next morning and paid his fine."

Miles turned back to the computer. "Hundred dollars plus court costs. Says here he had over six hundred cash on him. Guess he could afford it."

"Maybe he was anticipating a higher fine."

"What, like he thought he'd get arrested?"

Manny shrugged. "Can't say."

"What did he do exactly?"

Miles craned his neck around to face Willie. "Do? He showed up at the meatball dinner and started a food fight with some local toughs. My deputies said they weren't as tough as they thought, 'cause this Degas had three ranch boys laid out and was working over the fourth when the cavalry arrived. Degas just stopped fighting and said 'I surrender.' He gave up without so much as a twitch even when they slapped the cuffs on him."

Manny put his glasses on again and studied the photo once more. "I'd expect him to sport a fat lip, maybe a broken nose if he fought four big ol' ranch boys."

Miles shrugged. "I would, too. But the deputies were just glad he went without a fight as big as he is."

"Don't look so big," Willie said. He studied Degas's booking information. "Six two, one eighty-five. Little guy."

Miles smiled. "He was big enough to take care of four of our locals."

Manny leaned back and slipped Clara's glasses back into his pocket before Miles could comment on them. "Degas must have been pretty drunk."

Miles donned his glasses again and turned back to the computer. "That's odd."

"What?"

"We give everyone that comes into the jail a Breathalyzer."

"And?"

"For someone picking a fight, he blew zeroes."

>‹›‹›‹

"Don't mind if we stop for a beer?" Manny pointed to the VFW sign hanging outside the Four Aces Bar. "Getting a mite thirsty."

"Thought you didn't drink?"

"Only when I get some dry Montana dust stuck in my throat. Don't you?"

Manny regretted the comment even before it left his mouth. Willie had been fighting for his sobriety, and the last thing he needed was to go into a bar. "Sorry. I forgot."

"Like me offering you a Chesterfield."

"Camel."

"Any cigarette. You'd smoke horse shit rolled in that hard TP at the motel if you got a chance. Course, I might start drinking again after Lieutenant Looks Twice gets through with me when I get home."

Lumpy's voice had screamed in Manny's cell phone when he learned that Willie was involved in a Crow Agency investigation.

"Couldn't be helped," Manny explained. "We were there when it happened. What did you expect me to do, put Willie on the Hound and send him back home luggage class?"

Lumpy had simmered down after that. "What do you need, Hotshot?"

Manny had given him Degas's description from the jail booking form. "Big Horn County's going to TTY you Degas's photo. We need someone to find and detain him until I get there to interview him."

"Great." Lumpy's voice rose again. "How are we supposed to find him with a General Delivery address?"

"Most people on Pine Ridge have a General Delivery address. How do you find other people you're looking for?"

A long pause. "We'll try."

"And another thing," Manny was quick to say before Lumpy hung up, "this guy made short work out of four big ranch hands, and didn't get a scratch. When your guys go to hunt him up, tell them to be especially careful."

"We got it handled, Hotshot." And Lumpy abruptly disconnected.

They drove past the Four Aces and turned toward Custer's Revenge. "Why do you think Degas gave his real name?" Willie asked.

"He's not worried," Manny answered instantly. It had bothered him, too, that someone just involved in a homicide would give his real name. "He's not worried, even if someone would connect him to Tess's gun. Degas has the best alibi in the world—he was locked up at the time of the ammo swap. Or so he must think."

Willie nodded. "He must have driven like hell to get to the Meatball Dinner after he swapped the ammo."

"Then there's the matter of him claiming he was to be in the Hardin reenactment—that'd be easy enough to refute."

Manny undid his seat belt as Willie pulled into the motel parking lot. "The Indians that participate in Hardin's show make a few bucks on the side. My guess is that no one actually has a list of the reenactors on the Indian side. Whoever shows up for the show gets a job for the day."

Willie climbed out of the Olds and looked longingly at the Rodeway Inn across the street. "We could have stayed there." He chin-pointed.

"Better," Manny forced a smile. "We're close to Jackrabbit Red's Casino."

"Like either of us gambles?"

They entered their room, the lock still not fixed, and the door swung open on squeaky hinges. "Hope we didn't have anything taken," Manny said.

"Like your priceless Hawaiian shirt and funky shorts? Don't worry—they'd bring them back."

Manny clapped as they entered, but the light failed to come on. "You going to stand there all day and look foolish clapping?"

"One more thing to tell that slacker manager."

>‹›‹›‹‹

Manny pulled the Olds into the short-term parking lot at the Billings airport and walked Willie to check-in. Manny set Willie's bag on the scale. "Sorry about the vacation."

Willie shrugged.

"And for getting you in hot water with Lumpy."

"Not like it's the first time you've gotten me into trouble with the acting chief. I was lucky to talk him into giving me forty-eight hours to find Degas. He was half a step away from canceling my vacation and assigning me permanent animal control." He took the baggage stub and started for the security gates.

"You sure you're going to be all right back home?" Manny asked.

"More importantly, will you? You'll have to do all your own driving while I'm away . . ."

"I was driving when you were just playing with model cars."

"I had less scrapes and dents in my models than you got in that beater of yours."

"Just be careful back there," Manny urged. As their vacation had been cut short, Willie decided to go home and had offered to talk Lumpy into letting him find Degas. Manny's first instinct was to go to Pine Ridge himself, find Degas, and interview him, probably leading to an arrest. But he had been faced with a dilemma: leave the follow-up investigation on Crow Agency to Stumper, a rookie investigator, or leave finding Degas to Willie, a rookie investigator. No one was even sure if Degas had gone back to Pine Ridge, so Manny opted to send Willie home. "And if you find him, get backup before you take him in."

"I'm just going to interview him . . ."

"Willie."

"All right," Willie answered, but he didn't have as much conviction as Manny wanted. "I'll bring help."

"And call me right away when you got him. I'll need to interview him, too, before he gets a chance to lawyer-up."

Willie held up his hands. "All right, all ready. But you're the one that needs to be careful up here."

"Me? It's not like we're still at war with the Crow."

"It's not the Crow I'm worried about. It's turning you loose on Crow Agency behind the wheel."

"My driving's getting better."

"But in the meantime, you're driving a car with some serious iron. You scrape one of these modern cars and you'll total it."

"I'll be careful. But you be doubly careful. If Degas can swap ammo to get a man killed, he won't hesitate to kill an officer."

"He's no danger to me." Willie laid his hand on Manny's shoulder. "Degas thinks he has the perfect alibi. When I interview him, that'll give me a major advantage."

"With someone like Degas," Manny said, concern rimming his eyes, "I suspect no one really has any kind of advantage."

Chapter 12

Levi Star Dancer smiled at Hollow Horn. Intermittent suck-ing on Pretty Paw's breast caused milk to spill out of the baby's mouth. She dabbed at milk running down Hollow Horn's cheek, and looked up at Levi. He stood warming his hands over the fire in the middle of the lodge, content with his wife. And with Hollow Horn. The baby had been given the name just six days ago in the manner of the Apsa'alooke. Levi had humbly asked his friend and noted warrior Horse That Sings to honor his baby with a name. As was their custom, Horse That Sings appeared at the tipi of Broken Rib four days after the baby's birth. His friend had hoisted the naked and screaming baby in front of him, elevating him higher each of the four times before Horse That Sings pronounced his name: Hollow Horn. An honorable name.

Levi had thanked his friend with the gift of his best hunting horse, a bay that Levi had gelded when the colt was but five moons old. Levi had stood beside his friend stroking the pony, expecting Horse That Sings to ask about Hollow Horn's eyes that shone the color of a fall sky. But he had not, and neither had Levi's clan uncles and aunts who arrived to give Pretty Paw the cradle and moccasins as was their duty.

Levi smiled down at her, and she smiled back. They still lived in her father's lodge, and moments such as this alone with his new family rarely occurred. Levi bent and brushed the baby's hair hanging over his forehead and kissed him. He heard his father-in-law, his *iila'pxe*, untie the buffalo-skin flap, and Levi stood.

Broken Rib ducked inside. Frozen streaks of ice mixed with the old man's gray hair falling in clumps over his shoulder, hard droplets clinging to his battle-scarred arms. Levi had joined his *iila'pxe* one morning days before Hollow Horn came to Crow country. Broken Rib had chopped a man-sized hole in the ice with his trade ax. "The Old Man keeps his bows and arrows down there." He had smiled at Levi just before he jumped through the ice. He was under the water, lost somewhere down the hole for so long that Levi thought the old man had drowned. Then he had broken through the surface, shivering, unable to speak, his chattering teeth barely able to ask Levi for his buffalo robe.

"This is what the Creator intended for us Apsa'alooke," he had sputtered right before he nodded to the hole quickly icing over. "Now it is your turn."

Levi would have declined anyone else, but one did not say no to a warrior such as Broken Rib. Levi had stripped down, testing the water with his feet, shivering, holding his breath right before he dropped through the hole into the creek. He would later tell Pretty Paw he was certain his heart had stopped. The pain was like cactus slapping his whole body. Every day he awoke to Broken Rib greeting the Old Man as he brought sunshine just over the horizon to the east. And every day Levi managed some excuse not to join Broken Rib again in the frigid water.

Hollow Horn coughed and Pretty Paw tapped his back. She rolled over and covered herself with the buffalo robe as she resumed feeding the baby. Broken Rib turned his back on them and threw his robe off, flapping his arms. He straddled the fire wearing only a breachclout, and Levi feared the fire would burn the old man somewhere he didn't like.

Broken Rib eased onto the hide covering the tipi floor and scooted close to the fire. He nodded to woolen soldier blankets folded beside Levi. Levi handed his father-in-law the blankets and the old man wrapped himself with them, rubbing his hair dry and warming his hands over the burning cottonwood.

After several moments, Broken Rib got enough circulation back in his hands that he turned and grabbed his pipe bag, not the ceremonial one decorated with hawk feathers and dyed porcupine quills he'd used when Horse That Sings gave Hollow Horn his name, but the old man's everyday pipe. On mornings such as these, Broken Rib sat around the smoke hole, the aroma of cedar and sweetgrass emanating from his pipe, regaling Levi and Pretty Paw with tales of the old man's war deeds. Appropriately, his clan was *Ashke'pkawiia*, Bad War Deeds clan. Broken Rib enjoyed telling of his bravery, for such telling was rare with the Apsa'alooke: Humility was paramount in a warrior, and Broken Rib would never have bragged outside his lodge.

Levi sat silent as his *iila'pxe*, water-wrinkled hands trembling from the icy creek, packed the red clay bowl with the tobacco he'd traded from some trappers near the Shining

Mountains. He grabbed a smoldering, spitting cottonwood twig from the fire and touched the bowl. He watched transfixed as the smoke meandered around him before being sucked upward and out the smoke hole.

"A warrior needs times such as these," Broken Rib said, letting the smoke out slowly. "When a man spends his whole life caring for family, hunting, fighting the Lakota and Cheyenne from our lands, a man needs mornings to just pray to the Old Man." Broken Rib closed his eyes, his breaths grating, and Levi knew his *iila'pxe* was at the fall of his days.

"If we leave as you say," Levi blurted out, "I'll never have days such as this." He took a deep breath, calming himself, steeling for the argument that he knew would come from his father-in-law. "If I go to where the White man wants me, I'll never die a warrior."

Broken Rib tamped the ashes out into a small wooden bowl, quiet, as if he had not heard Levi. When he finished, he set the bowl aside and stretched out his hands to the warming fire. "It is said the Whites give each man forty acres . . ."

"What is forty acres?" Levi stood and started to pace. "A man cannot hunt buffalo on forty acres."

The old man's mouth drooped and his eyes held far away, sad times. "When was the last time you hunted buffalo?"

"We killed a cow and her calf . . ."

"And how long did that feed us? I tell you, there are no buffalo left. The *baashchiili* has killed them all. Hide hunters make their fortunes on killing what we need to feed our families."

"Then I'll hunt deer. I'll find *iichiilikaashee* . . ."

Broken Rib forced a smile. "And where will you find the elk? Or deer enough that Pretty Paw and Hollow Horn will not go hungry?"

Levi faced the fire, flickering flames framing the old man

in a warm glow. "But forty acres? We do not own land, because First Maker gives land to all."

"The White man owns the land." Broken Rib stretched out his legs and rubbed his calves. He left his feet close enough that spitting embers landed dangerously close to bare feet. "This is different times. The *baashchiili* tells us what we can own and what we cannot. You must leave."

Levi began pacing in front of the fire, careful not to step on the buffalo robe that covered Pretty Paw and Hollow Horn, both sleeping as if they heard nothing. "Forty acres is not enough to farm, even if I were a farmer."

Broken Rib nodded to the floor of the lodge, and Levi reluctantly sat. "All the young men will receive forty acres on this new reservation the soldiers formed?"

Levi nodded. "All will get only that small amount of land."

"But most will lose their land."

"Lose it? How?"

Broken Rib rotated his ankle, popping noises louder than the crackling of the cottonwood twigs. "They will take the White man's drink . . ."

"We do not drink their alcohol."

Broken Rib frowned at being interrupted, and Levi breathed deeply, regaining his composure so as not to disrespect the old man again. "Young men will drink the alcohol the White man gives them and they will lose their forty acres. They will lay lazy under the sun, wishing they were warriors once again. And they will lose their land. Some will simply walk away, but their land will remain. That is when you prosper."

Levi leaned closer. "Prosper? How?"

Broken Rib took his tobacco pouch from the bag hanging on the wall of the lodge. "When the young men no longer want the land, you will buy it—in some instances, even trade for things you have at hand—and you will gain more land. Soon, those forty acres will span as far as the eye can see. And you will raise crops that the *baashchiili* wants. And Pretty Paw and Hollow Horn will never hunger."

"But I am no farmer." Levi fought to come up with excuses why he should not give up the warrior life to farm the land. "I belong here, in the mountains, hunting, providing for my family."

Broken Rib refilled his pipe with tobacco. "You will learn to farm. And you will learn how to handle success in this new world that has come to Crow country."

Levi sat back, kicking around what Broken Rib said. As always, there was wisdom in the old man's words; wisdom that Levi suddenly realized would see him and his family through these times of great uncertainty.

He turned and grabbed his journal, but Broken Rib patted Levi's leg. "There is time enough to write the White man's words," he said, touching a burning twig to the bowl. The tobacco caught, and the old man closed his eyes, keeping the smoke inside for a long moment before exhaling and passing the pipe to Levi. "A warrior needs times such as these."

CHAPTER 13

Manny cussed himself for losing his sunglasses as he squinted against the sun driving west into Lodge Grass. He drove faster than he had a right to, hoping he'd get to Sam's house before the sun set. The last time he and Willie were there, the lights didn't work, and Manny wanted to get another look inside before darkness overcame the sad structure.

When he turned the corner onto Red Bird Lane, a truck sat crooked in front of Sam's house. The F350 Ford sprouted twin exhaust pipes jutting into the air beside the cab like twin fingers flipping off the world as if it didn't care. The truck, newer than it first appeared because of the dust and mud hiding the camouflage paint scheme, nearly concealed the exploding star, the STAR DANCER RANCH logo, adorning both doors.

Manny parked behind the truck, sharp noises coming from inside Sam's house as if someone were going through what few things lay piled in the middle of the floors. He reached under the seat of the Oldsmobile and cursed: he'd left his Glock in his motel room before he drove Willie to the airport in Billings.

He eased the Oldsmobile's heavy door shut and stepped over the fallen picket fence. He inched up to a window and shielded his eyes against the sun as he peered in. A large man hunched over the mattress on the floor. He tossed a sweat-stained pillow across the room and flipped the mattress over. Something scurried from under the mattress and disappeared somewhere behind the wall.

Manny duckwalked under the window until he reached the front door. He grabbed the screen door and jerked it open. The door ripped from the one remaining hinge. It fell to the porch. The man jumped. "Police!"

"Don't shoot." The man stood with his hands held over his head like he'd watched too many B-western movies. "I'm not armed."

Neither am I. "Sam give you permission to be here?"

"Can I put my hands down? I got a bum shoulder."

Manny nodded, keeping one hand behind his back as if he concealed a gun there. "What are you doing here?"

"I'd ask you the same thing. You don't look like any of the tribal or BIA cops here on Crow Agency."

Manny stepped over a pile of dirty clothes as he deftly flipped his ID wallet open.

The man exhaled as he bent to eyeball Manny's FBI identification. "You scared the shit out of me."

"Wouldn't want you to be shitless. People often get that way when they're caught."

"Caught?" The man slumped against a rain-stained wall, mold overtaking the blistering blue wallpaper hung about a century ago. He shook out a Marlboro and replaced the pack in his pocket. His hands shook as he brought his Zippo to the cigarette. Manny thought how un-Marlboro-Man this guy was, with his oversized ALL AROUND COWBOY rodeo buckle all but lost under his sagging belly. He took off his Stetson and ran a snotty bandanna around the sweatband, dropping it on boots caked dry with cow dung. He picked it up and shook it once before replacing it in his back pocket.

Surely the Marlboro Man never smelled this bad, and Manny was trying to figure out if it was the cow crap on the man's boots or his shirt with dark sweat stains under the arms. Or if he smelled this bad because he'd just awoke from an all-night bender with the bottle.

"I haven't been caught at anything," the man blurted.

Manny said nothing. Often, silence was his best weapon in getting at the truth.

"I said, Mister FBI man, I haven't been caught at anything."

"So you said." Manny smiled, enjoying the man's predicament. He had been caught at something. Manny just had to figure out what.

The man took a can of Copenhagen from his back pocket and stuffed his lip. Manny had never seen anyone dip snuff between drags of a cigarette.

"You stay here with Sampson?"

The man laughed and gestured around the room with his hand. "This pigsty? Not hardly. It's my brother-in-law's crib."

"So you're Iron Cloud?"

He drew in a deep breath that puffed his chest out, threatening to snap shirt buttons holding his belly up. An image flew by Manny, thinking that if the man did a handstand that belly would slap him in the face. "I'm Cubby Iron Cloud."

Manny nodded.

"And I'd have shit myself if you'd come in with your gun pointed at me."

"I did show restraint." Manny walked the small room.

Except for things being scattered about even more, the place looked as unlivable as it had the first time he was here.

Cubby seemed to anticipate his question. "I was hunting Sam."

"Under the mattress?"

Cubby's face flushed. "I thought I might figure out where he might have gone. Chenoa needs him to sign some papers. Ranch business."

"So she said earlier. Selling bred heifers to Wilson Eagle Bull. You must have better things to do than make a special trip into town."

"Tell me about it. Chenoa . . ."

"Got you wrapped around her finger?"

Cubby dropped his cigarette onto the floor and snubbed it out with his boot. A couple years ago, Manny would have bent and grabbed the snipe and smoked what was left. *In my smoking days.* Cubby looked at Manny and forced a smile. "The only time Chenoa sends me to this dump is when she needs me to hunt up her brother."

"She demands and you jump?"

"Every time." Cubby left it hanging in the air like the stale odor that permeated Sam's ramshackle house.

"And you always come in here tossing things around as if Sam's under all this trash?"

Cubby remained silent.

"Or were you looking for a journal that Harlan White Bird was to auction?"

Cubby's head snapped around and he glared at Manny. "I don't know anything about no journal." He looked quickly away, and Manny knew he'd just caught him in a bald lie. Manny let it rest, keeping it in the back of his mind that Cubby wanted desperately to find Levi Star Dancer's journal.

"I take it you didn't find Sam under the mattress, or piles of trash?"

"One day they'll find Sam floating in the Big Horn River with a point-three-oh blood alcohol content, and I won't have to worry about him anymore," Cubby blurted out. "But for now, it's important I find him and have him sign the sale papers."

"I detect a hint of hostility toward him."

"They teach you to pick up on obvious shit in the FBI academy? A first-year rookie could figure out I hate my brother-in-law."

Manny smiled. "It's an acquired skill. Like obeying the wife's orders."

Cubby spit onto a pile of newspapers stacked beside a pot-bellied heat stove. "I got no choice. While Chenoa and Wilson went to God-knows-where on business, I'm stuck with the dirty jobs."

"Well"—Manny gestured around the room—"it doesn't get any dirtier than this."

><><><

Manny rolled over and hit the snooze button, but the jangling continued and he hit it again before realizing it was the room phone jarring him awake.

"I didn't get any answer on your cell so I called the front desk and asked for your room." Manny was certain Willie smiled at him from the other end.

Manny rubbed his eyes and stared at the alarm clock. *Is Pine Ridge in another time zone? If not, why the hell's Willie calling at 5:00."*

"I found Carson Degas."

Manny clapped twice and the overhead chandelier came on. *Super finally fixed the damned thing.* He swung his legs over the bed and grabbed his socks stuck into his boots. "What did he say when you interviewed him?"

"I haven't yet. Last night I found out from your old chief . . ."

"What's Chief Horn got to do with you finding Degas?"

Willie laughed. "If you left it up to him, he'd come out of retirement and work the case himself. Acting Chief Looks Twice suggested I talk to Horn, as he knows everyone living on the rez. And most everyone that traveled the Spirit Road within the last century."

Manny cradled the phone in the crick of his neck. He moved over away from the spring poking him through the mattress and slipped a sock on. "So where's Degas?"

"Sitting down?"

Willie the drama queen. "Just tell me . . ."

"Degas works for Wilson Eagle Bull at his ranch south of Oglala."

Manny shook his head and stood on wobbly legs, stretching. It didn't work. He was still operating in sleep mode. "The same guy running for Senate? Chenoa Iron Cloud's boyfriend?" "Boyfriend" came out of Manny's mouth as if it had been lying in wait somewhere in the back of his mind to escape into the light of day. *Whenever the light of day finally arrives.*

"The same. Degas is Wilson's horse wrangler. Lines up stock for the Big Foot Memorial Ride for folks that don't have mounts. Rents horses to dude ranches in South Dakota and Wyoming, some in Montana and Nebraska. And—get this— he supplies ponies for actors at both Little Big Horn reenactments."

"You getting all this from Chief Horn?"

Willie chuckled. "When he's not raising hell with the other residents at the home, he talks to people. All sorts of people.

Including Wilson's former neighbor, who told him about Carson Degas."

"So Degas would be familiar with both Hardin's and Real Bird's reenactments. He'd have their times down pat?"

"No doubt."

"Where's Degas now?"

Rustling against the phone and Manny pulled the receiver from his ear. "Sorry," Willie said. "I've been living on Moon-Pies and root beer since last night. I'm sitting on Wilson's ranch house waiting for some lights to come on. As soon as I see some life around the bunkhouse, I'm driving down there and interview him."

A MoonPie, complete with a day's worth of sugar, would help kick-start Manny right about now. "Sure he's there?"

Manny could imagine thick, black hair falling over Willie's forehead as he nodded. "A couple of Wilson's ranch hands I let slide for public intox last month clued me in."

"They work for Degas?"

"They were adamant they worked for *Wilson*. They want no part of Degas. He scares the hell out of them."

Manny put the other sock on before he realized he needed to shower first. He went to the bathroom to splash water on his face in an effort to wake up from this sleep fog, thankful the phone cord had stretched ten feet. "Wilson's hands have problems with Degas?"

"Not yet. They've only worked for Wilson two months, but they expect to have a run-in with Degas eventually. They heard stories from a couple other hands Degas run off that he's way over the top."

"Over the top?"

"Stories. Rumors. About how Degas educates ranch hands in the back of the bunkhouse. People that got in his way. Or men that didn't do just what he wanted. Or just didn't do it fast enough."

"Sounds like he makes his own form of entertainment." The cold water helped Manny at least see his face through red-rimmed eyes. "Degas the foreman?"

Willie's voice was muffled as he scarfed down another MoonPie. "He's not, but it doesn't matter. Even Wilson's foreman gives him a wide berth."

Willie dropped his cell phone, but came back on the line. "Gotta run. Looks like that green Dodge dually Degas drives just pulled out from Wilson's equipment shed."

"Get backup before you drive down there," but Manny's warning fell on a dead line. "Be careful, my friend," he said aloud. He hung up the phone and turned to grab his shaving bag when the phone rang again. "Forgot to tell me something?"

"I didn't forget anything," Stumper said, talking fast. "I called to let you know Sam's been found. Better meet at his house in Lodge Grass pronto."

CHAPTER 14

Even before Manny turned onto the street leading to the cul-de-sac and Sam's house, thick smoke filtered through the vents of the Oldsmobile and found their way to Manny's nose, the taste of charred wood, siding, and electrical wiring making him retch. He pulled his car behind a Crow tribal fire tanker parked crosswise blocking the street. A Suburban sporting one crushed fender and COMMAND VEHICLE on one door sat next to the water truck, the red and blue flashing lights cutting through the smoke. The door of the command vehicle stood open as if someone had abandoned it there in a hurry.

Manny stepped over a deflated fire hose and stopped at the open window of the ambulance. "Someone hurt inside?"

An EMT behind the wheel tilted his hat back and glanced at Manny for a moment before replacing the hat over his eyes and resting his head back on the seat. "Someone's beyond hurt. Someone's dead. We're just sticking around in case one of the firemen sucks smoke or the roof falls in."

Manny walked around a smaller truck with a hose reel stretched across the road. He covered his ears to the hissing of water dousing charred wood, and wished he could cover his nose as well. He'd smelled enough burned corpses to know one waited somewhere inside Sam's house.

Stumper stood with a bandanna tied around his nose talking with a fireman wearing yellow bunker gear. He spotted Manny and turned on his heels and ran toward him. Stumper motioned for them to walk upwind away from the house. When they were half a block away, Stumper pulled his bandanna away and spit into the dirt. "Just shoot me if I ever say I want to be a fireman."

Manny forced a smile. "That I can do. Give me the headline version of what happened."

Stumper hocked up phlegm before grabbing his can of Copenhagen and stuffing his lip. He replaced the lid and held the can in front of him. "I can fall asleep with this in my hand and still be alive in the morning. Now I were a smoker with a cigarette . . ."

"That what you figured happened?"

Stumper brushed the excess snuff off onto his jeans and pocketed the can. "That's what the fire investigator thinks. It appears that Sam fell asleep with a cigarette." He chin-pointed to the house. "Looks like they're done."

Manny and Stumper walked to the command vehicle. Manny leaned against the dirty fender, black soot rubbing off onto his jeans and polo shirt, while Stumper stood away from the Suburban. "Getting a little filthy, ain't 'cha?" He smiled.

Manny smiled back. "Not as dirty as we're going to get once we go inside the house."

Stumper's smile faded. "We? I thought firemen investigated all arsons?"

"They do. We investigate homicides."

The color drained from Stumper's face as he looked over Manny's shoulder at the house leaking smoke and steam from windows and doors. "But the firemen said it looks like Sam fell asleep smoking a cigarette."

Manny sat on the running board and looked up at Stumper. "You've never investigated a fire-related death before, have you?"

"Of course I have."

"When?"

Stumper kicked the dirt with his boot and spit tobacco juice on an ant struggling with a tree leaf. "Okay, I've never actually investigated one."

"Or seen one?"

Stumper shook his head. "Just pictures."

Manny stood and patted Stumper's shoulder. "Then this will be your first. You'll do fine." He turned to the house, where firemen walked around stringing yellow crime scene tape.

At the front fender of the command vehicle, a heavyset fireman wrote on a clipboard, his THREE BITS name tag barely readable under the soot and dirt. Manny badged him, and he nodded to Stumper. "Is it clear inside to have a look?"

Three Bits turned his back and continued writing on the clipboard, and Manny thought he hadn't heard him.

"We need to go inside and . . ."

"I heard you," Three Bits said over his shoulder.

Stumper tugged on Manny's shirt and led him to the back of the command vehicle. "I'd like to say this guy's a prick, but that would be giving pricks a bad name," he whispered. "Hates everyone. Especially me."

Manny's eyebrows came together. "Problems with Three Bits?"

Stumper turned and looked at the fireman. "Went to

school with him. We used to tease him . . . called him Three Tits, and the fight would be on. Mostly, he wanted to fight me 'cause I was the smallest guy in school. The only thing he learned is that my smaller-size boot up his ass didn't hurt like it would with one of the bigger kids."

"Well, we got no choice. We got to work with him."

"You guys ready?" Three Bits called over his shoulder as he started for what used to be the front of Sam's house. "We don't have all night." Water, black char from the effects of the fire, ran into the street and mixed with mud. Manny stomped his feet, knocking off the mud before he entered the house.

"You won't get this place any dirtier than it has been," Three Bits said.

"Just don't want to introduce any more contaminants into the crime scene than we have to," Manny answered and stepped over the threshold. Stumper stomped his feet before entering as well and followed them inside.

Manny paused just inside the door, and Three Bits stopped. "I thought you wanted a walk-through?"

"In a moment." Manny stood in the center of what had been Sam's living room. The fire had destroyed much of the roof, and light flooded in. He turned to Stumper. "A lot of this contamination was introduced by the firemen . . ."

"What the hell we supposed to do when we get a fire? Take our shoes off?" Three Bits had turned to face them, anger spilling into his fists balling up. "We got to get inside. Save lives. Property . . ."

"It's sometimes referred to as spoliation." Manny ignored Three Bits as he continued instructing Stumper. As he had with Willie, Manny took the opportunity to teach Stumper about criminal investigation. And this might be Stumper's only chance to learn about arson the right way.

Three Bits stepped between them. "What's this bullshit about us firefighters?"

Manny turned to Three Bits. "Not a value statement, Captain . . ."

"Lieutenant," Three Bits corrected, his face losing some of the redness. "And we can't help it."

Manny smiled. "Never said you could. Just commenting on what's been introduced to a homicide scene."

"Homicide?" Three Bits looked quickly around, but no other fireman was close, and he lowered his voice. "Who said anything about a homicide?"

Manny shrugged. "I'm sure your assessment was correct—that Sam fell asleep with a cigarette in his hand and caught his ratty old mattress on fire. But we have to treat it as if it were a homicide. Don't you agree?"

Three Bits nodded. "Of course. It's just . . ."

Manny waved his hand. "Not to worry. Show us the body."

Three Bits put a bandanna over his nose as he led them into the bedroom.

"My God." Stumper turned away and Manny was certain he was going to heave, but he breathed deep and faced the body.

Little more than a skeleton with charred skin attached here and there, pieces of red flannel shirt sticking to burned muscle, lay on its back. The unmistakable stench of burned hair mixed with seared flesh reached Manny and he turned away. When he turned back, he had regained his composure and he squatted beside the body. The victim's hands were bent and held in front of his body, fingers burned back to reveal bone.

"What was he doing, fending someone off?" Three Bits asked.

Manny shook his head and pointed to the man's arms. "Coagulation of muscles from the intense heat causes the muscles fibers to constrict. Makes victims look like they're fighting. Called Pugilistic Attitude."

"We figure he was just laying there when the fire caught," Three Bits blurted out. "He wasn't fighting no one."

"Didn't figure he was." Manny stood and looked about the room. "How long was the fire going before your crews arrived?"

"Quite a while, the way I figure." Three Bits's voice was muffled through his bandanna. "We got here fast as we could."

"Of course you did. Just tell me how long."

Three Bits turned away from the corpse and stood as if talking with the wall. "No neighbor close to call the fire in until the house was engulfed. Then it took us fifteen minutes to get here. We did the best we could."

Manny put his hand on the man's shoulder. "We know you guys responded as soon as you could. But I need to treat this like a homicide."

Two Bits nodded. "What do you need me to do?"

Manny gestured out a charred window. "We'll need a building engineer here to see if it's safe to work in here."

"Got it."

"And your guys did right by running crime scene tape around the house. I'll request a crime tech to process the scene, but it might be a few days. I'll call the Billings office as soon as I'm finished here and put in the request. I'd like you to get enough plywood to seal off the house."

"You got it." Three Bits left, and Manny was certain he was grateful to be gone from where the seared body seemed to fend off his attacker with upraised arms. Hell, Manny wished he were somewhere besides smelling the odors and stepping around the filth that was once Sampson Star Dancer's house.

Manny waited until the fireman left before turning back to the victim. Stumper stood looking over his shoulder, unsure if he wanted to get any closer. "I think you may be right about this being a homicide." Stumper pointed to the man's head. "By the amount of blood in his skull—and the way his head came apart—we'll probably find an exit hole where the bullet came out."

Manny shook his head. "Intense heat often cracks the cranium, filling it with blood. It looks suspicious, but there's no bullet hole in his skull. But we won't know for sure until the autopsy."

Stumper nodded to the wall and window in Sam's bedroom. "It looks like the accelerant traveled from there." He indicated a spot on the floor beside the mattress.

Manny bent and patted the burnt carpeting, pulling fibers up and bringing them to his nose. "We'll make a note for the crime scene tech to take the carpeting for testing, but I don't believe there was any accelerant used to start the fire."

Stumper threw up his hands. He brought his bandanna away just long enough to stuff his lip with snuff before covering his mouth and nose again. "Then what started it? Look at that fire pattern . . ."

"Twenty minutes ago you were so certain it was an accident." Manny smiled. "It's like you want your first crispy critter to be a homicide."

Stumper shook his head. "I give up, oh Master. What the hell caused the fire? Spontaneous combustion? 'Cause if that's what you think, you're nuts."

Manny studied the fire pattern, the way in which the window in the room had been blown out, the mattress where the victim lay. "I think the fire was caused by a cigarette igniting

Sam's dried-out old mattress." He pointed to the pattern of the flames traveling to the solitary window in the room. "Just like Three Bits thought. Prior to flashover, fires grow by using fuel: wood, wallpaper, carpeting. Flesh. Once flashover is complete, the fire can only live with sufficient ventilation. It goes from a fuel-controlled fire to a ventilation-controlled fire."

Stumper nodded. "Good. At least we know it was accidental."

"Not so fast. It may be murder. We'll know more at autopsy."

"Then there's nothing left for us to do."

"We need to pay Chenoa a visit. If that's her brother . . ."

"If?" Stumper backed up and stumbled over what remained of the bedroom wall and knocked over a pike pole one of the firemen had forgotten. "That's Sam, all right. Look at that damned big turquoise ring that melted to his finger. His dad gave him that. He never went anywhere without it. It's Sam all right."

"Saw that." Manny stood and stretched his legs. "But you can buy those kinds of rings in most jewelry shops, not to mention tourist traps. We'll know more when we talk with Chenoa."

"What's this *we*, Kimosabe? I want no part of Chenoa when she finds out Sam's dead."

"I'm sure she'll take it as hard as most sisters would."

Stumper shook his head. "It's not that. She needs Sam's signature to make ranch business legal. Including sale of those heifers. Now what does she do?"

"She'll find a way around that. She'll involve the courts for temporary business dealings, at least until Sam's been positively IDed."

"So now you know why I want no part of telling her."

Manny studied Stumper eying the body. "Okay, I'll give

you a choice—come with me to talk with Chenoa, or babysit that poor BBQed bastard until the ME arrives."

Stumper's eyes darted between the corpse and Manny. "It's no choice at all. I'll stay with Sam, though our conversation won't be any more productive than when the rummy was alive."

"You'd rather stay here than come talk with Chenoa? You that scared of her?"

Stumper nodded. "I'm scared of what she can do. I want to keep my job, and pissing her off won't endear her to me. Or you when you give her the bad news. Let's say there's going to be some fireworks between one Crow lady and one Lakota FBI agent that might rival the old days."

CHAPTER 15

Manny turned onto the quarter-mile long driveway, passing under a black metal sign proclaiming STAR DANCER LAND AND CATTLE swinging from logs thicker than telephone poles. A branding scene had been etched on the sign, fashioned by some craftsman wielding a plasma cutter. Steer wrestlers throwing a cow down touched a hot iron to flanks, the image of bawling steers and flying ropes portrayed perfectly. Manny could almost smell the branding iron burning the cow's hair, much like the smell in Sam's house. Experience told him it would take days to purge that odor, and he pinched his nostrils as if the odor of the burn victim would be blocked. It wasn't.

Manny topped the hill overlooking the ranch house, a two-story log affair that had *Bonanza* written all over it. Manny pulled up beside Chenoa's pink Hummer and an International Harvester Travelall with the Star Dancer logo pasted on the door. He half expected Pa and Little Joe to come ambling out of the house, greeting him with thumbs hooked in the pockets of starched jeans, smiling friendly as Hoss joined them.

Instead, a man that would have towered over Hoss turned sideways to get through the door and onto the porch. His boots echoed heavily on the wooden walkway running the length of the front of the house. He stopped, eyes fixed on Manny. Thick cheekbones shadowed a nose broken in the past and sitting at an odd angle, his brown eyes glaring, threatening. He was the biggest Crow Manny had ever seen, and he made a mental note not to mention the Crow and Lakota had been bitter enemies back in the day.

"Can't read." The man stepped onto stairs Manny was certain would crumble under his weight. "Sign says no solicitors. We don't want what you're selling." *Selling* hissed through a limited number of teeth that Manny thought sounded like a diamondback. He nudged his side. He'd forgotten his gun. Again.

"Who says I'm selling anything?" Manny closed his car door and stood with his hand on the handle.

The man stepped down three steps at once and ambled toward him, towering over Manny. "Maybe I should toss you and this heap off the ranch." Knuckles popped on fists clenching and unclenching. The man had helped more than one victim off the Star Dancer Ranch.

"And who are you?"

"I work here. Jamie Hawk."

Manny smiled. "I got a niece named Jamie."

As dark complexioned as Jamie Hawk was, his face became a deep red. Manny thought bloodred as Jamie stepped toward him. Manny clenched his fist. Jamie might get a meal, but Manny intended getting a snack out of this dance.

"It's all right, Jamie." Chenoa Iron Cloud emerged from

the shadows of the doorway, black hair pulled into a tight ponytail revealing slight graying around the temples. "Let me introduce Senior Special Agent Manny Tanno."

Hawk's voice hissed, barely audible through clenched teeth, "The Sioux agent?"

Manny forced a smile as he looked up at Jamie. "The same. Not here to rekindle old feuds, big guy. I'm here to see your boss."

Hawk glanced over his shoulder, and Chenoa nodded. As noisily as he'd appeared, Jamie Hawk clomped up the steps and disappeared back inside the house. Chenoa watched him as he closed the heavy door. "He's just being protective."

"You hire him as protection?"

She laughed. "No, I hired him for his congeniality." She motioned to a swing on the porch and Manny joined her. "But he's especially hostile to federal law enforcement."

"From his days of getting into trouble?"

"Does it show?"

Manny nodded. "I suspect his cell number had nothing to do with his phone."

"How?"

"His stance. He blades himself like a cop. Or like someone used to fighting other convicts. Now, I don't think he was ever a cop, so that leaves him being in stir for some time."

Chenoa looked sideways at him, but said nothing, waiting.

"When he thought I was some Watkins salesman come peddling tit salve or something, he was forceful. When you told him I was the law, he got downright nasty." Manny avoided Chenoa's eyes. He could get lost in them if he wasn't careful. "You rehab Jamie?"

She nodded at last and looked out over the rolling, grass-covered prairie moving in time with the rising and falling of the wind. "My cousin's boy. He got into a little bit of trouble in a bar some years ago. Spent some time in Deer Lodge."

Manny thought of the reason a man would spend time in a bar that resulted in hard time at the Montana State Penitentiary. "Did he know the man he killed?"

"You knew about that?"

Now it was Manny's turn to remain silent.

After long moments, Chenoa nodded. "He didn't mean to kill the other guy. But when he busted Jamie in the head with a pool cue, Jamie reacted."

"And overreacted?"

Chenoa nodded. "But he's doing good now."

Chenoa rapped on the door, and a middle-aged lady appeared. She wiped her hands on her apron depicting pumpkins flanked by a headless horseman. Chenoa asked for iced tea and the lady disappeared. Chenoa looked after her. "Forget Jamie. Mary Slagy's the one you got to be careful of in this household. Iron-fist brutal."

Mary returned and placed a tray with a pitcher of iced tea flanked by sugar and Sweet'N Low packets and set them on the log table in front of the swing. Manny grabbed for the sugar, then replaced it with the Sweet'N Low when he realized he'd not run since his vacation started. His gut wasn't getting any slimmer, and he'd have to face Clara the Health Nazi when he went home.

Chenoa rubbed her ice-sweating glass against her temple and closed her eyes. A single drop of water escaped the glass and slid down her chest, drawing Manny's attention. She opened her eyes and caught him staring. She smiled, probably used to men looking at her.

"I took Jamie in. I felt benevolent I guess. They charged Jamie with manslaughter after he killed those two cowboys from Laurel." She sipped her tea delicately and turned in the swing to face Manny. "I made some calls. Talked to some people at state. Jamie was paroled early, providing I keep him on the straight and narrow."

"Have you?"

She paused, longer than she should have, Manny thought. "So far. And the last thing he needs is to go back for beating a federal officer."

"I'll second that."

"But you didn't come here to talk about Jamie."

Manny cleared his throat. "It's about Sam."

She laughed and grabbed her ponytail hanging over her back. She started unraveling her hair. "What's he done this time, steal jerky from the store again? Got thirty days the last time. And the time before that two weeks for defecating on the bench at the park in Hardin." She turned away.

"I need to tell you . . ."

She laughed and stood, her hair fully unbraided and hanging down her chest. "Sam and I weren't close when we were growing, but I love him . . ."

"Chenoa, it's about Sam . . ."

"I hope you found him. I got those bred heifers I need his signature on before they leave the state. Got the brand inspector waiting for my call . . ."

"Chenoa." Manny stood and put his hand on her shoulder. "Please sit down. I need to tell you something." The breeze carried her cologne past his nose, teasing him, and he turned to the swing. He stood and paced in front of her, gathering the courage. "I've never found an easy way to say this."

"Sam's dead?"

"Someone call you?"

Tears started running down her cheeks, tiny streaks of mascara running down with them. She wiped her face with the back of her hand. Manny struggled with the urge to go to her and hold her. "I figured it must be something serious about Sam if the other officers wouldn't have the courage to come out here and tell me."

"Sam's house burned down today."

"Good." She laughed. "I'm sure the neighborhood will be saturated with the cockroaches needing a new place to stay."

"A body was found inside. Burned beyond recognition. Firemen think it's Sam."

Chenoa drew in a deep breath, while Manny stood quietly in front of her, the only sounds the creaking of the rusty swing chains. When she stood and faced Manny, the tears were gone, replaced by the Chenoa he'd first met at Harlan's auction barn, tough and defiant. "The firemen think it was Sam, but you really don't know?"

Manny nodded. "We'll know for certain at autopsy." Manny described the ring that melted to the burn victim's finger.

"Dad's ring." She looked away. "How did the fire start?"

"Fire investigator thinks a cigarette in bed. I think so, too."

"Drunk as usual, no doubt." Anger filled her as her jaw muscles worked back and forth. "The damned fool fell asleep with a cigarette in his hand and Mister Mattress killed him. Damned fool should never have gone back to smoking. I told him a dozen times over these last years, smoking will kill him."

"Sam quit smoking?"

She jammed her fists into tight jean pockets. "He'd back-slide now and again. He said it was hard not to smoke when he drank."

Manny knew just how easy it would be to go back to smoking. He was just a matchstick away from starting back up, too. "Sure he quit?"

"I told him if he didn't quit I'd cut his monthly check."

"Can you do that?"

She laughed. "No, but he didn't know it. But I didn't want him hooked up to oxygen in some assisted living facility or talking through a hole in his throat, costing me thousands a month."

"So why didn't you get on him for his drinking?"

Her eyes narrowed and she took a step closer. "Sam always said that drink was the curse of the working class, and he lived it. I don't think he worked a day in his miserable life since he got back from Vietnam. Even I couldn't threaten him into stopping. My point is, if the fire was caused by a cigarette, someone may have started that fire. It might not have been Sam falling asleep with a smoke."

"We'll look into it."

"You'll do more than that, Agent Tanno." Chenoa's voice rose high enough that Jamie Hawk poked his head out the door, his eyes locked on Manny. Chenoa held up her hand and Jamie relaxed, waiting. "Someone may have murdered Sam. You open a homicide investigation, or you'll be working fugitive cases in Harlem. I guarantee it."

Manny caught his car out of the corner of his eye, calculating if he could reach it before Jamie Hawk put the grab on him. "We'll be looking at all angles."

"Then look into this angle." She stepped closer and jabbed her finger into Manny's chest. "Someone called me this morning and wanted to sell me that journal."

"The one missing from the Beauchamp Collection? How'd you know it was missing? Cubby?"

Chenoa shrugged. "People tell me things. All sorts of things on the moccasin telegraph."

Manny started pacing in front of the swing, as much as to think as to get out of finger range. "Who called you?"

"How the hell should I know?" Jamie stepped out the door

and stood leaning against the side of the house. "I didn't recognize the voice. It was like he talked through a bandanna or something. Hard to understand. He said there was damaging information in that journal that could ruin the Star Dancers. And the Eagle Bulls."

"And you turned him down?"

"In a heartbeat." Chenoa's eyes had dried so that it didn't look as if she'd mourned Sam's death for even that briefest moment. "I didn't even consider it."

"Because you don't think the journal contains any damning information?"

Chenoa picked up her glass and tossed the rest of the tea and ice onto the dirt in front of the porch. "I didn't say that. Rumor has it the journal contains some nasty historical gossip that could be, well, embarrassing at most."

Manny kept Jamie Hawk in his peripheral vision as he faced Chenoa. "Why didn't you agree to buy it? Contact the BIA police and set up a buy-bust for the journal?"

"I would have if I thought the caller actually had it."

"What makes you think the caller didn't have it?"

Chenoa tilted her head back and laughed, her chest heaving nicely. "Because of his price. A thousand dollars. If the rumors were true about what was written in the journal, he would have asked ten times that amount. Hell, just the value alone of a journal by one of Custer's scouts would be worth many times that."

Manny nodded. Her logic made sense. In another life, perhaps, she might have been an investigator.

"So you knew the journal could hurt your family?"

"So I've heard."

Manny thought back to what Itchy told them, that Sam had read the journal. He would know what damning information it contained, and he probably knew Harlan's safe combination. And Moccasin Top saw Sam coming out of the auction barn with an armful of old books. "Maybe someone thought Sam had it. Maybe someone torched Sam's house to destroy Sam and the journal." Manny glanced over at Jamie, who took a step toward him. Manny's hand went to the small of his back and Jamie stopped, as if Manny had, in fact, remembered his gun.

"I don't know what you're implying, Agent Tanno, but you listen to me: If that journal is still floating around, you give it to me and there'll be a hefty finder's fee for you."

> < > < > <

Manny drove out of the Star Dancer ranch road, his infatuation with Chenoa cured. From her feigned sorrow at hearing of Sam's death to her threats when she thought Manny wouldn't investigate the burn victim as a homicide, to her offer to reward Manny if he found the journal, she had lost her beauty. Her appeal had been replaced by the arrogance that people with power possessed when the weight they pushed around hurt whomever it fell on.

The image of beauty squandered stuck with Manny as he drove away, that and Jamie Hawk lording over Chenoa, pointing to Manny as he neared the hill. Chenoa nodded to Jamie, and Manny could only imagine the scheme they were concocting even as he dropped over the hill obscuring the ranch house.

CHAPTER 16

Manny drove under the Star Dancer Ranch gate and started onto the tribal road. A pickup was parked on the road facing the gate, "Cowboy Coupe" written all over it, as Willie was fond of saying. The bright candy apple red paint glittered in the sun, as did the chrome accents on the door handles, filler door, and window ledges. A chrome grill guard and bug shield announced to the world that CUBBY was behind the wheel of his gaudy Lincoln pickup. Manny pulled beside Cubby's truck and rolled the window down.

"The Princess give you what-for?" Cubby leaned out his window, one flabby arm hanging on to the steering wheel, the other dangling down, brushing over the door as if ready to hurl insults at Manny. "Bet she gave you your marching orders."

"When I was in the army I never did march very well." Manny smiled. "But I'll bet she has you doing the rout step to her tune."

Cubby's smiled faded and he quickly shook out a Marlboro from a pack on his dash. He lit an Ohio Blue Tip on his teeth and touched it to his cigarette, flicking it out the window.

"Good way to start a fire."

Cubby blew smoke in Manny's window. He leaned his double chin on his arm and jerked his thumb toward the ranch gate. "Not that I'd suffer if this place went up in smoke. The Princess owns it. And runs it."

"With Jamie Hawk's help?"

Cubby flicked ashes out the window. "All that big bastard does is make sure nothing happens to Chenoa. I ramrod the ranch. Not that I get any credit for it. And when she calls in the law, she doesn't even tell me why."

Manny popped a PEZ into his mouth, the tart orange causing his lips to pucker, and he cursed Pee Pee Pourier for getting him hooked on these. Manny sat silent, enjoying Cubby's unease.

"Well, why'd she call you?"

"I came here to tell her Sam may be dead," Manny said after a long pause.

Cubby slapped the steering wheel. "The drunk's finally worm food? What happened to the weasel?"

Manny explained that a body had been found burned in Sam's house, and that things indicated it may have been Sam roasting on that old mattress. "We'll know for certain when we get the dental records."

A broad grin remained across Cubby's face while he reached for another cigarette. "It's about time that pain-in-the-ass went to the Not-So-Happy Hunting Grounds."

Manny's cell phone tickled his chest. It vibrated again and he looked down at the screen: *Urgent*. He shook off the feeling of doom and stuck it back into his pocket. "You don't seem a bit upset, Sam being only your brother-in-law."

The smile remained plastered on Cubby's florid face. "Sam was trouble all his life. His and Chenoa's folks died a year apart—lung cancer both." Cubby patted his pocket for a match. "Got a light?"

"Quit."

"Wish I could."

Manny pushed the lighter into the dash of the Olds and waited for it to pop out. He handed it across, and Cubby touched the lighter to his cigarette. "Wish the hell these new outfits came with lighters." His cigarette flared, and he handed the lighter back. Manny stuck it back into the hole by the radio. "You were reminiscing about Sam."

Cubby laughed. "More like being thankful he's gone. Chenoa said Sam was all right before he went to 'Nam, but I didn't know him. After he came back, we let him stay at the ranch. We'd run the place since Old Smoke died, and Sam wanted no part of it. All he wanted to do was drink himself into oblivion every day.

"Somehow he'd manage to take the ranch trucks once or twice a week. He'd go into Crow Agency and get himself arrested for public intox. Or shoplifting. Or drunk driving. Once when we hid all the keys, he grabbed the Farmall— manure spreader and all still hooked up—and drove the damned tractor all the way into Crow Agency just to get arrested for fighting at the casino. The BIA cops damned near camped out on our front porch. Finally the Princess gave him the ultimatum—sober up or get the bum's rush. He didn't and she did. Can't say I was broke up over it."

Manny's phone vibrated again, but he ignored it. "He must have had some money to live in that house of his."

Cubby laughed hard enough that he started a coughing spell. He hit his chest hard and flicked his cigarette out the window. "Chenoa felt benevolent and bought him that rattrap in Lodge Grass. She figured it was close enough to Harlan White Bird's shop that Sam could crawl home if he couldn't walk. I'm sure she wasn't too broke up over Sam dying, was she?"

"Your wife was plenty upset about the fire."

"Bullshit."

"Those weren't fake tears I saw when I gave her the bad news," Manny lied.

Cubby reached into his cigarette pack for another, but it was empty. He wadded the pack up and grabbed another from a carton on the seat, tapping it hard on his hand before opening the pack. "Chenoa's good at producing tears on cue. Lord knows she's been in the public eye enough." He leaned out the window and met Manny's gaze. "But you can take this to the bank: Chenoa's damned glad Sam's gone. Once she gets things straightened out, she won't have to hunt his sorry ass up every time she needs something countersigned concerning the ranch."

"Why didn't she go to court and have the business arrangement modified years ago?"

"She tried." Cubby accepted Manny's Oldsmobile lighter again. "But Old Smoke had set the business arrangement up to be unbreakable. It was."

"Who gets Sam's money if . . ."

Cubby shook his head. "Chenoa was on him to have a will drawn up years ago. Even offered to pay for it, but he never did."

"Then Chenoa gets everything?"

"She's got everything now. Except with Sam dead, it'll be official." Cubby looked sideways at Manny. "You're not figuring Chenoa for burning up Sam?"

Manny held up a hand. "We don't know if the victim *is* Sam. It's officially accidental at this point. But if we find out

Chenoa set the fire and she goes up the river, your children will be next in line to take possession of the ranch."

"We have no children."

Manny smiled. Somehow it had been too easy to set Cubby up. "Then you'll get everything?"

Cubby's face flushed. He tossed his cigarette away and opened the door. "Now hold on . . ."

Manny smiled a wide, disarming grin. "Like I said, Sam's death is just an accident right now."

Cubby settled back in the seat and breathed fast like he'd been caught at something. "Sorry, Agent Tanno. It's just that I don't like to see my wife upset . . ."

Manny waved it away. "But there is one other thing."

"Shoot."

"Someone called Chenoa and offered to sell her the Levi Star Dancer journal."

"The missing journal?"

Manny nodded. "Or stolen."

Cubby slumped in the seat and closed the door. "Why did they think she would be interested?"

"Cubby—you know well enough that the journal purports to have damaging historical information that would hurt the Star Dancer family. And, ultimately, hurt you as well."

"My wife and I don't talk as often as we should," he sputtered. He took a drag on his smoke but his hand shook and he rested it on the windowsill. "Chenoa wouldn't be interested."

"The caller claimed the journal contained damning information about the Star Dancers. And about the Eagle Bulls from Pine Ridge."

"Him." Cubby's face reddened again and he looked away. "Did she buy it?"

Manny shook his head. "She said the caller lowballed her.

She figures the guy didn't have the journal, and was just trying to shake her down."

"It was a guy that called?"

"She wasn't sure. The voice was muffled."

"Itchy," Cubby said without hesitation.

"What makes you think it's your brother?"

Cubby stuck another cigarette in his mouth, then grabbed it and tossed it onto the floorboard. "The son of a bitch is a drug addict. And he crashed at Harlan's more often than not. That and he's not smart enough to know how much to ask for the journal."

Manny started the engine. The Rocket Motor sprang to life. "Any ideas where I might find Itchy?"

Cubby shrugged. "Most any rock on Crow Agency. Start looking for other meth heads—I think they gather in flocks somewhere and do their thing. Now I got to go, myself. After all, I am the working part of my marriage."

Cubby started his truck, but Manny stopped him. "And if you get wind of just who has the journal, you'll call me?"

Cubby laughed. "Sure."

Cubby started toward the ranch house, and Manny thought he'd lost interest in the journal that he was looking for at Sam's house. Either Cubby knew who had it, or he knew it had burned up in the house fire.

Manny waited until the dust had settled from Cubby's Cowboy Coupe before he fished his phone out and dialed his voice mail. Lumpy had called three times, and all messages were identical: "Call me at Rapid City Regional Hospital ICU. ASAP."

Manny drove to the highest point on the road so as not to lose the signal, and tapped in Lumpy's number.

CHAPTER 17

Willie shot bad. Hanging on by a thin thread. A dull rewind of Lumpy's voice kept playing in Manny's mind, the record skipping to the *thin thread* part. He floored the Olds and went around two Harleys as their riders gave him the finger when he passed them. If only they knew he needed to catch a flight from Billings to Rapid City.

"Willie had been staking out Wilson Eagle Bull's bunkhouse for Carson Degas," Lumpy had said in broken gasps. "I don't know why the hell I ever authorized Willie to help you. This is a federal case. And on another damned reservation at that!"

"Willie knew the risks," Manny tried to convince himself as well as Lumpy. But had Willie really taken Degas seriously? Willie stood a formidable foe, and at his young age, in his mind, he was bulletproof to boot. "He should have had backup."

There was a long pause on the other end. "I didn't have any officers to spare."

"Because it was my case?" Manny bit his lip, salty blood mixing with saliva on his tongue. He breathed deep, reminding himself that Willie came first now, and that there would be enough blame later to go around. If anyone were to blame. "I'm chartering a flight to Rapid City." But the charter pilot was four hours away. Four hours that could mean an eternity for his wounded and dying friend.

He turned off into Hardin, killing time more than anything else, to take his mind off Willie. He had stopped by the Custer's Revenge office and killed more time chewing the super's butt, getting the reassurance that he'd fix the door and the silly clapper light switch and the toilet seat that grabbed him with a vengeance. Ultimately, Manny ran out of things to take his mind off Willie. Manny had been bedside with a dozen wounded officers, tubes sticking out of every orifice, jutting from places where there was no natural hole, hooked up to monitors that brought nurses running whenever any slight change occurred. Manny needed to put that out of his mind for now, or he'd be a wreck on the flight to Rapid. He feared flying enough, let alone dealing with the anxiety of Willie's condition.

He drove to the Big Horn County Courthouse and jail and parked around back. Captain Miles had no new information about Degas. "Damned shame about your friend getting shot."

Manny thought he'd thanked Miles for the concern, but he didn't recall. He started driving out of town and passed the sign on the Four Aces Bar with the VFW Post 7481 screwed to the side of the building. He checked his watch: three hours and some change. He circled the block and pulled to the curb on Third Street. He had prayed to God. He had prayed to

Wakan Tanka. But now was one of the few times in his life when he *needed* to pray to a stiff drink.

He entered through the side door and sidled up to the long bar, taking a seat on the opposite end from two afternoon professionals who sat swapping war stories, both teetering close to the edge of their wobbly stools. One older vet hugged a boilermaker with an extra shot of house swill parked beside his drinks, his thin arm circling it as if someone intended sneaking up and stealing it from him. He paused in his story to his compadre to give Manny the once-over through bleary eyes.

His drinking buddy looked around his friend, coming dangerously close to falling off the stool. He tipped his glasses up and stared. A piece of peanut shell stuck to his scraggly beard, and he batted at a fly that strafed his mustache for last night's dinner. He downed his beer and turned his back on Manny as he ordered another.

"What'll it be, pardner?"

The bartender stacked glasses in a giant pyramid behind the bar and talked over his shoulder as he worked. A tire billy jutted from his back pocket, and his shirt bulged just under his left arm from the shoulder holster. *Cheers* this wasn't.

He turned and dropped a paper napkin onto the bar. "We got Bud and Miller on tap."

"You got Moose Drool?"

"A connoisseur." The bartender smiled, revealing a neat gap where his teeth had once been—the result of a fight? Or of opening too may beer bottles with his choppers. "You from the rez?" he asked from somewhere down inside a cooler in back of the bar.

"Does it matter?"

"Not particularly."

Manny sized him up. Younger than Manny, he stood a full

head shorter. He was thinner, with a scar that ran down one cheek to intersect with his mouth. Manny imagined he tried pushing one of the rez boys around once too often, as he was certain the tooth fairy hadn't snuck up and snatched his teeth. "Just killing time." *And killing this feeling of dread consuming me. Any other damned time visions come sneaking up on me when I don't want them. Why the hell not now? Why the hell can't I see if Willie is going to pull through?*

Manny stood, sipping the dark ale while the bartender draped a towel around his neck and went back to drying and stacking glasses, all the while keeping Manny in his peripheral vision. He sipped again, the bite of the ale just enough that Manny feared he could get used to drinking. But not today.

He walked to one wall and slipped Clara's reading glasses from his pocket. The bartender did a double take when he put them on, but Manny paid him no mind as he examined the military photos hung the length of the wall. The photos were arranged by service, the army taking up most of the space, with sailors, marines, and airmen competing for what remained, further clustered together depending on what war they represented.

Manny walked past the World War II photos, and something compelled him to stop at the Korean War area of one wall. A photo showed soldiers hunkered down inside a snow and frozen dirt barricade, the photographer catching their agony, their frozen beards bent against the wind. Manny fought the urge to reach out and touch the photo, but the urge won. As his hand ran over the photo, his fingers rested on two soldiers manning a Browning .30-cal, both men later dying in the battle when Chinese forces overran their position. How he knew this he suspected was his ongoing blight, and he silently cursed Reuben for convincing him that Wakan Tanka had gifted Manny with the powers of the sacred men.

Manny pulled away, careful to stay well back from the photos as he moved along the wall, sipping his beer, when he choked on it. He turned his head and coughed violently, clearing his throat. The two drunks at the bar turned rummy eyes his way, while the bartender reached to his back pocket for his tire billy. Manny cleared his throat and set his mug on a table. The bartender eyed him suspiciously for a long moment before turning back to his glass chore while he kept Manny in his side vision.

Manny walked down the wall to the Vietnam photos, and one picture drew his eye. He leaned closer and pushed his glasses farther up on his nose. There was no mistaking Wilson Eagle Bull, tall, sweaty green utility shirt rolled up over thick forearms, the faded eagle, globe, and anchor faded over one pocket. He stood beside a shorter, almost emaciated Marine, a green sweat-stained towel draped around his neck. They posed in front of a tunnel entrance, the camouflaged lid tossed aside. The small man grinned at the camera as he held up a stringer with four human ears.

"This picture," Manny called to the bartender. He draped his towel over his shoulder and walked to the wall. Manny tapped the photo. "You know this man?"

He shrugged. "Just another Indian." *Indian* sputtered from his mouth as if he were ashamed to have Indians adorning the walls.

"He's from Pine Ridge."

"So?"

"This other one isn't."

"Look, I got shit to do. You want a travel show, go someplace else." The bartender smirked and returned to his chores behind the bar, and Manny realized how he'd lost his teeth.

"He's a genuine tunnel rat." The drunk nursing the boilermaker had staggered over and stood reverently in front of the picture, one hand crossed over the other. He jerked his head at the bartender. "The kid's got no respect for those that fought for his silly ass."

Manny tapped the photo. "Know him?"

The drunk stood for a moment as if praying. "He's from Crow Agency. The big guy was only seen in here once. The little one the post commander says is a real hero. And he gets what he wants. On the house."

"I didn't catch his name."

The drunk laughed. "Did I forget? That's Sampson Star Dancer, and I'm proud to tip a drink with him whenever he drops in." The old vet grew silent once again and Manny stood quietly beside him. "Sampson earned four Purple Hearts," he slurred at last. "Last one when he stepped on a Willie Pete and busted hell out of his leg. I'm proud to tip the jar with him whenever he comes in."

"Come in often?"

He shook his head. "Just when he can catch a ride from the rez."

"How about the other one?" Manny tapped Wilson.

"Once. He came in with Sampson. Said the big guy was his CO in I Corps, and the owner bought everyone a round. It was great."

The bartender returned to the never-ending chore of cleaning and stacking glasses; the drunk returned to holding the bar stool in place, and Manny returned to studying the picture. Sam and Wilson had served together in 'Nam, and a dozen reasons why he hadn't mentioned that raced through Manny's mind, something he'd jump Wilson about. Right after he visited Willie in Intensive Care.

CHAPTER 18

1884
CROW AGENCY, MONTANA TERRITORY

Hollow Horn, all five developing years of him, nocked an arrow into his tiny bow. Missing the string, he fell to the ground and kicked his legs up in the air like a grounded turtle. Levi started to help his son when thoughts of his own father emerged. Bull Moose had watched as Levi successfully nocked his first arrow, sitting on the sidelines watching his son send the arrow over a cliff, forever lost. But forever proud of Levi.

Hollow Horn plucked the arrow from the ground, nocked it, and clutched the bowstring in his tough little fingers. He drew the bow and let loose the string, aiming it at the *pu pua*, the grass target Levi had fashioned and propped against a clump of sagebrush ten feet from Hollow Horn. He let loose the bowstring and the arrow dropped out of the string and stuck in the ground in front of the boy.

Soon, Levi thought, he'd be able to give Hollow Horn the bow he would carry all his life, one made from the mountain sheep covered in rattlesnake skin, one that would cost Levi a good war pony. *War pony*. What need would any Crow have now for war ponies? Or for that matter, when would Hollow Horn have need of a bow? Things had changed in Crow country faster than Levi could write about them, and he yearned for times past.

Hollow Horn gave a cry of frustration and dug the arrow from the ground. He nocked it once again, and once again the twang of the bow as the string rode past the arrow. It sailed two feet in front of the boy and dropped to the ground. *Perhaps tomorrow, little warrior.*

Levi stood from the chair made of willow, padded with a fine trade blanket, yet his back ached. The pain had become worse this past year, that sharp pain that was the running sickness digging itself deeper inside him. He had visited Seeds, a fine *as'bari'a*, a physician, of the Whistling Water clan. Seeds had given him herbs to chew and make into a drink. Levi had drunk the bitter tea and chewed the rancid herbs until his mouth puckered to the point where he could barely protest.

And still Seeds insisted Levi had no faith, for only with faith would he ever be cured. "Speak to *masa'ka*," Seeds had urged. "The god of the sun will hear your prayers."

"I have prayed to him until I am hoarse and my voice threatens to leave me forever," Levi insisted. "Still the pain persists. Perhaps if I visit the White doctor . . ."

"Then never come back to my lodge!" Seeds had turned his back and remained there until Levi assured him he was only thinking aloud, that he would never think about seeing the *baashchiili* doctor. And even though the running sickness had saved him that day the Lakota Eagle Bull had killed

White Crow and Eagle Bull's companion, he still cursed the pain that plagued him always.

Levi turned his attention to the field a half mile down the valley, and he shielded his eyes from the sun. His eyes remained keen, one of the reasons Colonel Custer had picked him to scout, one of the reasons General Crook had recruited him to scout for Lakota and Cheyenne after the Battle of the Greasy Grass. If Levi had that long scope of White Crow's that his friend had that day he was killed, Levi could better see the haying operation going on in those fields of his. He shielded his hand over his eyes. He barely recognized the tiny outline of a man walking behind a team of grays, imaging the reins slack in his hands, pulling another man sitting an iron seat atop the hay rake. He imagined the man pulled the rope whenever the rake became full, to be picked up and stacked in a wagon later.

In Levi's field to the west across from his hay field, corn stood taller than he. He had bought Poor Deer's forty acres two years ago when the young man tired of working the land. Levi had bought the land the same year he bought two other adjacent pastures, their owners lacking patience for farming. Levi had bought the deeded land cheaply from young men pursuing buffalo rumored to be plentiful at the base of the Shining Mountains to the west.

Buffalo they would never find.

Levi scooped Hollow Horn and his bow and hoisted him onto the wagon seat, then climbed beside him. He tripped the brake and slowly guided the wagon down into the valley, to the mud hut Poor Deer's sons had built and where their meeting would take place. Levi was certain that, by day's end, he would own the sons' land as well and would have to hire more farmhands. The one Crow and three White men that had failed in the Gold Fields of the Black Hills would be strapped with three more quarters of land as Poor Deer's sons fled to the buffalo. Except for the growing pain in Levi's inside, life was good for the Star Dancer family.

><><><><

Pretty Paw wiped beef stew from Hollow Horn's mouth. She swatted him on the rump and looked after him as he ran giggling, chasing his puppy running outside with a soup bone in its mouth.

Levi picked up his bowl, but Pretty Paw shooed him away from the dinner table and took the dishes to the washbasin.

Levi walked to the kerosene light dangling over his chair and touched a match to it before sitting. He grabbed his journal from the top of a small table beside the chair and opened it to the last entry, fishing inside his shirt pocket for his pencil. Pretty Paw laughed and reached over, grabbing the stub from behind Levi's ear and handing it to him.

"Guess I'm getting forgetful."

"Guess?" She grinned.

Pretty Paw turned back to the basin and began washing the dishes. Levi lit his pipe and sat back as he licked the end of his pencil.

"Why do you always write in the book? And why always in the White man's words?" Clanking of metal dishes mingled with the sloshing of water in the basin muffled her words.

Levi's pencil hovered over the paper as he paused. "By the time anyone wants to know what happened, there will only be the words of the *baashchiili*."

"But why?" she pressed.

"So that others will know about that murderer."

"Conte Eagle Bull?"

"Who else?"

Pretty Paw draped the dish towel over her shoulder. She

knelt beside his chair and stroked his head. "You should enjoy life more, my husband. You spend too much time thinking about that day."

Levi took off his reading glasses and rubbed his forehead. "The One Who Is Not Here was my *iilapaache*. He was my best friend in life, since we were boys. If I would have ridden to Pine Ridge and killed Eagle Bull, justice would have been served."

Pretty Paw frowned. "That was a terrible day, when you rode after Eagle Bull. If Lieutenant Magnuson had not stopped you . . ."

"If he had not, I would have killed the man that hung this curse around my neck." The memory of White Crow's death had haunted Levi ever since the murder. Levi second-guessed himself: If Eagle Bull had not shot him that day at the Shining Mountains, he would not have the running sickness. If the running sickness had not come upon him that day overlooking the Greasy Grass, he would have been at White Crow's side to fight Eagle Bull and the other Lakota warrior. If he had not hidden like a coward in the grass while Eagle Bull scalped White Crow and took their horses and rifles, Levi would not have this obsession like a hornet's stinger that festered in one's skin and wouldn't pry loose.

Levi had cursed his timing that morning five years ago when he planned to ride to Pine Ridge and avenge his friend's death. He had stowed a week's provisions in his saddlebags and draped his medicine pouch around his pony's neck. He had just finished praying to *masa'ka*, the god of sun, that morning when Lieutenant Magnuson rode up.

"I need a scout I can trust today."

"I have a trip to make."

"To Red Cloud's Agency?"

Levi looked away, certain that Pretty Paw had ridden for the soldier.

Magnuson coaxed his pony closer to Levi's. "Revenge for White Crow will do you no good, my friend. It will continue to eat away at you, and it will destroy you."

Levi looked away so that Magnuson couldn't see the tears. "Revenge is the *ira'xaxe*, the shadow, that wakes me at the first hint of day, and tucks me in at night. It is true I mourn for the One That Is Not Here. But it is justice I seek the most. It is justice I need the most."

Magnuson reached over and laid his hand on Levi's shoulder. "Eagle Bull will be tried by his own conscience . . ."

"He has none."

"Then justice will one day find him. This day I have need of you."

Levi started to protest when Magnuson interrupted him. "We had an arrangement, did we not?"

Levi nodded. "I got the first pick of the land. In return, I will scout for you when you need me."

"And I need you now."

"But fighting is over."

Magnuson shook his head. "There is rumor that Crazy Horse and his lodges are hiding in the Shining Mountains."

Pretty Paw had come out of the lodge, baby Hollow Horn sucking beneath the heavy buffalo robe. She had meant well by riding after Magnuson, and Levi could hold no anger toward her. In the manner of the Apsa'alooke warrior riding into battle, he nodded at his wife and fell in beside Lieutenant Magnuson. Pretty Paw had saved him from a soldier's hangman's noose that day.

>‹›‹›‹

Pretty Paw joined Levi on the bank of the slow-moving creek. She studied stones lining the bank and selected one, skipping it across the water. Five skips. "Bet you cannot do better than that."

Levi looked sideways at her. "No bet."

"You won't even try?"

He shrugged.

"What is bothering you?"

"Nothing."

She used his shoulder for support and sat beside him. "A wife knows her husband. You come here every day with that same hound dog look One Ear gets."

Levi smiled. One Ear did have a droopy expression, ever since that range bull hooked a horn into the dog's head and Levi had to slice off what was left of the torn ear.

Pretty Paw leaned around and took his face in her hands. "It is the same thing, is it not?"

Levi looked away, but he knew he could hide nothing from Pretty Paw. "The Indian agent at Pine Ridge Agency made Eagle Bull Boss Farmer." He picked up a rock and skipped it onto the water. One skip.

Levi had ridden beside Lieutenant Magnuson that day as they led Crazy Horse and his bedraggled band into Red Cloud's Agency—later Pine Ridge—weary and bedraggled from being pursued, their women and children starving, the warrior beaten out of them, with no choice but to surrender.

Levi felt a deep sadness and empathy for the Oglala Lakota, but none for Eagle Bull. Levi had started when he saw Conte Eagle Bull that day. Levi's hand fell on his rifle, but Lieutenant Magnuson held him back. Levi had glared with hatred at Eagle Bull, his hollow eyes set deep into gaunt, meatless cheeks, his teeth pulled back in a defeated snarl, for he, too, had had the warrior beaten out of him. And as suddenly as the bloodlust rose within Levi, it had faded. He was certain the murderer would soon die.

"I thought he was dying?" Pretty Paw skipped another pebble. Six skips.

"Some say a *ak'bari'a* healed him."

"But he was nothing. How could he be Boss Farmer?"

Levi shrugged. "His father-in-law. Stuck In The Clouds was named chief of the Oglala, vying for control with Red Cloud. And Stuck In The Clouds made sure his son-in-law was appointed Boss Farmer."

Pretty Paw moved Levi's arms aside and sat on his lap. "What the Oglala do is of no concern to us. The wars are over."

"It will never be over." Levi patted her head. "I love you dearly, my wife, but often you do not see everything. Eagle Bull will control people as Boss Farmer. He will prosper, when he should be dead. He will prosper on the backs of the Oglala."

"He would do this to his own people?"

He stroked her head. Pretty Paw always saw the good in people, even someone with a heart as black as Eagle Bull's. "If he murdered his own friend, surely he will not hesitate to hurt his own people if it profits him."

"But what can you do?"

Levi opened his book and grabbed the pencil stub and began writing. "This is all I can do."

CHAPTER 19

The drive from Rapid City Regional Airport through Rapid Valley on the way to the hospital took less than twenty minutes, but it seemed to take forever. Manny ducked around slower drivers, cussing at an elderly man taking up two lanes, even flooring the rental through a red light. Willie's condition replaced concerns about his bad driving, and he made it to Rapid City Regional somehow without an accident.

He double-parked in the loading zone and rushed to the hospital elevator. The ride to the fifth floor, like the ride from the airport, dragged on. His jacket caught on the door of the elevator and he ripped it free as he ran to the nurse's station outside Intensive Care.

"Mr. With Horn already has visitors," an RN sitting behind the desk said over a *People* magazine without looking up. "I can't allow anyone else . . ."

"You're telling me you're denying me access to a victim in

an attempted homicide?" Manny said, flipping his ID wallet open.

She dropped her magazine and stood. As she glared down at Manny, he figured she had him by thirty pounds. He sized her up in case she refused his request to see Willie, and figured on a good day he could take her. But this wasn't a good day. For him or Willie.

"Suit yourself, but the patient's not much of a witness right now." She jerked her thumb to a room across the hall. "You got ten minutes, then I test those self-defense classes you FBI are always stumbling through."

Manny ran across the hall and stood outside Willie's room, breathing deep, steeling himself for what he feared he would see. He shoved the door open. Doreen Big Eagle and Clara stood leaning on the bed railing looking down, obscuring Willie. Clara nodded to him and moved aside.

Manny gasped. He had seen far too many victims of violent crimes in his career, more than he dared recount, victims kept teetering in the land of the living by IVs and O2 and all sorts of drug cocktails shoved down their throats or in their veins or stuck up their rectums. But he wasn't prepared for Willie. He lay on his back, his thick chest not as thick and robust as Manny remembered it a few days ago. Willie's arm remained flaccid beside him, a host to tubes and IVs, and his breaths came labored past tubes sticking down his throat and nasal cavity. Willie gasped air, seemingly in time with the beep-beep-beeping of the monitor above his bed.

Manny bent to Willie's ear. "Willie, buddy. I'm betting you can hear me . . ."

"When the hell did he become your buddy?" Doreen stepped between Manny and the bed railing. "If you were his buddy, you would have encouraged him to get his teaching degree. Quit the tribal police. He wouldn't be in this position . . ."

"There's enough time for that later." Clara stepped around and rested her hand on Doreen's arm. "Right now, it's more important that Willie have quiet."

"I'll second that." The hefty RN had taken off her glasses as if she anticipated a fight. She even talked to Manny in a bladed stance as if she'd boxed a time or two. "I said you could come in if you were quiet. FBI or not, clear out Agent."

Manny thought for the briefest moment of arguing with her. But if she argued like she looked, he could end up in a crumpled heap on the floor. Images of Beetle Bailey after Sarge finished with him came creeping into his thoughts, supplanted by Nurse Ratched ordering Jack Nicholson around the padded room.

Clara saved Manny's pride when she hooked her arm in his and ushered him out to a waiting room down the hall. Nurse Ratched kept an evil eye on him from Willie's room before making her way back to the nurse's station.

"My God, he looks like hell." Manny eased himself into a hard plastic chair before he fell down. "But what did I expect with him being shot twice?" He looked up at Clara. "Will he make it? What did his doctors say? What can we do . . ."

Clara pressed her fingers to Manny's lips and sat beside him. She took his hand in hers. "I'm getting this through Doreen. The only reason the doctors told her anything is she's the closest thing to Willie's next of kin with his aunt Lizzy in the asylum. They figured they could trust his fiancée."

"And?"

"They're pushing it giving Willie a fifty-fifty chance. Doreen said she overheard one of the doctors saying he'd give better odds to someone hitting the slots in Deadwood than Willie ever walking out of that room alive."

Manny squirmed to get comfortable. Failing, he stood and paced the room. "What can I do now? I should have talked him out of the tribal police. You know he was a semester away from getting his teaching degree."

"Like I had any success talking you out of the bureau." She smiled for the first time. "Made no difference to you. Wouldn't have to Willie either."

Manny's decision to remain with the bureau had nearly cost them their relationship. Clara had accepted his wedding proposal, assuming he would be leaving the bureau for some safe job. When he didn't look into teaching college or private consulting, she had put their engagement on hold while she worked out the thought that—like Willie—Manny could end up in the ICU hanging on by a thin thread. She had finally accepted his career choice, and he still had her. He prayed Willie would have Doreen if he pulled out of this.

><><><><

Manny walked Clara past Nurse Ratched, who eyed him all the while. Doreen glared at him from the far side of Willie's bed as Manny kissed Clara and returned to the waiting room. Lumpy had slipped into the room. He slumped in a green plastic chair that had seen better days with its warped arms and one leg shorter than the rest. He thumbed through last month's issue of *Cosmopolitan*, tattered pages competing with ones that had been torn out. A large coffee stain graced the cover, obscuring the robust cleavage of the twenty-something espousing "Ten Techniques of the Highly Orgasmic."

Lumpy looked up and squinted as if seeing Manny for the first time, his lids drooping over green eyes that appeared to be swimming in red pools. Dark circles hung suspended under his eyes, and he hadn't shaved in days, his splotchy stubble making him appear far older than he was. He followed Manny's gaze to the *Cosmopolitan*, and quickly slipped it between a *Humpty Dumpty* and *Paternity Today*. He stood and stumbled to the one hundred-cup percolator sitting on a card table in one corner of the room. "Might be some left," he called over his shoulder.

"I'll pass." Manny sat in a chair in a long line of other plastic chairs, the only difference was his chair was missing a ragged chunk of plastic as if some rabid dog had gnawed through it. "What happened?"

Lumpy turned with his foam cup full of some dark, oozing liquid and walked back to the chairs. He hiked his dirty sweatpants up over his belly and dropped into a chair beside Manny, spilling week-old coffee onto the front of his T-shirt. He paid no mind to it and closed his eyes, while Manny sat quietly waiting for Lumpy to gather his words. "Willie did some impressive legwork," he said at last, sitting up and opening his eyes. "Chief Horn told Willie which place Degas might be working out of—Wilson Eagle Bull has four ranches—and Willie took Horn's advice and went to Wilson's Oglala ranch. I warned Willie to tread lightly . . ."

"Because Wilson's running for State Senate?"

Lumpy nodded. A trickle of coffee ran from one corner of his mouth, but he made no effort to wipe it away. "Willie was staking out Wilson's bunkhouse, and he radioed he was going in once he saw the ranch hands were awake."

"Why the hell didn't you send backup along with him?"

Lumpy shook his head. "All he was going to do was interview Degas. We never figured there was enough to arrest him, so I didn't send backup just for an interview."

Manny checked his voice and continued quietly. "Surveillance of someone potentially dangerous—if Degas meant

for Harlan White Bird to get killed—required two officers . . ."

"I had no one to spare, Hotshot," Lumpy fired back. He
stood and tossed the cup in the round file. "Maybe you're
forgetting we're running on quarter manpower here. Men are
working back-to-back twelves regularly. Besides"—he met
Manny's stare—"he was working on your case. It didn't even
happen in his jurisdiction. Why didn't you come back and
work surveillance with him? You sit there on your throne and
condemn me."

Manny dropped his head between his legs. "I should
have."

Lumpy sat back beside Manny and nudged him. "Guess
we both should have done things differently. Important thing
now is for Willie to get on the mend."

"If there's any mend in him."

Lumpy leaned back and looked at the ceiling. "Nothing
we can do now except to pray to God."

"And to Wakan Tanka." *Now where did that come from?
The old ways got us nowhere before, and they sure as hell
won't help Willie now.* "We know for certain it was Degas?"

Lumpy shook his head. "Probably was, but there wasn't
any witnesses. I got guys combing the rez looking for him now."

Manny closed his eyes, thinking of the last time he talked
with Willie. He said he was waiting for signs of life at Wilson's, and had blown off Manny's hollow suggestion that he
be careful.

"When Willie didn't respond to the periodic status check,
we started officers toward Wilson's ranch." Lumpy broke the
silence. "When the officers finally found him, he was about a
quarter mile from the ranch house soaking up dirt with his
own blood. He was barely hanging on. We life-flighted him
right away."

"He tell you anything?"

Lumpy shook his head. "He wasn't conscious when he was found, and hasn't regained it since."

"Did the crime scene tell you anything?"

Lumpy turned sideways in his seat. "Pee Pee worked his ass off over that scene, but didn't come up with much. Just two 9mm cases by the back of Willie's truck. And the surgeon in Rapid City recovered a 124-grain Hydra-Shok from his back."

Manny whistled. "Shooter was serious, using ammo like that."

"Tell me about it. Willie coded twice before they landed in Rapid." Lumpy's eyes clouded, and he looked around for tissue. Manny reached behind him and grabbed a Kleenex box from a table and passed it over.

Manny stood and stretched his back, trying to put the crime scene together in his mind from what Lumpy had told him. "We need to talk with Wilson Eagle Bull and find out where Degas is. And who else saw anything."

Lumpy straightened in his chair. "There's nothing to suggest Wilson knew about the shooting."

"You coming with me to talk with Wilson in the morning?"

"Much as I'd like to, this is now a federal case. You'll have to talk with him yourself."

"You don't want to risk pissing Wilson off, is that it? Save your cushy job . . ."

"No matter how you upset him, you'll still have your job," Lumpy blurted out.

"You want to find the man that shot your officer?"

Lumpy hiked his sweatpants up over his belly. "I'll go along in the morning if you want to interview Wilson," he said, red-faced. "But we still got to be careful even if Degas isn't there—Wilson's got some tough bastards working for him that don't like the law. And I got no one else to spare to bring along."

"Then I'll bring along some insurance."

"What kind of insurance?"

Manny smiled. "A first-rate insurance agent."

CHAPTER 20

Manny chanced Nurse Ratched's wrath and poked his head inside Willie's room. His shallow breathing had turned raspy, labored, and the irregular beeps of the monitor seemed to accuse Manny of sending his friend here. He motioned for Clara and she stepped into the hall. "I'm going to Pine Ridge in the morning and interview Wilson Eagle Bull, find out what I can about Carson Degas. You going to be all right? Going to get some sleep? You look . . ."

"Terrible?" Clara stroked his cheek. "I'll be fine. That nice nurse asked an aide to bring me a rollaway so I can spend the night beside him."

"None for Doreen?"

"I sent Doreen home," Clara said. "She needs rest worse than I do. She's been with Willie since they brought him here. I had a hard time convincing her that she needs some shut-eye."

"You look beat yourself." Manny squeezed her hand. "When was the last time you ate?"

Clara forced a smile and nodded to the nurse's station. "They don't bring enough to feed a sparrow."

Manny fished a twenty out of his pocket and handed it to her. "Go grab yourself something from the cafeteria."

"I'm not . . ."

"A sandwich or something."

Clara looked to Willie's room. "But if anything changes . . ."

"I'll call you on your cell."

Manny watched Clara disappear down the hall before he turned and entered Willie's room. He closed the heavy door and stood with his back to the bed, afraid to turn around. When he did, his eyes fell to the monitor, to the tubes, to the man partially covered with grim hospital sheets, a man that looked so much smaller than the one that began his vacation with Manny less than a week ago. "A person near death will seem to shrink," his academy instructor had drilled into him as a recruit nearly twenty years ago. "They will look smaller than is possible, but rest assured there is a human being fighting to pull through. Treat them kindly."

Manny pulled a chair near to the bed and leaned close. "You'll pull through this, bud," he whispered, but Manny was unsure if he were trying to convince Willie or himself. "For our vacation next year, we'll go to Yellowstone. Meet Old Faithful. Stay at the Lodge. I promise."

Manny heard his voice falter. Sticky, salty snot dripped from his nose and ran onto his lip, and he wiped it with the back of his shirtsleeve. He took Willie's limp hand and forced a laugh. "But this don't mean we're going to share showers or anything."

In Manny's mind's eye he thought Willie's lids flickered, but that was just hope and Willie continued lying motionless.

"Maybe I'll take driving lessons before our vacation. Help with the driving so you're not so exhausted." He stroked Willie's hand, over a saline tube taped to the back of his wrist. Did men kiss other men's hands? Manny didn't think so, but he looked around before he kissed Willie's, not expecting a reaction.

Manny closed his eyes, aware his face had been wet by tears flowing freely, the sound of his sobs mixed with the haunting monitor sounds that continued beeping.

Manny felt pressure on his shoulder and he opened his eyes. Clara stood over him, a foam container with steam escaping in one hand, a Minnie Mouse straw sticking out the top of another like a bizarre antenna. Manny wiped his face with his shirtsleeve before facing her.

"There's no shame in crying over your friend," she said as she cradled his face in her hands. "He would do the same for you."

"I put him here."

Clara shook her head. "Nonsense. He's here because he had an overwhelming need to put bad guys in jail. Same as you."

Manny looked over at Willie and squeezed his shoulder. "Guess you're right."

"And you will be cautious when you go to the Eagle Bull Ranch tomorrow?"

"I don't think a senatorial candidate will try anything with a federal agent."

Clara shook her head. "It's not Wilson I'm worried about. I've done enough consulting with Red Cloud Development around Oglala to recognize rough ranch hands when I see them. And the Eagle Bull Ranch seems to draw them like flies on a gut wagon." Her eyes welled up and she turned and threw her arms around him. "You just be careful tomorrow."

Manny moved her away and grabbed his bandanna from his pocket and started dabbing at her eyes. "Don't worry about me. I've got insurance."

"What insurance?"

"You don't want to know."

><><><><

Manny did the pecking bird as he pulled off Skyline Drive toward Clara's house, his exhaustion catching up with him. As he started to turn into the driveway, he noticed a decades-old Plymouth sat partially hidden by the side of the garage. He doused his lights and used the emergency brake to stop, careful not to trip the brake lights. He strained in the dark, trying to place the car. He would have remembered a car with a garbage bag for a back window and a trunk that looked like a semi-tractor had slammed into it.

He felt under the seat and found the holster containing his Glock and slipped it through his belt, snugging it up. He rolled quickly out of the car, illuminated only for a moment by the dome lights, and he eased the door shut. He duck-walked to the Plymouth, keeping the car between himself and the house. It was black as the night with numerous rust spots that bled through; Manny felt the primered hood: warm.

He crouched to get past the bay window and chanced a peek inside, but could see nothing in the dark house. He opened the screen door and tested the knob on the front door. Locked. He fumbled in his pocket for his keys and dropped them. He was certain if anyone was inside they heard the clanking of the key ring echoing off the concrete, and he expected someone to burst out of the house leading the way with a drawn gun.

After long moments when no one responded he breathed easier, and he silently inserted his key in the lock. He started turning the knob when he put his ear to the door. Someone walked inside. Or maybe more than one someone.

He cracked the door and paused, wiping away the sweat running into his eyes as he slowed his breathing. He peered inside, his eyes adjusting to the darkness inside the house, the only light coming from under the bathroom door. The only sound coming from there as well. Was the intruder after Clara? He couldn't imagine anyone wanting to hurt her. Perhaps someone was after Manny, and Degas popped into his mind.

Manny, still crouched and developing a nasty leg cramp, entered the room, gun leading the way, tiptoeing to the moving shadows of lights escaping under the bathroom door. A bottle dropped. Mumbled cursing followed. The doorknob turned, and Manny backed around the wall for cover.

The bathroom light went off. The door opened. A shape indistinct in the darkness, sensing someone else was in the house. "Who's there?"

"On the floor!" Manny's hand trembled, his voice broke, perhaps an octave higher than it should be. The intruder remained motionless. "I said . . ."

"That you, Agent Tanno?"

The bathroom light flicked on and Doreen Big Eagle stood silhouetted against the door. She hastily gathered her nightgown around herself as she nodded at Manny's gun. "Bad enough you got my man shot. Now you want to shoot me. What are you doing here?"

"I live here."

She brushed past Manny too startled to answer on her way to the kitchen. "Clara never mentioned you'd be staying here tonight or I'd have gotten a motel room."

She grabbed a mug and tea bag from the cupboard, and waited until she started the microwave before turning to

Manny. "I'm not particularly thrilled with this arrangement, either. Clara thought you were driving to Pine Ridge tonight and she offered me a place to crash. Fact is, I can't afford a motel room."

The microwave beeped and she took her cup out, studying the bag as she dipped it in and out of the hot water several times before going into the living room and dropping onto the couch. She sat her cup on the coffee table when her shoulders began shaking, and she buried her face in her hands. Steady, agonizing sobs came from Doreen, like the sobs that came from Manny the night Uncle Marion died.

Manny looked around the house as if scoping out an escape route. The bureau—and life as he'd lived it—had never prepared him to deal with a grieving girlfriend. *Go to her,* he heard Unc in his head telling him. *She's a human being in need of comfort. Go to her.*

Manny sat on the couch beside Doreen and started to drape his arms around her. He got no resistance and he pulled her close. She seemed so frail, so alone, so in need of someone. He stroked her head. "Willie will pull through."

She shrugged him off. Snot ran down onto her upper lip and Manny handed her a Kleenex. "How do you know he'll make it? You a psychic? Some holy man like Willie's studied to be? How do you know we won't get a call this minute telling us Willie died?"

Manny would have loved for his gift Reuben insisted he possessed to kick in and tell him what the future held for Willie. Manny felt his *wophiye*, his medicine bundle in the shape of a turtle, hanging from a leather thong under his shirt. But the medicine bundle, and his gift of visions from the sacred men, hung silent. All he had left tonight was grief. "Willie will make it. I won't think otherwise."

"And if he does, what do I have to look forward to, being

married to a cop? Worrying about getting the call in the middle of the night telling me Willie's been shot again?" She started to take a sip of her tea, but replaced it on the coffee table. "And maybe not being so lucky the next time."

"Would you rather have Willie die a slow death?"

She glared at Manny. "What crap you talking now?"

Manny stood and walked the cramp out of his leg. "Can you picture Willie teaching?"

"What's wrong with teachers?"

"Nothing. But it's not for Willie, spending days cooped up inside teaching grade-schoolers. Maybe spending nights in parent–teacher conferences. Coming home wiped out—not from teaching—but from pure lack of stimulation."

"You mean lack of excitement?"

Manny nodded. He knew just how Willie would feel, missing the sensation of your heart threatening to burst from your chest because you're so scared; the thrill of knocking on Death's Door only to find out in that last brief moment that Death locked you out. This time. "Willie's a cop. It's in his blood. He lives for the thrill of the hunt, for the thrill of slamming the cell door on scroats like Carson Degas."

"Just like you."

"And just like every other cop with stones."

Doreen blew her nose and dropped the tissue on the table. "Clara told me she couldn't convince you to quit the bureau, either."

Manny forced a smile. "I don't think she's totally given up. But if she were here right now, she'd tell you to support your man."

"I do support him."

Anger replaced empathy and Manny fought to control the resentment rising in his throat like an acid reflux attack. "You've already given up on Willie. You already have him flatlining. But Willie's going to pull through. I won't think otherwise. And neither should you."

She turned away and burst into tears, shoulders once again shaking. He started to sit, and paused, Unc's words coming through once again as they often did in times like these when Manny needed guidance: *Go to her. Comfort her. It's what I would do.* And Manny did just what his uncle Marion would have done, and he sat beside Doreen. She leaned against Manny and he wrapped his arms around her, rocking back and forth, stroking her head. At least for the moment, Doreen wasn't blaming him. At least for the moment, she was only concerned with Willie.

"Wakan Tanka won't allow Willie to die," he whispered, but he wished he sounded more convincing than he did.

CHAPTER 21

"You missed the turn to the Eagle Bull Ranch," Lumpy said between bites of a Snickers to replenish his strength. He wiped chocolate from his stubble, and bags under his eyes showed he hadn't slept any better than Manny had last night. But then Manny had slept on a lumpy couch and tried to block out Doreen's snores reaching him from the bedroom. "What you slowing down for? And will you turn down whatever it is blaring on your CD player."

"It's The Who."

"Who?"

"The Who. Rock group of the sixties and seventies."

"I know that." Lumpy stuffed the empty candy wrapper in the side pocket of the door. "But I thought you like that damned polka music?"

"I'm expanding my horizons." *And maybe because Willie got me hooked on rock and roll.* "We're going north of Oglala."

"I can see that, but what for? We passed the turnoff . . ."

"Picking up my insurance agent."

Lumpy opened a pack of Doritos. "What the hell we going to do, interview Wilson Eagle Bull or sell him a whole life policy?"

Manny smiled. "Like Clara pointed out, Wilson's got some genuinely nasty bastards working for him. We need an equally nasty insurance agent to handle them. And Degas if we find him."

Lumpy started to press Manny when they turned down a gravel drive leading to a boarded-up trailer, duct tape plastered over broken windows. A paint horse stood three-legged inside a corral that looked as if the next stout wind would topple it. Manny stopped the car in front of the trailer and honked.

Reuben walked from around the back of the trailer, hair braided with miniature beaded lizards for hair ties, T-shirt with a depiction of Sitting Bull plastered across the front.

"We're not taking *him*?"

Manny smiled.

"A felon? A murderer on an investigation?"

Manny so wanted to spill the truth about Reuben, a truth Manny himself had denied ever since his brother had gone to prison for a 1970s homicide. But Manny held his tongue as he watched Reuben amble toward them. At just over sixty, Reuben's six-foot-four frame still commanded respect. His thick chest and bulging shoulder muscles threatened to burst his T-shirt. "Can't hardly turn Reuben down now that's he's dressed in his best insurance agent clothes, can we?"

"But why him?"

"We might need help."

"We got a radio if we need help," Lumpy sputtered, his eyes fixed on Reuben. "And we got guns."

Manny turned to Lumpy. "Willie had a radio. And a gun. Didn't help him any."

Reuben stopped at the passenger side and motioned for Lumpy to roll the window down. "Acting Chief Looks Twice." His grin showed perfect teeth. "An honor to have you riding in the backseat with us."

"Does it look like I'm riding bitch?" He jerked his thumb toward the back. "Climb in if you're coming with us."

"And just how do you think I'm going to fit in back?"

"He's right." Manny smiled. "He'll have a hard enough time riding up front."

Lumpy cursed under his breath and grabbed his last Snickers and coffee cup and flung the door open. Reuben deftly sidestepped the door and waited until Lumpy had crawled in the backseat before he tackled entry himself. He leaned in and grabbed the aw-shit handle above the door, his braids falling onto his chest, and folded one leg at a time in until he was seated. Even with the seat scooted all the way back, his knees still rubbed the dashboard. He looked sideways at Manny. "Is this all the bureau can give a senior agent—a sedan instead of a Suburban? Maybe an Expedition? I'm going to get felony cramped."

"Your taxpayer dollars at work."

"Taxpayer dollars, my ass. If the government used money wisely, they'd have hired you a full-time driver."

Lumpy leaned over the seat. "Look at the bright side— Manny's driving will probably kill you before the cramps do."

When they reached Highway 18, they turned west, hitting the dreaded construction area that people hereabouts were so upset about. Manny read the police blotter where a pickup had dropped into a ten-foot-deep washout with no warning. Seems that the yellow warning signs and construction sawhorses had been stolen, and the flagman had left for an extended afternoon brewski in Hot Springs.

"You ever hear of this Carson Degas?" Lumpy's breath

smelled of chocolate and peanuts as he nudged Reuben. "Seeing you two are cut from the same cloth."

Reuben glared at Lumpy, who shrank back into the seat. Reuben started to turn toward him when Manny broke in. "What have you heard of him?"

Reuben eyed Lumpy one last time before he turned back around. "He showed up at Eagle Bull's last year. Claimed he was a horse whisperer. Claimed to know damned near everything there was to know about horseflesh."

"Does he?" Manny slammed on the brakes just before hitting a skunk crossing the road.

Reuben rubbed his forehead where he'd smacked the windshield. "Be careful."

"Put your seat belt on."

"Won't fit."

Manny slowed. "You were expounding on Degas."

Reuben nodded. "That what I was doing, expounding?" He laughed. "Word is, he's sharper 'n hell with horses. Knows everyone in the business it seems. Got contracts for Eagle Bull in five states, and . . ." He reached for the CD player but Manny slapped his hand away. "Can't you turn this to KILI? What is it anyway?"

"The Who," Lumpy said proudly from the backseat.

"Wrong." Manny turned the volume down. "It's Three Dog Night now. But continue."

"Degas came on the scene about the time that Wilson Eagle Bull fired his last horse wrangler," Reuben said, squirming in the seat, trying to make the seat belt stretch. It didn't. "Rumor has it that Degas spent some time in the hoosegow. Like a lot of Eagle Bull hands."

"Ever meet him?"

Reuben nodded.

"In stir?" Lumpy asked.

Reuben shook his head, staring out the window searching for the answer in the low-hanging clouds. He had spent twenty-five years in the state prison for the Billy Two Moons murder. For all Reuben's past faults, he was walking the Good Red Road now as a sacred man. "Degas came to the Rosebud Wacipi last year with a bottle of booze and a bad attitude."

"Can't have alcohol at powwows," Lumpy said. "They give Rosebud cops a call to have him booted?"

Reuben nodded. "They did, but there was no one available. Shorthanded. Anyways, Degas got in a row with the gate security. Kicked the shit out of two before they left him alone. He had everyone spooked, and picked a fight with some guy from Scenic riding saddle bronc. He was putting the boots to the guy big-time when one of the fancy dancers came and got me."

Manny popped a piece of sugar-free candy in his mouth and offered one to Reuben and Lumpy. Reuben grabbed one, but Lumpy waved it away. Manny never knew the man to ingest anything sugar-free. "And you stopped the fight?"

"I did, but I didn't faze him much." He grabbed Manny's bag of candy and popped three more pieces. "Even though I had him by fifty pounds and a couple inches, he wasn't scared of me one bit. I saw that in those black eyes of his. He didn't stop beating that guy because of me. He stopped because he wanted to. Me stepping in just reminded him of how tired his ass-kicking leg was getting."

They turned onto Tribal Road 41 on their way to Slim Buttes. "Another mile on the right"—Lumpy leaned over the seat—"to where we found Willie."

"And you didn't assign Willie any backup?" Reuben asked.

Lumpy snorted. "Now you, too. You a cop now or something?"

Reuben smiled. "No, but I've kicked ass on enough."

"There." Lumpy pointed.

Manny stopped beside a yellow evidence barrier tape stretched between two wooden fence posts. He started to get out and turned to Reuben. "You gonna get out and stretch your legs?"

Reuben sat back in the seat. "Just make it harder for me to get back in. I'll get out when it's necessary."

Manny shrugged and followed Lumpy to where faint orange spray paint revealed where Willie had lain, the outline nearly obliterated by the fine dust that blew into everything on the rez. *Like Willie's life that's fading away and nothing I can do about it.*

To one side of the tape flies had gathered around black blotches and had already laid their eggs in the blood. Willie's blood, and Manny turned away. P. P. Pourier, evidence tech extraordinaire, had worked the crime scene as a homicide. *Would it end up being a homicide? Manny found himself praying to Wakan Tanka and to God. It didn't hurt to cover all the bases.*

"We're not sure how long he lay there leaking blood." Lumpy seemed to read Manny's thoughts. "From the time of his last transmission until Officer Lone Tree found him, it was an hour. He said Willie's pulse was so weak he wasn't sure he had one."

"Witnesses?"

Lumpy shook his head. "At least none that would come forward." Lumpy nodded to Wilson Eagle Bull's bunkhouse a half mile to the south. The single-story ranch-hand quarters sat between the main house and a two-story barn. "We're just lucky that Willie wasn't shot at one of the other ranches Wilson owns."

"What do you think happened?"

"You asking a lowly tribal cop what happened, Hotshot?"

Despite their rivalry that went back to childhood days and later their tribal police days, Manny knew Lumpy had an analytical mind street cops envied.

"Willie was shot at close range. Powder stippling at the front and back of his uniform indicated two hits."

"I thought you said there were three cases found?"

Lumpy walked to where Willie had lain and shooed the flies away as he took out his bandanna and held it over his mouth. "There were. Two there"—he pointed—"and the third six feet away. Way I figure it, the first shot came when the shooter was six or seven feet to Willie's back."

"And he walked up to finish the job."

Lumpy nodded. "Way I figure it."

Manny bent and ran his hand over impressions, deep impressions that had survived the assault by the wind, Willie's impressions. "I'd say he put up a fight."

"He had a clump of black hair balled in his fist as the paramedics prepped him for the life flight," Lumpy said. "Like he knew we'd need it for DNA testing later if we found his shooter."

"Black hair. Doesn't narrow it down very much here on the rez."

"There were three shots." Lumpy paced across the scene. "Way I see it, Willie was shot, but managed to wrestle with the shooter, and the second shot missed. Went God-knows-where. But the shooter got the upper hand finishing Willie off with one to the chest. Contact wound."

Manny thought back to what Willie had said during their last conversation. "Willie told me he was sitting a quarter mile from Wilson, about twice this distance."

Lumpy rubbed his forehead and bent to the tracks. "Pee Pee said he cast two sets of tire tracks by where Willie was found. Might be that Willie found Degas, and was trying to get him to pull over. That'd account for two sets."

Manny nodded. Willie might have tried pulling Degas over and was shot when he stopped. Unless Willie chased someone besides Degas. "Good analysis."

"You just give me a compliment?"

Before Manny was forced to admit it, a black dually pickup kicking dust barreled toward them. "We got company."

The truck skidded to a stop, and the wind took the dust over them in a faint fog. Manny turned away and Lumpy held his hand tight around his mouth until the dust settled. The driver folded himself out of the one-ton and it rose several inches. The man that stepped toward them was big enough to be Jamie Hawk's twin. He put on a black Stetson that made him appear even bigger, and he stopped in front of Lumpy and Manny, looking down at them, his face contorted into a snarl. Manny nudged his side, realizing the holster was there but he'd forgotten the gun at Clara's.

"You're on Eagle Bull land," the big man spit.

Manny fumbled into his pocket for his ID wallet and flipped it open, holding it for the man to read.

"That supposed to mean something?"

Manny took a step closer, craning his neck up. "We're here on an investigation. An officer was shot here yesterday."

The man's fists balled up and his gaze settled on Manny's chin. "I'm telling you to scat."

"And who are you?"

"Just call me Harvey. I'm Mr. Eagle Bull's foreman. Now, maybe you didn't hear me right—get the hell off this ranch!"

"He heard, but I didn't quite catch that." Reuben had stepped soundlessly from the car and moved Manny aside. He stepped toward Harvey, winking at Manny in passing. "Guess it was necessary for me to get out after all." As big as Reuben was, he had to stretch his neck up to talk to Wilson's foreman. "Maybe we want to be here. Maybe we'll drive up that road." He chin-pointed to the road leading to the ranch house and bunkhouse. Reuben's right foot dropped back slightly, a move Harvey picked up on.

"Well, well." Harvey took off his hat and set it on the hood of his truck as he dropped his watch into the hat.

"We'll see how our agent sells a policy," Manny whispered in Lumpy's ear.

Harvey smiled when he turned back to Reuben. "And what name should I tell the gravedigger to chisel on your headstone?"

"Reuben Tanno."

Harvey's smile vanished. He jammed his fists into his pockets as he stepped back, just out of Reuben's reach. "I heard of you."

"From who?" Reuben stepped closer, to within finger-jabbing distance of Harvey.

Manny stepped back. He didn't want Harvey's blood splattering his shirt.

"Who told you about me, big man? Might it be that Carson Degas, beater of young boys?"

Harvey's face went blank and he shuffled back until the fender of his truck stopped him.

"Come on now, Harvey." Reuben smiled, enjoying putting Harvey on the hot seat. He poked Harvey in the chest. "How we going to be friends if you won't talk to me?"

Harvey had a wild bronc look in his eyes, pinned against the truck, and he nodded.

"I didn't hear that."

"Degas told me about you," Harvey said, barely audible. He looked around for a way out, but Reuben wasn't ready to let him slide just yet. Manny imagined a feral cat batting a field mouse around before biting its head off.

"What he say, Harvey?"

"He said you got a habit of sticking your nose in where it don't belong."

"Well, my nose is one piece, unlike yours in a moment if I don't get answers."

Harvey's eyes darted to Manny, then Lumpy. "Just tell me what you guys want," he blurted.

Reuben nodded to Manny.

"Tell me about the shooting yesterday." Manny held his notebook as if ready to take notes.

"I don't know a thing."

Reuben stepped closer, but Harvey held up his hands in front of his face. "All I know is your officer came to the bunkhouse. The kid was on the prod, big-time, demanding to talk with Degas. Said he was suspect in a homicide on Crow Agency."

"And that pissed you and the other ranch hands off, I'd wager?"

Harvey's face flushed, and his jaw muscles tightened. "Typical cop pushing his weight around." He spit out *cop* like it was an affront to even say it aloud.

"And my guess is you guys couldn't let a tribal cop push his weight around?" Manny said. "My guess is you set Officer With Horn up."

"Now wait a minute." Harvey stepped toward Manny; when he realized Reuben was still within striking distance, he stopped. "Sure we had some fun with him."

"Define *fun*?" Lumpy pushed past Manny and stood nose-to-nipple with Harvey. "If your idea of fun is trying to kill him . . ."

"We never. Honest." Harvey's eyes darted from Reuben to Lumpy, settling on Manny. "We never."

Manny took Lumpy by the arm and moved him aside. "Tell us just what you did to Willie."

Harvey looked away.

"Tell them what you did," Reuben said.

Harvey kicked the dirt with the toe of his boot and remained silent.

Reuben's hand shot out so quickly that Manny barely caught movement in his periphery. The slap sounded like a rifle shot as it landed on the side of Harvey's head. He slumped against his truck as his hand covered his ear. Reuben smiled. "These officers didn't hear you. Tell them what you did."

"We just scared him a little."

"Willie doesn't scare easily."

Harvey looked to Lumpy. "He did a couple days ago. Me and some of the boys surrounded him. We weren't going to hurt him. Really. We just jostled him around a little before we put the run on him."

"And what did Degas do?" Manny asked.

Harvey looked away again without answering, and Reuben took a step closer. Harvey cringed. His hands shot to his face. Reuben had clearly established himself as the alpha dog in this fight. "We told your officer that Degas wasn't on the place . . ."

"Was he?"

Harvey nodded. "He was in the bunkhouse. But we didn't tell the officer that. We told him to get the hell off the property."

"And he did?"

Harvey nodded again. "When he got back in his pickup and started to leave, we went back to work."

Manny flipped pages in his notebook. "What did Degas do?"

Harvey bit his lip.

"Harv?" Reuben said, raising his hand.

"He said he was going to stop the officer down the road and have a talk with him," Harvey blurted out. "He lit out in his truck and drove the right of way along the fence line. Last

we saw Degas, he was just getting ready to drop over the hill."
Harvey motioned to the hill a quarter mile north.

"So you figure Degas got ahead of him?"

Harvey held his ear and nodded. "He could have easily got
ahead of your officer and stopped him."

"Did you hear the shots?"

Harvey's hand dropped from his head and he straightened
up. "No way. It's a half mile north where your officer got
shot. Even if we were outside doing nothing, we wouldn't
have heard gunfire."

"So you stellar citizens would have reported it if you heard
gunshots?" Reuben said.

Harvey nodded. "We would have, but like I said we went
back to work."

Manny nodded toward Wilson's house. "Can your boss
verify that?"

Harvey shrugged. "Mr. Eagle Bull's busy."

"Where's he at?"

"Busy."

Reuben raised his hand, and Harvey jerked back. "All
right. Mr. Eagle Bull's at the house. But he's working on his
campaign."

Reuben grinned. "Surely he's not too busy for us voters."
He straightened Harvey's shirt and knocked the dust from his
cowboy hat before setting it on his head. He stepped close and
whispered in Harvey's ear: "I'm with you—I don't much cot-
ton to cops, either." He chin-pointed to Manny and Lumpy.
"But sometimes they're necessary. Now do us a huge favor
and lead us to the ranch house."

Harvey turned to his truck, and Reuben snatched his cell
phone from the holder on Harvey's belt. "I'll give it back as
soon we're at the house. Wouldn't want you lining up a wel-
coming committee for us."

They climbed in the car and waited for Harvey to turn his truck around. They followed him down the Slim Buttes Road, every twenty yards passing a red, white, and blue EAGLE BULL FOR SENATE campaign poster tacked to a fence post. Harvey led them past the long, single-story bunkhouse to the ranch house that loomed large on the other side. Manny hit the CD button and Crosby, Stills, and Nash faded. Manny nodded to a sign as big as a Volkswagen plastered on the side of the bunkhouse. "At least Wilson's hands will vote for him."

Lumpy leaned over the seat. "He'll get more votes than just his guys. Last poll I saw, Wilson was inching ahead of his opponent."

Reuben fidgeted in the seat. "Good Scandinavian name like Arvid Johansson will get a ton of votes in South Dakota. Voter perception."

Lumpy laughed. "That something you read in *Felons R Us* magazine?"

"No, that's something I learned working on my master's thesis."

"Master of what? Bait?"

"Sociology," Reuben answered.

"Where . . ."

"State pen." Reuben smiled. "What else did I have to do for twenty-five years but fold clothes in the prison laundry and get an education. Especially when you fine taxpayers picked up the tab." Reuben winked at Lumpy. "Which brings us back to Wilson Eagle Bull—his reputation for honesty precedes his campaign."

Manny agreed. Since meeting Wilson at Crow Agency, Manny had researched the senatorial candidate. Wilson traced his family history back to the Fetterman Massacre during Red Cloud's War. Wilson's great-grandfather, Conte Eagle Bull, was a young brave looking to prove himself against the

Whites when he volunteered to ride with Crazy Horse. What the Lakota referred to as the Battle of a Hundred Slain would remain prominent in their oral history as a great victory against White incursion.

Manny learned that ten years later Conte Eagle Bull had distinguished himself at the Battle of the Little Big Horn, and later Conte, peacemaker among the Oglala, would be confined to the Red Cloud Agency, later Pine Ridge. The man's exploits in battle had earned him the job of Boss Farmer, a high and treasured position that he held until his death three years before the Wounded Knee Massacre. Conte's reputation for honesty would stay with the Eagle Bull family their entire lives.

Manny swallowed. Soon he'd meet the stuff legends were made of.

CHAPTER 22

Harvey stopped in front of the log house as two men on horseback rode past them. They gave Manny's government car only a passing glance as they made their way to the barn. Manny stopped the car in back of Harvey's truck and started getting out when Wilson Eagle Bull emerged from the house. His turquoise-tipped braided ponytails bounced on his chest as he descended the steps. With his starched white shirt and bone choker, he gave the impression he was about to greet his campaign committee. He stood on the steps, arms crossed, looking at his foreman.

"Harvey usually tells me when we have company." Wilson's voice, a mellow speaker's voice, held a tone and timbre that demanded attention. Unc had told Manny about the great Lakota orators, those rare leaders who mesmerized crowds with just the sound of their voices: Spotted Tail and Red Cloud, Sitting Bull and Crazy Horse, commanding yet not demanding.

Harvey took the steps three at a time and stopped beside his boss. "I would have warned you but that one took my phone." He pointed to Reuben, who fished the phone from his pocket and tossed it to Harvey.

"Not old Harv's fault," Reuben said. "I held his cell phone for safekeeping."

Wilson nodded. "Then why the little parade here?"

Manny stepped between Wilson and Reuben and started digging his ID wallet out.

"I remember who you are, Agent Tanno."

Manny pocketed his ID case. "It was necessary to keep Harvey's phone so we could make it to your house without coming away in pieces."

Wilson turned to Lumpy and eyed his clothes. "And you are the acting chief?"

Lumpy nodded.

"Dressed like that?"

"We've been working on a case," he sputtered.

"And you?" Wilson asked, smiling. "Who are you that you intimidate Harvey?"

"Reuben Tanno."

Wilson's eyes widened for the briefest moment of recognition, and he turned to Manny. "Since when does the FBI employ felons?"

"Since when does a senatorial candidate employ thugs like Harvey and the rest of your crew?"

Wilson broke into a wide smile. "I'm glad I don't have to debate you during this campaign." He turned to Harvey. "Since when *don't* we cooperate with law enforcement?"

Harvey stood speechless, smashing a bug with the toe of his boot.

"Oh, just go help Pete and RePete with the horses. I'm hauling these mares up to Crow Agency myself Monday."

"Thought you were busy with your campaign, Boss."

Wilson dropped his eyes. "Sam Star Dancer's memorial service is Tuesday. Figured I'd take them up when I go."

"Kind of soon since we don't know for certain if it was Sam that got burned to death?" Manny said.

"Chenoa's convinced it was Sam who burnt up in that house fire." Wilson blew his nose with a white handkerchief bearing the image of an eagle sitting on the hump of a buffalo, the logo of the Eagle Bull family. "I understand the autopsy will be completed this weekend and Chenoa will have the closure she needs."

Manny was convinced legal closure, not emotional closure, was on Chenoa's mind. With Sam declared dead, she could go on with ranch business far more efficiently than with him alive.

"Must have been a real shock to have such a good friend die so suddenly?"

Wilson's eyes narrowed as he stared at Manny. "What do you mean?"

"Old Marine buddy like Sam was. I understand you were his CO in 'Nam."

Wilson locked eyes with Manny. "I was Sam's commanding officer in 'Nam. Back before he took to the bottle and disgraced himself and the Star Dancer clan. You might say we grew apart after the war. I only saw him a few times since we rotated back to the world."

Manny let it drop for the moment.

"I'm taking three registered Black Angus cows to Crow Agency." Wilson seemed to anticipate Manny's question. "The Star Dancer champion stud is waiting my ladies." He turned to Harvey. "Go get them loaded."

He watched as Harvey disappeared into the barn before turning back to Manny and Lumpy. "I appreciate his loyalty, but there's no reason to shake you down." He motioned to wrought iron chairs lined up on the porch. "Sit. Please."

Manny followed Reuben and Lumpy onto the porch and dropped into a chair across from Wilson. Reuben tried squeezing into a chair and finally stood and leaned against a porch support.

As he waited for Wilson to speak, Manny looked over the property to the stables painted bright red and with new green shingles, to the old outhouse behind it with the half-moon carved out of the door, listing slightly but still useable, to horses with their heads in a feed trough in an adjoining corral, their tails swishing flies, muscles twitching in the morning heat.

"I'm assuming you're here because of that officer that got shot down the road yesterday."

Lumpy nodded. "Officer With Horn. He is my investigator."

Wilson shook his head. "Terrible. Just terrible for the reservation."

"Even worse for Willie," Manny said.

"Of course. I didn't mean anything . . ."

Manny waved the comment away. "What can you tell us about the shooting?"

"Just what Harvey told me. The men went back to work after your officer left, and the next thing they know there's a helicopter coming in on an LZ. He and some of the hands drove down the road to see what was happening, but they couldn't get close. Tribal cops had both ends of the road blocked, so they returned and went back to work."

"And Harvey didn't talk with my guys?" Lumpy said. "Tell them the last they saw Willie was when Degas lit out after him?"

Wilson looked away. "Harvey doesn't like cops . . ."

"Can't say I do either," Reuben volunteered.

Wilson glanced at Reuben. "Harvey had a few nips of his hip flask that morning. He's a good man, but Harvey needs a drink now and again to get him through the day. He didn't go down to the roadblock 'cause one more DUI and he gets serious time. You know serious time, don't you?"

"The finest gated community in the state." Reuben smiled.

"Anyway, Harv gave the cops a wide berth getting back to the ranch." He turned to Manny. "And I know what you're thinking—same thing that Johansson would bring up during the campaign—what, do I have riffraff working for me."

"Carson Degas is a little more than just riffraff," Reuben said.

Wilson fidgeted with his hair ties. "Look, I got a soft spot for men working to turn their lives around, especially capable men like Harv. And Carson. Harv said your officer came to the house looking for Carson. Why?"

Manny stood and rubbed his butt, hoping the metal chair slats hadn't made permanent lines on his backside. He debated how much to tell Wilson, and concluded they needed to find Degas badly. He weighed Wilson's loyalty to Degas, and decided to chance confiding in him. Manny explained how Degas's photo had been captured on Thelma Deer Slayer's camcorder going into Ian Tess's tent and swapping the ammo. "Where is he?"

"That's why Pete and RePete . . ."

Avoiding the question? "Those two we passed on horseback on our way in?"

"Yes. Bob and Bo Myers."

"Twin brothers that went down for that Scottsbluff mom-and-pop stickup four years ago?" Reuben asked.

Wilson looked down at his boots. "Everyone needs a second chance. Anyone could screw up once. They did a year in the county . . ."

"Only 'cause they cut a plea," Reuben said.

Manny never asked Reuben where he got his information. He just knew it went beyond the moccasin telegraph. "It'd look bad during the campaign if it got out. Like hiring Degas. Where did you say he was?"

Wilson shrugged. "He disappears now and again."

Manny looked sideways at Wilson.

"It's true," Wilson insisted. "He's probably in some lockup. Degas likes his booze. Harvey tells me Degas goes out of his way to visit off-reservation towns that don't like us NDNs, or we aren't treated well. Degas looks enough like a Lakota he plays that part well in bars. Goads cowboys into fights and lowers the boom." A slight smile played on Wilson's lips. "If he wasn't such a genius with horses, I'd have put the run on him by now."

Manny grabbed his pen and notebook. People expected investigators to take notes, even if he didn't take them down or need them. "How long he work for you?"

Wilson looked to the clouds for the answer. "Year and a half about."

"Exact date?" Manny pressed. He often crowded people he interviewed: crowded people made mistakes, said things they hadn't wanted to come out. Wilson took no chances; his answers were weighed, calculated. Wilson had been grilled before. "It's important."

Wilson sighed and turned to Lumpy and Manny. "Follow me."

"Us felons will stay outside," Reuben said. "Wouldn't want candidate Eagle Bull shaking me down for stolen silverware or a crystal sugar bowl."

They followed Wilson inside through the portal to his world, a world populated with buffalo robes hanging on walls, deer and elk skins draped over chairs, and couches sporting antlered arms. Pendleton blankets and star quilts, uneven stitching telling Manny they were older than he by at least a century, adorned display racks situated around the room.

Wilson led them past a mountain lion mount snarling at a gray wolf above a fireplace mantel, both mounts showing patches of hide gone as if they'd had the mange, the mountain lion missing two claws on one foot. Wilson stopped and nodded to the scene. "They've seen better days." He reached up and brushed a cobweb off the wolf. "My great-grandfather, Conte Eagle Bull, killed those two the first morning his band was interned here."

"Odd choice of words, Mr. Eagle Bull," Lumpy said. "Interned."

Wilson leaned an arm on the mantel, his shirt pulling taut, revealing muscles that still held their youth despite gray hair around his temples and wrinkles around his eyes. "You're Lakota, and you don't understand our plight?"

Lumpy started to speak, but Wilson continued. "What would you call it if your entire family were uprooted from their hunting grounds. You ever been to the Powder River Country?"

Lumpy shook his head. "Not yet."

"Well you ought to go, and see what prime country we Lakota gave up to live on this barren land. I'd call that being interned."

But Manny understood. Unc would gather young Manny around the fire in their one-room cabin and tell tales of the Lakota. One of the stories Unc instilled in him was the forced move of the Oglala to Pine Ridge following the Battle of the Greasy Grass. The soldiers sought to avenge Custer's annihilation, and with the help of the Crow, they hounded the Lakota bands until, exhausted and faced with starvation, the

Oglala had surrendered. Only then did they learn they were to make Pine Ridge their new home, in a land that was nearly impossible to farm as their Indian agent demanded. And impossible to subsist on with hunting, as the game had gone the way of the buffalo.

They followed Wilson into his office, and he started plucking file folders from pigeonholes in his rolltop desk. "I got Degas's date of employment here somewhere."

Lumpy drew in a quick breath and nudged Manny. He motioned to a glass case in the room adjacent to Wilson's study. "Check that display out."

Many followed Lumpy into a great room lined with Navajo rugs and Hopi pottery displayed on oak stands. An Arapaho cradleboard hung next to Kiowa moccasins, both beaded on every inch of the deer hide. But it was the long glass display case, suspended at eye level and running the length of one wall, that caught Manny's interest. He stopped at one end of the case, his heart skipping a beat he was certain. Since the Red Cloud homicide, where he had had to rely on Willie and others for insight into Indian artifacts, Manny had begun studying his heritage. He had taken two online courses in Indian artifacts from the University of Wyoming and one on relics at Rapid City Community College. He had begun appreciating his roots. And he appreciated Wilson's display.

Manny stood in front of a beaded pouch, the light blue background a contrast with red and yellow hourglass patterns on the flap and pouch front. Sinew stitching had faded through the years, and the elk skin was cracked. The pouch may have hung from a hunter's saddle as he dressed a deer he had killed, his bloody hands brushing the side of the leather, a fleshing knife displayed beside it.

An assortment of belts hung next to the pouch, lazy stitched, others decorated with dyed porcupine quills, authentic all and old. Manny felt compelled to reach out and touch the glass as he closed his eyes. An Oglala wife had sat cross-legged around a tipi fire one wintery night, belt resting in her lap, porcupine quills soaking in her mouth until they were pliable enough to flatten and sew onto the deerskin.

The image of the hunter that had killed the deer the belt was made of loomed large. Manny opened his eyes, rubbing them, but the image persisted. The hunter stalked a two-point buck, rifle at the ready, brass tacks embedded in the stock reflecting the sun bouncing off the snow he crept on.

Manny forced himself to turn from the glass, shaking his head, clearing his mind of the scene. He had been witness to another scene from the past, and he'd talk with Reuben about it later.

He started walking away from the case when two scalp locks, grisly, long, wrinkled, and dried, fluttered inside the glass case. Manny struggled to turn away, but the need to know the scalps' story grew too strong. He turned, staring at them, his hand poised inches from the glass. Had the scalps actually fluttered? Had they called to him, or was that just another imagining like the woman sewing her hunter-husband's belt?

Manny's pulse quickened. Images flashed in his mind. The urge to run as strong as the need to stay. But his feet remained solidly planted in front of the case like cornstalks anchored into black soil. He reached out his hand, drew it away, dropped it onto the glass. A shock rose up his arm, through his body, the scalp locks talking to him.

Manny shuddered as a Crow warrior faced a charge by two Lakota overlooking the Battle of the Little Big Horn. The two warriors shot the Crow, one dropping off his pony and running to the corpse, knife in hand. The other Lakota, still seated on his horse, raised his rifle. Manny tried to scream a warning, his throat closed to any sounds, spitting the taste of black powder from his mouth as a cloud settled over the scene. When a breeze moved the powder cloud away, the Crow warrior lay on his back beside the lifeless Lakota his companion had shot, accusing eyes fixed on his killer.

Manny swayed, his knees buckling, weakening, and he leaned against the display case.

"That glass might break!"

Manny shook his head, the image gone, his balance returning.

Wilson hooked his arm through Manny's and steadied him. "Hate to have you fall through and cut yourself up. You okay?"

Manny looked back to the scalp locks sitting silent and immobile behind the glass. "Blood sugar spike. Damned diabetes."

Lumpy took Manny's other arm. "You want me to drive you to Indian Health?"

"No."

"Need a candy bar?"

"I might," Manny said, staring back at the display case. *As long as I keep away from those scalps I might not.*

Wilson followed Manny's gaze and nodded to the scalp locks. "I kept asking Grandfather Biford about those scalps. Grandfather was a *wicasa wakan*. I thought for sure a holy man would tell his grandson about them. But the only thing he'd say is that Great-Grandfather Conte scalped an enemy in battle at the Little Big Horn. I kept pressing him about it. I always thought there was more to the story, but he never said more. And my father never explained them. He always kept me away from the scalps."

"Was he?" Lumpy asked. "Was your grandfather a sacred man?"

Wilson laughed. "I guess, if there really is any such thing.

Tradition has it that someone's got to be a holy man, so I guess it was my grandfather's turn."

Manny nodded to the display case. "You must hold some store in tradition?"

Wilson laughed again and chin-pointed to the glass case. "I keep this collection because it meant something to my family. My family collection. That's as far as tradition will allow me to go."

"But you dress traditionally," Lumpy said.

"This?" Wilson flicked his hair ties and ran his finger under his choker. "These are just props. An Indian running for Senate is expected to look Indian."

"Doesn't sound like something you want to stump on the campaign trail."

Wilson's smile faded and he frowned at Manny, then at Lumpy. Gone was his naturally resonant voice, replaced by a low, guttural sound as he stepped toward them. "My attitude stays in this house. Got it?"

"I do," Lumpy said.

Wilson glared at him.

Lumpy put up his hand and forced a smile. "Honest Injun."

Wilson turned to Manny, silent, assessing Wilson's sudden change in demeanor. Wilson blinked.

"We'll leave you—and your attitude—as soon as we have the information we need on Degas."

Wilson turned away and walked to his desk. "Here's the information you need." He thrust a slip of paper into Manny's hand. "The date I hired Carson. His duties. Is there anything else, Agent Tanno?"

Manny, still unsteady on his feet, wanted to be out of the house and away from the scalps. "I may be back for more questions."

"Call next time before you come. Understood?"

When they walked out of the house, Reuben stood from the steps. He looked at Manny and wrapped his arm around his shoulder, leading him down the steps toward the car. "Again?" he whispered.

Manny nodded as Lumpy climbed behind the wheel. How Reuben always knew when Manny experienced a vision baffled him.

"I don't think you're in any shape to drive."

Manny could find no argument with that.

"We'll have to talk about it later, you know?"

Manny nodded again. For a brief moment before he climbed back into the car, he thought the scalps called out to him, but he wasn't entirely sure what they said.

CHAPTER 23

Manny sat toweling himself off as he sat on a tree stump over-looking the creek in back of Reuben's trailer house. They had emerged from the *initipi*, the sweat lodge that Reuben had permanently erected along the bank of the meandering creek. Reuben had tied willow boughs together and draped plastic sheeting and heavy canvas over that so no light could escape, so the cleansing heat would stay until he threw back the door. As always, this sweat had been brutal. Just how Reuben liked it.

Manny turned his head and shoulders to the west, savor-ing the cooling breeze. Reuben had soaked him with a garden hose, and Manny wanted to sit all afternoon with his shirt off enjoying the air. But he had an investigation to conduct, an investigation that competed with his attention to Willie lying on his deathbed.

Manny grabbed his Dockers and shirt draped over a bicy-cle with one wheel missing. The rusty bike provided the perfect clothes hanger, having been left there for so long the cottonwood tree had grown up around it. He tucked his shirt in and slipped his ID wallet into his trousers.

Reuben sat in a lawn chair, his butt sticking through missing slats, sipping a Coke and fiddling with his sunglasses. As was Lakota custom, Manny had brought a gift when he visited Reuben, his Ray-Bans the only thing he had on him to give.

"What are you smiling about?"

"You." Reuben straightened one bow and slipped the glasses on. "You are still fighting against it."

"I told you, I didn't have a vision at Eagle Bull's."

"Then what do you think happened—Disney animated those scalp locks so they could talk to you? You got to come to grips with the fact that visions find you now and again, even when you don't want them. And there is meaning to every one of them."

"That my big brother talking shit?"

"This is your brother the sacred man talking. And I do not shit you."

Manny held up his hands. "Don't start with your holy man analysis."

Reuben sat relaxed in his chair as if talking with a group of schoolkids. "Then what do you think happened?"

Manny sat back on the stump and started pulling on his socks. Sometimes, Reuben was such a pain in the ass, prodding on subjects that Manny had no desire to talk about. "Just what I said, that my blood sugar spiked. I felt better once I had a sandwich." Manny tried to convince himself as much as Reuben that he had not had a vision at Wilson's.

But Reuben was right—Manny denied his visions taking over his mind, taking over his body at the least opportune times, visions of things he couldn't explain. Since returning to

Pine Ridge last year, a lifetime of disallowing his native roots had caught up with him. What he couldn't figure out was if it was a curse—as he thought it was—or a blessing from Wakan Tanka as Reuben believed. Either way, it scared the hell out of Manny.

"Why don't you admit what happens when you see these things?"

"If what you call visions don't help me solve cases, I got no time for them. I came here to sweat. Maybe come up with an answer for my hallucination today. Besides my diabetes acting up."

Reuben uncapped a root beer and handed it to Manny. "You got the right answer, *kola*. Those scalp locks told you a story. Now you'll have to make room in your heart to hear what they had to say."

Manny drank half the root beer in one gulp, feeling his strength returning. The *initipi* always rejuvenated him, just as Reuben espoused, with the heat and the water and the dome representing Mother Earth and the breath of life healing his body. But today, his mind was in more need of that healing.

"Something else bothers you, *kola*."

Manny turned to him. "You the Amazing Kreskin or something? How'd you know I . . . got problems?"

Reuben shrugged. "I just know things. I know something has upset you besides Willie's condition."

Manny turned to him, taking a deep breath before he confessed. "I felt pride when I was in Harlan's shop among the artifacts. I felt pride when I looked upon Wilson's display of relics."

"Pride in what?"

Manny pushed an ant out of his boots before slipping them on. "That the Lakota—our ancestors—defeated Custer so soundly. When I went to the Little Big Horn Memorial the other day, I only felt pride in those warriors."

"Pride is not necessarily a bad thing." Reuben toweled the sweat off his chest and shoulders, the water pooling in deep scars across his chest and neck. "As long as you do not use pride for your own gain." He stood and stretched as he looked at the steep bank they'd have to climb to get back to Reuben's house. "I have always felt pride in what our warrior-ancestors did. They did nothing else that other people would not do. They protected their families, and were willing to die for it. Tell me that is not something to be proud of."

Manny nodded. As always, Reuben was right. Now all Manny had to do was get past the feeling of pride that Manny had for Reuben for his involvement in the American Indian Movement. But that would have to be a discussion for another day, for another sweat. For the moment, he had an investigation to conduct.

>‹›‹›‹

Manny left his rental parked at Big Bat's after he'd finished his breakfast burrito and walked across the street to the justice building. It had seemed so strange having breakfast at the convenience store alone. Whenever he worked a Pine Ridge case, he and Willie would usually have breakfast there together, two men on Indian time and in no hurry. This morning Manny realized just how much he missed his talks with him. He shuddered when he thought of Willie being fed his breakfast through a tube stuck down his throat.

He walked up the flight of stairs and into the building. Someone on the other side of the smoked glass buzzed him through the security door, and he walked the long corridor to Lumpy's office.

"I wouldn't get too close." A secretary stuck her head out of a cubicle. "The bear got here just twenty minutes ago, and he's crankier than usual. If you can believe that."

"Thanks for the warning," Manny called over his shoulder. He continued until he reached the door with ACTING CHIEF LOOKS TWICE in letters painted across the door. He rapped, but got no answer, and rapped again. Silence. He turned the knob and cracked the door. Lumpy sat in his velvet Elvis chair, hands cradling his head as his elbows rested on his desk, looking like Manny felt. Dark circles under Lumpy's eyes melted into puffy cheeks sporting yesterday's stubble. A large yellow stain followed his gig line on the front of his shirt, which could have been breakfast or last night's supper. "Bad night?"

Lumpy used the edge of the desk and stood. He shuffled to the coffeemaker and began scooping grounds into the pot. "The worst. While you were at Reuben's doing God-knows-what, I sat with Willie all night."

Manny dropped into a chair opposite Lumpy. "You gonna give me the update?"

The coffeemaker started dripping dark liquid into the carafe, but Lumpy kept his back to Manny. He sighed deeply. "Willie's lungs filled with liquid last night. We damned near lost him." Lumpy turned around, tears starting at the corners of his eyes, and he turned back to the pot.

Now maybe you'll treat Willie better if he pulls out of this, Manny thought, but he said nothing as he walked to the coffee cart and grabbed two cups. "Maybe I'd better get up there . . ."

"I wouldn't." Lumpy filed both cups and turned back to his chair. "Doreen spelled me this morning, and she's even more pissed at you than she is at me. She thinks I should have let Willie go from the department, and blames you for encouraging him to stay."

Lumpy dropped into Elvis and Manny swore the King shed tears in solidarity. "I'd still be up in Rapid if I didn't have to put out fires here."

Manny wrapped his hand around his coffee cup, feeling the warmth, waiting for Lumpy to tell his problems at his own speed. "I got a call from the tribal councilmen from Porcupine and LaCreek Districts. And the Fifth Member. All about Wilson Eagle Bull."

"Don't tell me: Eagle Bull complained we harassed him?"

"You got it. He complained about the acting police chief coming to his house with a known felon, and about you implying he knew where Degas was but wasn't saying."

"I didn't imply anything. I know Wilson knows where Degas is and I said so." Manny smiled. "I'd say that's a direct accusation."

"Either way, this is strictly a federal case from here on. Wilson's got a good chance of being the next state senator from Pine Ridge and they don't want bad PR mucking it up for the tribe."

"So your department won't help me?"

Lumpy stood quickly, Elvis rolling and hitting the wall with a dull thud. "Dammit it, I got no choice. The tribal council made it plain: with Eagle Bull and Chenoa both active in the National Congress of American Indians, their working together will bring animosities between our tribes down. Either I toe the mark, or they'll replace me with someone who can."

"So you won't help?"

Lumpy remained silent over the coffeepot.

"We weren't raised that way," Manny said. "You and me, we were raised to help people. And especially now, we need to help each other to find Degas. Or whoever shot Willie."

Lumpy turned around, empty coffee cup dangling beside his leg.

Lumpy turned back to the coffeemaker and grabbed the carafe, putting it down before he could refill his cup. "If something comes up that I can help on the sly, I will," he said over his shoulder. "But it's strictly unofficial."

Manny nodded. "Thanks."

"Unlike the official bitch they pitched to your senior agent in charge."

"So I can expect the SAC to chew my ass as soon as I hit the office?" But Manny already knew the answer: "Hard Ass Harris" would salivate with the opportunity to chew Manny's butt again. "Last time I couldn't sit for a week."

Lumpy nodded. "I wouldn't answer any cell phone calls either."

CHAPTER 24

Manny timed his drive to Rapid City to coincide with lunch break, and arrived at the FBI office while everyone, including Senior Agent in Charge Hard Ass Harris, was out of the office. Manny peeked inside before making his way to his office. He grabbed a stack of messages from his mailbox in passing and closed the door. The jeweler had called with price quotes on his and Clara's wedding rings. Clara had convinced them they should get married while they both had the courage to go through with it, while Manny was still in the "let's get an engagement ring first" mode.

He thumbed to the next message, where Queen City Motors in Spearfish had finished the front fender and quarter panel from where the tree had come out of nowhere in the city park to hit Clara's Cadillac. Manny hadn't thought at the time that he deserved Clara's wrath for wrecking her "baby," even though he was driving.

The last message was from Stumper LaPierre this morning,

and Manny cursed the secretary for not calling him. He snatched his cell phone from his pocket and dialed Stumper. "What we got?"

"First, how's Willie?"

"Not good. Sounds as if his fifty-fifty chance went south."

Manny imagined Stumper picking his teeth with his pocketknife. "The medical examiner completed the autopsy."

"Was he able to ID Sam?

Paper shuffling. "No. He hasn't received Sam's military record to compare X-rays and dental records yet, but he's got an expedited request in. Also, he sent DNA samples and toxicology to the FBI lab in Quantico with a 'hurry-the-hell-up note' as per Senior Special Agent Tanno."

"Oh that'll get quick action. Now give me the quick and dirty of what the ME did find."

Stumper shuffling papers. "No soot in the airway. Means Sam was dead at the time of the fire."

Someone else tried the outside office door and Manny paused until they gave up opening it and left.

"Sam had to be alive or else if he died of smoke inhalation, he would have sucked in soot," Stumper added.

"Not necessarily." Manny lowered his voice. "Soot isn't always present with burn victims. Anything else?"

"The ME left a note for you that Sam's hyoid bone was broken."

"Broken?" Manny sat down, thinking of the strangulation cases he had investigated where the U-shaped bone at the larynx had been snapped off, the only times he had seen such injuries. "A man passed out in bed—whether he died naturally or by smoke inhalation—doesn't get his hyoid bone broken unless . . ."

"Unless someone strangled Sam before the fire was set."

"Have to have been," Manny agreed. "Whether it was

Sam or not remains in the hands of the ME once he gets that information from the Marine Corps, and we get the tox report from Quantico. I think it's even more important that we talk with Itchy again."

"I just haven't had time to look for him," Stumper blurted out. "Between Della Night Tail bitching about Little Dave's still out catting around, to the two meth search warrants we served last night, I've been just a little tied up. But I put the word out on the moccasin telegraph to turn over every rock looking for him."

"Thanks."

"And one other thing, the son of that Beauchamp— Emile—called. Yesterday, which is like, last week in France with the time difference."

"Not quite." Manny jotted down Beauchamp's phone number and checked his watch: early evening in France. He had just enough time to call and make his escape before the office people returned.

He punched in the international code and Emile Beauchamp's number. After a long interval, a man spoke French with a voice so deep Manny barely caught it. Manny identified himself.

"Ah, Agent Tanno." Gone was but the slightest accent, his English near perfect. "My father said you needed to speak with me about items he donated to the Crow Tribe for auction."

"Your father said you knew the items well."

An easy laugh crossed thousands of miles in a heartbeat. "I loved playing with the artifacts when I was a young boy. I would grab the knife—the one with the black stone imbedded in an antler horn—and stick it in my belt. You do not know how many forts I raided with that knife. Did you ever play Cowboys and Indians, Agent Tanno?"

"I guess I was always stuck playing the Indian."

"So it was with me." Beauchamp sounded as if he wanted

to play the Indian once again. "I guess it was the spirit of Blaise Beauchamp calling to me, because I felt alive when I played Indian. Sometimes, I just felt ghosts calling me."

You ought to come to Pine Ridge and play Indian. Give you a perspective other than a romanticized one of what it's like to be one. Wouldn't take you long and you'd be scrambling for a cowboy hat. "I sometimes feel the spirits calling me as well," he found himself telling this stranger, and he wished he had more time to talk with Beauchamp about his trapper relative who once lived among the Crow. "I understand your grandfather came by the artifacts unusually."

"Quite." Beauchamp paused, and Manny recognized a match being drawn across a striker, and could imagine Emile drawing on a cigarette, could almost see the gold cigarette holder. Manny instinctively patted his own pocket where he once stashed his smokes. "Blaise lived with a Crow woman in the Valley of the Giveaway, but left the area shortly before the Custer Massacre. Did you know a developer put forth plans to build a Little Big Horn theme park some years ago on the outskirts of Paris like the western theme park in Sweden? But it never got off the ground. What a shame."

"A shame indeed. People would have loved to see men dying and scalps being lifted all over the battlefield."

"Exactly!"

Manny breathed to gather his composure. "Blaise brought the artifacts with him when he left Crow country?"

"Some of the items," Emile explained. "When he left to return east, Blaise carried many of the Indian items. He formed a freighting company and went west many times, though never back to Crow country. Whenever he came back east, he had other relics with him. Sioux. Arapaho. Shoshone."

"And he never connected with his Crow woman again—Pretty Paw?"

"Most lived on reservations by the time he started his freight company."

Interned is how Wilson aptly termed it.

"He made a fortune in freight and moved back here to France. Does this answer your questions?"

"It helps," Manny said. "But I'm most interested in a journal your father included in the things Harlan White Bird was to auction off."

"The journal. Of course." Beauchamp pulled the receiver away and hacked a lingering smoker's cough, just like Manny was developing before he quit last year. When Emile stopped, there was another long pause. Another drag. "Blaise's Crow woman—Pretty Paw—would eventually marry a Crow man."

"Levi Star Dancer."

"Yes. She outlived Star Dancer by many years. Shortly before her death, she asked the Indian agent at Crow Agency to send Blaise some of her personal things from the time he lived in her father's lodge. Simple things her family was not interested in. Star Dancer's journal was among them."

"What was Blaise's reaction to receiving the relics?"

More coughing. "Blaise was dead by then, but she had no way of knowing. Grandfather tossed the things in a trunk with the other Indian relics Blaise had collected, and it was forgotten by most of my family."

"Except by you?"

Emile laughed. "I was a ten-year-old boy sitting beside a musty old trunk in his father's attic, reading a hundred-year-old journal. I imagined I was a Crow warrior, playing Cowboys and Indians. No, Agent Tanno, I did not forget about the relics."

"Tell me about the journal."

"The journal." Emile Beauchamp paused so long Manny feared the line had disconnected. When he began speaking

again, Emile measured every word so Manny could understand. "Levi Star Dancer witnessed his friend—White Crow—
killed by two Sioux warriors overlooking the Custer battlefield.
He was indisposed at the time of the attack on his friend. Running sickness he called it."

"Running sickness?"

"What you would call diarrhea. Star Dancer had suffered
from colonic problems ever since the Sioux warrior—the
same one he witnessed killing White Crow—gutshot him in a
fight years earlier. It is what killed Star Dancer so young."

"He wrote about this sickness in the journal?"

"He felt guilt that the sickness caused him to be off in the
grass the moment his friend was attacked and killed. He was
guilt ridden the rest of his life because he could not help his
friend."

"I can imagine."

"And there was more," Emile continued. "The Sioux that
killed White Crow next murdered his own friend."

"The other Sioux warrior?"

"Yes. That is what Star Dancer wrote in the journal."

Manny thought back to Wilson's display case, to the scalp
locks that seemed to talk to Manny. Somehow, he knew the
answer before asking it. "Did the journal name White Crow's
killer, the one that killed the other Sioux?"

"He wrote the man's name many times: Eagle Bull. Seems
like Star Dancer developed an obsession with him. He set out
to avenge his friend many times, but Pretty Paw always
stopped him."

Manny closed his eyes, letting Emile's revelation soak in.
Eagle Bull would have rode back into camp, victorious that he
had killed a Crow warrior. He would have hoisted the scalp
high for all the lodges to see. He would have showed his own
friend's scalp around, his war deeds claiming White Crow

had killed Eagle Bull's friend, and he avenged his death. He would have been an instant hero. His war deeds would be told for many generations; young boys would look up to him, try to emulate Eagle Bull's deeds.

"One thing I'm still curious about—why did Pretty Paw send her things to Blaise, when Star Dancer's own children may have wanted them?"

"Hollow Horn Star Dancer was Blaine's natural child," Emile said. "You'll read that in the journal as well."

"So Hollow Horn knew Blaise was his natural father?"

Static over the lines. "He did. But Blaise did not know she had been pregnant when he left Crow country, or he would have stayed and honored her, I believe. But Hollow Horn never wanted anything to do with his natural father. And kept Blaise a secret all his life. Only when I read the journal did I realize Blaise had a Crow son—long after Blaise died. This bothered my grandfather, and is why my father decided to donate the artifacts to the Crow Tribe."

Manny thanked Emile and disconnected, sitting quietly at his desk digesting what he'd just learned. The journal could harm Wilson Eagle Bull. His renowned reputation for decency, handed down through generations, would be tarnished. The sins of the father revisited the sons, or in Wilson's case, the sins of the great-grandfather. But would that be enough to want to kill someone over? Or have someone do the killing for him, like Carson Degas? As a Vietnam Marine, Wilson had surely seen—and done—his share of killing. Perhaps one more would make little difference. Perhaps this was the real Eagle Bull curse: treachery.

And the journal revealed the half-French child Hollow Horn. Levi Star Dancer and Pretty Paw had kept the family secret. Such a child from a Crow woman and French trapper would prove Chenoa hadn't the Crow purity she claimed.

Had Chenoa found out who had the journal and arranged to have someone steal it back? Or was the information contained so damning that she arranged for Sergeant Tess's ammunition to be switched to prevent Harlan from telling the world what it contained? Or was Harlan putting the bite on her, receiving periodic blackmail money?

Sampson Star Dancer had been an unexpected iron bar jammed in the cog of whoever wanted the journal's secrets to remain so. Sam had read it. Sam could tell the world what it contained. And someone had strangled a man presumed to be Sam in his ramshackle house before setting fire to it.

A door slammed outside Manny's office and he peeked out. Hard Ass Harris walked to the coffee station and grabbed the pot in passing as he headed for the watercooler. Manny eased his door closed as he flattened himself against the wall and silently made his way to the front door, escape just feet away. His cell phone beeped a message. The SAC spun around, eyes wide, a slight grin widening across his face.

"Just the man I want so see."

Manny dropped his head and started for the ass chewing, and checked his message from Clara just before he closed Hard Ass's door: "Get to the hospital ASAP."

CHAPTER 25

Pretty Paw dabbed sweat from her husband's forehead with her apron. Levi forced a smile. "*Aho.*" Thanks.

With one hand Hollow Horn squeezed his father's hand, the other wiping tears from his eyes with his shirtsleeve. The boy had just turned ten, yet he was much older, having seen death many times before. Hollow Horn turned away, and Levi knew his son didn't want his father's last image of his son to be crying. Levi painfully sat a little higher on the pillow. He brought Hollow Horn's hand to his parched and cracked lips and kissed the back of the boy's hand. Even that slight movement brought pain shooting through his gut and he slid lower, flatter on the bed.

"Lay there," Pretty Paw scolded him. "The sacred man is coming . . ."

Levi laughed, and he was rewarded with an intense pain that shot clear through his gut. "Can't you leave me and my *baachilape* in peace, woman." Levi knew that inner person that always dwelled within him, his constant companion, perched on the end of the bed. His *baachilape* would be with him when he traveled to the *Ammilliwaxpe,* west where the sun sets, west where the dead have gone. West where First Maker waited for him.

Pretty Paw's sobs brought him around, and he patted her hand. "Even on the other side there are homes. I will be all right."

"Lay there quiet."

"And linger another hour?" Pain shot through Levi anew, pinning him to the feather-ticking mattress soaked with sweat from hours of agony.

His breathing came in gasps now, and sweat stung his eyes as he forced them to remain open, wanting to see his family to the end, wanting to tell the Old Ones what a blessing they had been his entire life.

Pretty Paw laid a wet rag across his head, but he brushed it away. "The journal," he said to Hollow Horn. "Get it for me."

Hollow Horn grabbed Levi's possible bag from where it hung from antelope horns beside the fireplace mantel and withdrew the journal. He held it away in front of him as if, by bringing it close, some terrible affliction would consume him. Levi tried untying the thong holding the journal closed, but dropped it. He moaned in pain, and Pretty Paw untied it and took out the journal. Levi flipped to the middle pages and grabbed a stack of folded-up papers and handed it to Hollow Horn. "These are land deeds, and one day they will make a difference to our clan."

Hollow Horn clutched them close and backed away as if

the deeds were deeds to a gold mine. "I will keep them safe until your return."

Levi nodded his approval and turned to Pretty Paw. "A pencil. Please."

She reached behind his ear and grabbed a stub with just enough lead left for one entry. "What will you write, my husband?" Her sobs drowned out Levi's grated breathing. "If you stay with us, I'll let you teach me the White man's words."

Levi smiled.

"I promise I will learn."

"I do not have time." He patted her hand again. "The One Who Is Not Here awaits me on the other side."

Pretty Paw stroked Levi's head. "Do you not think the Old Ones will forgive you if you speak White Crow's name just this once?"

He shook his head; he dared not speak, his strength was fading so quickly. He had just enough strength to wet the pencil with his tongue and make a final entry before leaving to meet White Crow, his final entry cursing *Eagle Bull*.

CHAPTER 26

The elevator thumbed its nose at Manny, taunting him, as it rode slow enough for a second chorus of "God Rest Ye Merry Gentlemen." Christmas music in June made no sense to Manny, and he sure as hell didn't feel merry. Clara's text to get to the hospital had betrayed Manny as he tried sneaking past Hard Ass Harris, and Manny had been brought into his office for a closed-door session. The senior agent in charge had grilled him about his questioning of Wilson Eagle Bull. The bureau, Manny had reminded him, often stepped on toes during the course of an investigation. Manny just had to convince him toe flattening was needed in this case, and he was grateful Hard Ass had let him off with just a brief ass nipping.

He slapped the button for the fifth floor as if doing so would make the elevator go faster. "Come right to ICU," Clara had texted again. Manny leaned his head against the elevator and closed his eyes, praying Willie's condition had improved. He became aware of gears whining, of the elevator shaking ever so slightly as it crept upward, of the odor he had not noticed before. *The odor of death?* Manny shook his head to clear it. No, this was the odor of a hundred people riding the elevator today, and he had newfound respect for wee people riding elevators with smelly, gassy people.

The tiny bell brought him off the wall and he poised, the doors remaining closed long enough that Manny felt the taunt as if the machine fueled his anxiety. When it finally opened, Manny squeezed through before the doors fully opened and ran down the hall. He passed the nurse's station, grateful the bulldog-jawed biddy that had kicked him out before was not on scowling at him from behind her magazine. The duty nurse gave Manny a curious look before she went back to charting.

Clara met Manny at Willie's room and stepped into the hall, closing the door after her. She hooked her arm in his and led him to the waiting room.

"Willie's come out of it and he wants to talk with you."

"That's great." Manny turned to Willie's room, but Clara held him back.

"He's come out of it long enough to make a declaration."

"Declaration?" Manny struggled to make meaning out of it. "Declaration of what?"

Clara's mouth turned down and she ran her sleeve over her eyes. "His dying declaration. At least that's what Lumpy called it."

Dying declaration. Then Willie thinks that his death is imminent. "Dying? I thought the doctors drained the fluid in his lungs?"

"They did," Clara muffled through her hand covering her mouth. She turned back, eyes red, regaining her composure. *At least one of us has it under control.* "He developed pneumonia, and the medication's not working."

"What do the doctors say? He's not going to die?"

Clara squeezed Manny's arm. "What's important is that Willie thinks so. He's lucid enough that he ordered the nurses to take the feeding tube out of his stomach. He's given up."

Manny patted his back pocket for his bandanna, anticipating his condition when he talked with Willie. If Willie intended making a dying declaration, Manny intended holding it together long enough to record it and convict the SOB that shot him.

Manny eased the door open, and Doreen stood from the chair beside the bed. She glared at Manny as she brushed past him. "He wants to talk with you alone."

"I understand." What Manny understood was that Willie was about to make his way to the Wanagi Tacna, and he didn't want to travel the Spirit Road alone.

"Hell of a predicament I got myself into this time."

Manny barely made out Willie's whisper, and pulled a chair close. Willie's heavy eyes, red and bleary, found Manny. He turned away for a heartbeat, breathing to control himself. He needed to maintain composure in order to get through this, but it was difficult for Manny to see his friend's sallow, drooping cheeks. Willie had lost twenty pounds in the few days since the shooting despite the feeding tube, and Manny wouldn't have known him in the dark.

"Doubt if I'll get a chance to top this." Willie coughed violently. Manny grabbed the call button but Willie waved his hand away.

"I'm all right for now." Spittle dripped from one side of Willie's mouth, and Manny dabbed it with a towel draped over the bed stand.

Manny patted Willie's cold, clammy, fragile hand, Manny's palm resting on the IV tube sticking out. He never thought he'd ever see his friend this fragile.

"I need to make a statement."

"You of all people know Lakota tradition," Manny said. "First we jaw a little before getting down to business."

Willie's eyes closed, and Manny's heart jumped. He couldn't tell if Willie was breathing, and only the steady beeping of the monitor above him showed he was still living. "I got no time to jaw," he said at last. He looked around the room as if seeing it for the first time, and his eyes met Manny's. "I need to make a statement. For court. When you catch the bastard."

"There'll be time enough for that when you get up on your feet."

"I won't be around to make a court appearance." He lapsed into another coughing fit, and Manny held the towel under Willie's chin. He slumped back onto the pillow, his breaths coming in wheezing gasps. "You need to get this asshole. Before he kills someone else."

Manny suddenly became very proud of his protégé—putting others ahead of himself. With fortitude like that, the Old Ones would be proud of Willie. "Of course."

Manny grabbed his notebook and pocket recorder from his briefcase. Although he rarely needed notes, this was different. These would be Willie's final words, used to catch and convict the shooter.

"I spotted Degas coming out of Wilson's barn in that big Dodge dually. I didn't . . ." He started coughing, chunks of green spitting onto his bedsheets, and Manny grabbed for the call button. Once again, Willie stopped him. "I don't want that female drill instructor coming in here and kicking you out."

"She's not on duty."

"She's always on duty." Willie smiled for the first time, and continued. "I learned Degas was working for the Eagle Bull Ranch and waited until I saw some activity down at the bunkhouse." Willie sputtered, coughing. Manny grabbed for a metal pan beside the bed. Willie spit phlegm into it and wiped his mouth with his hand.

"I put the binos on them. Cubby Iron Cloud was riding in the passenger seat." Willie breathed, rasping breaths coming hard. "They got to within a hundred yards of where I was hidden and turned around. Like he forgot something in the barn."

Manny wrote legibly. *For court*. "What did they do then?"

Willie closed his eyes. "They went back to the bunkhouse and parked. I was sure they didn't spot me, but I'd been sitting there all night waiting for Degas; I was running out of gas myself. I decided to drive in there. Talk with Degas. Arrest him if I could."

Manny started to speak, but Willie interrupted. "I know what you and Chief Looks Twice said about confronting him alone. I messed up." His eyes closed, and Manny quickly wrote what he had just told him. Willie remained motionless and Manny nudged his arm. Willie opened his eyes.

"I'm not sure what happened then."

"Wilson's foreman said the ranch hands surrounded you."

Willie nodded. "That's right. They started pushing me around when I told them I needed to talk with Degas."

Manny wrote quickly. "And Cubby?"

Willie shook his head. "Don't know. I didn't see him after that time riding in Degas's truck."

Manny waited until Willie found the strength to continue. "After they let me go, I took off down Wilson's driveway. Got a quarter mile when I saw Degas was parked across the road. Hood open. I didn't know it was him at the time as it was a different truck than he drove earlier. I stopped. Thought someone had problems. But it was him."

Willie slumped back on his pillow and motioned for the

water glass. Manny held it up and Willie sipped through the straw. "He was friendly enough. At first. He said he'd come into the police station for an interview. But wanted to know what I wanted him for. I said he was a suspect in Harlan's death. At the reenactment.

"He laughed. Said he wasn't there. Said he was in jail in Hardin when Harlan was shot. I told him we had him on a camcorder swapping ammo."

Manny flipped the page and finished writing what Willie had told him. "Maybe you ought to rest a bit . . ."

"I got no time," Willie sputtered. "Listen, Degas started getting real agitated when I said we had proof he was in Harlan's tent. He demanded who else knew. He was especially interested if you knew about it."

"What did you tell him?"

Willie motioned for another sip of ice water. "I didn't. I kept quiet. That's when he pulled that gun from the small of his back. I knew Degas intended killing me," Willie said, opening his eyes and staring at the ceiling. "I could see it in those black eyes of his. Heartless eyes. I'm not ashamed to say he scared the hell out of me."

Willie gasped, wincing in pain, shallow breaths coming in spurts. "He wanted to toy with me. Like a wildcat with a field mouse. A big, mean cat. I talked to him. Tried to distract him. Thought if I got him to talking I could pull my own gun."

Manny wrote, aware Willie's words were coming at more effort.

"I got him to talk. Asked him why he switched that ammo that killed Harlan. Why he killed Sampson Star Dancer. He got madder 'n hell. Shouted. Demanded to know who else knew about them. I told him you did. And that you kept the tape with you all the time."

Even with Willie staring down the barrel of a gun, he kept his wits. "So he'd come hunting me up?"

"Sorry," Willie gasped. "But I knew he'd have to come after you. And when he did, you'd get him. Sorry."

Manny patted Willie's arm. "You did good. He will come after me. And when he does, I'll be ready. What happened then?"

"That's when I saw my chance. I sprang for him. Just as the gun went off, I landed a right cross on his chin. We went down in a heap."

Manny wrote, imagining Degas would be sporting a swollen jaw, or worse, broken, given Willie's strength. At least up until he came to call ICU his last home.

"I landed on my back. Tried to get up," Willie gasped, and Manny wiped spittle from his chin. "But it was like I was paralyzed. Couldn't move. But at least Degas's jaw was at an odd angle. I knew I done damage. He had a hard time talking. But he got up. Asked again what you knew about Harlan and Sam."

"And you said?"

" 'Stuff it in your ass.' That's when he pressed the gun to my chest and touched off a round."

Manny wrote, watching Willie out of one eye. "Where was Wilson's other ranch hands all this time?"

Willie shrugged, and he winced in pain. "I'm sure we were too far away from the house for them to have heard. It was just me and that son of a bitch on the road. He stood over me for the longest time. I kept my eyes closed. Finally heard him moving off. He thought I was dead. And you know the funny thing?"

"What?"

"I had a vision. Right there on Eagle Bull land I had a

vision. I was almost sorry the cavalry arrived and carted me off."

Willie's eyes fluttered and Manny was quick to keep him talking. "What was the vision?"

Willie's yellowed eyes focused on Manny. "You know that's a private matter. You know I can't tell you."

Manny nodded.

"Now let me sign. While I can. You're my witness."

Manny held the statement up in front of him, his fingers wrapped around the pen, his signature little more than a scribble. He dropped back onto the pillow. "That will stand up in court, won't it?"

"It would, but we won't need it." Manny tried sounding confidant, but anger replaced his deep sadness. For once, he did his best to clear his mind, to learn if Willie would live or travel south along the Milky Way. *What the hell good are visions if they won't come when you need them?* "This is no dying declaration."

"It is."

"Bullshit. You got too much to live for."

Willie laughed, but a coughing fit overcame him and Manny held the pan for him to spit phlegm. A large piece cascaded off the side and dropped onto the floor with a dull smacking noise.

"What do I got for me here?"

"Doreen for one."

A faint smile crossed Willie's face. "Who, if I pull out of this, will leave me."

Manny glanced at the window as Clara talked with Doreen just outside the door. "I'm certain when you finally make the break from this place, Doreen will be there for you."

Willie started coughing, his shoulders shaking violently, his IV popping out of his arm. Manny hit the call button and the charge nurse burst through the door just ahead of Doreen. The nurse started rethreading the IV tube. "He needs rest," she ordered.

"Of course." Manny met Doreen's glare for a brief moment before he turned back to Willie a last time before leaving. His coughing had stopped and he lay motionless on the pillow, eyes closed, breaths little more than shallow gasps.

The beeping of the monitor went steady, and the nurse yelled "Code Blue." She pushed Manny and Doreen out the door and out of the way of the Code Team rushing inside pushing a medical cart.

Manny stared after the closed door until Clara took hold of his arm and led him toward the waiting room.

>‹›‹›‹

"If—and this is a big if," Clara said, "if Willie pulls through this, Doreen is resigned to stick with her man."

Manny dried his face and neck with his snotty bandanna. He stuck it in his overnight bag and grabbed a fresh one. The Code Team had kick-started Willie's heart that stopped just now. They were uncertain if they could do it again. "Doreen will stay with him even if Willie remains with the tribal police? Why didn't she tell Willie that while he could understand her?"

Clara shrugged and sipped her tea. "She's not any happier with his choice of profession than I am with yours, but at least she realizes that Willie can't get police work out of his blood."

"So she didn't suggest he take a job as a funeral director?"

Clara laughed and scooted closer to Manny on the couch. "No. But I convinced her when Willie pulls through this to sit down and talk every night with him. Like we should be doing."

"About what?"

She elbowed him and massaged her ring finger. "About the wedding. Or did you forget so soon?"

Manny forced a smile. He had found scarce little to smile about lately. He zipped his overnight bag shut. "How can I forget that?"

He kissed Clara as he started out the door for the airport, making a mental note to have Lumpy call regional hospitals for anyone matching Degas's description coming in with a broken jaw. And for Lumpy to hunt up Cubby Iron Cloud if he's still on Pine Ridge.

CHAPTER 27

Even before the charter plane's prop stopped washing hot air over the Beechcraft, Stumper LaPierre was running across the Billings Airport tarmac. He held his cowboy hat on as he grabbed Manny's bag with his other hand. "In answer to your question, we found Cubby. But he's not under arrest."

Stumper had called Manny while the plane was still in the air to tell him he'd located Cubby and was bringing him in for another interview. "But you know where we can put the grab on him?"

Stumper nodded. "He came into the police department on his own. He's waiting for your bright smile."

"Is he still going to be there when we arrive?"

Stumper shrugged. "Let's hope so."

On the drive to Crow Agency, Manny filled Stumper in about the shooting and about Willie's condition. "Willie said he landed a right flush on Degas's jaw. As strong as Willie was . . ." Manny caught himself. "As strong as he is, we put a

BOLO out at hospitals for someone coming in looking like a range bull had just kicked the shit out of him."

"What's the odds that Degas will learn that Willie's still alive? What if he makes an appearance to Rapid City Regional to finish what he started?"

"I thought of that, too. Lumpy's making arrangements for round-the-clock protection, in case Degas comes visiting."

"Thought he wouldn't help?"

Manny wanted to say something sarcastic about Lumpy. But all he had was gratitude for him making arrangements to protect Willie. "He got volunteers to stand watch at Willie's door. On the sly. If the tribal council found out Lumpy disobeyed orders, it'd be Katy bar the door."

"I hear you there," Stumper said as he pulled out of the airport parking lot. "You got Wilson Eagle Bull there, I got Chenoa Iron Cloud making things miserable here at Crow Agency."

"And tell me you've found Itchy."

Stumper shook his head. He steered with his elbows as he stuffed his lip with Copenhagen. "Not yet."

"You know how important he may be?" Manny snapped. "Itchy's bound to know something about Degas, hanging around with Sam and Harlan like he did."

Stumper threw up his hands. "Give me a damned break. Della Night Tail's been on my ass about Dave 'teepee-creeping' again. She pitched a bitch to Chief Deer Slayer, and I had to put another meth search warrant on the back burner while I looked for him." Stumper glared at Manny. "I'm doing the best I can."

Many sat back in the seat and rubbed his eyes, convinced Stumper was doing all he could with the time he had. "I apologize. I know you're doing what you can to find Itchy."

Stumper looked sideways at Manny and smiled. "That an official apology?"

"Don't push your luck," Manny answered. "It's the only one you're going to get today." Thinking of Willie's condition lying in ICU had clouded Manny's rational thinking, a cloud he didn't need right now if he wanted to find Willie's shooter.

They pulled into the justice building at Crow Agency. Cubby's shiny bright red Lincoln truck waited in front. Stumper led Manny past the dispatch and into the interview room. He put up the INTERVIEW IN PROGRESS sign outside both doors and shut them.

Cubby sat with his ostrich boots propped up on the table, Stetson pushed back on his head, cigarette dangling out of his mouth. Manny eyed the smoke. "Put it out, please."

Cubby smiled. "I talk better with a smoke."

"It's just that I quit last year and would love to start again. Better to get rid of the temptation."

Cubby eyed him suspiciously, but he came up with no argument for Manny. He took a last drag and dropped it into a Pepsi can. "Stumper tells me you want to find out my relation with Carson Degas?"

Manny nodded and grabbed his pocket notebook as if he intended referring to nonexistent notes. It had been three hours since Stumper called and said he'd located Cubby, three hours that he'd had to anticipate questions and formulate lies. Manny had had the three hours flight time to rehearse what he intended asking Cubby. A draw. "Where do you know Degas from?"

"The ranch, of course. He's one hell of a horse wrangler. Knows horseflesh better than anyone I've worked with." When Manny said nothing, Cubby continued. "We swap stud service. He brings his studs up here, or we ship to Pine Ridge."

"And what do you swap?"

"You've never worked a ranch, have you?"

"I have." Growing up, he had hired out to ranches skirting

the Badlands, haying, branding, everything else a laborer does on a working cattle ranch. "But I'm not intimate with stud service."

Cubby chuckled. "Then you got to take some Viagra or something." When Manny and Stumper failed to laugh, Cubby continued. "We've got four champion Black White-Faced bulls that the Eagle Bull Ranch uses in stud, and he has registered Appaloosa and paint stallions we use. Makes for a handy swap."

"So you spend a good deal of time with Degas?"

Cubby paused, sensing a trap yet not sure how Manny would spring it. "I do, but it's strictly business."

"Shooting a policeman business?"

Cubby shook his head. "I heard about that two nights ago. Damned shame."

"Who'd you hear about the shooting from? Degas?"

Cubby paused, one foot tapping the floor, eyes darting to the door. "I didn't see Carson two nights ago. I stayed at Wilson's that night. First I knew a cop had been ventilated down the road is when Harvey came into the bunkhouse and told me. Damned shame he's going to die."

"He's not." Manny hoped he sounded convincing, as he wasn't certain himself if Willie would pull through. "The tribal policeman—Officer With Horn—is recovering fine."

Cubby sat silent for long moments, looking at the floor. He rubbed his palms against his jeans and started to grab a smoke from his pocket when he put the pack back. "He's going to pull through? That's great."

Manny nodded. "He recalls a fight with Degas, and Degas shooting him."

"A shame," Cubby repeated, avoiding looking at either Manny or Stumper.

"And he remembers you riding with Degas an hour before he was shot."

Cubby looked to Stumper.

"Maybe you went back to the bunkhouse when Degas turned around on the road," Manny pressed. "Maybe you convinced the other ranch hands to stay away from where you knew Degas intended stopping Willie."

Cubby stood, knocking his chair over as he started for the door. "I'm outta here. Last thing I need is to be accused of helping someone shoot a cop."

Cubby started for the door, but Stumper moved to block it. Cubby glared at him, spittle flying out of his mouth, fists clenching. "Get outta my way if you want to keep your job!"

Manny stood. "Sit back down."

Cubby started around Stumper. Although Cubby had him by fifty pounds, the smaller man grabbed Cubby's shirtfront and spun him around. He shoved him into a chair and stood over him.

"I'll make a call to the tribal chairwoman and you can kiss your job good-bye, little man."

Stumper smiled down at him. "My job is the only thing that prevents me from stomping your fat ass. Now, you get me fired, and I got no reason for restraint. No reason not to wait for you some dark night when you least expect it."

Manny leaned over the conference table. "And if I add accessory to attempted homicide, Cubby, you'll be looking over your shoulder every time you go to the prison shower room."

Cubby's lips quivered, and his foot tapped incessantly. He looked first to Manny, then to Stumper, rubbing his hands together. "I told you guys all I know about the shooting. I didn't know he'd shot your officer."

"But you were with him that morning. At about the time of the shooting."

Cubby nodded. "I jumped in when he said he was driving into Pine Ridge to mail a package, but he forgot it. He turned and dropped me off at the bunkhouse while he grabbed the package. He was gone by the time I was done."

"How long was he gone?"

"Four beers."

"How long's that?"

Cubby shrugged. "As long as it took me to knock back four cold ones from the cooler he always keeps in the bunkhouse. When he came back, we took off for Gordon and some serious drinking."

Stumper nodded. "You must have heard gunshots? Willie was shot"—he turned to Manny—"a half mile from there?"

Manny nodded.

Cubby shook his head. "Wilson's bunkhouse has been standing for a hundred years. It's built like a fortress. I wouldn't have heard the shots if it had been outside the front door."

"Why Gordon?" Manny asked.

Cubby shrugged. "Closest place to drink."

"But if you had beer in the cooler, why go to Gordon?"

Cubby looked away.

"Why!" Manny said, pulling up a chair and sitting nearly on top of Cubby. "I'll find out with a few phone calls. Now, why Gordon, or do we hook you up as an accessory?"

Cubby slumped in his chair. "When he came back, his jaw looked like hell, all swollen. He could barely talk. Said after he came back from the post office he was leading a mare into another pasture before we lit out, and she kicked him in the jaw. Looked like it was broke, so I drove him to the ER in Gordon."

Stumper came off the wall and leaned over, close to Cubby. "Didn't that seem odd—driving to Nebraska when Pine Ridge and Hot Springs hospitals are closer?"

Cubby shrugged. "All I know is he needed a little TLC from the ER in Gordon, and a little CLC from the bar afterward."

CHAPTER 28

Manny herded the Oldsmobile down the long driveway behind a stream of cars on their way to Sampson's memorial service. He wished he had gotten the air conditioner fixed, and rolled the window up against the dust settling inside the car. He swiped at the sweat running down his forehead stinging his eyes, obscuring his vision as he parked beside a line of other cars and walked toward the ranch house. Chenoa stood bent over tables as she arranged buckets of food for the mourners. Jamie Hawk walked behind her easily carrying two twenty-gallon water bottles in each hand. He glared at Manny as he set the bottles on the table. He bent and whispered to Chenoa. She nodded, and the big man disappeared into the house. She stood and smoothed her dress as she waited for Manny to approach.

"Your brother must have had a lot of friends." Manny jerked his thumb over his shoulder at the cars lining both sides of the driveway, at elders painfully and slowly climbing out of cars, at kids bounding ahead of their parents, all here to send Sampson Star Dancer off. They milled around the porch, waiting for direction, when Wilson Eagle Bull emerged from the house. His gaze fell on Manny for a brief moment before turning to the crowd, his arms crossed, looking down as if he were going to give a campaign speech. Beaded lizard hair ties held his salt-and-pepper hair that lay on his chest. A bone choker of red and white and black dyed porcupine quills circled his thick neck and set off his starched pleated pearl shirt. He turned to the crowd and led them around back of the house to the Star Dancer family cemetery like a Pied Piper of the dead.

"You here for the funeral?" Chenoa was dressed more for a Montana Tourism shoot than her brother's funeral. Beaded geometric designs adorned her muslin dress, and her multicolored flared top was open to reveal more cleavage than a mourner should be allowed. Manny looked away as she bent over the table arranging food bowls. A shallow breath of wind caught her cologne and drifted past Manny. He swallowed, fighting urges that, as he approached middle age, still ran strong. Feelings earmarked for Clara.

"You here for the funeral or the food?" She motioned to the bowls on the table, to the stack of plates adorned with the Star Dancer logo, to neatly arranged dinnerware, all looking like she'd prepped for a state dinner.

"Fact is, I'm hungrier than a woodpecker in a steel mill."

"You don't look hungry."

Manny patted his stomach. "This is just my disguise."

"Well, I'm sure you didn't come all the way out here to snack. Have you caught Sam's killer yet?"

"Not yet. But I'm working on it."

"Then I don't want you here, Agent Tanno."

"Because I haven't found Sam's killer yet, or because I came down hard on Cubby yesterday?"

Chenoa nodded to Cubby following Wilson around back to the cemetery. "Got nothing to do with my husband. I just want some answers about Sam's death, and if you're here you're not looking for them."

"I'm here for answers." Manny took out his pocket note-book and flipped pages.

Chenoa stopped arranging the food buckets and squared up to Manny. "What answers?"

"About Sam's death?"

"I got no answers."

Manny ignored her and flipped pages as if he had written questions. "Like where was Cubby when Sam's house was torched?"

"How should I know?"

"As owner of this ranch, I'd think you'd know the where-abouts of all your ranch hands. Especially your husband."

She glanced at Cubby as he reemerged from around the back of the house and disappeared inside. "Reality's the only obstacle to true happiness. My reality of happiness with my husband went south about the time his belly did. But he comes and goes as he pleases." She stepped back as if realizing Manny's question for the first time. "Surely you don't suspect Cubby?"

Manny gave her the headline version of Cubby riding with Degas in Pine Ridge the morning Willie was shot, and how Cubby had lied about it initially. "I understand the ranch would run even smoother with Sam out of the way. When I connect the dots, Cubby's always there."

Chenoa lowered her voice. "Back when Cubby was a rodeo champ and competing around the region, I competed in bogus beauty contests . . ."

"Stumper tells me those bogus contests are what landed you a lucrative Montana Tourism contract years ago."

"Do I look like I need the money?" She laughed, waving

her hand around Star Dancer pastures visible for miles. "When Cubby and I competed in the same circuits, we grew close. Very close." She looked out into the field in back of the house with a faraway look. "He was something back then, sitting a bull for a full eight seconds, or riding saddle bronc without losing even his hat." She turned back to Manny. "He cut a dashing figure back then, with his broad shoulders and slim hips that swaggered when he walked. Yeah, we grew close, and I've grown to know him like I know myself. I can tell you, Cubby had nothing to do with the fire."

Manny shrugged and flipped a notebook page. "Just to satisfy my curiosity, where was he at the time of the fire?"

"Who knows? I run the ranch: hire and fire hands, pay bills, oversee investments in the Star Dancer name. Cubby runs the horse and cow part of our operation, and I don't see him much these days. I'm plenty busy with other things."

As if to punctuate her statement, Wilson Eagle Bull walked from in back of the house and smiled at Chenoa before leading more mourners around back. She caught Manny looking after Wilson. "And no matter what you think, Cubby and I both loved Sam."

"You're mighty fast to bury your brother when we don't have positive confirmation it was him in that house fire."

Chenoa turned to the tables and began taping plastic tablecloths down against the strong wind. "I said I loved my brother. I didn't say I was overly upset by his death. Burning up in that house was a lot quicker death than him drowning in the bottle."

"That's pretty cold."

Chenoa stood and faced Manny. Had another button came undone from her top, or was that Manny's imagination? He averted his eyes while she moved food buckets back onto the tablecloth. *Stalling.* "Look, Sam had a chance to walk the Red Road, same as the rest of us. Instead, he chose the Black Road, drinking and wasting the life the Creator gave him. I needed his signature on most things ranch-related. It was nearly impossible to find him when he was on a bender." Chenoa smoothed her skirt. "I know positive ID hasn't been made yet. But it's better to start the process to declare him dead now."

"What if it wasn't Sam?"

"Of course it was," she snapped.

"I don't think so," Manny lied. "Sam was a bona fide war hero . . ."

"What's that got to do with his death?"

Manny had called the medical examiner in Billings. The autopsy wouldn't be filed for another forty-eight hours, when Sam's military medical records would be sent from Kansas City. Manny had a little wiggle room until Sam was identified. "His wounds." Manny flipped pages as if he needed to refresh his memory. "He earned his last Purple Heart when he stepped on a Willie Pete," Manny repeated what the old vet in the Four Aces had told him. "Damned booby trap shattered his leg. Left him with a unique set of breaks the ME didn't see at autopsy."

Chenoa walked around the table, her face red. She stood nose-to-nose with him, her jaw tightening, pointing to the driveway leading out of the ranch. "I want you out there finding my brother's killer instead of wasting time badgering me."

Manny nodded to the ranch house. Jamie and Cubby stood looking at them. "No matter how close to home it gets?"

"I want you off my property. Now!"

She turned and stormed into the house, slamming the door. Manny waited until she'd disappeared, waited until he was sure Jamie Hawk wasn't rushing out of the house with bad intentions, before he turned to his car.

"Agent Tanno." Wilson brushed past Mary Slagy carrying pots of food to the table. Manny stopped and waited for him. "Chenoa's understandably upset over Sam's death. Don't hold it against her."

"Then she mentioned the victim might not be him?"

Wilson turned away.

"I thought you'd be happy."

Wilson adjusted his turquoise bolo tie. "How so?"

"You and he were friends."

"I was just his company commander."

"I saw a picture of you and Sam taken when you were together in Vietnam. You looked closer than mere CO and grunt."

Wilson looked to a butte to the east as if gathering courage to talk about the war. "Sam was the best tunnel rat we had. Nothing scared that little bastard. I was grateful to have someone like Lance Corporal Star Dancer under me."

"Why didn't you mention this before?"

"I didn't think it was relevant." Wilson rubbed his forehead and looked to that same butte. "Sam and I got together after we'd rotated back to the world after 'Nam. In fact, he introduced me to Chenoa."

Manny smiled. "Sam must have been an unlikely matchmaker."

The hair ties bounced on his chest as Wilson turned around and sat on the hood of the Oldsmobile. "Not like that. Chenoa was involved in tribal politics, and involved in the National Congress of American Indians. I'd just been appointed Fifth Member of the Pine Ridge Tribal Council, and Chenoa thought I'd be a good contact person there." He smiled. "Sam figured we'd get along, her fighting for the rights of her people here at Crow Agency, me on Pine Ridge."

"Didn't hurt that she's as beautiful as she is?"

"She was married."

"And still is."

Wilson's face flushed, and he turned away.

"Look, Wilson, I'm not here as moral arbitrator, or to expose anyone's indiscretions. I'm here to find out who killed Harlan White Bird and Sam. And to find Carson Degas for shooting Officer With Horn."

Wilson turned back. His brows came together and seemed to wrestle with his answer. "When I heard about your officer being shot, I asked the ranch hands what they knew. Harvey said Carson might have done the shooting, though Harvey had just a feeling."

"And you believe old Harv?"

Wilson nodded. "It took a lot for Harvey to suggest Carson. Harvey knows if it got back to Carson, that his life wouldn't be worth much. You know, the son of a bitch has been more trouble than he's worth."

"I heard he had a habit of finding trouble."

Wilson forced a laugh. "But nothing really serious. Nothing like shooting an officer. If he did. He'd go into Gordon or Hot Springs. Pick fights with cowboys, like it was his hobby or something. He'd get locked up and me or Harv would have to bail him out. He'd be good for a while, then all of a sudden, he'd get the call of the wild and go into town again and go ape-shit again."

Manny flipped his notebook open. "And where can I find him?"

"Wish I knew. I haven't heard from him since that morning your officer was shot."

"Any suggestions?"

Wilson stood from the hood of the car and brushed dust off his jeans. "He could be anywhere." He looked out to the pasture as if Degas lay in wait there. "Wish I could be more help. I'd like to get this cleared up before the election."

Manny nodded, studying Wilson for any signs of deception, any facial giveaways, any micro tics. He saw none. "Let's talk about your association with Sam a little more. I'm trying to get a handle on who he hung around with besides Harlan, who he might have talked to or seen before he died."

Wilson's mouth drooped, and a sadness overcame his normally vibrant eyes. "Sam was different when he came back from the war. We saw each other less and less when I came to Crow Agency on business. Sam would drink. Raise hell. When I entered politics, I knew I had to distance myself from him. I didn't need to be associated with a drunk and a troublemaker. As far as I know, Harlan and Itchy were his only friends."

Manny nodded to a yellow Cessna cabled to the ground in the flat pasture west of the house. Winds buffeted the wings with every gust and got the rudder kicking sideways. "Thought you drove here?"

Wilson shook his head. "I got a fund-raiser in Rapid City tonight so I thought I'd better fly." He smiled for the first time. "Helps me think, being up there alone. My vehicle of choice when I can." He turned back to Manny. "Sam was a good friend. Once."

"You think it was Sam in that fire?"

Wilson chin-pointed toward the ranch house. "Chenoa thinks it was. I got to respect her opinion."

Manny pocketed his notebook. "I may have more questions later." He turned to his car when Wilson stopped him.

"Have you got anywhere on Harlan's murder?"

"I can't tell you much. It's an open investigation."

"I just want to know if my horse wrangler is involved in that for certain, too."

Manny shrugged. "We'll know once we find Degas and I can interview him."

"You mean arrest him?"

Manny nodded.

"Can you at least tell me if you've located the journal?"

"Not yet."

"It must contain something important to have started these killings."

Manny turned and faced Wilson. "Levi Star Dancer's journal contains some . . . interesting things."

Wilson's eyes narrowed, and the veins at the side of his head started throbbing. "How could you know what the journal contains if you can't find it?"

"I talked with a man that read it."

"What man?"

"For now, just a man."

Wilson moved closer to Manny, looking down on him, an imposing figure, a figure used to having his way. "What did the journal have to say?"

"You don't have any idea?"

"None," Wilson answered, but he looked away and his voice wavered. Gone was the tone and timbre of the seasoned politician, replaced by a face as devoid of emotion and flat as the scalp locks in his glass display case. *He knows just what the journal contains.*

CHAPTER 29

As Manny topped the first tall hill east of the Star Dancer Ranch, his cell phone beeped. Lumpy had left a message to call and Manny hit speed dial.

"You took your sweet ass time getting back to me, Hotshot."

"Cell service is no better here than at Pine Ridge. What you got?"

"A letter from the Marine Corps for you that came here to Pine Ridge for some ungodly reason."

"I figured I'd be working there more than out of the Rapid City office. Certainly more than here at Crow Agency. Guess I was wrong."

"Marines probably want you to enlist." Lumpy laughed. "At your age, that'd be interesting."

Manny had sent a request to the Marines for service records on both Sam and Wilson. "What's it say?"

"How the hell should I know? I don't open other people's

mail. Haven't you heard, that's a federal offense? I do that and some hotshot FBI agent will have to spend more time here than I'd like."

"Just open it and read it to me."

Lumpy swore at the other end between paper rustling. "Cut my damned thumb opening the envelope."

"Just man up and tell me what it says."

After long moments Manny was certain Lumpy had fallen asleep. "Well, what's it say?"

"I'm still reading."

"Is English your second language? Tell me what it says."

"Looks like Sampson Star Dancer and Wilson enlisted in the Corps a month apart in 1967, and both went to boot camp in San Diego."

"They would, living in the western part of the country. What else?"

"Sam was shipped straight to 'Nam out of basic. 0311 it says."

Grunt. Manny found himself nodding. From what Reuben had told him, nearly every Marine coming out of boot camp went to 'Nam as infantry. Wilson had been one of those "nearlys."

"Wilson got selected for Officer Candidate School."

"And went straight to 'Nam right out of OCS I'd wager."

"Seems like it." Lumpy swore into the phone again, and Manny imagined him sucking blood from his thumb. "Wilson was assigned to Sam's rifle company right out of the chute. Looks like they served under a First Lieutenant Osmon."

"Any trouble with either of them?"

More rustling. "Just one speed bump."

"Is it bigger than a breadbox?"

"What?"

"Is this twenty questions? Just tell me what the hell their service records say."

"Okay." Lumpy dropped something, accompanied by another round of swearing. "Here's the skinny. This Osmon got the company shot up in some firefights. Testimony by Naval Intelligence was that Osmon was a real screwup. Had complaints up the ass from the Marines of Echo Company. Command did nothing about them. So it looks like someone solved the problem for them."

"How's that?"

"Someone fragged Osmon in the crapper."

"And Second Lieutenant Eagle Bull was next in line to lead the rifle company?"

"You guessed it," Lumpy answered.

"Was Wilson a suspect?"

"Doesn't look like it. Wilson and Sam corroborated each other's whereabouts—they were in a poker game at the time. Looks like they interviewed everyone in the company, but no one knew who lobbed a fragmentation grenade into the shitter while Osmon sat reading *Stars and Stripes.*"

"Killer ever caught?"

"Doesn't sound like it."

"Thanks," Manny said, then: "Anything new on Willie?"

Lumpy choked, and Manny imagined tears leaking from his bloodshot eyes. Just as they'd be if Manny was there with Willie all night. "They drained his lungs twice since you left. Sergeant Hollow Thunder's guarding Willie's room. I'm heading up to Rapid to spell him now. Good thing you took his dying declaration," Lumpy added and disconnected.

Manny looked at the dead cell phone for a moment before pocketing it. Had Second Lieutenant Eagle Bull fragged his own CO? Manny recalled what Emile Beauchamp said Levi

Star Dancer had written about Conte Eagle Bull killing his companion. Given the history of the Eagle Bulls, it wasn't a far stretch to imagine that Wilson had killed a fellow Marine, with the only other person knowing Wilson had lied being Sam, supposedly in a poker game with him. Dual alibis. Too pat.

And had Sam slipped far enough that he'd stooped to blackmailing Wilson on the eve of his senatorial election? The drive to drink caused men to do some desperate things.

As Manny's thumb poised to hit Stumper's speed dial, Manny prayed he'd have information that would allow him to leave Crow Agency and return to Willie's bedside.

CHAPTER 30

"We found Itchy." Stumper's voice rose an octave. "Finally."

"Good. Get him ready in the interview room and I'll be there . . ."

"I said we found him, but the only thing he's ready for is an autopsy. His own. We found Itchy deader'n shit."

Manny closed his eyes. A key witness—and the person who may have called Chenoa with the threat of the journal— was dead. "Give me the headline version."

"Surveillance cameras at the Little Big Horn Casino caught Itchy playing penny slots yesterday. He looked more nervous than a cat in a Chinese restaurant playing that machine, looking around constantly, like someone was after him."

"Sounds like the last time we spoke with him, climbing the walls, needing to score some crank."

"I thought of that." Clicking in the receiver, and Manny was certain Stumper had a toothpick jammed between his teeth. "But I looked at that surveillance tape until I was blue.

Itchy kept shelling in pennies, looking around like he expected someone. After about an hour of playing, he jerked around and said something to someone in back of him."

"Recognize who he was talking to?"

"Dead spot in their system. Anyways, Itchy left the pennies in the tray and ran out the door."

"Check with the security guards?"

"Think we fell off the turnip truck yesterday?" Stumper snapped. "Of course I checked with them. All they remember about the guy that Itchy met was that he was wearing a yellow hoodie and you couldn't see his face. That's it."

Manny leaned back in the seat, sweat rolling down his forehead, and he grabbed for his bandanna. He rubbed his eyes against a rising headache. "All right—where'd you find Itchy?"

"Moccasin Top found him under one of the bridges he slept under now and again."

"Natural? Awfully cold last night after the sun went down."

"Not unless you consider a hole in the back of his head big enough to put a pencil in natural."

Just what I needed, another body to extend my sentence to Crow Agency. "Got an estimate of the time of death?"

Stumper paused; the sound of paper shuffling made Manny's headache throb even louder. "Sometime yesterday, we're thinking. And we're basing a lot of that on the security camera catching Itchy running out of the casino."

"Tell me someone heard the shot. Saw a car. Saw Itchy."

Stumper laughed nervously. "The bridge is two miles from the nearest ranch. Six miles from Lodge Grass. No one we talked with heard a thing."

"How did Itchy get to the bridge?"

"What?"

"The bridge?" Manny repeated. "Itchy didn't drive. And Mr. Spock damned sure didn't beam him over there."

"Give me a break—I've been busier than a one-legged man in an ass kicking contest tracking a fresh shipment of meth that came in yesterday."

"Well, look into it when you get a chance. What was he wearing?"

"Itchy's usual dress rags—blue jeans with more holes than OJ's alibi, and holey tennis shoes that matched. And that filthy watch cap he always wore to give lice a covered home."

"Was what Itchy was wearing consistent with where you found him?"

Stumper paused again. "Shit!" he said at last. "His stocking cap was caked with dried leaves. Under the bridge is all dirt—there's no trees for miles."

Manny knew Stumper hadn't been a lawman long enough to develop his street eyes, seeing things other people didn't. "And I'll bet there's little blood at the scene?"

Stumper cursed again. "Way too little for a head wound."

Manny dabbed at the sweat on his face and neck, letting Stumper work it out for himself. "I think Itchy was killed someplace else. Stuffed under the bridge."

"I think you're right." Manny smiled, thinking how alike Stumper was to Willie, with gobs of confidence, yet willing to learn when the opportunity arose. As Stumper hung up, Manny leaned back and closed his eyes. Willie's image came through again, tubes stuck where they had no right to be, breaths coming in gurgling gasps, hanging on by a sinew. "Fight it, my friend," Manny breathed.

He reached in the backseat to the CDs that Willie had packed for their trip. Harlan White Bird's homicide had started Manny on a journey he hadn't wanted: working Crow Reservation for Harlan's killer, along with Sam's. And now Itchy's murder. It would be a matter of hours, perhaps minutes, before the Billings SAC would call him and assign him

Itchy's homicide as well. Unless Hard Ass Harris demanded Manny return to the Rapid City Field Office. Which was slim. He considered calling Hard Ass, but thought better: He could do little in Pine Ridge right now. His best shot at finding Degas was to remain on Crow Agency.

Manny needed relaxing music, and he rummaged through Willie's CDs. What he found was Willie's rock collection, and Manny loaded the first CD he grabbed: ZZ Top. He stuck it in the player hanging under the dash. Manny hadn't developed a taste for rock, but it did remind him of their trip from Pine Ridge to the reenactment, and Manny dearly wished he could turn the clock back a week.

He adjusted the volume, the heavy drumbeat reminding him of polka music. And of powwow drums. He closed his eyes and thought of Itchy. Where had he stayed these last days when he couldn't be found? With Cubby perhaps? Cubby didn't seem the benevolent type to let a druggie stay under his roof. Besides, he'd kicked Itchy out of the house years ago.

Manny thought that even Itchy didn't sleep under bridges unless he had no other place. He had crashed at Harlan's shop so many times, he could probably find it with his eyes swollen shut. But Stumper assured Manny that Harlan's building was sealed, with step-up patrols making security checks periodically. Still, Itchy had known the building, knew no one else would be inside, knowing there was a bunk with his bedbugs on it, waiting.

Manny turned the CD up and started for Lodge Grass, his heart only half into the investigation. Willie filled his thoughts, and he swore to Wakan Tanka and the God of the Jesus people that he'd get with Reuben when he got back to Pine Ridge and sweat and pray for Willie. If his friend hadn't already traveled along the Spirit Road.

CHAPTER 31

Manny squinted against the bright sun as he ducked under the crime scene tape. He reached above the door for the key and opened Harlan's shop. *So much for a secure building.*

By habit, he paused just inside the door, listening. A radio in a far room played country music, and a sparrow that had made its home in the auction barn chirped as if feeding young. Somewhere in the back of the shop a fan circulated air. Manny dropped into a crouch. An odor hung in the air, the odor of something he'd noticed before that couldn't place. He only knew the hairs on his neck stood at attention for a reason. He'd gotten his street degree picking up on things others didn't.

He duckwalked farther inside the building. He leaned back against one wall while his eyes adjusted to the darkness. He strained, but caught no further odor, no sound besides the chirping. Yet, he couldn't ignore his instinct, couldn't get it out of his mind that someone else was inside Harlan's shop. His hand fell onto his empty holster. He had taken off the gun in the car, and could envision it lying on the seat. Just where he didn't need it.

His hand ran along the wall and he found a light switch, but he waited, ears catching something besides the fan coming from the office. A light played off the walls, flickering on and off, casting delirious shadows through the blinds over the windows.

Manny rubbed his eyes, his vision slowly adjusting to the darkness as he struggled to remember the layout of the shop. He could go straight in and buttonhook to the right, giving him good coverage of Harlan's office.

Manny drew his legs under him and wiped the sweat from his palms. He breathed once and sprung, flattening when he got inside the room. Chenoa Iron Cloud screamed and papers flew into the air. She stumbled backward and ran into a file cabinet. She dropped her flashlight just as Manny tripped the light switch. Chenoa looked wide-eyed at him, caught in some act that Manny knew she'd try sweet talking her way out of.

"Agent Tanno?" Chenoa turned around, her hands behind her. She dropped some papers on the floor. "What are you doing here?"

"I'm conducting investigations into several homicides. I'd ask the same of you, since you have a memorial service to conduct."

"It's done." Chenoa smiled, and Manny got the feeling it was as phony as those tourism smiles. "Jamie and Wilson are handling things while I . . ."

"Mourn for Sam in Harlan's shop?"

"I don't have time for this." Chenoa brushed past Manny. He grabbed her arm and spun her around.

"Get the hell out of my way or I'll . . ."

"What? Call the BIA or tribal police? Tell them you got caught breaking into a crime scene? How about I make that call for you." Manny took out his cell and flipped it open. She reached out and wrapped her hand around his. Manny's eyes found hers, as thousands had been drawn in before by posters and tourism brochures. And her cologne, the same he'd recognized on entering Harlan's shop, the same at Sam's memorial service, wafted past his nose. "Don't embarrass me by doing that. I'll tell you what you want to know."

Manny closed his cell and stepped back. He didn't trust himself this close, and he brushed a Cheetos bag and candy wrappers off Harlan's desk before sitting on the edge. "Start by telling me how you got in."

"Same as you." She rolled Harlan's chair around and sat down, crossing her legs, the same dress she'd worn at Sam's memorial service riding over her knees. Manny looked away, and she smiled at his predicament. "We always knew Harlan kept his key above the door. Whenever I needed Sam to sign papers, I'd send Cubby over. If Harlan wasn't around, Cubby would grab the key and go inside. More often than not, Sam would be passed out in the spare room."

Manny gestured around the room, and to the papers that Chenoa had dropped when Manny surprised her. "But there's no papers for Sam to sign now, is there?"

Chenoa started to speak, but looked away.

"Maybe you were looking for something else. A journal perhaps? Maybe land deeds that were stuffed inside?"

"All right. I was looking for the journal. I'm convinced it was Itchy who called me offering to sell it."

"And you couldn't take a chance that he actually had the journal?"

She smiled, but her eyes darted around the room as if forming an escape plan. "Wilson told me you had talked with someone who had read the journal."

Manny nodded. "And you were interested in the journal."

She smoothed her dress. "What makes you say that?"

"Harlan kept a list of bidders, people who came into his auction barn prior to the sale. He might have been a slob, but he knew how to keep his business profitable. You came by two days before the sale by the looks of his sign-in book."

"So I came by. A lot of people came by."

"When I looked at Harlan's list, I saw the only thing you were interested in looking at was the journal."

"Nonsense. I was interested in the entire Beauchamp Collection. It's an amazing piece of history of the Star Dancer clan. Who better to have it? I'm certain if I pushed it, the courts would award it to me under NAGRA."

Under the Native American Graves Repatriation Act, relics and artifacts throughout the country were being returned to the rightful heirs. "But Pretty Paw gave the collection to the Beauchamps. You had no standing to get it returned through the courts. I'm sure Harlan told you the same thing when you confronted him about giving you the journal."

Chenoa stood, and the chair rolled back and banged into the wall. "He smiled when he told me to go ahead and take my case to court. I could have slapped the smug bastard. But I held my cool. I made a respectful offer."

"I understand Harlan intended donating his auctioneer fee to the tribe for the sale of the Beauchamp Collection. He have a change of heart?"

Chenoa shook her head. "That was before he knew the collection contained the Star Dancer journal."

Manny flipped his notebook open. "I see you offered to buy just the journal before the auction. Harlan recorded it. Guess it wasn't enough for him."

She turned and faced Manny, her arms crossed, no façade of the proper lady remaining. "Harlan laughed at me," she blurted out. "Said it would bring five times what I offered at auction."

"That make you mad enough to want him dead?"

Chenoa turned away.

"If he were dead, you might be able to retrieve it. Like now."

She turned back, her face contorted, clenching her fists, and spit flew from her mouth. "I told you, I wanted the entire collection."

Manny stood and pocketed his notebook. "But the offer was just for the journal. I wonder why that is the only thing that interested you. Was it because the journal revealed things you didn't want made public?"

Chenoa walked to the Montana Tourism calendar on Harlan's wall and seemed to be talking to herself as she kept her back to Manny. "I didn't know what was in the journal. Harlan never let me—or anyone else interested in it—read what Star Dancer had recorded."

"But you had an idea there was information in that journal that shattered the notion of Star Dancer purity? It showed there was a White man in the Star Dancer lineage?"

She turned around, hands on her hips, hair falling over her chest, and Manny averted his eyes. "If it ever got out that the Star Dancers weren't as pure, weren't as holy as people thought, they would shun you, would they not? And calls would be made to the state, and your lucrative tourism contract would be canceled. Am I right so far?"

"I've had enough of this." She brushed past Manny and headed for the door. "Call the tribal police if you wish." And she headed out of the auction barn.

Manny sat back on the edge of the desk looking after her. He had seen a side of Chenoa few people saw, and her professional world—that of the face of Montana and the face of Crow purity—was in danger of toppling down around her. If she had read the journal. Manny believed her when she said

Harlan let no one read it prior to the sale, but someone had told her what Levi had written. Harlan, when he put the bite on her for money?

He closed his eyes and tried to imagine their argument when Harlan refused to sell her the journal outright. Had he wanted a piece of the Star Dancer Ranch in exchange for the journal, and for keeping quiet about what it contained? Manny made a mental note to check into Chenoa's bank records and, in particular, any payments to Harlan White Bird before his death.

Manny stood and stretched before turning to the spare room that Sam and Itchy had often crashed in. The plastic chest of drawers lay on its side minus one drawer, overturned since the last time he and Willie and Stumper had been there. A pile of dirty clothes in one corner had been kicked apart, one sock dangling nose-high from a nail sticking out of the wall. Ceiling tiles had been ripped down, and one section of wallboard had been cut open.

He sat on the edge of one bunk, unsure if it was Itchy's or Sam's. Someone had been in Harlan's shop looking for something. But it hadn't been Chenoa, at least not today. Her clothing had been as clean as when he talked with her at Sam's memorial service, not a spot of dust or ceiling tile or wallboard on her.

So someone else had ransacked the room, and Carson Degas floated immediately to the top of the dung heap. He had been seen coming out of Harlan's shop the day before the man was killed, and Degas would know where Harlan kept the key. Had he been looking for the journal? The safe in the corner of the office had been opened, a place where Harlan probably kept the one thing valuable to him: the writings of Levi Star Dancer. Nothing else from the collection was missing.

Manny used the edge of the bunk to stand, and a crackling sound accompanied him. His knees? He felt over the cot and his hand replicated the sound, coming from under the green wool army blanket. He stood and turned the cot over. Stuffed between the canvas cot and the blanket a business-size-envelope lay crumpled. He opened it and held it to the naked lightbulb swaying from the breeze coming in through the broken window.

He pulled the lined notebook paper out. Scratching from a shaking hand had scrawled across the paper, the envelope addressed to Cubby. The writer demanded a thousand dollars, explaining how damaging the information in the journal could be to the Star Dancers. The note had been signed "Your Estranged Brother."

Manny tapped the envelope against his leg. So Itchy had blackmailed Cubby, or so it seemed. Did Itchy have another copy that actually had gotten delivered to Cubby? Or was this a practice note so Itchy could get it right when he delivered the actual blackmail letter to Cubby? Or had Itchy hid this note where someone could find it in case anything happened to him?

Manny stepped around dirty clothes and the overturned plastic dresser, pacing as best he could, tossing the possibilities back and forth in his mind. *Mental ping-pong.* Itchy had been content to have nothing to do with Cubby, relying on Harlan for his drug money. But with Harlan dead, Itchy had to do something, and this might be the boldest thing he'd done in his short life. Manny needed to reinterview Cubby.

He slid the letter back into the envelope and slipped it inside his shirt, his hand poised beside the chain dangling from the weak light. He studied Harlan's office one last time, noting what had been rummaged through, before pulling the chain and plunging the room into darkness. He shuffled into the shop, skirting rows of tables, their relics slowly becoming more than shapes as his eyes adjusted to the darkness. He felt the wall and made his way toward the lighted EXIT sign above the door.

A noise bounced off the far wall, a scraping noise, unnatural for a building. Unless someone was in there with him. He paused, his ears straining to locate the source of the noise, willing his breathing to slow, willing himself to think, to evaluate. He wished his gun, only a short ways from the door in his car, were in his hand as shuffling neared.

An artifact fell from a table that Manny couldn't make out. Something rolled along the floor. Closer.

Manny kept his back away from the wall, careful to avoid contact, careful to avoid making any noise, working his way toward the EXIT sign, when his back ran into a picture hanging on the wall. It crashed, glass breaking. Manny instinctively dropped to his knees a moment before a shot splintered a support beam beside his head, sending splinters into his cheek.

He sucked in air, the veins in his neck and head pounding. Footsteps neared, sounding as if they echoed off every wall in the large shop, and Manny crawled on all fours away from the sound.

He squinted in the darkness. Tables covered with auction items blended into the darkness to become mere shapeless outlines. His legs cramped as he peeked over a table.

Another shot, and pottery next to him shattered, shards falling down his shirt collar, cutting into his skin. He dove to the floor and scrambled away from the table. He crawled under the first row of tables and paused on the other side, rising off the floor so his heaving chest could gulp air.

His eyes adjusted to the darkness and he chanced a look over the table. He spotted the gun display four tables over. Manny recalled ammunition in original boxes had been set up for the sale and prayed it still worked after a century of sitting in someone's collection.

He ducked under the table as another round went off inside the auction barn, the sound deafening. Manny saw the muzzle flash by the EXIT sign at that last random shot, scrambling so he could reach the gun display without getting ventilated.

He crawled under tables displaying beaded purses and possible bags, under another with saddles and tipi bags and halters, reaching the gun display as another random shot erupted. A pinging sound as the bullet went through the metal barn.

Manny reached up and over the table, his hand falling on a revolver. He grabbed it but lost his grip, and it fell to the floor. Immediately, the attacker fired two quick rounds in Manny's direction, hitting a beaded cradleboard. Beads flew into the air and rolled onto the floor. Manny slipped, but caught himself on the edge of the table. The shooter knew where he was.

Manny crawled to the far end of the display as a shadow moved across the EXIT sign. Manny's hand grasped a box of ammunition, .45-70, of the type used by Custer's troops. He saw a row of rifles on the opposite end of the table, and he duck-walked to where the display was. His hand found the butt of a rifle. He brought it down, along with a rifle sling that clattered on the concrete floor. Another shot, this time kicking up pieces of table only inches from Manny's face, and he sat on the floor as he fumbled opening the ammunition box. The brittle one-hundred-year-old cardboard came apart and spilled cartridges onto the floor. The shadow moved, nearer, shoes scraping on the concrete.

Manny grabbed two rolling rounds and slid along the floor to the next table over, his eyes finding a shape closing in.

He sat back against the table and cradled the Springfield in his hands. He had never fired a trapdoor Springfield before, and his hands shook. Manny imagined Custer's soldiers loading their rifles, hands fumbling to reload, as the enemy closed in for the kill.

He found the lever that opened the rifle's action, exposing the rifle's chamber. Manny felt the tip of the bullet and shoved it into the breech, the closing seeming louder than he could ever imagine, expecting another shot his way. *Please Wakan Tanka, let this old rifle and ammo work just this once. I promise never to forget my gun again.*

Manny fished into his pocket and grabbed a quarter. He drew his legs under him and shouldered the rifle, tossing the coin across the other side of the room. The shooter touched off a shot. Manny estimated the flash to where he thought the shooter was and squeezed the trigger. Click. The ammunition failed, or else the rifle was too old to fire.

Manny paused for a moment, his FBI instructors yelling at him to wait for a ten count, that it might be a hang-fire caused by moisture. But Manny didn't have ten seconds. He opened the breech and extracted the round, thumbing another in and closing the action.

He grabbed the bad cartridge and cocked his arm while he shouldered the rifle once more, finding the sights in the dim light. He took a breath, squatted, and tossed the round across the room. It hit the far wall a heartbeat before the shooter sent two more rounds in that direction. Manny estimated back from the half-foot flame and squeezed the trigger. The rifle slammed into his shoulder, sending him back on his haunches, black smoke engulfing him, burning his eyes and spreading a bitter taste in his mouth, powder mingled with the taste of fear.

The shooter yelled, metal clanged to the floor, a table

overturned as Manny crawled to where the ammunition box had been torn open. His hand fell on two more rounds. But he didn't need a follow-up shot. Footsteps ran toward the exit, the shooter briefly silhouetted as the door flung open.

Manny breathed deep, his heart just now calming enough that he could think. He waited for what seemed like an hour before he crept to the exit door and shut it. He fished his cell phone out of his pocket and hit buttons with trembling hands, punching in the police dispatcher at Crow Agency.

He sat with his back against the wall and patted his pocket. What he wouldn't give for an old, calming friend and a Zippo lighter right about now as he waited for the cavalry. He laughed to himself: an Indian waiting for the cavalry. That was a new one. He hated to admit it, but at times like these, Clara was right: He lived for the rush that police work brought, treasured times such as these that brought him a heartbeat away from buying the farm.

Sirens approached, growing louder, cutting off as they reached the auction barn. Manny left the rifle on the floor as he stood and opened the door, careful to keep his hands high. It would be a damned shame to survive an attack only to be smoked by a policeman who didn't recognize him.

Matthew Moccasin Top stood from behind his car door and turned off his spotlight. "What happened, Agent Tanno?" The BIA officer holstered his gun and walked toward him. "Dispatch said you reported a shoot-out here."

"I did, but the shooter fled."

"Who was it?"

"Couldn't see. But there ought to be a few slugs buried in the walls hereabouts. And I think I hit him."

"Or her?"

Manny hadn't thought of that possibility before. "Or her. Let's see your flashlight."

Moccasin Top grabbed his Streamlight from his belt and handed it to Manny. Large droplets of blood tapering to witch's tails showed the direction the shooter had run.

"How bad do you figure he's hit?"

"Not bad enough," Manny answered. "See anyone while you were driving up?"

Moccasin Top shook his head. "A few cars on the interstate, but nothing from when I turned off to here. What we do now?"

Manny started rolling up his sleeves as he walked toward the trunk of the police cruiser, where he knew Moccasin Top would keep an evidence kit. "Get your grubbies on. We got a crime scene to process."

CHAPTER 32

Manny set his cooler with sodas, sandwich, and salad on the seat beside him as Stumper closed the door and leaned in the open window. He wiped perhaps the only clean spot on his Jeep with his shirtsleeve. "Hope this comes back in one piece."

"What makes you think it won't?"

Stumper had balked when Manny asked to use his Jeep, insisting he needed to use it to get places around the Star Dancer Ranch that his Oldsmobile just couldn't go. He had broken Stumper's will when he suggested Chief Deer Slayer could assign him the tedious and always boring chore of surveillance for Manny. "Besides, you got my car to use if you need it."

Stumper choked on his toothpick. "That old beater? The air-conditioning doesn't work."

"And your Jeep does?"

Stumper looked away.

"You're free to conduct the surveillance yourself."

Stumper fidgeted with his flayed toothpick sticking out the end of his pearlies. "Even looking for Little Dave is more interesting than parking in Star Dancer pasture. Especially when it'll be a waste of time."

Manny buckled the seat belt, surprised it even worked. "If you'd look past Chenoa's charm and chest, you might realize she was at Harlan's shop yesterday for no good reason. I thought for sure she was there looking for the journal; now I'm not so sure. She may have been there looking for that blackmail note Itchy left for Cubby."

"Still a long shot connecting Wilson Eagle Bull with your shooter."

Manny grabbed his bandanna and wiped the sweat from the inside of his hatband and set his hat on the seat beside him. "Wilson's arm wasn't bandaged yesterday."

Stumper flicked the toothpick and fished into his pocket for a fresh one. "I told you when I talked with Chenoa yesterday Wilson met me at the door. I asked him how he got his arm cut, and he said on the edge of a metal table at Sam's memorial."

"And you believe everything people tell you? Did you actually get a look at the arm? Talk to the ER folks?"

"He never went to the ER."

"How you know?"

"He said he hadn't. Said it wasn't bad enough. Besides, he had a campaign function he had to get to." Stumper smiled. "But I did get him to commit to a DNA sample to see if it matches with the blood you found on Harlan's floor where the shooter ran away."

"And when does he plan to give this sample?"

"As soon as he returns from that fund-raiser in Rapid City." Stumper grabbed his can of Copenhagen and stuffed his lip full. "Look, Wilson's about as guilty of bad intentions as Chenoa . . ."

Manny held up his hand. "I don't want to know how she's done so much for the Crow. Fact is, either one of them could have been my shooter last night. If there's a silver lining, it's that we must be getting close if someone's coming after me."

"Still no reason to suspect Wilson, just 'cause he cut himself on a table."

Manny turned the ignition switch off and the Jeep shuddered before it coughed once and finally died. "Wilson's got no fund-raiser in Rapid tonight. I had one of the field agents check. I want to be here when he takes off for home."

Stumper kicked the dirt with the toe of his boot. "What do you want me to do?"

"Touch base with the ME. Nail him down on the tox report on whoever burned up in Sam's house . . ."

"You mean Sam?"

"I mean whoever was in that house fire. Until we get a positive ID."

"So between looking for runaway husbands and investigating the newest meth delivery, you want me to call the medical examiner?"

Manny nodded. "And find out where Itchy was staying the last days of his life."

Stumper forced a laugh. "Great. This is a big reservation. Where the hell do I start?"

Manny shrugged and coaxed the Jeep to life. "Find out who Itchy was getting his shit from, and you might find out who was benevolent enough to let him crash."

"Did it ever occur to you we may never solve Itchy's murder? I tell you, Itchy's a luncher."

Manny shook his head. The last homicide case he had to

eat was Jason Red Cloud's. He didn't intend to ever have another luncher.

><><><><

Stumper's Wagoneer had no air-conditioning. For that matter, it had only one wiper that wiped, and the second gear was shelled out so Manny had to shift from first right into third. Air passed easily through the back window—knocked out two winters ago, Stumper claimed—and Manny had to roll down his side window with a pair of vise grips. But it did have a perfectly good operating four-wheel drive system, which enabled Manny to traverse deep gullies and steep rock-covered hills along the back side of the Star Dancer property.

He came to a gate and got out. Cows thinking Manny had brought hay walked bawling toward the Jeep, and he was quick to shut the barbwire gate behind him before they could get out. He drove around the cows, across a trickle of dirty water running through a creek bed to a pasture overlooking the Star Dancer ranch house. He jockeyed the Jeep between two high buttes, and parked sideways so he could watch Wilson's 180 Cessna. Manny shuddered: Flying worked on his gut so he could barely sit in the seat of an aircraft. He had reasoned that it was because he had no control of the outcome of the flight. On a more primitive level, though, he was just scared to fly.

Manny took a sip of his root beer and set it on the transmission hump before he grabbed onto the vise grips and rolled his window halfway up. He opened his duffel and grabbed his window clamp and screwed it tight to the side glass. He secured his spotting scope to it and adjusted the focus. Satisfied, he settled back and took a sip of the Hires. Fizz shot up his nose and onto his cheek and he wiped his face dry with his bandanna.

He grabbed the salad the casino had made up for him and opened the packet of dressing. He checked the label before trickling vinaigrette over his greens. Clara would be proud as he grabbed the croutons sealed in a tiny plastic bag tough enough to resist everything except a pocketknife. Which he grabbed and cut the top. It had always amazed him that croutons came in airtight packages when they were just stale bread, anyway.

He had just readied his salad when he caught movement a half mile down, and he dipped his head to the scope. Cubby emerged from the house and walked to the plane. He opened the outdoor storage door and slipped a bag in before turning to the chains and unhooking the cable tethering the Cessna to the earth. Why was Wilson leaving Crow Agency so soon? He'd just flown in for the memorial service, and said he needed to attend a fund-raiser in Rapid City. But there was no fund-raiser.

Wilson emerged from the house and Manny trained the scope on him. Chenoa appeared alongside Wilson, standing apart, looking after Cubby. "Did you have a lover's spat with Chenoa?" Manny said aloud. "She's not giving you a good-bye kiss. Or did you and Cubby get into an argument when Cubby found out?" Cubby was no fool: He would have figured out their affair long ago.

But Cubby returned to the house and disappeared inside. He reemerged within moments with a suitcase and followed Wilson across the pasture to the airplane. Cubby started to open the door, but Wilson took his case and set it inside the plane, before turning back to him. Words between them went unheard, and Manny could only speculate what they talked about. But even as darkness camouflaged the plane and the two men below, their conversation appeared amiable, with nothing to indicate hateful words passing between them.

Manny took his last bite of salad and washed it down with root beer as his eye strained into the spotting scope. Cubby smiled and slapped Wilson on the shoulder before turning back to the house: not exactly the image of the jealous husband. Or the grieving brother. Stumper had given Cubby the death notice, explaining how Itchy had been found shot in the back of the head and dumped under a bridge. Stumper said Cubby had taken it well, showing no surprise, even shrugging as he thanked Stumper for the message. Had Cubby already known his brother was dead?

"That son of a bitch is colder 'n hell," Stumper had said. "He didn't tear up even a little bit when I told him."

"Some men handle grief differently." Manny had found himself defending Cubby. Or was he teaching Stumper about investigations, teaching him about people, like he did with Willie? "Some men just don't cry with such news." *Will I cry if Willie doesn't pull through?* Manny had been close to death his entire law enforcement career, yet he had been so distant, telling himself the murders he investigated were just a job, denying the corpses had ever lived, with family and with people that cared for them. He forced himself to work that way. For in the end, so many times he was the only one that spoke for the victims.

He had been close to a loved one's death only a few times. He had cried at Unc's funeral, a grown man with shaking shoulders, and loud sobs that no one else paid any attention to at graveside. Would he handle Willie's death like Cubby handled Itchy's? Or would he break down in blubbering sobs? He shook his head to clear it. *Me and Willie will go on that Yellowstone trip. Willie will pull through. I won't have it otherwise.*

Movement in the fading light caught Manny's attention and he bent to the scope. Wilson walked around his plane, checking aileron movement, rudder extension, doing his pre-flight inspection before folding himself behind the wheel of the Cessna. The motor coughed out black smoke for a moment until the prop started revving. Dust kicked back as the plane started a slow roll into the wind. Stumper had been right: This was a waste of time.

He looked through the scope a final time, intending to unscrew the window mount when movement through the plane's side window caught his eye. He adjusted the focus while he tracked the Cessna with the spotting scope. Wilson half turned in the seat, his arm resting on the seat back, his lips moving, the plane picking up speed. He talked with someone in the backseat. Someone that had hidden there while Wilson was still in the house with Chenoa and Cubby, hidden back there before Manny took up position.

Manny scrambled to start Stumper's Jeep, to get into a position where he could look down into the cockpit. He fumbled for the ignition key and it stuck. Manny jiggled it and it finally started, coughed, and spewed blue smoke, but Manny ran out of time: Wilson had started his takeoff roll.

Manny broke the window mount as he jerked the spotting scope free and trained it on the aircraft. Just before it disappeared from Manny's view, he was sure someone's head popped up from the backseat.

CHAPTER 33

With the Jeep's back window out and the passenger side window fallen down into the door, it was typical Indian air-conditioning. Manny turned onto the gravel road from the Star Dancer pasture, the Jeep kicking up dust, blowing through the windows the more he picked up speed. His eyes gritted, and he spit dust from his teeth. He wished he had brought water to clear his eyes instead of root beer, and he ran his sleeve across his eyes to clear his vision.

When he was sure he was far enough from the ranch no one would spot him, he pulled the light switch: The beater had two headlights, even if the dimmer was inoperable. An approaching truck flicked its headlights on high, then back to dim.

"Sorry, buddy, all's I got is high beam." The driver laid on the horn as he passed, and Manny was sure a finger was jutting outside as the truck went by.

Manny dropped over the first hill away from the ranch,

and he relaxed, sitting back and fumbling in the cooler for another Hires. He popped the top just as diesel smoke reached inside a heartbeat before a truck slammed into back of the Wagoneer. Root beer spilled onto his hand, instantly sticky as Manny fought the wheel.

He floored the accelerator, mushy linkage responding slowly. Even if the Jeep had had all its gears, it wouldn't have been any match for the truck that kept tapping his bumper more violently each time, playing with Manny. He feared the coup de grace was just around the next sharp curve, but the old Jeep was maxed out.

The truck laid on its horn, bright lights inches from Manny's bumper. He spotted an approach to a pasture just ahead and he jerked the wheel hard right. The Jeep veered off. Manny crashed through the fence, pumping the brakes. Barbwire caught under the Jeep, slowing it, finally stopping it as the fence wrapped around the driveshaft.

The truck shot by and the driver laid on the brakes, obscured by heavy dust as it skidded to a stop. Reverse lights came on as the driver floored the truck backward. For once, Manny had remembered his Glock and he grabbed it as he bailed out the door, grateful that the Jeep's dome light was broken. Bright floodlights above the truck's cab switched on as the driver steered toward the Jeep, hunting him.

He used the fender for cover as he crouched down, hand shaking as much from fear as the adrenaline dump. He wiped his palm on his jeans and gripped the Glock, waiting for the driver to get out. He didn't have long to wait. The truck door slammed. Footsteps neared, kicking up gravel. A rock banged off the fender of the Jeep as the driver approached.

Manny breathed deeply, what his academy instructors termed "Survival Breathing," meant to calm oneself before making a crucial move. And a crucial move was soon to be in order. Manny crouched low and peeked around the bumper. A figure bent over, head inside the Jeep, and Manny jumped up. "Show your hands!"

The man's head hitting the doorjamb sounded like a rifle shot as he backed out, his hands high above his head.

"Turn around so I can see you."

Cubby Iron Cloud turned slowly, silhouetted against the headlights of his powerful truck. With his hands held high, his belly was away from his pants and Manny saw Cubby's championship rodeo buckle for the first time. "You trying to kill me and make it look like an accident?"

Cubby's hands came down a few inches. "That you, Agent Tanno?"

"Who'd you expect to run off the road?"

"I got no gun."

"Turn around slow and pull your shirt up."

"I said I'm not armed."

"Do it!"

Cubby pulled his shirt up, exposing his belly as he turned slowly around. He faced Manny. "Satisfied?"

Manny motioned with his gun and Cubby lowered his hands, shaking as he grabbed a pack of Marlboros from his shirt pocket. Manny looked lovingly at Cubby shaking out a cigarette, and he fought down the urge to bum one. "Now why the hell you run me off the road?"

Cubby kicked the side of the Jeep. "Didn't know it was you. I would have thought the bureau could give you something better than this hunk of crap metal to drive."

"That doesn't answer my question."

"You were trespassing on Star Dancer land." Cubby blew smoke rings that lingered around his headlights before the wind ushered them away. "Wilson called me on his cell right after he lifted off. Said he saw headlights in the west pasture.

Thought it might be spotlighters looking for deer—we get those now and again. My guess is you weren't hunting deer up there."

"With this?" Manny holstered his Glock. "And why didn't you call PD dispatch if you had trespassers?"

Cubby tilted his head back and laughed. "Way the hell out here? By the time they could respond, the spotlighters would have the deer gutted, loaded, and be halfway back to Billings." He leaned against the fender of the Jeep. "But I might just call in a trespassing complaint on you, unless you can come up with a good reason for being on our land without permission."

"I was watching Wilson."

"For what?"

"I'm sure you heard: Someone tried killing me in Harlan's shop last night."

Cubby nodded. "But what's that got to do with Wilson?"

"I hit the shooter . . ."

"So rumor has it. With a damned buffalo gun from what I heard."

Manny nodded. "But not too bad, or I'd have found him bleeding to death outside the shop. Wilson didn't have his arm bandaged when I talked with him at Sam's memorial service."

"He cut his arm changing strut bolts on that plane of his."

Wilson told Stumper he had cut his arm on the metal edge of a table. "He got witnesses?"

"Me and Jamie Hawk."

"Oh that's a pair to draw."

Cubby shook out another cigarette and grabbed his BIC from his pocket. "Look, I could care less about Wilson Eagle Bull. If you winged him, I'd be the first to tell you."

Manny mulled that over. Either Cubby was an accomplished

liar, or he hated Wilson. Because he knew about his affair with Chenoa?

"Then tell me who's Wilson's passenger."

Cubby stood and walked closer to Manny. "There was no one with him. He flew out alone like he always does." Cubby rubbed his forehead. "Wilson never mentioned anyone. You sure?"

"As soon as Wilson got airborne, someone crawled into the front seat."

Cubby shook his head. "I can't think of anyone who'd want to fly to Pine Ridge."

"He's not flying to Rapid City?"

Cubby shook his head and snubbed his butt out with the toe of his boot. "Sounded odd to me, too. He said he's flying to Pine Ridge, but I wasn't aware they had a lighted runway there."

"Neither was I," Manny said. "And for now, I believe you don't know. Thing we need to do now is get this heap off your fence so I can limp back into town."

Cubby squatted and looked under the Jeep. "You're not going anywhere tonight. Driveshaft's locked up solid with barbwire. I'll have Jamie lift this thing up with a tractor tomorrow. Some of the boys can untangle the fence." Cubby grinned at Manny. "I could give you a ride into town, though I don't know why I should. Give me one reason why I shouldn't call in a trespassing complaint on you."

"'Cause it's preferable to being arrested for assaulting a federal officer."

"Who was on my property without permission."

Manny threw up his hands. "Looks like we got an Indian standoff. Like a Mexican standoff only simpler. Want me to help fix the fence?"

Cubby grabbed the handle of the Jeep and stood. "Naw,

we're not running any cows in this pasture anyway. I'll have Jamie fix it after he pulls this thing off the fence in the morning. But stay off Star Dancer property."

Manny leaned inside the Jeep and grabbed his duffel and cooler. He grabbed the ah-shit handle above the door and hoisted himself into Cubby's truck. Cubby sat staring straight ahead, avoiding eye contact, and Manny thought back to that note Itchy had scribbled demanding money for the journal. "When was the last time you saw your brother?"

"Like I told Stumper, last week when Itchy called and hit me up for some lucky bucks."

"A thousand lucky bucks?"

Cubby laughed and turned in his seat. "With Itchy, it was usually a ten-spot here, twenty there, whenever he thought he could con me into thinking he was hungry. Only thing he was hungry for is another hit of crank. Damned fool."

Manny slipped on his seat belt as Cubby started the truck. A rumbling of diesel accompanied a puff of smoke before the truck smoothed out. "You don't sound like the mournful brother."

Cubby lit a cigarette, the glow of the ash momentarily illuminating his face like a cynical jack-o'-lantern. "Itchy had the same opportunities as the rest of us, but he chose drugs, petty thieving to support his habit. I always thought if Harlan hadn't kept a bunk open for him and slipped him money now and again, Itchy would have had to straighten up."

"So you didn't like Harlan?"

Cubby inhaled, the red glow of the cigarette contrasting with the green dash lights. "Most folks liked Harlan, but I saw through him years ago. He was all about his bottom line, how much money he could make."

"Ever fight with Harlan?"

Cubby slowed to allow a doe to pass, her eyes translucent

in the darkness. "I argued with him more than once about letting Itchy crash at his auction barn. But I sure didn't hate him enough to want him dead." He snubbed his Marlboro in the ashtray. "And I held the offer open to Itchy: He could come back to the ranch whenever he got clean."

"That must have been a pretty safe offer, knowing Itchy would never stop crankin'."

Cubby shrugged, looking over his shoulder as he took the interstate on-ramp toward Hardin. "What the hell do you want from me?"

"The truth."

"I've been honest with you."

"About Itchy's note demanding a thousand dollars in exchange for the journal?"

Cubby shook his head. "I got no note, and I don't know about this phantom journal you and Chenoa and damned near everyone else is looking for."

If Manny had been more flexible, he would have kicked himself in the ass for questioning Cubby in the dark truck, too dark to gauge Cubby's answers, too dark to tell if he lied or not. Now he had nothing to go on with Cubby, and he vowed the next time he questioned him it would be face-to-face in the light of day.

CHAPTER 34

Cubby dropped Manny off beside his car parked at the hitching rail in front of his room at Custer's Revenge. The key chain dangled from the ignition, and Manny left it there. No one in their right mind would want to steal a '55 Olds with enough dings and dents it should be headed for a demolition derby.

Manny sat on the hood and tapped in Rapid City Regional ICU. "Chief Looks Twice said to notify him whenever you called. He's in Officer With Horn's room now."

Manny suffered through Perry Como elevator music, soothing in mental institutions. But he wasn't in an institution, unless he had to listen to the music much longer. Even powwow tunes would be preferable to Tony Bennett or Mel Tormé. Or Perry Como.

"He's still with us." Lumpy sounded out of breath when he at last came on the other end. But then anyone five foot five and two fifty would be out of breath just waddling down the hall of the hospital. "At least he's no worse."

Manny let out a sigh. "Tell me what happened after I took his statement."

"The nurse called me and Doreen when she heard you'd taken his dying declaration, and we've been here since."

"You got an officer that can check something for me?"

"We're working quarter staffed now," Lumpy said, sounding as if he cradled the phone. Paper shuffled on the other end. "What you need?"

Manny gave Lumpy a condensed version of what had happened since he returned to Crow Agency, and Wilson Eagle Bull's actions leading up to whisking away some unknown passenger tonight. "He's got to have one of his pastures rigged for lights. I need an officer to be there when he lands."

"Which pasture?"

Manny shook his head. Wilson had four ranches that he might land the plane on. "Can you have an officer stand by each of them?"

Lumpy sighed. "Look, I got officers working their second twenty-four-hour shifts, busting their butts with family fights, DUIs, normal stuff we policemen deal with. Sitting security outside Willie's room. I got no one to spare on your hunch that Wilson's flying someone that you need to ID."

"Would you have people to spare if it wasn't Wilson?"

The line went dead, and Manny stared at his phone before pocketing it. Lumpy didn't think much of his theory about Wilson and a passenger. Then again, Manny wasn't so sure he would send busy officers to sit on a pasture waiting for Wilson to land on Manny's split-second glimpse as Wilson got airborne. But he needed to know, and there was only one other man Manny trusted to watch for a powerful man like

Wilson Eagle Bull, someone that didn't care if Wilson was running for Senate. Or president.

Manny punched in Big Bat's number, praying that Philbilly was cooking on the swing shift. A woman answered the phone. "Is Phil working?"

She chuckled. "If you call what he's doing, working. He spends more time on his ass than he does in front of the grill. But he's here somewhere—let me wake him up."

Manny thanked Wakan Tanka that Phil was at the convenience store tonight as Manny suffered through more elevator music. Did Big Bat's and Rapid City Regional enter into a conspiracy to drive him nuts with their music? "What y'all need, man?" Phil's thick Arkansas drawl was even harder to understand over the phone than in person. Luckily, Philbilly was too lazy to use long words in conversation, and Manny suspected Phil never got the full benefit of alphabet soup.

"I need you to do me a favor."

"My back's been giving me fits lately, Manny."

"It's nothing that needs heavy lifting or moving."

Philbilly's voice perked up. "Then I'm your man."

"You got a cell?"

Philbilly laughed. "Of course I got a cell. Everyone's got a cell. What you think I am, dumb?"

Manny bit his lip. He was tempted to tell Philbilly he was not only dumb, but was perhaps the laziest man Manny had ever met. Rumor on the rez was that he married his former wife's older sister because he was too lazy to break in a new mother-in-law. "Reuben doesn't have one."

"He needs one."

"I couldn't agree more. He needs yours."

"Mine?"

"I need you to run your cell phone out to Reuben."

"Reuben?" Philbilly said after a long pause. "Your brother?"

"The same. And he doesn't have a car either, so you'll have to drive out to his place and drop your phone off."

"In the dark?"

Manny understood Phil's predicament. Manny could think of no one on Pine Ridge that wanted to approach Reuben's house in the dark, unannounced. "Look, drive in slow with your lights on and make a lot of noise. Put on your dome light so he knows it's you."

"I'm working," Phil stuttered. "I can't leave."

"You owe me, Phil. How many times have I covered for you because you claimed a bad back or a sniffle?"

Phil coughed into the phone. "I feel the flu coming on now."

>‹›‹›‹

The room phone's persistence brought Manny dripping out of the shower. "We found where Itchy was killed." Stumper sounded out of breath. "That Caddy Degas rented was never returned to Avis—it's stuck in a riverbed north of Crow Agency."

"Good work."

"Wasn't nothing I did. Dispatch got a 911 tip that the car was there. It was down the bank so no one could see it unless you were walking or riding in that area."

Manny patted his legs dry. "What's that got to with Itchy?"

Stumper took a breath. "Blood everywhere inside that car. And like you said, there's trees lining the river—same kind of leaves we found stuck in Itchy's clothes and watch cap."

Manny dried his face with a towel depicting blue jays that looked more like purple jays for all the stains. He didn't want to think what the stains were from. "Pick me up."

"Why don't you drive over here. You can drop my Jeep off . . ."

"I don't have it," Manny said. "It's a long story. We'll talk when you get here."

Manny pulled on Dockers, then thought better. He'd have to work around and in the car, and decided on grubby blue jeans and a faded Big Bat's T-shirt instead. He started putting his holster on and tossed it into his duffel. He didn't need the extra weight on his belt when he crawled around the Caddy. But at least he kept his promise to himself never to forget it again.

>◇◇◇<

Stumper tooted the horn, and Manny hopped into his cruiser.

"Way to go, waking everyone up."

"You see any other car parked at this rattrap."

Stumper was right. Manny remained the only boarder at Custer's Revenge.

As Stumper pulled out of the motel parking lot, Manny gave him the short and dirty of how his Jeep had come to be hung up on Star Dancer barbwire. "Don't you beat all. I loan you my Jeep in good faith and you manage to wreck it."

Manny forced a smile. "We'll laugh about this someday."

"Yeah, like when the bureau pays for fixing it."

I wonder how much the SAC will laugh when I give him a bill for a new transmission and driveshaft for a '63 Jeep Wagoneer.

Stumper drove the service road south. When they were a mile before reaching Crow Agency, they turned east on a gravel road. "Anyone approach the Caddy?"

Stumper shook his head. "Just me, and then I got only far enough to see the blood and gray matter on the dash that didn't come from the factory. That's as close as I wanted to get in the dark."

"Who's watching the car?"

"You're looking at the only guy in this district tonight,"

Stumper said. "I had to run up to Hardin just long enough to pick you up."

They turned down a gravel road and had only gone fifty yards when the lights of the Tahoe reflected off the roof of the Cadillac nearly hidden down the creek bank. They stopped two truck lengths from the edge and climbed out. Manny motioned to tracks in the field. "Let's see your flashlight." Manny squatted and studied the tracks leading over the edge of the bank to the car. He shined the light on the ground as he walked the tracks back the way they had come.

"What you see?"

Manny shone his light onto a small barn thirty yards away. "Looks like the driver just missed that shed." He ran the light the length of the tire tracks. "But there was no skidding to indicate the driver lost control. I think someone drove it off the bank on purpose."

"Why wouldn't Degas—if he had been the driver—conceal the car any better?" Stumper said.

"Why indeed?"

Manny returned to the embankment with Stumper close behind. Manny bent and played the light down at a sharp angle. Boot prints shone where the driver had climbed out of the car and scrambled up the steep bank. Manny sat in the dirt and eased himself down, grabbing onto a tree root to slow his descent. By the time he'd gotten to where the car sat, Stumper had jumped down and helped him stand. He stood apart from the car.

"How long do you figure this has been here?" Stumper asked.

Manny squatted and ran his hand over the tire marks, but wasn't sure how to age the tracks. The car rested in axle-deep mud, and the only thing Manny knew was the tracks were fresh: half a day at the most, an hour at the least. "Only thing

I can say is that if Itchy were killed in the Cadillac, it hadn't happened where it is now." He motioned up the bank. "Not even Degas could have carried Itchy's body up the steep and slippery embankment."

Manny inched his way down far enough to illuminate the inside. "Open the door."

Manny waited, but Stumper stood with his back to the bank eying the car.

"Come here and open the door so I can look inside at a different angle."

Stumper's wide eyes reflected moonlight as he stared at the car.

"What's the matter with you?"

"Didn't you hear that?"

Manny stood and cocked his head. "I don't hear anything."

"Sounded like an owl."

"I said I didn't hear anything. Why?"

Stumper shook his head. "Itchy's *ira'xaxe* remains close."

Manny turned off the light and walked to Stumper. "Explain."

"Itchy's soul is close by. Can you not feel it?"

Manny felt the hair rise along his neck and the backs of his hands. He had heard nothing. But if Stumper felt Itchy's soul remained near the car, Manny knew no amount of prodding would convince Stumper otherwise. Besides, with Manny's experiences with *wanagi*, he believed Stumper.

"Okay," Manny said. "Just sit there and catch your breath while I check the car out."

Manny opened the door and propped a broken cottonwood branch in the doorjamb to hold it open while he shone the light inside. Blood and brain matter had been blown straight into the passenger side dash. Blood spatter showed

Itchy's outline where he had been slumped back in the front seat when the killer shot him in the back of his head.

"What you make of this?" Stumper yelled.

Manny turned to where Stumper knelt halfway up the creek bank. His flashlight illuminated a boot print laid over a cigarette butt stuck in the mud. Even before he picked it up, Manny smelled the odor of smoke. *Finally, one advantage of being an ex-smoker: knowing if a butt is fresh.*

Manny stood, looking about. "This is recent. Last hour, perhaps. Someone wanted this car found."

"Why?"

"Knowing that I'd respond," Manny said immediately, his hand going to his belt: He'd left his gun and holster in his duffel in Stumper's cruiser.

Out of the corner of his eye, Manny caught light reflected in the barn window thirty yards away. He dove for Stumper, his shoulder hitting him and knocking him to the ground just as two quick shots kicked up mud where they'd stood a moment before. They rolled down the bank and hit the side of the Cadillac. Stumper half crouched, his sidearm already in his hand, and he looked at Manny with a wild-eyed, questioning stare.

"I left mine in your Tahoe."

"Lot of help you'll be." Stumper started up the bank, but Manny grabbed the back of his belt and pulled him back down. "He's just waiting for us to poke our heads up."

"What the hell you want us to do, stay here and hope someone heard the shots? Wait until the shooter gets a bead on our asses? It's a long way from anyone. We got to move."

"Of course we do, but we move smart." Manny peeked over the bank and studied the terrain, the muddy creek bed, the steep bank that would provide them cover, analyzing the best way to get to the shooter. Just like Lakota back in the day would have done. "We'll split up. You go along the creek bed to the east, I'll stay below the rim and make my way west, closer to the barn."

"You think the gun fairy's going to pay you a visit—you're not even armed?"

"I will be when I grab my Glock from your truck." Manny peeked over the bank again, and a bullet kicked up mud and dirt a foot to his right. He dropped back down, rubbing a piece of tree leaf from one eye. "You give me twenty yards and start lobbing rounds. That'll give me time to put the sneak on whoever's in that shed."

"You? Put the sneak on someone?"

Manny drew his legs under him. "Just like we Lakota did when we won against you Crow."

"Seems like it was the other way around."

"Whatever. Just lob a few rounds without exposing yourself. That'll give me time to work around to the back of the barn. Then get on your cell and call for backup."

Stumper shook his head, but did as Manny instructed. Manny duckwalked twenty yards before crawling up the bank and grabbing tree limbs drooping toward the creek. He pulled himself up the bank just as Stumper fired two quick rounds. One that hit the barn with a solid whump, and the shooter answered with four quick shots that kicked up mud where Stumper had crouched only seconds before.

Manny made it to the Tahoe and kept the cruiser between him and the barn as he leaned inside the open window and grabbed his handgun. He knelt, waiting for the shooter to fire again, for the telltale muzzle flash to tell him where the shooter was. But it didn't come, and Manny imagined their attacker waiting until Stumper shot again.

Manny dropped behind the Tahoe and low crawled until he reached a stand of cottonwood, his palms bleeding from rocks and cactus, and he picked a barb out of his palm with his teeth. He breathed heavily as the huge cottonwood tree—alive since the Old Time—shielded him from the barn. He silently thanked Wakan Tanka for the protection the Cottonwood Oyate afforded.

Manny chanced a look around the tree. Clouds moving in and out of moonlight cast odd shadows over the barn, eerie movement reflected off the few remaining windows. Manny prayed a final time to Wakan Tanka to give him courage to sprint across the open field to the barn. He gathered his legs under him, breathed deeply, and darted out of the safety of the cottonwood. He zigzagged across the field, stumbling on downed branches, tripping, catching himself as he dropped beneath the window where the shooter had last fired.

Manny strained to detect where the shooter was in relation to the window, to the door that Manny would have to rush through. *How the hell stupid is this?* If he were training a new agent, he would have washed him out for doing something as dumb as running across an open field, just praying the shooter wouldn't get a bead on him. Why had he done something any rookie would not have done; the answer came to him immediately: *I might have already cost Willie his life. I don't intend losing Stumper as well.*

Moonlight faded in and out and Manny waited for clouds to momentarily obscure the light. He sprang around the corner, gun muzzle leading the way, searching for a target. Moonlight reflected off chicken-crap-covered walls, off stalls that once housed working draft horses, off a loft with only faint tendrils of hay hanging over the edge. But no shooter.

A flashlight shone into his eyes, destroying his night vision. Manny's hand shot to his face, shielding his eyes, and he strained to make out the gun barrel inches from his face. "I saw that quarterback shuffle across that field," Stumper said, lowering his gun. "That was one dumb move."

Manny blinked to restore his vision. "Can't argue there."
He grabbed Stumper's flashlight and shone it around the
barn. "Looks like our shooter didn't want to play after all."

"You mean Degas?"

Manny shrugged. He had felt all along it had been Degas—
the man had the most to lose, and the most to gain, if Manny
failed in his investigation. Now he wasn't so certain. "One
thing's for sure, whoever's our shooter, he set us up like we
were a couple rookies."

Manny played the lights onto the dirt floor, where a half-
dozen butts lay snubbed out beside the window where the
shooter had stood waiting in ambush. Manny grabbed a twig
and circled them for photographing and collection later.

Sirens neared, and Manny leaned back against a wall. His
legs buckled and he slumped, thinking of the dash across the
open field, of how the outcome might have been different if
the shooter had stuck around to play. Manny put his head
between his legs, feeling his heart rate slow, the veins in his
neck throbbing a little less violently.

Stumper nodded to two cruisers turning onto the field.
"Just be thankful it's not late or we wouldn't have been able
to round up any backup." He walked out into the field and
talked briefly with two BIA policemen exiting their cars. The
officers nodded and started working their way in a tight
perimeter looking for the shooter. Stumper joined Manny
back inside the barn. "What you find?"

Manny shone the light at a boot print imbedded in bird
poop. He placed his own boot next to it. "Size nine or there-
abouts."

"Pretty small for a man as big as Degas," Stumper said.
"Any ideas?"

"Think."

"I am, but I'm coming up blank."

"Chenoa comes to mind."

Stumper laughed. "And she could keep us pinned down?"

"How many ranch women you know could outshoot their men?"

Stumper nodded. "I see your point. Still, she'd have to have a hell of a motive to call in that car just to ambush us."

Manny wanted to tell Stumper what the journal contained, that Chenoa's future would be in jeopardy if the contents of the journal were made public. A made-for-TV motive for murder.

"But Chenoa doesn't smoke." Stumper nodded to the butts. "And it looks like the shooter waited quite a while for us to arrive."

"We're running out of suspects," Manny said. "If we don't come up with another winner, we'll have to award Chenoa the suspect prize."

"Cubby," Stumper blurted out. "He's got pretty small feet for a fat guy. And he smokes."

Manny thought back to Cubby running him off the road. If Manny had been slower to drive the Jeep through the fence, Cubby would have gotten a notch on the fender of his truck. "You might have something there. We better pay Cubby a visit, then."

"Sure, first thing in the morning."

"Now."

"Now?" Stumper checked his watch. "It's ten thirty."

"Then if Cubby's our shooter, we'll just catch him coming home."

"But this time of night is ridiculous."

"You're the one that suggested Cubby." Manny smiled. "You afraid of tribal politics?"

"Damn you." Stumper turned to an officer shining his light down the bank for the wrecker driver. "Have it taken to the impound yard," he called to the officer. "We'll process it tomorrow. And cast these boot prints in the barn." He tore pages from his notebook and handed it to a younger officer who had just walked into the shed. "And make sure you're at the PD at 0700—I got Della Night Tail and Big Dave coming in to make a statement about meth activity they claim to know about."

Stumper started for his cruiser. "Damn you," he called over his shoulder, and Manny ran to catch up for the ride to the Star Dancer ranch.

CHAPTER 35

Manny's cell phone buzzed just as he turned off Interstate 90 toward Lodge Grass and the Star Dancer Ranch. He checked the number: Philbilly's phone. "Pull over so I don't lose the signal."

Reuben's voice sounded faraway and faint, but then Reuben always sounded faint and faraway, soft, and a little hard to understand. Manny pressed his phone tight to his ear. "Wilson was here, and gone. That quick. I drove Philbilly's outfit to the Pine Ridge airport—you know how embarrassing it is to drive a bread truck at forty miles an hour, chasing Wilson Eagle Bull's plane?" Philbilly had bought an old Wonder Bread truck at auction and repainted it. As with all Phil's schemes, his latest one of selling Indian tacos on the side of the road wasn't panning out.

"But did you see who his passenger was?"

"I missed it," Reuben said. "After he didn't land at the airport, I drove to his west place first, and just got there as he was taking off in his pasture again. His foreman caught me in Wilson's driveway and damned near ran me off the road as I was leaving."

"Harvey?"

"Call him Harvey Broken Nose now. The SOB must have thought I was Philbilly driving onto Eagle Bull property, 'cause he blocked the road. When his fat ass came lumbering up with that toothy grin and tire billy slapping his hand, he expected the driver to lie down and bleed." Reuben laughed. "That lasted just long enough for me to climb out of the bread truck and educate him."

"Did Harvey know who Wilson's passenger was?"

Reuben chuckled again. "You mean Harvey Missing Teeth? He claimed Wilson had no passenger tonight or any night."

Manny closed his eyes, and prayed Harvey didn't file an assault charge on Reuben. "He didn't know or wouldn't say?"

"All Harvey knows is that Wilson radioed him when his plane was a half hour out. He and Pete and RePete positioned their pickup lights so Wilson could land. Like they'd done a hundred times before, according to Harvey Split Lip."

"Who was with Wilson?" Stumper asked.

Manny held up his hand for silence. "You think Harvey told you the truth?"

"I do." Reuben laughed again. "After a few whacks, me and Harvey bonded, in that special way a coyote bonds with a prairie chicken a moment before the coup de grace. Harvey said if Wilson had a passenger, he would have had to hustle to get away. It only took Harvey a few minutes to walk to the plane and grab Wilson's baggage."

"Keep your ear to the ground. Someone got out of Wilson's plane. The ranch house is close enough his passenger could have made it there."

"Or the bunkhouse. I'll see what I can find out. You know," Reuben said, "this cell phone technology is pretty cool. I might even get one myself."

Manny hated to ask: "You got Philbilly's cell, *and* you still have his bread truck?"

"I do," Reuben answered. "It's not much, but Phil was glad to let me keep it for as long as I needed it. He didn't even argue with me, and I got the impression he was a little intimidated."

"You think? You don't have him tied up in back of your house or anything?"

"Of course not," Reuben chuckled. "I'm civilized. I woke up Crazy George, and said that Phil wanted to stay there for the night. Or until I was done with his truck."

Manny shook his head. "Great, staying with a man that dresses in skirts, and has a junkyard horse that'll eat Phil alive. Next thing you know he'll be hightailing it off the rez."

"Now, wouldn't that be a shame," Reuben said, and disconnected.

Manny pocketed his cell and told Stumper what Reuben had said. "Any ideas who Wilson might have given a ride to?"

"If that's what Wilson did."

"Why else would he have set down in his pasture just long enough for him to let his passenger off? I know what I saw. Someone was climbing into the front seat after he lifted off."

Stumper turned onto the long drive leading to the Star Dancer ranch house. "We'll start by seeing who's missing at the Star Dancer place."

As they topped the hill overlooking the ranch house, Stumper started turning around on the road.

"What you doing?"

"Going back to town." He nodded to the house invisible

in the darkness at the end of the drive. "Looks dark to me. I told you they'd be sleeping. We can come back tomorrow."

Manny squinted. "I see light between the curtains. Drive down there, and we'll bang on the door until someone answers."

"What if Jamie Hawk comes crashing out. I'd hate to tangle with that big bastard . . ."

"I got faith in you to keep him busy while I interview whoever's inside." He chin-pointed to the house. "Someone tried killing us tonight and I want to see who's playing, and eliminate who's not. Now drive down there."

Manny recalled Jamie looking through him, no emotion showing, and he was with Stumper on one thing: He didn't want to tangle with that big bastard.

>◇◇◇<

But that big bastard's voice surprised Manny as he banged the door knocker. "You guys lost?" Jamie stood in the shadows at the end of the porch, ass-whipping muscles bulging under a white T-shirt. "We're all sleeping."

"You're not."

He took a step closer. "I was until you drove in here and woke me up."

"We're here to see Chenoa."

Jamie stepped toward them, and Manny was surprised how easily he drew his gun and pointed it between Jamie Hawk's legs. "I'm not much of a shot, but I'm good enough to hit your big ass from here. Someone shot at us tonight, and I'm in no mood for you to interfere with an official investigation. Take another step closer and you'll be the morgue's newest resident, or you'll be someone's girlfriend in a federal slammer."

Jamie saw the gun for the first time, his eyes widening, stepping back.

"I thought you'd recognize official. Where's Chenoa?"

"She's not here."

Manny tapped the door with his hand. "I got a sneaking suspicion she is. Now, run along, and I'll tell her you did your best to keep us away."

Stumper looked after Jamie's disappearing form. "You wouldn't have shot him, would you?"

Manny holstered his gun, expecting Jamie to come back for round two. "He had bad intentions written all over him. Besides, you pay any attention to his feet? As big as Jamie is, he's got pretty small boots. And he wasn't just sleeping like he claimed."

"You don't think Jamie was our shooter tonight? The guy that was holed up in the barn took off pretty fast."

"Just 'cause he's so big," Manny said as he rapped hard on the door, "doesn't mean he's not nimble." He dropped the door knocker again. A voice called out, "Wait a damned minute." And it wasn't Cubby's voice.

The door swung open, and Wilson Eagle Bull stood with his tighty-whities inching a bit south over a slight paunch, revealing what Reuben referred to as "rear cleavage." Wilson stood with mouth agape for long moments before he sputtered, "I thought it was Jamie."

Manny smiled and exaggerated giving Wilson the once-over. "I'm sure you did."

"Who is it, baby?" Chenoa glided down the winding wooden staircase, her sheer negligee clinging to shapes, barely covering legs that belonged to a twenty-something rather than a woman of fifty. She didn't bother hiding taut nipples that threatened to escape the thin fabric.

It was Manny's and Stumper's turn to stand with mouths agape, and Chenoa smiled at their discomfort. She slipped her arm around Wilson's waist. "Guess the cat's out of the bag or"—she nodded to the bulge in Wilson's shorts—"it would have been if you hadn't interrupted things." Her smile faded. "Just what do you want at this time of night?"

Wilson stuck his head out the door and looked. "Maybe they'd like to come inside in case someone else comes calling."

"Like Cubby?" Chenoa said, stepping aside. "He's too busy doing his own thing." She turned to Wilson. "Take them into the kitchen."

Chenoa turned and ascended the stairs while Wilson led them into the kitchen and nodded to stools situated around a breakfast counter. When Chenoa entered a few moments later, she had wrapped herself in a terry cloth robe and she handed Wilson one. The yellow and blue star of the Star Dancer logo adorned pockets on both robes. Wilson turned away while he hid his embarrassment and tied his robe shut.

"So you got us dead to rights." Wilson scratched his groin. "What you intend doing with it?"

"Depends on what your answers are."

Wilson hung his head while a sly grin crossed Chenoa's face, enjoying his predicament, and Manny realized Wilson running for the South Dakota State Senate meant nothing to her. And neither did Wilson. "What do you need to know?"

"Who shot at us tonight?"

Wilson looked sideways at Chenoa. Her smile faded and she leaned closer to Manny. "Someone shot at you? Are you all right?"

Manny nodded. "We're curious as to where all the players were."

"Players?" Chenoa sat on a stool next to Wilson, her bathrobe riding up over her thighs and revealing her legs again. She made no effort to cover them. "Players in what?"

"Murders. Sam's. Itchy's. Harlan's. They're connected by only one thing—the theft of Levi Star Dancer's journal. I'm looking at the two people who would profit the most if I failed to solve the murders. At the people who'd least want me to find that journal and return it to Harlan's estate for public auction."

Wilson wiped his forehead with a dish towel. "I got nothing to gain by killing anyone. And neither does Chenoa."

"No?" Manny rested his elbows on the counter and formed a tent with his fingers. "How about the renowned Eagle Bull reputation?" He turned to Chenoa. "And the Star Dancer purity?"

Manny eyed Wilson's size thirteen slippers and nodded to Chenoa's manicured, blue-painted toenails dangling from the stool. "I'd say you're about a nine?"

"No, I'm a size 36. D to be precise."

Manny felt his face warm. "I meant your shoe size."

Her grin widened. "I knew what you meant. Yes, I'm a size nine. Why?"

"Our shooter tonight wore about a size nine cowboy boot, with a walking heel by the looks of the impression in the barn where he—or she—waited to shoot us."

"Lot of people wear size nine," Wilson volunteered. "Cubby does, too. And Jamie's shoes are not much bigger."

Chenoa scowled at Wilson and he turned red.

"That true?" Manny asked. "Cubby wear a size nine?"

"More like a nine and a half. And if your next question is could he shoot at you, he's a ranch man. He's got guns. And he knows how to use them."

"But is he smart enough?"

"I don't understand," she said.

Manny paused, letting them think he knew more about the shooter than he did. "Is Cubby smart enough to set us up? Drive that Caddy that Degas rented to that creek bed, knowing we'd investigate all the blood inside. And call in an anonymous tip?"

Chenoa tilted her head back and laughed. "I see your point. My husband's capable of shooting at you, but I'm not so sure if he could have arranged something as complex as that." She stood and grabbed a teapot and began filling it with water.

Wilson stared at the floor until Manny asked him, "Who'd you fly to Pine Ridge tonight?"

Wilson's head snapped up. "What makes you think I flew back home tonight?"

"Harvey said you did."

"Harvey? Even if he saw me, he wouldn't tell anyone. The man's got loyalty in spades."

"He got religion tonight."

Wilson leaned forward. "How's that?"

"He confessed to a holy man."

Wilson threw up his hands. "All right. I flew back home, but I flew alone. I had a fund-raiser in Rapid tonight, but it was called off an hour from home. I set down only long enough to give some paperwork to Harvey and I flew back here."

"Any particular reason you didn't stay in Pine Ridge?"

Chenoa sat beside Wilson and cradled a cup of tea in her hands. She kissed him lightly on the cheek. "Wouldn't you come back," Chenoa asked, "if the sex was so good even the neighbors had a cigarette afterward?"

Manny looked away, aware that Chenoa's smile widened at his embarrassment. "Tell me what you know about the journal."

Wilson shrugged. "I never knew until the journal surfaced that Conte Eagle Bull murdered his own friend. I'm running an honest campaign . . ."

"Based on the integrity of the Eagle Bull name?"

He nodded. "If the contents of that journal were made

public, it'd give that damned Arvid Johansson more than a few mud pies to sling."

"Did you get a chance to read it? You seem to know a great deal about it."

"Sam," Wilson answered. "He told me what Levi Star Dancer had recorded."

"I thought you hadn't talked with him."

Wilson turned away. When he looked back, tears had formed in his eyes, but Manny couldn't tell if they were genuine sorrowful tears, or those conjured up by a politician. "Sam called me the day before he got burned up. He told me what the journal contained, how he thought it would ruin my chances for the Senate."

"And advised you to bid on it at Harlan's auction?"

"Not exactly." Wilson stood and paced in front of the counter. "Sam offered to steal the journal for me. For a price."

"I'm thinking you declined?"

Wilson faced Manny. "I told Sam I wouldn't pay one cent for any stolen artifact. But I would bid on it, like anyone else."

"I didn't see your name on the bid sheet."

Wilson nodded to Chenoa. "That's 'cause we decided to pool our money. With the publicity the journal received worldwide—the only surviving written account of the battle, and the times after, by one of Custer's scouts—we knew it would bring six figures."

Manny turned to Chenoa. "That so."

Chenoa set her cup on a woven coaster and turned to the coffeepot. *Stalling.* "We planned to split the price if we won the bid and burn the damned thing."

"You stand to lose as much as Wilson?"

She nodded. "If the contents get out that I got a *baashchiili* in my gene pool, Montana may still keep my contract, but the

Apsa'alooke tribe will cut ties. I've still got my ranch, so it's not like I'd be out bumming on the street."

Like Sam used to do, Manny thought. "That's why you went into Harlan's shop looking for it?"

Chenoa nodded. "I heard Harlan had hidden it in his office. You caught me snooping around his shop like an amateur, but there was no sign of it, even though Itchy claimed to have it."

"And you thought you'd find it . . ."

"Somewhere under all that trash," she said. "But you interrupted me."

"Which brings us back to Itchy's murder and who shot at us tonight."

"We were together all night," Chenoa said. "Ask Jamie."

"Oh that's a credible witness to corroborate your tale," Stumper said.

Chenoa glared at Stumper and the kitchen went silent until Wilson asked Manny, "When will this get out?"

"This?"

He wrapped his arm around Chenoa's waist. "Our affair."

Manny swiveled in his stool and leaned closer to Wilson. "Not from me, and I doubt Stumper will want it getting out a Lakota was sparking the face of the Crow Nation. What you do is your business. But there's another thing that'll hurt you far worse than your affair."

Wilson dropped his head. "Degas?"

"Degas. I want him, and you can give him to me."

"What makes you think I know where he is?"

"Mr. Eagle Bull," Stumper cut in. He grabbed his can of Copenhagen, but slipped it back into his pocket when he caught Chenoa glaring at him. "We know now you hired Degas right out of Folsom prison, and that he'd do most anything to protect you. Including making sure that journal never surfaces."

Wilson stood abruptly and his stool rolled back and banged against the refrigerator. A magnet dropped onto the floor, and a copper decorative clock dropped onto the counter, but neither man made a move to pick it up. Wilson stood chest-to-nose looking down on Stumper. "I don't like your implication."

Manny stepped between them and eased Stumper back onto his stool before he turned to Wilson. "Then maybe you like this implication: Degas switched ammo and got Harlan White Bird killed. He probably killed Sam—probably for information about the journal—and he'd be good for Itchy's death, just in case his threat of exposing you were true. And for icing on the cake, he shot Officer With Horn. Remember that loyalty you mentioned Degas had? And this piece of shit works for you."

"You can't convict me of anything . . ."

"Don't need to," Manny said. "All I need to do is leak this to the press and they'll convict you in their papers. *And I'm sure Sonja Myers will be more than happy to run an exposé in the next issue of the* Rapid City Journal *on senatorial candidate Wilson Eagle Bull.*

Wilson's jaw muscles tightened and he stepped closer. "That how the FBI works—use threat and intimidation?"

"Is that how politicians work—threats and intimidation?"

"Leave him alone." Chenoa stepped between Wilson and Manny. "He doesn't know where Degas is . . ."

Wilson pressed a finger to Chenoa's lips. "I may be able to help you find him."

Chenoa took Wilson's head in her hands and looked up. "Why would you help find one of your ranch hands? And someone who knows horseflesh like he does?"

"Why?" Wilson forced a smiled that faded as quickly as it came on. "For the reasons Agent Tanno mentioned—Degas arranged for at least one man to be killed. And he shot Officer With Horn. I might be able to help."

Manny sat back on the stool. "Go on."

Wilson paced in front of the counter, rubbing his forehead. "Carson has called me four times since Harlan's death."

"Where is he?"

"Can't say."

"Can't or won't?"

"He wouldn't tell me where he was calling from." Wilson slumped on the stool, while Chenoa stood behind him, looking over his shoulder and glaring at Manny. "He called wondering if he still had a job."

"After we arrest him?"

"He said there was no proof that he switched ammunition that killed Harlan. Said he was in jail in Hardin at the time."

Manny thought back to Degas's loyalty to his boss. Did the loyalty go both ways? Was Wilson protecting him? From what he had uncovered about Degas, Manny could easily put together a scenario where the man killed to protect his boss, killing anyone who might expose him with the journal.

And did Wilson or Chenoa know who killed Sam and Itchy? Manny rubbed a rising headache away. Something just out of the reaches of his reasoning eluded him.

"And he said he wasn't even on Crow Agency when Sam and Itchy were killed," Wilson added. "Said he was on Pine Ridge. Said he couldn't get here in time to kill them." Unless they had a ride, Manny thought. Like in the passenger seat of a Cessna.

"And you believe him?"

"Carson's never lied to me before," Wilson said, but his

voice lacked conviction. "He assured me he didn't have anything to do with Sam's or Itchy's death."

"And Officer With Horn?" Manny felt his anger rising, and he breathed to control it. "Is Willie's dying declaration a lie?"

Wilson shook his head. He stood, looking down at the floor, and started pacing again. "There must have been some mistake. Maybe Carson thought Willie was sneaking around the ranch waiting to steal something. We've had some cattle thefts this last year."

Manny remained quiet.

Wilson's shoulders drooped and he faced Manny. "His alibis don't hold water."

Manny nodded.

"Okay, Agent Tanno, what can I do to help?"

Manny stood and walked a cramp out of his calf. "Here's the deal: The next time Degas calls, you tell him you need to meet him at your ranch, or here if he's still on Crow Agency. I'm not buying it that he's been in Pine Ridge all this time."

"What will you do when you find him? I don't want Carson hurt . . ."

"We'll do our best to take him alive," Manny answered. "Dead men don't interview well."

Wilson's lips moved as he paced, talking to himself, until he stopped and faced Stumper and Manny. "I'll do it."

"Wilson . . ."

"I have to." He laid a hand on Chenoa's shoulder. "The sooner Agent Tanno and Stumper corral Carson, the sooner he can clear his name. I just know there's some mistake. I'll tell Carson I need to meet him."

"And one other thing"—Manny swallowed hard, sweat forming on his forehead just thinking about it—"if Degas goes to your Pine Ridge ranch, you fly me there."

Wilson looked to Chenoa for approval, her face unreadable. Wilson agreed. "He'll probably call soon, as I haven't heard from him for a couple days. He'll have heard about you and Stumper being shot at, and he'll wonder if he's a suspect in that, too. What do I tell him?"

"The truth—that you don't know anything about it."

Wilson straightened. "I'll call you when he does."

"And Wilson, I'll know if you're setting me up."

Wilson shook his head. "I won't. I don't think Degas is your killer, and I want him to have a chance to prove it. But if your trap fails to catch him and he escapes, you've got to promise to protect me."

Manny eyed Wilson's trembling lips, and he sat on the stool to ease his shaking knees. "Vietnam Marine vets usually don't frighten easily."

"You don't know Carson."

Manny turned to Chenoa. "I'm going to have to seize your boots. Jamie's and yours, too, Wilson."

"What the hell for?" Chenoa asked.

Manny shrugged. "Compare them to those prints we found in that barn tonight."

><><><

Manny put the boots in the back of Stumper's Tahoe and climbed in. Manny turned and looked out the back window as they drove out the long driveway. Wilson looked after them, backlit by the lights in the open door as he watched them disappear over the hill. "Wilson might set you up," Stumper said, filling his lip with Copenhagen. "He might want to win the senatorial race so badly, he'll have Degas waiting to kill the chief investigator in the case."

"I've thought of that."

"And you're not scared?"

"I didn't say that. But as long as I'm scared, I won't make stupid mistakes."

Stumper pulled onto the gravel BIA road Cubby had tried running Manny off earlier. "What are you going to do until Degas contacts Wilson?" Stumper asked.

Manny smiled. "I'm going to hang out with my friend and colleague Stumper LaPierre tomorrow. See what the evidence tech found in that Caddy, after which we'll take a trip to Billings to talk with the ME."

"And wait around to fly to Pine Ridge?"

Manny's smile faded. "*Now* you do got me scared."

CHAPTER 36

They were close enough to Custer's Revenge that Manny could almost feel the lumpy mattress under his head; smell the stale cigarette odor permeating the walls; hear the drip-drip-drip of the running stool with a crack in the seat that pinched his butt at least once a day.

Until Stumper got a call on his cell. "Where'd you get the info on the shipment?" he said into the phone. He kicked on the overheads and siren and cut through the interstate median on his way back toward Crow Agency.

"What's going on?" Manny asked.

Stumper held up his hand. "Make sure Jerry doesn't share the interview room with anyone else."

"What?"

Stumper closed his cell and floored the Tahoe, setting Manny back against the seat. "Some CI that's been working with DCI tipped our guys off that Jerry One Feather was heading to Billings with an ounce of crank. My guess it came from a cook in Denver. I'm going to interview Jerry while he's fresh."

"Mind if I sit in?"

Stumper laughed. "Like you're going anywhere until I'm done with him? Not that I'm going to get anything out of him."

"You don't sound too optimistic."

"Jerry's a tough nut. Been around the horn. He's been a suspect in a jail homicide in Rawlins, and another in Sioux Falls, but never proved up on any of them. Spent time in Leavenworth, and a bunch of jails across this part of the country had the Jerry One Feather memorial jail cell in his honor. We used to joke that he was trying all the lockups in the country so he could write an article for a travel magazine, like those guys that go around the country sampling restaurants. Until he started dealing meth. Then the joking stopped."

They pulled in to the justice building and Stumper grabbed his notebook as he led Manny past the dispatch center to the interview room. Jerry One Feather stood bent over a garbage can brushing ashes into the round file. "You guys got a real pigsty here, Stumper."

Jerry towered over them, scarred fists clenching and unclenching, the picture of unchained anger begging for release. Manny recognized the swollen knuckles, the nose set at an off angle, one cheekbone that protruded more than the other when it didn't heal right. His joint body, bulging muscles developed by someone with little else to do besides work out eight hours a day, showed through his white T-shirt. Manny recognized Reuben in Jerry One Feather.

"Anytime I was in stir, I kept my house immaculate. Always." He slapped the tabletop with his bandanna to clean the ashes off. "And you expect cooperation from me in *this* room?"

"Just sit, Jerry."

Jerry dropped into a metal chair chained to the floor. He crossed his arms and chin-pointed to Manny leaning against the door. "Who's your chubby partner?"

"FBI Senior Special Agent Tanno."

Jerry's eyes narrowed. "You federal bastards railroaded me six years ago. What you say to that, chubby?"

Manny reached his arm above his head as if pulling on a steam valve release, and did his best imitation of a train whistle.

Jerry started to stand, but Stumper put a hand on his shoulder and eased him back into the chair. Not that Jerry couldn't have stood if he wanted to. He continued staring at Manny until Stumper opened a file and laid out the field test. "An ounce is what you had in your hot little pocket when you were stopped."

"So?"

"You've been dealing."

"I don't deal . . ."

"Like those quarter-gram Baggies were going to some charity? You've been drugging long enough to know . . ."

"I said, I don't deal . . ."

". . . when you've been cheated."

Jerry's eyes narrowed. "How so?"

Stumper filled his lip with Copenhagen and offered Jerry a dip.

He shook his head. "Tobacco's bad for you."

Stumper pocketed the can. "If you bought an ounce—like our information had—you were cheated out of four grams."

Jerry's grin faded.

"Unless you smoked it yourself."

Jerry stood. The table groaned under his weight as he leaned over, veins in his neck throbbing. "You know I don't use that shit."

Manny came off the door. "But you don't mind ruining other people's lives with it."

Jerry chin-pointed to Manny. "Tell your chubby friend to stay out of this, or he'll get more than he bargained for."

Manny walked to the table and stood looking up at Jerry, inches from his face, smelling the odor of the steak and onions he had recently eaten. "You'll get more than you bargained for, too. This is a felony, and we hold the future of your ass in our hot little hands."

Jerry laughed nervously and felt for the seat. His eyes remained locked with Manny's as he eased himself into his chair. "Okay, little man. We'll do it your way. For now."

Stumper turned the chair around and sat across from Jerry. "Who you getting your shit from?"

"Stumper, you're dumber than I thought."

"The dummy is the one with three strikes hanging over his head. Looking at life being some other guy's wife in the slammer."

"How's that?"

"Three felonies. You made a home run on this one. This makes three, and you'll be tried as a habitual criminal. Mandatory life."

Jerry came off his chair and it fell over as if playing dead. "What the hell you mean, three strikes? This would be only my second felony: the carjacking in Billings and that stop and rob in Sheridan. The others happened before that habitual law was passed."

Stumper shuffled through the file and slid a court disposition across the table. "You seem to have forgotten about that bum check to the car dealer three years ago."

Stumper turned to Manny as if Jerry wasn't in the room. "Dumb shit tried to leave the state with a car paid for with a no account check." Stumper laughed. "Nothing in the universe travels faster than a bum check."

"I spent misdemeanor time for that," Jerry sputtered.

Stumper grinned. "No, that stay in the county turned into felony time. Only if you abided by the plea agreement would it be considered a misdemeanor. Which included the probation appointments you failed to make. As per the plea."

Jerry wiped his forehead with his bandanna and paced the room. "I only missed one."

"You only made one." Stumper winked, enjoying Jerry's predicament. "And the conviction went back to grand theft. Felony. Sit down."

Jerry righted the chair and slumped into it.

Manny sat in a chair next to Stumper and leaned his elbows on the table. "Stumper's right. Judges got no wiggle room on this. It's mandatory life."

"Shit."

"Sure you will, in an open toilet shared by some other schmuck. Maybe you'll work yourself up from prison laundry to book server," Manny explained, slowly as if educating a Boy Scout troop. "Maybe even get your jailhouse lawyer license. Help other inmates file for appeal, maybe sentence reduction. Help everyone except you, 'cause no habitual ever gets out early."

Jerry seemed to shrink in his chair. "What you guys need to know?"

"Jerry," Stumper said, shaking his head. "Now who's dumb? You know I need your supplier's name here on Crow Agency."

Jerry rubbed his stubble. "You know I can't snitch on my supplier."

"Even though you were cheated out of those four grams?"

Jerry looked down at the floor, but said nothing. Stumper shut his notebook and stood, while Manny held the door for him.

"Wait," Jerry said. "Can't we make a deal here?"

"Who do I look like, Monty Hall. What door you pick depends if you're the girlfriend or the wife when you go up the river."

Jerry nodded to the door and Manny shut it. "I'll talk about dope, but I can't talk about my supplier."

"What, like the meth fairy just drops it into your lap once a week?"

Jerry kept silent, and Stumper motioned to the door.

"Wait," Jerry said. "You'll put in a word for me, right? That's only fair."

"Life's not fair, Jerry." Manny leaned over the table. "Life's like a shit sandwich—the more bread you have, the less shit you gotta eat. The more you give, the less you'll get."

Stumper looked to Jerry. "What I recommend to the prosecutor depends on what you give up."

"Fair enough."

Stumper took out his notebook again. "How much crank comes onto the rez every week?"

"A quarter pound."

Manny whistled and scooted closer to Jerry. "Every week?"

Jerry nodded.

"How's it coming in?"

"I don't know."

Stumper started closing his notebook again when Jerry held up his hand.

"I honestly don't know. All I know is I take delivery of an ounce a week from . . ." Jerry kicked an imaginary rock on the floor with the toe of his boot.

"Jerry," Stumper said, leaning over and looking at him. "Now's not the time to test our newfound friendship."

"The guy I get my shit from is not the one who hauls it from Denver. Understood?" Jerry's foot started tapping the floor and he fidgeted in his seat. "This guy's just small potatoes, like me. After . . . the big guy picks it up in Denver, he hauls it to the rez and gives it to the guy I get it from. Understood?"

Stumper nodded.

"Okay," Jerry muttered. "When my guy gets it, he gives me a call and we meet. Slips me an ounce. Sometimes an ounce and a half."

"Who, Jerry?"

"Little Dave Night Tail."

Stumper scooted his chair back. "You have got to be shitting me."

Jerry held up his hand. "No shit. Little Dave's got a thing for the ladies. Likes buying them nice things. And he's got expensive tastes himself: clothes, jewelry, new trucks. Last year he bought a damned Shetland pony just to give to one of his girlfriend's boys living in downtown Billings."

Stumper nudged Manny. "Oh that must have been a hit with the neighbors."

"That information should be enough to keep me locked up in here, right?"

"What you mean?" Stumper closed his notebook. "You can make bond as soon as I talk with the magistrate."

"I don't want to make bond, Stumper. I make bond, the guy bringing the load up from Denver will slit my throat." His foot started tapping again, and he wrung his hands. "Just let me sit in jail and wait for trial. Think you can swing it?"

Stumper shrugged. "What are friends for?"

"Take Jerry over to Detention," Stumper told Moccasin Top as he passed out of the interview room.

Stumper led Manny to his truck and hit the remote. "He was damned afraid of being cut loose," Manny said.

Stumper started the cruiser and backed out of the lot. "I've never known Jerry to be afraid of anything. The main supplier must be one tough bastard to get him riled like that."

"Degas?"

Stumper nodded. "As good a suspect as any."

Stumper started onto I-90 and half turned in his seat. "Guess Della Night Tail wasn't just imagining Little Dave teepee-creepin', though I'd have rather found out Little Dave was getting stray on the side rather than dealing meth. Makes a lot of sense, all the times he was gone. I'll go back to the records and cross-reference those days Della reported him gone to shipments of meth coming onto the rez. Now all we got to do is round up Little Dave."

Manny popped a PEZ and let the bittersweet candy dissolve under his tongue. "You said she reported him missing what, four days ago?"

Stumper nodded.

"And you haven't found him?"

"Not a sign."

"Maybe he left for greener pastures. Maybe someone gave him an all-expenses-paid lift off the rez."

Stumper looked sideways at Manny. "What you getting at?"

"Wilson," Manny said. "If Little Dave was making deliveries for Degas, it wouldn't be such a stretch that Degas would want him whisked away before the law got to him first."

"And maybe he was the one you saw climbing into the front of Wilson's plane right after takeoff."

"Maybe."

CHAPTER 37

Loud banging on Manny's motel door woke him with a start. He swung his legs over the side of the bed, and cursed as he stubbed his toe against the nightstand. "Who is it?"

"Me. Stumper."

He brushed past Manny and closed the door. Stumper squinted as he smiled at Manny standing beside the closed door clapping. "I really didn't need any applause."

Manny ignored him, and his last clap turned the light on. He walked to his bed and bumped his head on the low-hanging chandelier.

Stumper smiled when the light came on. "Red skivvies with pink hearts FBI issue?"

"Gift from Clara," Manny said as he hunted for his socks and boots. "What the hell did you wake me at six o'clock for? I thought you were going to get me after you talked with Jerry One Feather again." Manny crow-hopped, one leg stuck into his trousers as he fought to stick the other one in before he fell over.

"Better sit down for this."

"That amazing?"

"No," Stumper laughed. "But you better sit down before you fall down."

Manny sat on the edge of the bed and managed to wrestle his other leg into his trousers. "What's so important?"

Stumper waved a manila folder in front of him. "Completed autopsy report from the Billings ME came early this morning. He finally got Sam's military records."

Manny slipped the socks on and the material dangled over his toes. The only ones at Last Stand Western Wear were the 12–16 size. "So we're back to twenty questions. Just tell me what it says."

Stumper pulled up the only chair in the room, an occasional with, by the looks of stains on the seat, only occasional cleaning. He flipped the folder open on the bed. "The crispy critter in Sam's house wasn't him."

Manny stopped mid-sock. "If it wasn't Sam, who was it?" Manny dropped his sock and grabbed the medical examiner's report. He snatched his reading glasses off the *Cosmopolitan* lying open on the nightstand.

Stumper nodded to the magazine. "Another FBI issue?"

Manny looked over his half-glasses. "Clara's idea of getting in touch with the feminine perspective."

Manny flipped the cover page and read where the ME had estimated the victim as being between five five and five nine, based on long leg bone measurements. "The victim's left arm had healed at an odd angle from an early break," Manny said aloud.

Stumper propped his feet up on the table and flipped through the *Cosmo*. "The ME compared Sam's Marine medical records with the victim's. Sam never broke his arm like the victim. And Sam's right foot was shattered when he stepped on a personnel mine in Vietnam. Victim had no such breaks."

Manny closed the folder. "And Sam picked up a nasty skull fracture in a tunnel when an NVA frag detonated close by." He held up the report. "So who is this?"

"Wish I knew." Stumper tossed the *Cosmo* on the bed, and it flipped open to an "Eight Ways to Make Him Scream" article.

Manny dropped the ME's report on the nightstand and went back to putting on his socks and boots. "This burn victim had Degas written all over it. Several scenarios come to mind."

"Me too," Stumper said. He'd flipped open his pocketknife and begun picking his teeth. "The intended victim might have been Sam."

"Killed by mistake?"

Stumper nodded. "Maybe over drugs?"

Manny shook his head. "Sam didn't sound like the kind to deal. Or use."

"Then the journal," Stumper said. "Maybe it was Sam that tried to squeeze money from Chenoa."

Manny stood and tucked his shirt into his trousers. Like his socks, the shirt was several sizes too big, as if the only men buying clothes in Hardin were giants. "Possibility. Itchy said Sam had read the journal, and that Harlan locked it in his safe afterward. As good friends as they were, Sam could have known—probably did know—the combination to Harlan's safe and taken it after the reenactment."

"Which leads us back to the Star Dancers." Stumper closed his knife and stood. "I liked it better when we thought Sam was a drug dealer connected to Degas. Now we have to tiptoe around the Star Dancers again. Cubby called the tribal office the last time we were out there and bitched to Chief Deer Slayer."

Manny caught a look at himself in the mirror listing to the starboard on a wall stenciled with a cavalry-Indian scene. He looked silly and sloppy in the overgrown outfit. "We need to ID the burn victim. Get out a BOLO for anyone missing . . ."

"Including Little Dave?"

"Including him. And anyone else that may have failed to show for home. And"—Manny smiled at Stumper—"we'd better drive out and give Chenoa the good news about Sam."

Stumper groaned. "You mean bad news. Now she's back to needing Sam's signature on ranch business. She'll be madder 'n hell."

Now it was Manny's turn to smile as he tossed Stumper the *Cosmo*. "Look at the bright side—we've got the drive to Lodge Grass for you to figure out how to give her the news."

>〈〉〈〉〈

On the way to give Chenoa the news that her brother wasn't the victim in the house fire, Manny called Rapid City Regional. Willie had lapsed into a coma, and Clara said the doctors feared the worst. Miraculously, Doreen insisted Willie would fight through it. "I don't know what you said to her the other night," Clara whispered into her phone from the waiting room, as if Doreen could hear from inside Willie's room, "but she's thumbing through bridal books. Planning their wedding while he's lying there. Something we should be doing, too."

"Losing cell service," Manny said, and hastily closed the phone.

By the time they pulled onto the Star Dancer ranch, work trucks stood in a row by the bunkhouse like horses tied to a hitching rail. Manny thought how every truck in the Star

Dancer fleet must be there, except for Cubby's fancy red Lincoln.

Jamie Hawk stood blocking the doorway even before they'd climbed the steps. "The missus and Mr. Eagle Bull are just finishing lunch."

Manny stepped around him, but Jamie moved to block his way. He stood a few inches shorter than Reuben, but was no less intimidating, with a head perched on neckless shoulders, the kind that could snap yours if he desired. Manny moved his jacket aside just enough that his holster was exposed, grateful that he'd remembered his gun. Manny recognized the indecision in Jamie's eyes, a strained desire to break Manny in two for last night, and the fear of getting shot or doing hard time in doing so. Jamie dropped his eyes and stepped aside.

Manny grabbed the door knocker, but Wilson opened the door before he could drop it. "This is getting to be a habit, you two coming out here. It's like you're looking for work."

"With these hands?" Manny held up hands so soft they could be in a Palmolive commercial.

Wilson stepped aside to allow them in. His blue and red and black bone choker contrasted with his ivory shirt and pleated slacks, so unlike the man answering the door last night in tighty-whities, not nearly as regal-looking as he was now. A slight bulge under Wilson's shirt hid the bandage on his arm.

Stumper jerked his thumb at Jamie still staring at them from the porch. "He a bodyguard?"

Wilson shook his head. "With Chenoa's popularity and notoriety, he makes sure nuts don't come calling."

"Like us?"

Wilson said nothing.

"We need to speak with Chenoa," Stumper said.

"I need to speak with you first," he whispered, and led them into a den adjacent the kitchen. "Carson called a short time ago."

Manny tried to hide his excitement. How would he react when he found Degas? Would he goad him into a fight, or kill him outright? Manny thought a lot depended if Willie pulled through or not, but he drove the thought of killing another man from his mind. "Where is he?"

Wilson shrugged. "He wouldn't say, but I told him I needed to meet him at the ranch this afternoon."

"Did he agree?"

"Sort of. He said he had things he needed to do. Said he could meet me there tonight."

Manny calculated the drive from Crow Agency to Pine Ridge. Degas could have been the shooter that tried killing him and Stumper last night. "He doesn't know about your passenger?"

"I told you, I had no passenger."

"What passenger?" Chenoa came into the study, transformed as Wilson had been since last night, wearing black jeans and a sheer white top with the top two buttons undone as if to distract Manny. It did. "Agent Tanno, I'm getting tired of this. I can't do anything about the FBI, but him." She jerked her head at Stumper.

"He's my driver today," Manny said quickly.

Her chest rose and fell nicely as she sighed. "What is it this time?"

"Sam," Manny answered. "We need to talk."

She studied him a moment. "You look serious. We better get some coffee." She led them into the living room and nodded to chairs while she disappeared into the kitchen. "Did you find something out about Sam's death?" Wilson asked.

He bent and whispered to Manny: "She's pretty upset about it."

"And have you been upset about his death as well?"

Wilson looked away. "In life you have friends that stand with you no matter what. Sam was that friend. Once. Of course I was upset to hear he died in that fire."

Manny squinted, trying to read Wilson's sorrow, but found none. Perhaps Sam wasn't as good a friend as Wilson claimed. Perhaps he wasn't any more upset over Sam's death than Chenoa had seemed. Or perhaps it was that Vietnam was so far removed that Wilson no longer cared.

Chenoa cursed at the crash of a cup, followed by water running in the sink. When she reappeared, she carried a platter with cups and a carafe of coffee. She held her cup in one hand as she sat on the arm of the couch beside Wilson and draped her arm over his shoulder. "I assume you finally found Sam's killer?"

Manny struggled not to smile. "You'll be pleased to know it wasn't Sam who died in that fire."

She stopped mid-sip, her mouth wide. "Then who?"

"Might be Little Dave Night Tail," Manny said, gauging Wilson's reaction. He showed no more emotion than when Manny told him Sam wasn't the burn victim. "Little Dave's been missing four days. Or it could be any other acquaintance of Sam's who was unfortunate enough to sleep in his bed the night the killer came to pay your brother a visit."

Wilson scooted to the edge of the couch. "Then Sam's alive?"

"He could be," Stumper said, his mouth slightly upturned, enjoying this as much as Manny. "We haven't found him yet, so there's a good possibility Sam's still alive."

"I don't believe this." Chenoa stood, coffee sloshing onto

the floor. She paid it no mind as she paced in front of the couch. "If Sam's alive, where could he possibly be?"

Manny shrugged. "He could have felt threatened and gone underground. With his Marine experience, he could have, right?"

Wilson nodded. "If he stayed off the sauce, he might make it in hiding."

"Or he could be lying dead somewhere here on the rez," Stumper added. "Just waiting for some hapless hunter or rancher to find him rotting."

Chenoa set her cup down and rubbed her face that had paled the last few moments. "But Sam was identified."

"An ID based on probability." Manny topped his and Wilson's coffee cup off and motioned to Chenoa. She shook her head, and he set the carafe back onto the serving tray. "The ME positively ruled Sam out as the victim."

"Now what the hell am I going to do?" She stopped and faced them, once again in control, the color returning to her face. Her anger had reddened her cheeks and her eyes narrowed, focused on Manny and Stumper, the bearers of bad tidings. "I just signed papers on selling another eighty heifers, and signed lease papers on the section to the north."

"You sound so concerned about your brother," Manny blurted out. "Don't you even care where he is?"

"Of course I care. But if he's alive—or at least not declared dead—none of this ranch business this week will be binding."

Manny stood, and Chenoa stepped closer, glaring at him. "You'd better find Sam, Agent Tanno, whether he's alive or dead. Or I will make a call to the Billings FBI office and have you replaced on the case."

"Promise?"

"What?"

Nothing would make me happier than to be replaced by another agent on Crow Agency. "We're all looking for him, now that we learned he may still be alive. But look at the bright spot." He smiled at her as he started for the door. "At Sam's memorial service, you put on a good feed. And you had a lot of friends over. There's not much that can replace good times like that."

CHAPTER 38

Right after takeoff, Wilson told Manny they'd be flying at eight thousand feet at one hundred forty knots. But the only knot he remembered the whole flight was the one in his gut, twisting, churning, and twice he'd grabbed for an barf-bag. And twice he'd managed to keep his supper down.

"Now after we land, Harvey will pick me up in his truck. You stay hunkered down and he'll never know you're there."

"Like the passenger you had a couple days ago?"

"I told you, I had no passenger. What you saw—or thought you saw—was me grabbing my duffel from the backseat."

Stumper had checked the reports when the BIA knew meth came onto Crow Agency to the time Wilson visited the Star Dancer Ranch. In nearly every case, Wilson was on Crow Agency during those delivery dates. Stumper argued that Wilson was dirty, that he made deliveries of drugs onto the rez for the main supplier, Carson Degas. Manny wasn't so sure. Was he defending Wilson because he's Lakota? But what

Manny was certain of was that he could lead him to Degas. If this little aerial jaunt wasn't a setup.

"You ask me, it's stupid to trust Wilson," Stumper had argued. "He's got too much to lose if you find Degas."

"He's got too much to lose if I don't. He knows if I don't find Degas soon, the newspapers will pick it up that senatorial candidate Eagle Bull has been harboring a suspected murderer. Now think what that would do for his Senate chances against Arvid Johansson?"

"His chances will greatly improve if you're out of the way."

"If Wilson is setting me up on the Pine Ridge side, that means he'll have to make arrangements for others privy to the investigation to be taken care of." He nudged Stumper. "So I'd watch your ass up here as well."

The Cessna hit an air pocket, and Manny's gut fought to catch up. "That wasn't a duffel you were talking to the other night."

"You're the first rider I've had in years."

"Sure." Manny held his roiling stomach.

"It's true. I gave up passengers when I gave up giving flight lessons. It'd take someone special to get me to give them lessons. And to give them a ride. Count yourself privileged."

"You flew home for a three-hour pleasure ride, landed for ten minutes, then back to Crow Agency again that night? My money's on you flying someone to Pine Ridge. No other reason to be on the ground only a few minutes."

And I don't buy that your fund-raiser was called off in-flight. You'd have lain over in Pine Ridge."

"Like I said before, don't you think Chenoa's worth coming back for?"

She was worth it, with her timeless beauty that took Manny's breath—and every other man's in the room—whenever she entered, or when he opened that tourism brochure or flipped pages on that Montana calendar. He thought of last night, when she'd sashayed down the staircase, her robe falling away revealing her negligee clinging in just the right places, making no attempt to hide herself from him or Stumper.

Manny believed she was worth it, up until the time they gave her the news that her only brother might still be alive. Her beauty had faded as she ranted on how ranch business would be more difficult now that Sam might be alive. "Unless he's found," she'd said last night. "Dead or alive. Makes no difference to me." Suddenly, Chenoa's beauty had left her as surely as if she'd aged before his eyes, and he thanked God that he had Clara to come home to.

The Cessna dropped a hundred feet and Manny grabbed for the air bag. Wilson laughed. "I thought you FBI guys were supposed to be tough? But don't worry, I'm sure the worst is yet to come."

Manny kept his mouth tightly closed as he shut his eyes, leaning back in the seat, hoping the drone of the aircraft would settle him and override his fear of flying, like the motor drone when he was a boy. He had been four or five—he wasn't sure, only that Reuben had been deployed to 'Nam by then. His folks had driven to Hot Springs for Christmas shopping, the steady motor of their old Pontiac driving over the expansion stripe on the highway, their slap-slap-slapping keeping time with the heavy snow, putting Manny to sleep.

That had been his last memory of his parents before the fatal accident that sent them to an early grave and sent him to live with his uncle Marion. *"Close your eyes and imagine you are on Oglala Lake with the wind gently lapping the bank,"* Unc told Manny during one trip to Rapid City when Manny felt sick riding in Unc's old pickup. *"That will relax you. That will take you to other places in your mind."*

And Manny had taught himself to relax, a skill that he used whenever the bureau flew him somewhere.

"Let your mind calm itself and the Old Ones will speak with you later in your life."

"But Unc, I don't want to speak with anyone except you. I don't want to speak with the Old Ones. When they try to speak with me, I see scary things."

Unc smiled and drew Manny close to him. "One day the wisdom of the Old Ones will come to you."

Manny wrapped his arm around him and shuddered. "But they show me bad things . . ."

"Not bad things." Unc stroked Manny's head and scooted closer to the fire. "True things. Things that you need to deal with in this life, so when you travel the Wanagi Tacanku you will meet me waiting for you."

"No, Unc, you won't ever die."

But Unc's image, and their conversation so long ago, abruptly ended when the Cessna hit another air pocket and Manny woke with a start.

Wilson chuckled but said nothing, and Manny shook his head to clear his thoughts. Wilson, descendent of the Eagle Bull who had murdered his own friend, flew him into danger that Manny might not recover from. He told himself Wilson was basically a good man, and refused to believe Stumper's theory about Wilson being in cahoots with Degas in selling drugs. Would Manny one day meet Wilson along the Spirit Road? He was uncertain, but Manny was sure he wouldn't meet Conte Eagle Bull there, his treachery against his fellow Lakota warrior sentencing him to eternity never finding the Milky Way, never finding the Wanagi Tacanku.

And would Wilson follow in his great-grandfather's treacherous footsteps, setting Manny up so Carson Degas could kill him? Manny was unsure enough that he had dialed

Philbilly's phone on the way to Wilson's plane earlier, hoping Reuben would answer. He had.

"I thought you were going to give Phil his phone back?"

Reuben laughed. "I told him I'm kinda getting used to this thing. I told him I'd give it back in a couple days. It must have been all right with him 'cause he didn't argue any."

Manny explained he was flying to Wilson's Oglala ranch, and asked Reuben to be there when they touched down. "Lumpy's got no one to spare."

"Because it's Wilson Eagle Bull?"

Manny had nodded into his cell. "He says because it's just another of my cockamamie theories. Can you put the sneak on Wilson's ranch by the time we land?"

"I'll have to steal a car."

"What about Philbilly's bread truck?"

"I gave it back. It smelled like greasy Indian tacos. Besides, it was about out of gas anyway."

"Can you get it back?"

Reuben laughed again. "I doubt Phil would answer any phone call from me after I sentenced him to an evening entertaining Crazy George."

"Well find a car. I might need you."

Their conversation faded as Manny became aware of a gradual descent. He sat up in his seat and looked out the side window just as Wilson grabbed the CB mic and spoke with Harvey. "I'm entering landing pattern in five minutes."

Lights below flicked on.

"That where we're landing?"

Wilson nodded.

"Not much to land by."

Wilson pulled the throttle gently toward him, the motor slowing, the nose dipping slightly. "I've flown this so many times I probably wouldn't even need Harvey and the guys down there with their truck lights."

"Wouldn't it be easier just to install landing lights in that field?"

Wilson shook his head. "We raise corn in that field in the off years. I'd have to move the lights to a different pasture. But sit back and relax." He nudged Manny. "We'll probably land safely." The green glow of the instrument lights cast an eerie light on Wilson's smile. "Statistically, most aviation accidents occur on takeoff or landing."

Manny groaned and cinched his seat belt tighter.

"We're on the final leg. Better climb in the back and scoot down."

Manny eyed Wilson. "I'd have to take off my seat belt."

Wilson laughed. "A seat belt's just to make us feel good as we plow through the windshield or get crushed by the weight of the plane in a crash. It's just for looks."

The nose dipped steadily down as Wilson put on ten degrees of flap. Manny scrambled into the backseat and hugged the floorboard. "Where will Degas be?"

Wilson made a correction and the wings dipped slightly as he kicked the rudder to ease into a cross-wind landing. "He wouldn't say, except that he'll come to the house tonight. Wait the better part of an hour before you chance slipping out in case he's hiding and watching the plane. I'll leave the yard light on so you'll know where to go in the dark."

The Cessna's tail swung into the wind and the plane rolled onto the ground, choppy as it bounced over corn stubble and clumps of dried field dirt. Wilson eased the throttle back while he taxied to where headlights illuminated the far side of the field. "When you go in the house, skirt the steps leading up, and wait in the hall closet until you hear him."

"How will I know it's him?"

"I'll call his name."

"And Harvey?"

The plane bounced along corn stubble. "I'm sending him and the other hands in those pickups into Hot Springs. Twofers at the Legion Club Saturday nights." Wilson eased back on the throttle, the plane moving at walking speed toward Harvey's headlights. "And I'll put the dog in the garage."

"I appreciate it, but tell me just why I should trust you? Seems like I'm trusting you with my life. Seems like I'm taking all the risks here."

Wilson kept his gaze steady out the window as he spoke out the side of his mouth. "You can trust me because I wouldn't do anything to hurt that lady at Crow Agency. If scandal comes back to her, she'll be ruined. Besides, I'm taking a big chance, too. If Carson finds out I've set him up, he'll slit my throat as surely as he will yours."

Wilson pushed the throttle in slightly. The prop moved the plane toward the waiting headlights, and Wilson cut the power. Manny resisted the urge to fall out of the plane and kiss the ground.

"Hey Boss," Harvey called. He slammed his truck door and approached the plane. "I'll get your bag?"

"I'm good," Wilson answered quickly and grabbed his duffel on the seat beside where Manny lay.

He remained hunkered on the floor until he heard Harvey's truck driving away before he took a chance. He rose from the floor enough to stretch out a cramp forming in his calf as he peeked out the window at the disappearing taillights. He grabbed his bandanna from his back pocket and wiped the sweat from his face and neck, his polo shirt soaked despite the cool air. He shuddered with the realization that he'd just survived a plane ride with Wilson. Or did he sweat from fear of an Eagle Bull setup, where he would face a killer cunning and ruthless enough to get the best of Willie?

CHAPTER 39

Manny eased the door open and stepped down to the ground, using the fuselage of the Cessna to shield himself while he worked the cramps out of his legs. He was grateful for the thick clouds that had moved in and covered what small moonlight there might have been. He stood alone in total blackness, like the times he sat in an *initipi*, all light in the sweat lodge blocked.

He peered over the cowl and spotted the yard light a quarter mile away. He could just make out Wilson's ranch house under the glow of the halogen light like a lighthouse beacon waiting to guide him.

Wilson's shepherd barked at something, and Manny hoped Wilson would remember to put the dog in the garage. Given Manny's track record with animals, he didn't want another trip to the ER messing with the rest of his vacation. If he ever got another vacation.

He started across the empty cornfield, the yard light

guiding him. He tripped on stubs of cornstalks and fell, his hands cut by last year's crop. He tasted blood on his hand and he rubbed it onto his trousers before he continued plodding toward the light.

Manny arrived at the house and crouched just out of the yard light's periphery while he caught his breath. The wind had picked up, bringing the odor of the horse barn, as well as the barking of Wilson's dog inside the garage. Harvey's truck sat in front of the bunkhouse, but the other trucks he'd seen in the field lighting the way for the landing were gone. Manny mentally ran scenarios through his head, the least attractive one that Harvey was working with Degas. After what Reuben did to the big man, Manny didn't relish having to deal with Wilson's foreman any more than he did Degas.

And maybe with Wilson. He had agreed a little too readily when Manny suggested he fly both of them to Pine Ridge whenever Degas called. A little too readily to set up a meeting. If Wilson was as wary of Degas as he made out, setting him up was a risky move. Unless Manny was the one being set up.

Manny breathed deeply, his lungs hurting, not only from the effort of walking the cornfield, but from something he recognized: fear. He had scoured the area as he approached the house and could see no sign of Reuben. He was about to go into a house alone, about to put his life in Wilson's hands, about to trust a man that had little honor in his family dating back all the way to Conte Eagle Bull. He was about to confront Carson Degas alone. Manny had felt the gut-wrenching fear before, so he was no stranger to it. If he could manage his fear and turn it into controlled anger, he might get through this alive.

Manny shuddered while he unsnapped the restraining strap on his holster. Just what he knew about Carson Degas would fit in a thimble. Manny knew Degas had been dishonorably discharged from the army for black marketing arms and ammunition in Iraq. He knew the man had disappeared into Folsom prison for a manslaughter conviction in Barstow, resurfacing twelve years later. A man with Degas's record didn't stay out of the spotlight for long, and Manny guessed those twelve lost years were spent honing his skills in Folsom. Manny found it hard to swallow that Wilson was so into rehabbing bad men that he had hired Degas knowing his record.

That Degas was the point man for the recent rise in methamphetamine on Crow Agency was undisputable. But had he seized the opportunity to make a bundle more on the journal, blackmailing both Chenoa and Wilson? Wilson said Degas was loyal, but loyalty only went so far to someone as ruthless as Degas. And he would be smart enough to know that both wanted the journal contents silenced.

Manny skirted the yard light and slipped around the corner of the house. He stood, listening to people talking inside, but he couldn't make out who they were or what they said. He tried the screen door. As Wilson promised, it was unlocked, and Manny opened it slowly, rusty hinges loud in the still night air. Manny froze, certain those inside had heard the noise. But the talking continued, and Manny opened the door the rest of the way and gingerly closed it behind him, buttonhooking around it and flattening himself against the wall of the mudroom.

He chanced a look around the corner of the wall to the top of the stairs. A hall closet stood at the top and to one side of the stairway where Wilson had drawn it on Manny's notepad. He hugged the wall while he inched his way up, careful to avoid pictures hanging on it.

When he reached the closet door, he strained to hear what

the voices said several rooms over. He caught people arguing about a horse trade with the Star Dancers, and about delivering some shipment to Crow Agency. Just as Manny turned to the closet door, something cold and hard pressed against the base of his neck.

"Don't turn around." A man with a nasally voice kept the gun barrel against his neck while his other hand reached around and lifted Manny's Glock from the holster. Quick, like he'd done it a time or two.

"Now get in the living room." The man laughed as he shoved Manny down the hall. "Funny place where you'll die—living room."

Manny cursed himself for trusting Wilson, but only for a moment. The man kicked Manny's legs, and he fell to the floor beside an overstuffed chair where Wilson slumped, handcuffed to the chair's arms. A trickle of blood started at the back of Wilson's head and followed his shoulder line down to the front of his white shirt.

"Is he dead?" Manny asked.

"Not yet," the tall man said. He wiped fresh blood onto his jeans. "He'll come around in a minute. Sit there on the couch."

Manny studied the long, angular nose, the hard cheekbones cloaked in a gauze bandage taped from his jaw to the top of his head, from where Willie had hit Degas on the way down, the close-set eyes that darted around the room, taking in everything in a glance, like a wolf looking for prey. And this man was the predator. "Carson Degas I'll wager."

"They do hire sharp agents nowadays."

"You look just like you do in the video at the sergeant's tent."

Degas stepped closer. "What do you have on that?"

Manny shrugged. "Enough."

Degas flicked out a slap that landed flush on Manny's face, knocking him to the floor. Degas drew his gun back to hit him, but paused as he nodded to his bandaged shoulder.

Manny used the arm of the couch to pull himself from the floor, his face stinging as if he'd been kicked by a cow. Even without the six-inch revolver, Degas was intimidating. As Reuben had described, Degas stood several inches shorter than Reuben, and was thinner, but with every cord of the man's muscle devoted to keeping him alive, and keeping others from talking about what they knew. And constant survival, which he had done by the looks of him. A scar ran from his jawline down to his collarbone, crude stitches having once closed the angry wound. One earlobe had been lopped off, and an old bullet wound to his forearm added to his sinister look. As Degas thrust the gun in his face, Manny noticed Degas was missing one finger, and he regretted it wasn't his trigger finger. "What did you do to Wilson?"

"Love tap."

"No loyalty to your boss."

"My loyalty ended when he flew you here tonight."

"How'd you find out? Did Wilson tell you?"

"I told him." Cubby Iron Cloud emerged from a side room carrying a .45 automatic by the side of his leg. "My good wife called and said Wilson was flying you here to put the grab on Carson, and she needed me at the ranch. I told her I was in Chamberlain at a horse sale and couldn't get back until tomorrow."

"You lied."

Cubby laughed and pointed at Wilson with his gun barrel. "Trade one sin for another. Which is worse—lying or adultery?"

If Manny could keep them talking, maybe he could work out a plan. He scanned the room looking for an escape route. Wilson slumped in his chair blocked the main door, and

Cubby stood between the living room and mudroom. And a door out of the house. Cubby stood just out of reach of a gun grab, and Manny prayed he'd get close enough for one. "Chenoa tells you when to come and go, doesn't she?"

Cubby's face flushed. "Chenoa and me got an understanding. I look the other way when she beds fools like Wilson, and she lets me come and go as I please."

"But every now and then she needs you around? Does having a has-been rodeo champion around make her feel special?"

"I went out a champion."

Manny forced a laugh, careful not to fixate on Cubby's gun pointed at his chest. "It's hard to make a comeback when you haven't been anywhere. Way I heard it, you fell on your fat ass once the competition level got higher."

Cubby stepped close and cocked his gun arm back, but Degas's hand shot out and grabbed Cubby's arm. "Don't be a fool. The son of a bitch is just goading you. You can have at him once he tells us what he knows."

Cubby pointed the muzzle at Manny's chest. "I ought to . . ."

"Just watch him while I clean this blood off me." Degas nodded to an occasional chair beside Wilson's that faced the couch. "And keep back. He wants you to get close enough to grab your gun."

Degas disappeared into the bathroom and shut the door just as Wilson's head rose slowly and he shook it. Blood droplets fell to the floor from the gaping cut on his jaw and head. He strained to focus with his one good eye, the other closed and swollen shut.

Manny nodded to Wilson. "You do this?"

Cubby shook his head. "I'm not into the killing part, if that's what you mean. Carson did that. But just when it was necessary."

"You free us now," Manny whispered, watching the bathroom door, "and you'll get a fair trial. Testify against . . ."

"Bullshit," Cubby spit out. "Put my fate in the hands of a jury? You know that all a jury decides is which side has the best attorney."

"You'll fry along with Degas for murder."

Cubby dropped the gun a little. "Harlan was necessary."

"And the man he killed in Sam's house before torching it? It wasn't Sam, so who was it?"

Cubby shrugged. "Ask Degas. All's I'm saying is that was an accident. Degas thought it was Sam when he went in there."

Wilson spit a piece of a bloody tooth. It hit the arm of his chair and bounced under the couch. "I could have told you Sam wouldn't kill easy. Drunk or not."

"My guess is, the little bastard's hiding out under a bridge on Crow Agency." Cubby took a step closer to Wilson, and Manny measured the distance to Cubby. "Or he could be dead. I got some feelers out in case someone runs into him. Alive or dead. We can't take the chance that the journal will get into the wrong hands."

Wilson shook his head. Blood flipped onto the beige carpeting. "You think whatever the journal revealed about me— and about Chenoa's side of your family—justified killing Harlan? And whoever was in Sam's house?"

"And don't forget Itchy." Manny started to stand, but Cubby's finger whitened on the trigger and Manny sat back down. "Your own brother." Manny shook his head. "You pop him in the back of the head for the journal?"

Cubby's mouth turned down for a brief moment. "Now that was unfortunate. We gave Itchy a chance to say where the Star Dancer journal was. I recognized his hen scratching on that crude blackmail note he slipped into the ranch mailbox, and thought there was a chance he might just have it. All he'd say was that Sam had it."

"But Degas didn't believe him?"

Cubby nodded. "Not for a second. And he killed Itchy. Would have gotten you and Stumper, too, if you had been a mite slower."

"So that was Degas in that old barn?"

Cubby shrugged. "Who else? Rumor has it that you got spirits watching over you. Not that they'll help you any this time."

"All that killing for a damned journal?" Wilson struggled against the handcuffs, but he remained shackled to the chair arm.

"It wasn't the journal, now was it?" Manny said. "What it contained was just an afterthought. My guess is that Degas didn't set Harlan up because he'd read it."

"Got things figured out, don't cha?" Degas emerged from the bathroom wiping his hands with a hand towel bearing the Eagle Bull logo. Blood had crusted under his nails from where he'd worked Wilson over, but he made no attempt to clean them. "I guess that's what federal agents do, figure things out. Not that it'll help you any."

"Can't we just get rid of them now?" Cubby said, pacing the floor in front of where Manny and Wilson were seated. "They know too much already."

Degas went to the window and looked out. "Pete and RePete are just now fixing to head for Hot Springs. Soon as they're gone, we'll march them out into the south pasture and be rid of them."

"Harvey?" Cubby asked.

Degas shrugged. "He got drunk on my beer earlier today and is sleeping it off. He won't hear a thing."

"But why Harlan?" Wilson spit more blood onto the carpet, his handcuffs rattling against the chair.

"Harlan found out about your drug dealing on Crow Agency, didn't he?" Manny said. "That's why you needed him dead. Itchy said Harlan kept notes inside the journal."

Degas turned a chair around and sat backward, draping his arms over the chairback. "Harlan was an opportunist. He got wind of our business through Itchy. The damned fool spilled his guts to Harlan for the price of a quarter gram of crank."

"How much did Harlan demand to keep his mouth shut?"

Degas nodded to Cubby. "They're not leaving this room alive, anyway. Tell them, fat boy."

"Don't call me that."

Degas laughed. "Okay, fat boy. Just tell them what Harlan wanted."

Cubby turned his back on Degas and faced Manny. "Itchy was tweaking bad one night. Needed his shit, and he had no money. But he did have information that he'd trade for some crank. He told me all about how Harlan had us figured out."

"Let me guess—Harlan's demands to keep his mouth shut got pricier. Like most blackmailers."

"That's when fat boy here screwed up."

"I did not screw . . ."

"What do you call flat-out refusing Harlan's demands?"

Cubby looked away, and Degas continued. "When fat boy here told Harlan to shove his demands, Harlan threatened to go to the law. Cubby never was much for thinking, guess that's why his woman runs the ranch."

Cubby's face reddened, and Degas laughed. "The amount of money we were pulling in, we could have easily met Harlan's demands. But after fat boy refused to pay more, we couldn't risk Harlan going to the law."

"And you." Manny nodded to Wilson. "When did you decide to run drugs for these two?"

Wilson strained in his chair to look at Manny with his one good eye. "What the hell you talking about?"

"Stumper crossed the times shipments came onto Crow Agency with the times you were up there. He figures you were transporting the shit for them."

Wilson strained against the cuffs, trying to stand from the chair. "You asshole . . ."

Degas shoved the chair back onto the floor. "Easy, Boss. Can't blame Mr. Agent Man for suspecting you."

Cubby smiled at Wilson. "You were the perfect fool. Sometimes we stuck the shipment in your pickup and someone picked it up at Crow Agency. Sometimes we needed it there quicker, and you flew it for us."

Wilson glared at Cubby. "I brought no drugs to Crow Agency . . ."

Cubby laughed. "Sure you did. Every time you headed out of here, Harvey would carry your bags for you. Remember?"

Wilson shook his head.

"And every time you landed on Crow Agency, Jamie Hawk grabbed your bags. Bet you thought Harvey and Jamie were kissing your ass being your bags bearers."

"And the drugs were in there," Wilson breathed. "I flew them for you."

Degas stood and looked out the window. Manny followed his gaze to the backup lights on the truck backing from the bunkhouse. He turned back to Manny. "Not much longer."

"Did you ransack Harlan's auction barn?"

Degas nodded. "I found a notepad, made a rubbing. Harlan had written down everything he knew about our operation, I'm assuming in case anything happened to him. It's what I would have done. I looked everyplace in his office, including his safe, and found the only thing missing was the journal. I figured his notes were inside it."

"That's when you went hunting Sam?"

Degas's hand shot to the bandage on his jaw. He rubbed it. "Harlan's safe was open when I got into his office. So I asked myself, who would Harlan trust with the combination? Cubby had told me Harlan and Sam were inseparable if Harlan had beer. But the little bastard got to the safe first."

Manny stretched his legs and Cubby pointed his gun at him. Manny dropped back on the couch. "There never was anything in the journal to worry the Star Dancers and Eagle Bulls?"

Degas shook his head. "Not that I'd kill anyone over."

"And Sam?" Wilson said, his speech becoming more difficult to understand as his face became more swollen. "He knew about you?"

"Had to have." Degas glanced out the window again and walked to the coat tree. He snatched his jacket and turned back to Wilson. "That day I saw Sam coming out of Harlan's shop with a bunch of papers and old books in his hand, I just thought they were junk. But I realized one had to be the missing journal."

Degas chin-pointed to Wilson. "And Sam would have given you the notes, and you'd have gone to the law."

"And reveal the contents of the journal?" Wilson said. "We were willing to pay big bucks not to let that come up for auction."

"Ain't you the pious one, not wanting the public to find out about your great-grandfather murdered his friend. You wouldn't have wanted another murder on your hands."

Manny looked sideways at Wilson. "What's he talking about?"

Wilson looked away.

Degas stuck one arm through his jacket as he held the gun on Manny with his other one. "You mean the great man didn't tell you? About his good buddy Sampson Star Dancer, tunnel rat, Marine to the bone, sworn to protect one another. Tit for tat in 'Nam, wasn't that right?"

Wilson kept silent, and Degas squatted in front of him. He grabbed Wilson's face and turned it toward Manny. "Sam had a mouth when he was drunk, huh Cubby?"

Cubby nodded. "Big-time. He'd cuss his own mother when he had a head on. He told me about a trifle incident in Vietnam one night. Seems like Lieutenant Eagle Bull played second fiddle to some butter bar. Dangerous though he was to his men, I'm not so sure he deserved to have one Lance Corporal Sam Star Dancer toss a fragmentation grenade into the crapper one night, giving Wilson the command of the company."

Wilson strained against his cuffs, and Degas stepped back. "Sam wouldn't tell anyone . . ."

"He would for a twelve-pack," Cubby said.

"But the ranch," Manny said. "You had everything—the finest ranch in the state, a beautiful wife who's a celebrity."

Cubby laughed nervously as he paced in front of the couch. "The ranch is Chenoa's. She just gives me an allowance, which is why I decided to supplement my income. As for her beauty"—he jerked his gun toward Wilson—"she saves the romance for men like him."

"And what does Chenoa have to do with this little cottage industry you've been conducting?"

"Enough."

Manny followed Degas's gaze as he watched Pete and RePete's taillights disappear down the gravel. He turned to Manny sitting on the edge of the couch. "Now it's time you tell me who knows about us. And especially about Harlan's murder."

Manny remained silent.

"That scrawny BIA cop there at Crow Agency know everything?"

Manny shrugged.

Degas turned his gun on Wilson and cocked the hammer. "Unless you want the future senator ventilated, answer me."

"You'll kill him anyway."

Degas shook his head. "I don't think so. Way I figure it, my boss here wants that senator seat so bad he'll just want this to go away." He brought the barrel of his gun down on Wilson's head, the high front sight cutting a deep furrow across his forehead. Blood flowed from the gash, making his salt-and-pepper hair appear rust colored.

"Don't hurt him anymore." Manny stalled. "I made a call to our Rapid City office before lifting off from Crow Agency. They should be rolling up with a Hostage Rescue Team any moment."

"That so?"

Wilson forced a nod.

"Maybe we better get out of here . . ."

Degas backhanded Cubby. He fell back against the wall, and his .45 covered Degas for the briefest moment before dropping beside his leg.

"Wilson's lying, fat boy. I've been in stir enough times to know when a man's lying. I can't tell if Mr. Agent Man is lying, though it's doubtful the Rapid City Field Office has enough for a Hostage Rescue Team. They might come from Denver, but even if they did, these turds will be worm food by the time a team arrives."

Degas faced Manny, a smile crossing his lips. "You got one last chance to save Wilson before I cap him. Now who else knows about our operation?"

CHAPTER 40

"I hate being lied to." Degas raised his gun to Wilson's chest, fingers tightening around the revolver grips. And when he smiled at Wilson, Manny knew Degas intended killing him. Manny judged the distance across the room, judged how many shots Degas could get off before Manny could cross that distance. He had drawn his legs under him, his hand grabbing the arm of the couch, when Degas swung the gun toward him.

A blur passed the corner of Manny's eye, the glint of steel reflecting from the chandelier in the center of the room. Sam Star Dancer sprang on Degas. Sam clutched a KA-BAR knife in one hand, and for a moment Manny envisioned Sam clearing tunnels of NVA and VC with such a weapon.

Degas caught the movement out of the corner of his eye. He jerked back. Sam's knife missed his throat, slicing his shoulder. His gun discharged, missing Manny by a foot, the sound deafening. Manny rolled onto the floor, sticky from the blood coming from the knife wound in Degas's shoulder.

Cubby swung his gun at Sam and fired twice, missing. Manny sprang for the gun, knocking it from Cubby's hand. It slid under the couch. Manny lunged for it. Cubby leaped on Manny, his arm encircling his neck, cutting off Manny's air, tightening. But Manny had wrestled too many years in high school, and taken too many Custody Control classes with the bureau, not to recognize his immediate danger.

Cubby stood behind him, thick arm lifting Manny off his feet, and he turned his face into the crook of Cubby's arm, his airway freed for the moment, sucking air. Manny grabbed Cubby's arm and held it while he dropped to one knee. Cubby flew over Manny and into Wilson chained to the chair, knocking him over. Wilson struggled against the handcuffs as another shot erupted as Sam dove behind the couch.

Manny stood, rubbing his neck, regaining his airway just as Cubby lunged. Manny sidestepped the larger man and hit him on the side of the head as he passed. Cubby dropped to the floor, struggled to get his wobbly legs under him, but fell back, lifeless.

Degas shot four times into the couch where Sam had leaped. His revolver clicked on empty cylinders and he swung it open, fumbling in his pocket for fresh rounds.

"Get out of here," Wilson yelled from the floor. "Sam's hit bad. Degas won't hurt me until he finds out what you know."

Manny bent to Wilson as Degas shut his revolver cylinder. "Go!"

Manny sprang for the door. A bullet kicked up wood splinters next to his face, a piece of mahogany lodging just under one eye, another round whizzing just over his head. He ran zigzagging from the house. Degas fired again before Manny reached the temporary safety of the darkness just past the yard light.

He squatted, breathing hard. He watched the house as he

picked the splinters from his face, his eyes adjusting to the darkness. He checked himself for injuries: Degas had missed, but Cubby's choke hold had badly bruised his neck and it was beginning to stiffen.

Manny fished his cell from his pocket and checked for bars: none. The closest bar was in Hot Springs with the ranch hands. Except Harvey. Manny knew he would have heard the shouting and the shooting, unless the man was so dead drunk he couldn't hear it, and Manny recalled how the bunkhouse had been described: a hundred years old, built like a fortress, with little sound reaching inside.

Manny low-crawled, watching the house, expecting Degas to come running out. Or come slipping out unseen through a side door.

Manny sat with his back against the side of the bunk-house, breathing deep. Behind the door, Harvey lay passed out. And although the big man had no use for the law, he must have loyalty to Wilson. Unless Harvey was working with Degas and had known all along what was in the luggage each time he carried Wilson's bags to the plane. Harvey might be more of a threat than Degas.

Manny tried the knob and the door swung open to a dark room. He duckwalked inside and eased it closed. He felt along the wall and his hand fell on the light switch. He paused. Degas would suspect Manny had gone to the bunkhouse for help. He didn't need to confirm it for the man.

Manny crouched in the darkness, the yard light filtering through blinds running the length of the building letting in just enough light that Manny could make out the room. A potbellied stove sat in one corner, while the cookstove and fridge stood guard over a long plank table. A row of bunks, two high, ran along one wall, enough for twenty men. Except they were all gone drinking for the night.

Manny skirted the outside wall, feeling for a phone jack, just as another shot came from the house. Degas had just finished off Sam, Manny was certain, and he bet Wilson's life that Degas would keep his boss alive. At least until he learned from Manny who knew about their meth ring.

When Manny neared the end of the row of bunks, light reflected off a chrome cross lying on the floor. Harvey's cross. Manny crouched beside the bunk where the man lay covered. He listened intently. No snoring, no movement, came from under the covers.

Manny stood and approached the bunk. If Harvey awoke now, he'd be a handful, and he might not give Manny time to explain why he'd crawled into his house at night. Harvey would surely take great pleasure in squashing one federal lawman. If he woke up.

But Harvey wouldn't be waking up anytime soon. Manny pulled the covers back and stared into his lifeless eyes, rolled back in a head turned at an odd angle, as if his neck had been contorted and stretched before Degas broke it. Manny felt for a pulse that would never be there again. Harvey's face was contorted, bruised and broken, and Manny speculated that had been a result of Reuben's roadside talk. Harvey surely wouldn't be pressing charges now.

Footsteps outside. Gravel kicked against the door. Manny ducked under the cot beneath Harvey. Manny pulled the blanket over the edge of the bed. The heavy door swung open. It hit against the wall, and for a moment Degas stood silhouetted against the yard light, blood covering one shoulder, leading the way into the bunkhouse with his long-barreled revolver. "Yoo-hoo, Mr. Agent Man. Come out and play," he said, holding his jaw that Willie had broken. "We need to talk. Just for a little while."

Manny held his breath, feeling his heart quickening,

feeling with his hand if there was enough room to shuffle out the other side of the cot.

"You'll be glad to know I took care of that little cockroach Sampson." Degas shuffled along the row of bunks, looking under each. "Wilson, now he's a different matter. I'm pissed at him for setting me up, and I might work on him a little more, but for now he's taking a nap. But you're a different story altogether. You come out so I don't have to work looking for you and I'll kill you quick."

Manny unbuckled his belt and rolled it in his hand, the only thing he might use if Degas got close enough.

"Maybe me and old Harvey can use some light." When Degas turned and walked to the light switch, Manny scurried from under the bunk, belt wrapped around his hand, buckle dangling nearly to the floor, stepping toward Degas.

Degas hit the light switch. Manny swung the belt at Degas's gun hand. He yelled and dropped the gun. Manny swung the belt again. The buckle hit Degas on the shoulder Sam had sliced. He yelled in pain, and again Manny drew back. But this time Degas caught the belt and jerked it from Manny's grasp.

Before Degas could savor his victory and attack him, Manny dove for Degas's legs, catching him on the knees. They fell to the floor in a tangled mess, and Degas swung at Manny's head. Manny pulled back, the buckle glancing off his head, slicing his temple, and he wrapped his legs around Degas's belly. If they stayed on the ground, Manny had a chance. Upright, Degas was too powerful, too agile, even with a knife wound to his shoulder to handicap him.

Degas rolled on top of Manny and drove an elbow into his face. Manny deflected the blow, yet it landed on his cheek, the swelling immediate. Degas reared back for another elbow when two quick gunshots came from the ranch house, stopping Degas midswing. Manny drove his knee into Degas's side and rolled away, leaping for Degas's revolver. He felt the large grip, sticky with blood, and he rolled onto his back.

Degas froze when he saw the gun pointing at his chest. He bent over, panting. "Guess you got me, Mr. Agent Man. Now what you going to do with me?"

Manny chanced a look around the room for a phone, spotting one by the cook's cabinet. Degas picked up on it.

"You won't be able to summon the cavalry in time."

"In time for what?"

Degas smiled. "Those shots. I told Cubby to kill Wilson if he managed to get loose. Fat boy will join us in just a minute." Degas stepped toward the door.

"Stop right there!"

Degas turned and smiled. "I'm leaving now, and you won't shoot me. It's not in your nature to shoot an unarmed man, no matter what a bastard I am. You just can't hurt me."

"But I can." Reuben's fist shot out, catching Degas on the side of the head. His legs buckled, but he sprang up, rushing Reuben. He hit Degas again. Even twenty feet away, Manny heard the snapping of bone, and Degas slumped to the floor.

Degas rolled over, brushing blood from his eyes, and leaped for Reuben's legs. Reuben kicked Degas full in the groin and the man dropped, groaning and holding his testicles. As if that'd help.

"At this point," Reuben said, sitting on the edge of a bunk, "you'd toss your handcuffs to your partner to cuff the bad guy. If you had a partner. And if you managed to keep your cuffs through all this."

Manny grabbed his cuffs from his belt holder. "Want me to . . ."

Reuben held out his hand and Manny tossed them to him.

"I've had enough practice with these things. I'd suggest you go to the house and capture Cubby."

Manny started out the door when he turned around. "What the hell took you so long?"

Reuben ignored Degas's moans as he wrenched one arm behind him and snapped a cuff on, prying the other from his groin. Reuben dragged him to the Franklin stove and cuffed Degas to one of the heavy cast iron legs. "If you only knew how long it took me to convince Crazy George I only wanted to borrow his car this time. Then we had to find jumper cables and hook it on his tractor. Then round some gas up . . . Well, you get the idea. Better get to the house."

Manny grabbed Degas's revolver and opened the cylinder: four rounds left.

"Just so you know," Reuben said, and Manny paused in the doorway, "Clara called. Willie came out of the coma. The docs say two weeks in physical therapy and he'll be a pain-in-the-ass tribal cop once again."

"How'd she call you?" Manny closed the cylinder so that the next round up was live.

Reuben held up a cell phone.

"Pink? Doesn't seem your style."

"It's not. It's Philbilly's."

"Thought you were going to drop it off."

Reuben shrugged. "I'm kinda getting used to this technology stuff."

Manny approached the house from the side away from the yard light, squatting under low windowsills. He heard shuffling inside. Something dragged across the floor. His hand poised above the doorknob, his sweaty hand on Degas's gun. He rubbed his hand on his pants, and breathed one last time before he gathered his legs under him and burst through the door. He ran up the landing to the living room, gun leading the way.

Cubby Iron Cloud lay on carpeting soaked with his own blood, one wound to the side of his neck, another to his chest. Wilson lay on the floor, one free hand holding Cubby's auto. He brought up the gun, and quickly dropped it when he recognized Manny. He nodded to the chair with one arm splintered. "Nicest Queen Anne I ever had. Hated to bust it up."

Manny motioned to Cubby. "You?"

Wilson nodded. "Cubby thought Sam was dead. But when the scrappy little guy came up over that couch, Cubby shot him twice more. I went ape-shit. Managed to bust this one arm up and get a hand free. You'll find two big slugs in Cubby."

Manny checked Cubby's pulse, but he'd already gone the way of Harvey.

"Don't just sit there feeling dead people. Get your cuff keys and get me off this chair." Wilson jerked on the cuffs. "I got to help Sam."

CHAPTER 41

Manny fished his key ring from his pocket and grabbed his cuff key. As soon as he freed Wilson's hand, Wilson stumbled around the back of the couch. Manny pocketed his keys and joined him. Wilson sat on the floor between the wall and the couch holding Sam's bloody body, rocking back and forth, tears mixed with his own blood streaming down his cheek. His one good eye focusing, he looked up at Manny, wanting to say something, yet not able to.

Manny turned to the phone and called the Pine Ridge Police Department dispatch. After explaining he had dead men and one with nuts swollen like softballs by now begging to be arrested, he hung up and sat on the floor beside a senatorial candidate all beat to hell.

After what seemed like an hour, Wilson's weeping stopped. Manny stood and rested his hand on Wilson's shoulder. "We can't do anything for him. Come over here. Sit with me. I got the paramedics coming."

Wilson made no attempt to move, and Manny gently took Sam and lowered him to the floor before he helped Wilson stand. Manny led him around to the front of the couch and they sat. "He remained your buddy, even after returning from 'Nam, didn't he?"

"Sam saved my ass more than once in 'Nam." Wilson nodded and wiped tears and blood from one eye, the other swollen and stuck shut by sticky, dried blood. "When he came back to the world, he hit the bottle. But we still kept in contact. I owed him."

Manny turned back to Wilson. "I got to read you your rights," he said and fished into his notebook for the Miranda warning card he carried.

"No need for that. I'll tell you whatever you need to know."

Manny nodded and pocketed the card. "You said you owed Sam. Like with the fragging incident? You knew about it."

Wilson nodded as he rubbed circulation back into his wrists cut by the handcuffs. "Our company CO was an idiot, but a dangerous idiot. He must have found those lieutenant bars in the Dumpster or something, 'cause he sure had no business leading a Marine rifle company."

Manny nodded. He knew officers in law enforcement who should have been assigned to conduct background investigations, desk assignments, anything other than working violent crime cases that they usually botched.

"The butter bar made some bad calls, and we were shot to hell every mission. We'd lost half the company, and replacements were slow in coming." Wilson looked over his shoulder as if he expected Sam to rise from the dead. "Sam talked about getting rid of the LT before he got the rest of us killed. I knew what he meant. I just chose not to act on it. That was wrong, wasn't it?"

Manny shrugged. "Legally, yes. Morally, I can't judge you. Or Sam."

Wilson nodded. "Thanks. There'll be enough judging to do later, won't there?"

"'Fraid so."

Wilson sat quiet for a moment before continuing. "We'd drawn a mission along the DMZ, five klicks from Con Thien. The CO ordered us along a corridor we knew to be NVA controlled, but he ordered us to go anyway. We had three KIA and three more we had to call in a dustoff for. Medics saved two but another died en route to the base medics."

"And Sam couldn't take it any longer?"

Wilson nodded. "That night when the rest of us were licking our wounds at base camp, Sam was watching the latrine. When the lieutenant went in, so did a grenade."

"You covered for him?"

Wilson nodded again, droplets of blood staining his carpeting. "I said we were both playing poker when the LT was fragged."

Manny folded his bandanna and held it against Wilson's head. "And you got a field promotion to lieutenant?"

"I did." Wilson held the bandanna tight. "We never lost another man while I was in charge of the company. After the war, I stayed in the Corps. Rose to the rank of major . . ."

"So your military records said."

Wilson smiled, but he winced in pain against a split lip. "I would have made a career, but Dad died and I got willed the ranches."

Wilson sat quiet, until he asked: "Where's Degas? Forgot about that bastard." He looked wildly around to the door and reached for Cubby's gun. "If he comes back . . ."

"He won't," Manny explained. "Remember that felon you were complaining about?"

"Your brother?"

"He's watching Degas until the police arrive."

Wilson looked out the door, expecting Degas to come charging in and finish the job. He turned back to Manny. "What do you think this will do to my campaign?"

"I'd worry more about what it'll do to your freedom. Sam murdered a man in '68 and you covered for him. There's no statute of limitations on murder. But," Manny said, "the man that committed it is dead, and any witnesses are probably not alive. You just might luck out."

Manny nodded to Cubby. "I'd be more concerned about how it'll look, you killing your lover's husband, and how your horse wrangler ran a major drug operation under your nose. With you transporting the shit to boot."

Sirens neared, their whelp-whelp-whelping rising and falling in the still night air. Wilson dried his eye and blew his nose before handing the bloody bandanna back to Manny.

Manny stood and went to the windows, pulling the curtains back. Red and blue lights filtered through the shelter belt lining the long drive. Manny turned back to Wilson and sat on the sofa beside him. "Sam was your passenger two nights ago?"

Wilson dropped his head between his knees. "Harlan had let Sam read the journal. Joked how it contained things Chenoa would like kept quiet. Harlan figured he could squeeze her to keep quiet. And me. Sam wanted to buy the journal outright . . ."

"Where would he get the kind of money it would bring at auction?"

"That monthly pittance Sam got from Chenoa—plus disability from the VA—mostly went into savings. Sam saved his money, buying up artifacts he thought might have been detrimental to his kid sister. He spent very little on beer. Harlan was generous in that regard, at least." Wilson laughed. "Sam said Harlan hated to drink alone." He looked to the couch. "Sam figured Chenoa didn't deserve a scandal because some French trapper drifted through the Valley of the Giveaway in 1876. And he wanted to protect me."

Emergency lights flickered off the windows as Manny helped Wilson stand. "It wasn't the historic contents of the journal that Degas was after. Degas said Harlan had written down everything he knew about their drug dealing. Just in case."

Wilson held his head, the gash in his forehead bleeding anew. "Degas figured Harlan kept the journal in his safe." Manny handed Wilson his bandanna again, and he held it against blood leaking from the head wound. "But the only way to get to it was with Harlan out of the way. So Degas had to set up Harlan to get shot."

"That's the way I figured it." Manny leaned Wilson against the doorjamb on the front door. "But Sam must have gotten to it before Degas?"

Wilson held the bandanna to his head but it had little effect. Blood seeped down and stained his shirtfront, his trousers. "Sam knew the items would go on auction once Harlan's estate was probated. Sam knew the journal held damaging evidence on both our families. What he didn't know is that Harlan's notes were stuck inside. Once Sam read them, he knew his life was in danger and he went underground. Even I didn't know where he was until he called me two nights ago and needed off Crow Agency pronto."

"Why didn't you tell me all this before?"

Wilson closed his eye. When he opened it, tears had once again mixed with dried blood. "I only knew about all this the night Sam called and wanted me to find him a safe place. Once Sam told me what he knew, I figured there'd be a way of clearing this up before the election."

"Hard to clear things up when Degas left bodies behind."

"I know. I was a damned fool."

"Can't argue there." Manny smiled. "So who was in Sam's house when it burnt?"

Wilson shrugged, bringing another wince of pain to his swollen face. "Sam had no clue. Sam had an open invite for anyone to crash at his place if they needed it. That fire just drove him deeper. Sam planned to hide out in the basement here until he could figure out what to do with Harlan's notes. Guess he ran out of time."

"You have Harlan's notes?"

Wilson nodded. "They're stashed in the basement. We'll get them as soon as I get patched up."

Officer Jumping Bull was the first through the door, and he holstered his gun when he saw Manny. "Secure the house," Manny instructed. "And the bunkhouse. We got a croaker there, too. We'll get Pee Pee Pourier in here to start working this crime scene."

Jumping Bull looked at Cubby's faceup death stare and the blood soaking the carpeting beside the sofa before turning and stopping paramedics from entering.

Manny slipped his arm through Wilson's and helped him onto the porch. He handed him off to paramedics and grabbed a lady EMT with the name tag A. S. SHOLE.

"Shole, we got . . ."

"Adriane Shole. Adriane Susan."

"Okay. Adriane, grab your jump bag. We got another man wounded in the bunkhouse."

Degas's screams reached them even before they burst through the bunkhouse door. He still lay handcuffed around the base of the potbellied stove, blood caked on the floor from where Sam had sliced his shoulder. "That son of a bitch left me like this. Get me loose."

Manny looked around for that son of a bitch, but he was gone. Reuben never was one to stick around and chat with the law. "I don't see anyone."

"That big bastard that came after me when I should have killed your ass."

Manny shrugged as he exaggerated looking around.

"Well at least get me some ice on my nuts."

Manny grinned and turned to the paramedic. "You want to handle his nuts, Adriane?"

CHAPTER 42

Stumper stood beside Manny, both men holding their hats, as Sam was lowered into the same hole Little Dave Night Tail had occupied the week before. Chenoa had insisted Dave be removed from the Star Dancer cemetery as he didn't possess the purity of Crow heritage. As the Star Dancers did. The American flag draped over the casket fluttered, revealing the eagle, globe, and anchor adorning the finest casket that Wilson could buy.

"Guess Cubby wasn't pure enough to be planted here," Stumper whispered. "Guess that's why he's fertilizing the Lodge Grass cemetery."

Manny watched Chenoa dab at her eyes that were as dry as the Badlands. "That, and he had brought shame to the Star Dancer name with his drug operation."

Stumper fought down a chuckle. "Now if the journal ever went public, Chenoa would have a cow."

Manny agreed. When Wilson had gone to his basement to

gather what few things Sam brought with him when he hid out there, he brought out the journal stashed between two pairs of jeans.

"Believe me," Stumper said, "I'm tempted to let that information leak to a newspaper."

"Just be glad Jamie Hawk didn't know anything."

Jamie stood beside Chenoa, glaring at attendees, daring anyone to bother Chenoa at Sam's funeral. Manny bent and whispered in Stumper's ear: "I'm glad Jamie was as dumb as he seemed to be and didn't know squat about Cubby and Degas's drug operation. I'd have hated to try handcuffing him."

As if he could hear Manny, Jamie flexed his massive shoulders and stared at him.

Chenoa stood beside a tall man wearing a perfectly cut suit and black armband, his salt-and-pepper hair contrasting with his California tan. Chenoa's eyes darted between the casket and Wilson standing apart from the others as the sacred man completed the service. Chenoa led the attendees past the coffin, each tossing a handful of Star Dancer dirt on the casket. Chenoa's eyes met Manny's, a knowing look for a secret shared between them, and she tossed a worn and cracked brown leather book onto the casket as she passed, a moment of faded blue and yellow beading on the journal's front catching the sun before it disappeared with Sam.

The tall man hooked his arm in Chenoa's and they led the funeral goers to the food tables in front of the house.

Wilson stood staring at the hole in the ground, tears flowing, and he swiped at them with the back of his silk shirt. Manny rested his hand lightly on Wilson's shoulder. "In the end, he was there for you once more."

Wilson looked to the hills to the west. "I should have insisted he get treatment when he rotated back to the world. If I had of . . ."

"If you had, he probably would have ended up just where he is now. It was his choice to drink."

"But the things he saw when he entered those tunnels in 'Nam . . . he had no choice—he had to drink to forget."

"He lived life as he chose," Stumper added.

"And he chose to live in obscurity, protecting the Star Dancer name."

Stumper chin-pointed at Chenoa disappearing around the house. "She knows you read the journal. She's waiting to counter the FBI's public statement about the lack of purity in the Star Dancer line leading to Sam's disappearance, and how it connects to Harlan's and Itchy's murders."

"What journal?" The sound of dirt hitting the metal casket accompanied two men with shovels burying the journal—and the Star Dancer secret. Manny had been tempted to expose Chenoa. He suspected she had told Cubby that Wilson and he were flying to Pine Ridge that night, knowing Cubby was dirty, knowing he would tell Degas and be waiting for them. Manny suspected all these things, yet got only a wry smile when he questioned Chenoa. Now her world was all right, with her husband and brother in the ground along with the journal. Now all that was needed to mend the Star Dancer name was to explain how she knew nothing of the drug operation.

Manny patted Wilson's shoulder. "I take it that guy with Chenoa is her new squeeze?"

Wilson nodded. "Once Cubby was dead and buried, the thrill of the hunt was gone. She gave me the bum's rush."

"That's Chenoa's style," Stumper added. "That guy looking like he came out of GQ magazine is an assistant attorney general. But she'll dump him once that thrill wears off, too."

"What's in store for me now?" Wilson asked.

Manny looked out into that pasture that Wilson had taken

off and landed in so often. "I've sent my report to the U.S. Attorney, though I suspect he'll figure a murder that happened in 1968, with a suspect dead and buried, won't take up much of his time. I'd be more worried about the publicity."

"You pulling out of the Senate race?" Stumper asked.

"I thought about it," Wilson said, standing straight and smoothing his pleated slacks. "But I haven't quit anything yet. I'll tell the truth—that I knew nothing of my horse wrangler and Cubby running drugs. Let the public decide."

"Well, you can decide on lunch." Manny slapped Stumper and Wilson on the back. "I'm buying in Crow Agency."

Wilson looked sideways at Manny. "Just as long as you don't drive us there."

Epilogue

"You up to this?" Manny asked.

Willie nodded as he began standing from a lawn chair on a tall hill overlooking the Eagle Bull Ranch. He had started sitting back down when Doreen hooked her arm in his and helped him stand. Willie's strength had come back quicker these last weeks than Manny had expected. Still, he tired easily. But this was something he had to do.

Reuben opened a cedar box and took out an eagle feather fan and handed it to Willie.

"What's he going to do now?" Wilson whispered.

"He's going to smoke us."

Willie lit the braid of sweetgrass, smoke thick in the windless afternoon. He moved the smoke over him and turned to pray to the four directions, the earth, the sky, before turning to Reuben. Reuben closed his eyes as Willie fanned the smoke over him, before turning to Manny and Clara and Wilson. The sweet odor filled Manny's nostrils, and he inhaled deep, taking in the sacred sweetgrass, the clean, clear air here on the rez. During moments like these, he didn't even miss his Alexandria, Virginia, home he'd given up when he moved here last year.

Willie's voice rose high, shrill, then dipped low as he continued signing, the heavy drumbeat echoing off the hills. They each stood, silent and reverent, until Willie stopped. He set the drum on the ground beside him and turned to Wilson. "The dead."

Wilson bent and picked up a metal box and passed it to Reuben, who opened it and handed Willie the two scalps from the Eagle Bull collection. Manny swayed, yet there was no wind. He smelled the odor of blood, yet there was nothing killed here recently. He heard the cries of Levi Star Dancer's friend, White Crow. He stared into the pleading eyes of Conte Eagle Bull's companion, Stone Thrower, just before Conte killed him.

Reuben slipped his arm around Manny's shoulder and whispered, "You all right, *misun*?"

Manny nodded, his head clearing.

Reuben nodded as if he could witness the terrible scene as Manny had, a scene forgotten until the journal resurfaced. Manny had read the journal before giving it to Chenoa: It was exactly as Manny's visions had depicted.

Willie wrapped the scalps in a red muslin cloth, yellow and blue and black geometric designs painted across the front. Doreen helped Willie bend down and lay them into the deep hole in the pasture Pete and RePete had dug earlier. *Crow and Lakota together*, Manny thought. *Enemies until united by the evil of Conte Eagle Bull. At least Conte's descendent proved he had honor. At least Wilson had wanted them buried together.*

Willie grabbed for the shovel and swayed; Doreen helped

him into the lawn chair, and Reuben took the shovel and began moving dirt over the two scalps.

When the ceremony was completed, Doreen and Reuben helped Willie down the gentle slope with Wilson close behind.

Reuben walked beside Manny and Clara as they picked their way around clumps of cornstalks. "One thing's been bugging me," Manny said to Reuben. "How come you didn't finish Degas off when you got a chance?"

Reuben smiled. "Some people make the world a better place, *misun*. Some by leaving it. The world would be a better place without the likes of Degas. But a *wicasa wakan* can't hardly be going around bumping off bad people. No matter the reason. I had a choice to make."

Reuben went ahead and walked on the other side of Willie, helping him down the hill.

Clara nudged Manny. "That was honorable of Wilson— wanting both scalps buried together."

Manny chin-pointed to Wilson. "He's not a bad sort. I think he would make a great senator if he can get elected over all that's happened with him."

"I noticed the papers weren't too sympathetic to him. Hard to overcome that."

"It will be."

"Another thing I noticed," she said, looping her arm in his.

"What's that?"

"There were two scalps buried. At the same time."

"And?"

"Don't you see?"

"No," Manny said.

Clara smiled. "Things that happen in twos go better than things done singly. Like marriage. Doreen and Willie set their wedding date. We could, too. At the same time."

"You mean a double wedding?"

Clara nodded.

Manny groaned. Just what he needed—going down the aisle with the mad Lakota woman Doreen Big Eagle waiting for him by the altar.